HALO®
MORTAL
DICTATA

HALO®
MORTAL
DICTATA

KAREN TRAVISS

TOR

First published 2014 by Tor, Tom Doherty Associates, New York

First published in the UK 2014 by Tor
an imprint of Pan Macmillan, a division of Macmillan Publishers Limited
Pan Macmillan, 20 New Wharf Road, London N1 9RR
Basingstoke and Oxford
Associated companies throughout the world
www.panmacmillan.com

ISBN 978-0-230-76710-2

Printed and bound by CPI Group (UK) Ltd, Croydon, CR0 4YY

For Alasdair,
for many fascinating discussions on the emotions
we have in common with other animals

ACKNOWLEDGMENTS

343 Industries would like to thank Kendall Boyd, Ben Cammarano, Scott Dell'Osso, Stacy Hague-Hill, Matt McCloskey, Whitney Ross, Bonnie Ross-Ziegler, Dave Seeley, Rob Semsey, Matt Skelton, Eddie Smith, Phil Spencer, Karen Traviss, Carla Woo, and Jennifer Yi.

None of this would have been possible without the amazing efforts of the Microsoft staffers, including: Christine Finch, Mike Gonzales, Kevin Grace, Tyler Jeffers, Carlos Naranjo, Tiffany O'Brien, Frank O'Connor, Jeremy Patenaude, Jay Prochaska, Brian Reed, Corrinne Robinson, Chris Schlerf, Kenneth Scott, and Kiki Wolfkill.

HALO ®
MORTAL
DICTATA

PROLOGUE

My name is Staffan Sentzke, and I never planned to be a terrorist.
It's not the kind of life you aspire to. It was simply what I had
to do. Terrorism is Earth's word for it, a moral judgment, as if
your warfare's somehow noble and mine's cowardly. But it's a
unit of measurement; nothing more, nothing less. When your
enemy is an empire and you're just a few guys, a handful of little
people, then the biggest punch you can land is called *terrorism*.
That's all you've got.

Like I said, it's a measure of magnitude, not morality. And
I'm really particular about measurements. I used to work in a
machine shop in Alstad before Sansar was glassed by the Covenant, and I still like to make things to keep my skills fresh.
Here: what do you think of this? It's a scale replica of an
eighteenth-century Gustavian dining chair—I'm making a doll's
house for Kerstin. Edvin says I'm spoiling her, but what else is a
granddad for?

I'd give anything to be able to spoil Naomi again.

There's not a day goes by that I don't think about her. She'd
be nearly forty-two now, well past the age for doll's houses, but
still my little girl.

Anyway, I need to finish this chair before dinner. I use a set
of dental drills for the small detail. The upholstery's the hardest thing, getting the right fabric so that the stripes are to
scale. If I can't make something myself, then I can acquire
what I need because I know people who can get me pretty well

anything—a scrap of satin brocade, a birch plank, even tiny brass pins.

Or a Sangheili warship. I can get one of those, too.

I think I've got one now, but I have to see Sav Fel again to iron out some details. Earth thinks it's back in business now the Covenant's collapsed. It won't be long before it tries to stick its nose into our business again. We need to be ready. And what better time to prepare than when the black market's awash with weapons and ships? When empires fall, there's always a fire sale.

For the moment, though, I'm making doll's house furniture, not arming Venezia. The workshop door opens behind me. This is the only place I'd ever sit with my back to the door, but then I know everyone who comes and goes in my own home.

"She's going to love that," Edvin says, peering over my shoulder. "Is it a set?"

"I've still got to make the matching table."

"Nice work, Dad. I wish I had your patience."

Oh, yes. Patience. I've got it in spades. When you have to wait for answers, for revenge, for justice, you can learn to wait as long as it takes.

I was forty when Edvin was born, and Hedda came along two years later. This is my second family and my second homeworld. I had a wife and a daughter on Sansar, but it wasn't the Covenant that took them from me—it was my own kind. *Humans.* Maybe it was the colonial government, or maybe it was Earth's, but it was human nonetheless.

And that's how I ended up as a terrorist. That's your word for it, remember. Not mine. I bet there are UNSC personnel out there right now doing exactly what I'm doing. I'll use any means necessary, so I can't object if my enemy does the same thing. Rules of engagement are just cynical games for politicians to play. It's a war. People get killed. There's no way you can make that look reasonable.

"So did you visit your sister today?" I ask Edvin. I know what's coming next. "What's she made me this time?"

"She sent you some *surströmming*. She says it'll do you good."

"God Almighty, you've not brought it in here, have you?"

"No. Take it easy. I've set up a cordon around it."

"Good. Otherwise I'll have to have the place fumigated."

"Mom said you'd say that. Just pretend it was yummy, will you? For Hedda."

"You can have it. Just take it outside the city limits before you open it."

I'm not much of a Swede at heart. I don't even like pickled herring, let alone the fermented variety, and anyway, we don't have herring on Venezia—just some oily eel-type thing that's even worse when it's been turned into *surströmming*. Hedda, on the other hand, clings to her diluted heritage more fiercely every year, even though she's never seen Earth, let alone Sweden. Cultures can get pretty warped in diaspora. They become weird fossilized parodies of themselves that seem to distill their worst features, but I'm afraid Hedda's like me. She *focuses*, and then she can't see anything else to either side. Edvin takes after Laura. He lets things wash over him.

But they both know they had a half sister who was abducted, and that when she came back she was . . . different. And then she got sick and died. They know I think the government took her and replaced her with a double.

You think I'm crazy? Everyone did. Even me, for a while. But then I started looking, and found a few other families out in the colonies who'd lost children the same way. The kid went missing, then came back a little later, a little different, and finally went down with multiple organ failure or some metabolic disease.

So either we're all mad, or something awful was going on long before the Covenant showed up. A few dead kids aren't even a drop in the ocean considering the billions who've died in successive wars. But they're *our kids*. Thirty-five years doesn't even begin to numb the pain. I still need to find out what happened to Naomi and why. Before I die, I want to *know*.

Damn, it's getting late. I need to finish this and call Sav Fel. It sounds too good to be true, but if he's got a warship to sell, he's come to the right place. Imagine it; he just strolled off with a vessel that can glass entire planets. Would *you* trust a Kig-Yar crew to look after your battlecruiser? The Sangheili took their eye off the ball.

Never turn your back on someone you've screwed over. You might want to make a note of that.

I smooth the tiny legs of the chair with an emery board, then blow off sawdust as fine as flour. It's going to look great when it's finished.

Edvin laughs to himself. "If your buddies could see you now . . ."

"Yeah. They say Peter Moritz knits. Real hard case."

"You want me to go check out that new shipment?"

"No, it's okay. I'll be finished soon. You've got a living to make."

What, you think terrorists sit around scheming and playing with firearms all day? We've got factories to run, food to grow, families to raise. We're pretty much like you. This is our home. We have a functioning society, and the Covenant never bothered us. We do okay. Leave us alone, and we'll leave *you* alone.

I've got time to put a coat of primer on the chair before I leave. This is one of my many regrets: I never did get around to making a doll's house for Naomi. She really wanted one. I planned to make one when I had more time. She was such a bright, happy kid, always out exploring, always with lots of friends around her, which makes it even harder to understand how nobody saw her being taken.

I want to believe she's still alive. She might not know I survived, and that's why she hasn't come looking for me. Maybe she doesn't even know who she really is. They say that happens to kidnapped kids.

But if she's still out there somewhere, I hope she's among friends.

There. Finished. It's a lovely little chair. But now I've got to go talk to a buzzard about a warship.

CHAPTER
ONE

ONI SPEC OPS AI BLACK-BOX (BBX-8995-1)
RECORDING 4/5/2553
PARTITION SECURITY FAILSAFE ACTIVATED

I don't actually *need* to record any of this, but my memory isn't what it was.

Let me put that another way. I recognize its potential fallibility after that unpleasant business of reintegrating my damaged fragment. Not that I misremember, lie to myself, or acquire false memories like humans do. I might have missing segments and damaged clusters, but what I actually recall is real, and it doesn't change or get overwritten. So, reminder to self: memory gaps hurt, a preview of death by rampancy. Second reminder to self: yes, I'm reminding myself to remind myself, because Mal says the best way to stop worrying about your inevitable demise is to dwell on it morbidly until you're so bored that you forget it.

Anyway, I'm securing this data so that it can't be retrieved by hostiles if I find myself in the same pickle again. My name is Black-Box, generally called BB: I work for Captain Serin Osman of ONI, who would have been a Spartan-II now if the program hadn't nearly killed her, and I serve with her personal black ops unit, Kilo-Five—Sangheili cultural expert Professor Evan Phillips; ODST Marines Staff Sergeant Mal Geffen; Corporal Vasily Beloi; and Sergeant Lian Devereaux; and a Spartan-II, Naomi-010. We also have two Huragok on board, Requires Adjustment, aka Adj, and Leaks Repaired, known as Leaks. We've been covertly supplying arms to the Sangheili rebels to keep a civil war with the Arbiter on a steady simmer, because all the time they're busy killing each other, they're not regrouping to kill humans. They're a tad disorganized since the collapse of the Covenant— job jobbed, as Mal would say—and the rebels have misplaced a battlecruiser. Like everything else, it'll end up in the wrong hands unless we go and retrieve it. Or blow it up. I'm easy.

There's also the added complication of Naomi's father showing up on Venezia. I suppose it was inevitable that the ugly past of the SPARTAN program would come back to bite us one day. Vaz and Naomi are on Venezia now, undercover. This will *not* end well.

But now I have to go bake a cake. I just need to enlist some organics. Meatbags have their uses. They have *hands.*

And, I admit, some of them are my friends.

RECORDING ENDS

ALSTAD, SANSAR, OUTER COLONIES: SEPTEMBER 10, 2517

"Honey, where's Naomi?"

Staffan Sentzke hung up his jacket and looked for his daughter's satchel and coat on the hook halfway up the wall, set as high as a six-year-old could reach. If the bus hadn't dropped her off yet, he still had time to sneak the box into his workshop. It was five days to her birthday. She was already keeping an eye on everything he did with the unblinking vigilance of a security guard.

Lena wandered into the hall, wiping her hands on a dishcloth. "Music practice, remember," she said. "She won't be back until five."

"You think she's a bit young for all these extra classes?"

"If you think she's old enough to go to school on her own . . ."

"Okay. You win that round."

"So did you get it?"

"Yeah." Staffan put the box on the kitchen table, pleased with himself both for finding such a uniquely Naomi kind of gift and for the overtime he'd had to work to buy it. It was a mini planetarium the size of a table lamp. "I bet she can name all the stars. You can get different discs to show the northern and southern hemispheres. Even views from other planets."

Lena opened the box and lifted out the projector. "At least she won't think it's the doll's house before she opens it." She had to move the toaster to plug the lamp into the wall socket. "Too small."

"You think she'll be disappointed?"

Lena flicked the switch. Sansar's night sky came to life in the kitchen as constellations began tracking slowly across the walls and ceiling. Naomi would love it. She could leave the projector running all night if she wanted to. It was a grown-up kind of night-light for a smart little girl who was sometimes still afraid of the dark.

"No, she'll forget all about the doll's house as soon as she sees it," Lena said. A slow smile spread across her face as her gaze flickered from star to star. "It's pretty magical, isn't it?"

"You can change the colors." Staffan turned a dial on the side. "Look. There's even a rainbow setting. And you can zoom in on individual stars and planets. Look." He pressed a key and a blue-green planetary disc sprang out of the heavens. "Just like landing on Reach."

"Okay, let's wrap it and put it away before she gets home."

Staffan rummaged in the kitchen drawers for scissors and tape, and noticed that the collection of tiny, handmade furniture on the shelf had grown an extra chair. Ever since Naomi had spotted the doll's house in an expensive toy store in New Stockholm—no Daddy-I-want, no wheedling, just that rapt look on her face when she saw it—she'd been collecting all kinds of scraps, and spent hours cutting and gluing them to make furniture. There was a table, a bed, and now a dining suite. Staffan picked up one of the fragile chairs and studied it with his own craftsman's eye, marveling at how square the angles were and how neat the glued joints.

Pride overwhelmed him for a moment. Naomi would be six in a few days. She shouldn't have had that level of dexterity or precision. Average six-year-olds were struggling with joined-up writing while his daughter was measuring angles and working out scale.

Every parent thought their child was uniquely perfect, but Staffan knew the difference between fond delusion and the realization that Naomi was a gifted child. A few months ago, an educational psychologist from the Colonial Administration Authority had visited the school to carry out batteries of tests on her class, and Naomi's teacher had told Staffan and Lena what they already knew: Naomi was exceptional, in the top small fraction of a percent—one in millions, maybe one in a billion. He just hoped that a small colony world like Sansar would have enough to offer her when she grew up.

It was funny that she was so taken with the doll's house, though. She didn't even *like* dolls. She wasn't interested in being a princess, either. There was something about the detail of the house, the creation of a separate world, that seemed to absorb her.

Staffan turned the miniature chair over in his fingers. The cushion fell off. He swore under his breath and took it out to his workshop. He'd stick it together again and hope she didn't notice, but she never missed a thing.

A dab of wood glue put the tiny cushion—the fingertip of a knitted glove—back in place. There: good as new. Then he wrapped the planetarium projector in the red-and-white striped paper that he'd sneaked into the house last week. He'd have to lock it away somewhere. Naomi had a lot of self-control for a small girl, but she was a very curious child, always busy searching for something to do or make.

He parted the blinds with his finger to look across the yard. It was getting dark. She'd be home soon. He hid the parcel in his rifle locker and went back inside the house.

"Where's she gotten to?"

Lena stirred a pot on the stove. "I just called the school. They were running late. She's on the bus now, so I make that ten minutes."

Staffan wanted to wrap his daughter in cotton wool, but if he did then she'd grow up afraid of everything. She was smart enough to catch the right bus and not talk to strangers. She had a watch—a proper adult one, not some glittery pink toy—and the drivers kept an eye on the kids and old folks anyway. Lena didn't approve. It was one battle that Staffan had won.

He worried, all the same. Dads couldn't help themselves.

And then before I know it there'll be parties, and dating, and all that to fret about.

While he watched TV, he could hear Lena walking back and forth between the kitchen and the hall. Then the front door opened. He expected to hear Naomi's voice. But the door closed after a few seconds, and Lena came into the living room, pulling on her coat.

"I'm going to walk to the bus stop," she said. "I don't want her wandering around in the dark. Which wouldn't have happened if you'd let me pick her up."

Staffan checked his watch. Damn, it had been nearly half an hour since Lena had called the school. There was probably a perfectly good explanation. "Honey, you know she likes to feel grown-up. She's not an idiot."

"I know. But she's five."

"Six."

"I'm going. Keep an eye on the stove."

Staffan fretted for a few moments, trying to work out if this was Dad worry or rational anxiety. Naomi wasn't the kind of kid to wander off or lose track of the time. Okay, he'd do some more overtime and get her her own phone. That would keep Lena happy.

He opened the front door to take a look. The bus stop wasn't that far: he could see the string of streetlights dotted along the road in the distance and the silhouette of the climbing frames and swings in the park. He expected to see Lena and Naomi walking back across the grass, but there was just Lena. And she was running.

Oh God. Oh God, no.

Some things were instantly understood.

In the moments it took to close the distance between them, Staffan had thought a hundred terrified, stomach-churning thoughts about perverts, road accidents, ponds, and *God I should never have let her go out on her own, I shouldn't, I shouldn't, I shouldn't—*

He ran down the drive. Lena almost cannoned into him and grabbed his arm, wide-eyed and distraught. "She's *gone*. He called the depot."

Staffan could hardly breathe. "Whoa, slow down. Who?"

"The bus driver. He just called the other driver, the one on the earlier bus. He said she got off a stop early. She just got off the bus. I *told* you. I told you she was too young—"

"Then she's just walking a bit farther. Nothing to worry about." It was a lie and Staffan knew it. There was *everything* to worry about. His heart pounded. He thought immediately of his neighbors, trying to work out which of them had always seemed a bit odd. Everyone warned kids about strangers but forgot to mention it was the people they knew and trusted who were the biggest danger.

Did I do that? Did I teach her to be too trusting? Is it my fault?

Staffan fumbled in his pockets for his keys. "I'll drive back down the route. I'll find her. You stay here in case she's taken a shortcut."

Lena was shaking. "He said she's done it before. This is your fault."

"Yeah, I knew it would be."

"If anything happens to her, I'll never forgive you."

"Jesus Christ, Lena, this isn't the time, okay? Stay here. She'll probably be back before I am."

He backed the car out of the drive and headed for the main road. Naomi would have been home by now if she'd walked that distance. *Please be all right, sweetie. Please. God? God, if you're there at all, if you're listening, you haven't done a whole lot for my family, so maybe now would be a good time to show yourself. Let her be okay. Please.* He drove along the bus route back to the school, now shuttered and in darkness, before looping around to scan both sides of the road. He didn't even pass anyone out walking. Maybe she'd taken a shortcut through the new houses that were springing up to the west of the park. He doubled back and turned into the tract.

Or maybe she cut through the construction site.

Staffan slowed to a crawl to press the receiver into his ear and call Lena, but the number was busy. She was probably ringing around Naomi's friends' moms to see if she was with them. Which direction would Naomi have taken? He drove around every possible permutation of roads he could think of, but he knew damn well that she would have been long gone if she'd actually walked through here.

So am I looking for a body? Am I? Is that what I'm doing?

He could hardly bear to listen to his own thoughts. He headed home and turned into the drive, willing Naomi to be back and in need of nothing more than a talking-to about staying on the bus and not scaring Mom and Dad, followed by being escorted to and from school for a few weeks. But Lena was standing at the front door, eyes glassy with unshed tears.

"Nothing," she said.

He wasn't sure if it was a statement or a question. "Well?"

"Everyone's calling their neighbors. They're going to search for her. I've called the police. They're putting out alerts."

"I'm going back out, then." For no good reason, Staffan was suddenly grateful that his mother was days out of communication range and Lena's folks hadn't spoken to him—or her—in years. It was one less set of explanations and recriminations to think about. "Someone's got to organize this. How could she go missing between a couple of bus stops?"

It was a stupid question because the answer was both obvious and terrifying. He wished he hadn't said it. As he checked the map of the area on his datapad, he was still thinking through the list of everyone he knew in the village, trying to work out which one was the pervert that he'd never suspected. Naomi would never have gone off with a stranger.

Or she's lying in a ditch, hurt. Or worse.

"I've got to look for her," Lena said.

"No, stay put. Someone's got to be here to talk to the cops."

Staffan had already covered all the roads he could think of. The places he hadn't searched—the construction site, the stream, the farm—were the kind of hazard-ridden places where kids were found dead. In less than two hours, he'd gone from worrying if Naomi would be disappointed by her birthday present to not knowing if he'd ever see her again. Lena stood with one hand to her mouth, tearful and accusing at the same time, while he rang friends and tried to coordinate the search.

Alstad was a small place. All the kids who went to Naomi's school were from three villages in an eight-kilometer radius. This wasn't like a big city where a kid could vanish in seconds.

But we don't have all the street cameras that a big city would have, either.

Someone hammered on the front door. Lena rushed to answer it, but it wasn't the police. Twenty or more neighbors, including a couple with dogs and night hunting scopes, stood outside, clutching flashlights and looking grim. It seemed like the entire village had turned out in a matter of minutes.

"We'll find her, Staf," said Jakob. He was the district councilman, the kind of guy who always stepped up with a plan. "She's only been gone a few hours. She can't get far. They've got cams on all the buses."

It was just comforting noise. If she'd been taken by someone in a car, that meant nothing. She could be anywhere by now, unseen and unheard. Staffan gave Lena as reassuring a hug as he could manage.

"Call me if you hear anything," he said, as if it needed saying. "I'll keep my line clear."

Jakob took over as if he knew Staffan was now going in circles and needed steering. He'd already divided everyone into teams and given them areas to search—the sheds and slurry pit at the dairy farm north of the main road, the construction site, and the park. Others were tasked to go door to door, asking people to look in their sheds and outhouses. Nobody suggested waiting for the police. Staffan felt useless. He wasn't sure what the dogs would be able to achieve, either, but everything was worth trying.

Every minute that passed became the worst of his life, a steady downward path. The construction site was a list of fatal accidents waiting to befall a kid, from the holes full of water to the stacks of building materials that could fall and crush the unwary.

"She wouldn't come in here voluntarily." Staffan poked a long piece of wooden batten into a water-filled trench. Reflections of the security lights danced on the surface. "I know my daughter."

While they were dragging the ditches, the construction manager showed up with half a dozen guys and started opening every storage hut and locked door, working through half-built houses with no floors or stairs. When the search party drew a blank on the site, they moved on to the occupied houses. With every door that opened, someone offered to join the search. Even strangers cared what happened to a little girl.

Staffan's phone rang a while later, showing 20:05 on the screen. He realized he'd completely lost track of the time. His heartbeat and the strangled sound of his own breathing almost drowned out Lena's voice.

"I gave the police one of her blouses from the laundry basket," Lena said. "For the canine unit. They've called in a Pelican with thermal imaging to scan the ground."

"Yeah, well, we're going to carry on anyway," Staffan said. *Thermal imaging.* That meant they thought she was alive. That was a good sign, wasn't it? He clung to the belief like a life belt. "We've got half the village out here now. We'll find her. I promise."

Staffan went back to sit in the car for a few minutes to check the local news, just to be sure something was being broadcast and that they'd gotten the detail right. He didn't catch anything on the radio. But his datapad showed an appeal for sightings on the local news site, complete with a picture of Naomi.

A police car with a flashing light bar slowed to a stop alongside him. The driver got out and Staffan lowered the window.

"Have you found her?" Staffan asked.

"Not yet, sir." The cop's comms unit was burbling quietly on his lapel like a second conversation in the background. "The dog's tracking right now, and we've got the bus security footage, so we know that she got off at—"

"Yeah. We knew that *hours* ago."

"Look, most kids usually turn up again safe and sound. Sometimes they forget the time and go playing somewhere, and then they're too scared to face the music for being late."

"Yeah, but not Naomi," Staffan said. "Not my daughter."

He drove back to the bus stop and sat watching the police dog and its handler. The dog was wandering back and forth on a long leash about fifty meters from the road. In the distance, flashlight beams crossed and wobbled between the trees as people searched the woods. Staffan decided he'd had enough and went to talk to the dog handler.

He stopped on the paved path. "What's the dog found? I'm her father. I want to know."

"He's picked up a trail from the bus stop, sir, but it doesn't go very far." The handler nodded in the dog's direction. "Let's not jump to conclusions. It might not be the right one."

Staffan wasn't stupid and he knew the dog wasn't, either. The trail ended abruptly a distance from the road because someone had lifted Naomi off the ground at that point. It was the only explanation.

"She's been taken," Staffan said. The words were strange and distant, completely unreal. "Some bastard's snatched my little girl. You know it."

In three hours, Naomi could have been a long way from Alstad—or dead. Staffan had no idea what to do next except *not* stand here talking a second longer. He got back into his car and just drove blindly. He should have been home with Lena, but he felt helpless, useless, *guilty*. He had to do something or go crazy.

Lena was right. He should never have let a six-year-old out on her own like that.

He headed for New Stockholm, praying one minute and swearing the next, cruising the streets while he scanned pedestrians and every single car that passed. There was no reason to think anyone would have brought Naomi here, but he didn't have a better idea. It wasn't until his phone bleeped again that he snapped out of it and accepted this was all random and pointless.

"Come home," Lena said. "I can't stand everyone calling to tell me it's all going to be all right."

It was nearly midnight. It was shocking how much life could change in a matter of hours.

I could have just driven to the school and picked her up.

Why the hell did she get off the bus early?

When he got home, there were neighbors' cars still parked in the road outside, but Lena was alone, sitting in the kitchen with her arms folded on the table. She had the radio and TV on at the same time. The competing audio streams merged into a quiet babble in the background.

She looked like she'd been crying. Staffan waited for the what-ifs and if-onlies.

"I'm sorry, sweetheart," he said. "I'm so sorry. But we'll find her. She can't just disappear like that."

"But they do, don't they?" Lena had that look on her face, the one that stopped short of saying *this is all your fault.* He didn't need reminding. "You've only got to watch the news."

Staffan knew he wouldn't get through the next hour if he let himself think that. He'd expected to find himself crying and pacing the floor, but he and Lena just sat at the kitchen table, not talking, not looking at each other, just fending off sporadic knocks at the door from well-meaning neighbors. The police called pretty well on the hour, but they had no more news.

"I should go out again," Staffan said. It'd be light in a few hours. His eyes kept closing. How could he be tired at a time like this? "I really should."

Lena poured a pot of cold coffee down the drain. "I'll go. You stay here."

"You sure?"

"I've done all the sitting and waiting I'm going to do." She took the keys. "She's out there. I know she is. I refuse to believe she's gone. Don't you dare tell me she is."

"Okay, honey. I know. I know."

Staffan had expected himself to be *more* than this somehow: more decisive, more logical, more grief-stricken, more angry. He felt like he was bargaining with fate. If he didn't actually say the words or think the worst, then it wouldn't happen. Naomi was still alive; he'd see her again. Repeating that mantra was the only way to cope with the unthinkable.

He switched to another TV channel and rested his head on his hands, trying to think of something that he'd overlooked. Had anyone rung around the hospitals? Maybe she'd been hit by a car and they couldn't ID her.

Maybe . . .

This is crazy.

His head started to buzz. He closed his eyes for just a moment.

The phone rang and woke him. He hadn't even realized he'd fallen asleep at the table. Lena was back. She stood with the handset pressed to her ear, sobbing. "Are you sure? *Are you sure?* Oh, thank God . . ."

Staffan jumped to his feet, heart pounding, trying to listen in on the call. Lena put the phone down and cupped her hands over her mouth, eyes tight shut.

"Jesus, honey, just *tell* me."

"They've found her. She's okay. They've taken her to the hospital to check her over."

The relief was so powerful that his legs almost buckled. "Where?" He looked at the clock on the wall. It was just before six in the morning. Was he really awake? Yes, he was. The nightmare was over. "Goddamn it, you should have let me talk to them."

"She's *okay.* Come on. Let's go."

"Who took her? What did they do to her?" Staffan's dread was already giving way to a panicky anger. "I swear I'll kill the bastard if he's laid a finger on her—"

"They said she's fine. She's *safe.* Come *on.*"

"What the hell happened? Where was she?"

"Five klicks southwest of New Stockholm," Lena said. "She was sitting at a bus stop. A bus driver stopped to check on her and she asked him to help her find her way home."

That was an hour or so from Alstad. "What was she doing out there?"

"No idea. She can't remember. She didn't show up on any other bus cams, so they'll want to talk to her again later. She certainly didn't walk there on her own."

Staffan had to search for his keys. He realized he hadn't called the factory to let them know he'd be late, either. Well, too bad. He struggled to keep his mind on the road while he tried to make sense of what he knew.

"I don't believe it. Six in the goddamn morning? Nobody notices a kid out on her own all night?"

"Someone *did* spot her. Eventually."

"But where was she for the rest of the time? She was gone for *twelve hours*. She couldn't have done that on her own. What were the goddamn cops doing? They couldn't even find her with a dog and a dropship. Useless assholes."

Lena held up her hands to silence him. "Look, we'll find out later. All that matters is she's alive and she's coming home. Just stop this. Please."

Staffan hardly dared say it. But Lena had to be thinking it as well. "I swear if anyone's touched her, I'm going to find him and cut off his balls. Because all he'll get from the judge is a rap across the knuckles and his own personal social worker to—"

"Staffan. Please. *Don't.*"

"Why aren't they telling us what happened?"

"Because they *don't know*. For Chrissakes. Just stop it."

It confirmed the worst for him. Naomi was probably too traumatized to speak. When they got to the hospital, they had to wait with a woman police officer for the best part of an hour before the doctors were ready to let them see Naomi. Staffan braced himself. When he and Lena were shown into the private room, Naomi was sitting cross-legged on a metal-framed bed, hands folded in her lap, still wearing her bright red dress and blue jacket. She looked more baffled than terrified.

Lena grabbed her and crushed her in a tearful hug. Staffan had to wait to get a look in. When he cuddled Naomi, she looked at him blankly for a second, as if she was working out who he was, but then she smiled. It worried him. Maybe they'd sedated her.

"Wow, you're away with the fairies, aren't you, baby?" he said. "What did they give you?"

"Breakfast," she said. "I had eggs."

Staffan looked at the doctor. "Have you given her any drugs? She seems pretty spacey."

The doctor shrugged. He had no way of knowing what was normal Naomi. *This* wasn't. "No sedation," he said. "She wasn't agitated. And she has no injuries at all. Which is odd, given that she can't remember how she got to the bus stop. Has she ever had seizures or blackouts before?"

"No." *Seizures? My little girl?* "She's perfectly healthy. Lord knows she's had enough medical examinations at school this last year. They'd have spotted anything odd. Look, when you say no injuries . . ."

"No, she hasn't been molested, if that's what you're asking. We do check in these cases."

It was a massive relief. Staffan found himself breathing normally for the first time in what felt like forever. "Well, she's never had fits. Are you sure she wasn't drugged by whoever took her?"

"We've run a tox screen—all clear so far. And nothing on the brain scan. She just doesn't remember anything before she arrived at the bus stop, let alone anyone taking her, and she still seems disoriented." The doctor ruffled Naomi's hair and gave her a big smile. "But you ate a pretty good breakfast, didn't you, poppet?"

"Where are all the other doctors?" Naomi asked. "There were always more than this."

That made no sense at all. Staffan glanced at Lena. She looked worried too. Just when he thought it would be enough to have Naomi back alive, it looked like they had a new problem.

"Keep an eye on her for the next few days," the doctor said. "I'll refer her to the consultant neurologist. It's the memory loss that concerns me. She might just be scared of a telling-off, but let's err on the side of caution."

Staffan carried Naomi to the car and put her in the backseat. She was still clutching her satchel. He watched her for a moment, desperate to see some hint of the normal Naomi, but maybe that was asking too much. She opened the satchel and looked inside as if she wasn't sure what was in there. Lena drove while he sat in the back, holding Naomi's hand. It was more for his benefit than hers.

"No school for a few days, sweetie," Lena said. "You've had a nasty fright, that's all."

Staffan didn't think that Naomi would ever be too scared to tell him anything, but there was always a first time. Maybe the doctor was right; maybe she'd behaved like a little girl for a change instead of a child prodigy.

"We're not angry with you, baby," he said. "But did you go into town to look at that doll's house again?"

Naomi gazed up at him, baffled. "What doll's house?"

"Doesn't matter." That was weird. She couldn't have forgotten it already. "I've got you something even better for your birthday."

"Okay." That was all she said. "Okay."

Staffan was really scared now. There *was* something wrong. When they got home, he tucked her up in a blanket on the sofa and sat watching her for the rest of the day, frightened to take his eyes off her. Whatever had happened, she was a lot quieter than normal. When she got up to go to the bathroom, she stood in the hallway for a moment as if she was working out where it was, and Lena had to lead her upstairs. When she came back and started reading her book, she turned it over from time to time to frown at the cover, and she didn't finish her favorite sandwich—crustless triangles filled with mashed egg, dill, and mayonnaise. Lena put her to bed early and she didn't beg for a few more minutes to finish the chapter. She didn't do anything that she usually did.

Weird. Wrong.

"Yeah, I think she's ill," Lena said, folding the blanket. "Whatever the doctor said, she's sickening for something. Flu, maybe."

"I hope that's all it is."

Lena just looked at him, arms folded. "And we'll keep a closer eye on her, because Naomi or not, we nearly lost her. She'll grow up fast enough. Until we know exactly what happened, she isn't going anywhere on her own again, okay?"

"Okay."

It was strange how Naomi had forgotten all about the doll's house. Some kids had a different fad every day, but once Naomi set her mind to something, it was hard to derail her. Perhaps she'd been into the shop after all, seen how much the doll's house cost, and realized that she was expecting a very expensive thing. Maybe she'd felt guilty about that, and was too embarrassed to come home and admit it until she'd worked out a way to change her mind without sounding like she felt her dad had let her down.

Come on, she's smart, but she's still five—okay, six. On the other hand . . . she's like her grandma. She'll pretend she didn't really want it after all.

Staffan couldn't afford the doll's house, but he could certainly make one like it. How hard could it be? He worked in a machine shop. If he could cut and grind metal to fine tolerances, he could make a wooden house and all the furniture that went in it. And he could make it special and personal for her.

But that would take time. Naomi needed something special right now. He unwrapped the planetarium lamp and put it on the table next to her bed. She opened her eyes just as he switched it on and filled the room with drifting stars.

"There," he said. "You've got the whole galaxy now. And all the galaxies beyond it. See that one? And that? Can you remember what it's called?"

Naomi gazed up at the ceiling. She seemed mesmerized. "No. But it's pretty."

She could normally name the constellations. Staffan put his hand on her forehead, but she didn't feel feverish. "We got it for your birthday. But you deserve a treat right now."

"Thank you, Daddy. I'm sorry for not remembering."

"It doesn't matter, sweetheart. You'll be right as rain before long." He turned the dial to the rainbow setting. If she woke in the night, the first thing she'd see would be the soothing play of lights. He stroked her hair as she watched the ceiling. He had his little girl back, and right then nothing else mattered. "Just enjoy the stars."

CHAPTER

TWO

EVERY VESSEL COUNTS. WE CAN'T YET REPLACE WHAT WE LOSE, SO THE WAR AGAINST THE ARBITER AND THE OTHER BLASPHEMERS MAY BE WON OR LOST ON A SINGLE HULL. WE NEED TO RECOVER *PIOUS INQUISITOR* FROM THE KIG-YAR. THE SIMPLEST WAY TO FIND HER IS TO PAY AN-OTHER KIG-YAR TO BETRAY HIS OWN KIND. THEY HAVE NO HONOR—FORTUNATELY.

—SHIPMASTER AVU MED 'TELCAM, SERVANT OF THE ABIDING TRUTH, ADDRESSING REBELLION COMMANDERS AT HIS HEADQUARTERS ON LAQIL, FORMERLY THE HUMAN COLONY WORLD NEW LLANELLI

UNSC *PORT STANLEY* IN STEALTH MODE, OFF VENEZIA; THIRTY-FIVE YEARS LATER—APRIL 2553

"Smooth icing," Mal Geffen said, gesturing at Adj. "Come on, BB. Can't you make him understand? I thought you'd fixed his translator."

BB projected his plain, box-shaped avatar into *Port Stanley*'s galley, where Mal, Devereaux, and Adj were putting the finishing touches to a cake for Osman. Adj floated around the table, occasionally reaching out a tentacle to tease a layer of navy blue frosting into even more ragged peaks. On closer inspection, the curved tips of the frosting turned out to not to be random; they were fractals. Huragok didn't do anything by halves. The common name for them, Engineers, didn't even begin to cover their skills.

"Serves you right for using the galaxy's most sophisticated organic computer as a food processor, Staff."

"I was trying to be *inclusive,*" Mal said. "You know. Team building."

BB projected two holographic tentacles to begin signing. Huragok appreciated someone talking to them in their own language. *<Fractals? Smartass.>*

<I cannot do random things.> Adj's translucent mantle shimmered with a hint of violet bioluminescence. If he'd been agitated, he'd have lit up like a Christmas tree. *<And an uneven surface makes the substance taste more appealing to humans.>*

<They need it to be smooth and level,> BB signed. Huragok knew best, and it baffled them that humans sometimes didn't *want* what was best. *<It has to be written upon.>*

<Mal should have specified that.>

<You know what humans are like. Vague. Just make the surface completely smooth.>

Mal leaned against the counter, arms folded, and fixed Adj with a narrow-eyed stare. "Is he pissed off because he thinks cooking's beneath him?"

"No, he's fine, and he understands you perfectly well."

It was clear to BB that Mal was joking, but maybe not to Adj. "Just being arsey, then."

"Let's say *perfectionist.*"

Huragok didn't care what they were doing as long as they were busy and improving things. Sometimes that meant more elegant patisserie; sometimes it meant a more lethal nuclear missile. They didn't seem to make moral judgments. BB marveled at the human capacity to see that as innocence rather than an inherent danger.

Adj switched to his translator's quiet, monotone male voice. *<It would have tasted better with an uneven surface.>*

He'd had the last word, which seemed to make him happy. His mantle sparkled with bioluminescence as he reworked the frosting. BB wondered if that was the Huragok equivalent of whistling while he worked.

"Can you write 'Congratulations Rear Admiral Osman' on the top as well, please?" Devereaux asked. "In gold?"

<*Yes.*> Adj waited.

"And in English," Devereaux said, taking the hint.

<*You were imprecise again.*>

BB took that as a scolding. Adj pounced on the cake and in seconds it was as smooth as a Johansson block. His tentacles plunged into the bowl of sugar again, worked furiously, and strands of gleaming gold paste emerged. One paid out like a rope trick onto the top of the cake to form the lettering, and two more—one wide strip, one narrow—appeared as a replica of a rear admiral's lace. How he'd managed to build metallic color into the sugar was anyone's guess.

Adj placed the sugar braid around the sides of the cake, then licked one tentacle with a tiny anteater tongue. Huragok could adapt to survive on any energy source, and even recharge from a power outlet, but when given a choice they seemed to prefer something sugary. It just added to their deceptive cuteness as far as BB was concerned.

"Thanks, Adj." Devereaux put her hand on his back like a favorite child. "You'll never be unemployed. Do you want us to save a couple of slices for you and Leaks?"

Adj drifted away, job done. Sharing food was one thing, but the minutiae of human social customs appeared to be of no interest to him. <*Puréed, please.*>

Mal slid the cake onto a tray and stood back to admire it. It really was very professional. "Okay, BB. Where's Phillips?"

"Moping around on the hangar deck."

"Really?"

"He's preoccupied."

"The hinge-heads."

"He felt he should have saved them."

"Hinge-heads."

"He sees them as women and children."

"Okay, I'm going to put my boot up his arse and *un*-preoccupy him." Mal would probably take Phillips to one side and give him a sympathetic sergeantly chat instead, but BB could translate Geffenese now. The time to brace for impact was when he went quietly polite. "Christ, you can't save every stray in the kennels. Are you going to round him up, or shall I?"

"I'll do it," Devereaux said. "I've got the special touch."

"Don't leave any bruises."

Devereaux made a show of tucking her shirt in her belt and tidying her hair as she headed for the door. "Poor old Phyllis. He's got to learn not to make pets of species we might have to kill."

She had a soft spot for Phillips. BB wondered whether to give the relationship a gentle nudge in the right direction, but decided to mind his own business for once. Mal adjusted the cake on the tray and sighed.

"Do you want a single red rose to put with that?" BB teased.

Mal raised a middle finger. "Vaz is the one with a thing for Spartans. Not me."

"Oo-oo-ooh . . ." Sometimes Mal would respond to a heart-to-heart, but sometimes dressing things up in a joke worked better. "Is it Naomi you're worried about, Staff? Or are you missing Vaz? You do get stroppy when your little chum's away."

"I worry about everybody. It's my job." Mal fidgeted with the cake again. "Osman doesn't seem delirious about her promotion. Is she okay?"

"Oh, it's just the sobering reality of coming one step closer to omnipotence. That's *much* healthier than the alternative. Look, would you excuse me a moment? I have to pay a courtesy visit to Admiral Parangosky."

Mal opened the galley lockers to collect plates and napkins. "I thought you could do fifty things at once."

"*I* can, but *you* get confused by it. Linear time. Don't you just hate it?"

BB could spread his attention through a thousand separate systems in locations light-years apart, but he tried to keep his visible presence restricted to one place at a time. *I'm not going soft. No face, no limbs, none of that cutesy-pie corporealist nonsense. Really. It's just good manners.* He wasn't trying to be human, just considerate of his human crewmates. He split off a fragment of himself and rode *Stanley*'s instant comms channel to appear in Margaret Parangosky's office, light-years' away in UNSC's Bravo-6 HQ in Sydney.

Parangosky looked up from her elevenses—Kona coffee, one sugar, two ginger nut biscuits—and smiled. "Morning, BB. How's our brand-new admiral?"

"We're waiting for the List to be formally promulgated before we wheel out the cake, ma'am."

"I'll send her a Bravo Zulu later. Everything okay?"

"We're expecting a sitrep from Venezia in a couple of hours."

"I'm not stepping on Osman's turf."

"Of course you're not."

"Just curious. Mainly about the Naomi situation."

BB thought that over for several nanoseconds, an AI's eternity. It was a delicate topic. "How would you feel if you discovered your father was not only still alive but living on Venezia under surveillance by DCS counter-terrorism?"

"That wasn't quite what I was asking."

"Naomi's a Spartan, ma'am. And a Spartan-Two, at that. If you can't rely on a Spartan, who *can* you trust?"

"*That* wasn't what I was asking, either."

"Ah. I see." BB read between the lines. "Kilo-Five is very close-knit. Very supportive of their *oppos*. Very loyal. But they do the job, regardless of their personal feelings, or else Dr. Halsey would be frozen solid and floating somewhere in space by now. Wouldn't she?"

Parangosky laughed, a throaty chuckle. "I'll cherish that image on dull days, BB. It'll be my *happy* place." She checked her watch. "CINCFLEET's releasing the List at noon, Alpha Time. Do you think Osman's getting cold feet about doing the job?"

The job meant only one thing; Parangosky's job, Commander in Chief of the Office of Naval Intelligence. BB fully understood her fixation with making sure she was succeeded by someone with the right stuff, which in ONI's case was best described as the *bad* stuff. Parangosky had transformed the branch from just another tribe within the rivalry-ridden intelligence world to effectively its sole power—clear in its purpose, unflinching in its resolve, and free of the budget squabbles that made agencies put preserving their own existence before the needs of Earth. BB had no illusions about the bodies that Parangosky had buried to achieve that, but only the very mean-spirited would deny that the woman was brilliant. Even as a mere captain, she'd punched well above her weight and brought down senior officers. When nobody wanted the Department of Colonial Security after the CAA fell from grace, she took it on as a doer-upper and acquired her own instant spy army of civilians with no preexisting loyalties to anyone else in the UNSC.

That took vision. Parangosky had it in spades. It extended beyond her own lifetime, too, which was where Serin Osman came in, because this wasn't about empire or the exercise of power, but the pursuit of a goal that would span generations. BB, doomed to a seven-year life span, took enormous comfort from a human who refused to let a small detail like being dead stop her from finishing what she'd started.

"I think Osman just needs a sustained run of unsavory choices to harden her casing," BB said. "That's the trouble with spending her formative years in the Spartan program. Her default setting is to seize the initiative and go it alone. To take one for the team. Not to send someone else to die in her place."

"And to bond with her squad. I *am* aware, BB."

BB picked his words as carefully as someone trying to avoid the coffee cremes in a box of chocolates. *Coffee cremes. Why did I think that? I've never even seen them.* "I know you couldn't possibly have set this up, Admiral, but I imagine the dilemma presented by Naomi's father will be rather character-forming for Osman."

There was a hair-fine line to walk between serving Osman and knowing what *not* to tell Parangosky, and Parangosky made it clear that she knew BB walked it. Sometimes he wondered whether it was a test to check that he would side with Osman instead of her if push came to shove—as he had to, as Osman would need him to when she became CINCONI. Parangosky was ninety-two and had ruled the Office of Naval Intelligence with a rod of unforgiving iron for decades, making some people disappear and others wish that they could. Osman was only forty-one, which was nowhere near enough time to build a throne of skulls like Parangosky's. On the other hand, her early childhood had been one of life-or-death survival in Halsey's boot camp on Reach, so he wondered how fast the adult Osman would revert to that primal ruthlessness when her back was against the wall.

And she'd been raised on the concept of killing a human enemy, colonial terrorists, not the clear-cut and easily digested threat of invading alien monsters. She was used to morally dirty warfare. No, she'd be fine. BB was sure of it.

He felt he'd been waiting minutes for Parangosky's reply, but that was the price of being an AI, running so fast that a blink for a human was an hour's internal debate for him. She'd simply paused for a second to brush a crumb of ginger nut off her jacket. The biscuits sounded like concrete when she crunched on them. Even in her choice of cookies, the old girl liked something that put up a fight.

"Very well, BB," she said. "Keep me posted."

He rode the comms channel back to *Port Stanley* in an upbeat mood. There was good news to impart, even if it wasn't actually news to anybody, and he enjoyed being the bearer because it was always in short supply. He changed his box-shaped avatar into a gold envelope and projected himself at eye level above the desk in Osman's day cabin.

"Ta-*da*." His hologram glittered with a ripple of light. The latest Fleet promotions list, known simply as The List in every wardroom across the fleet, was the UNSC's official notification of which officers had been promoted and which were doomed to toil in the same rank for another year, or maybe forever. BB opened the envelope's flap and slid out a holographic sheet of paper with an accompanying drum roll. "And the winner is . . . gosh, *not* Captain Hogarth! Not even nominated for best-supporting minion. No, it's *Rear Admiral* Osman."

Osman leaned back a little, almost cringing from the news. "I'm not breaking out the Krug for this, you know. Maybe a cup of ONI's finest Jamaican, though."

"Oh, go on." BB reverted to his blue-lit box form. "Allow yourself some pride in achievement."

"I haven't done anything to earn it yet."

"I meant surviving the bear-pit of ONI thus far. Not the admiral bit."

"Thank you, BB."

Osman didn't even smile. She'd known it was coming for years, part of the necessary process to groom her as the most powerful officer in the UNSC—in reality, if not on paper—and by default the most powerful person on Earth. It was a prospect that BB knew weighed more heavily on her with every passing week.

Osman shrugged and looked past him, apparently studying her reflection in one of the nav displays. "I didn't have this many gray hairs six months ago."

"They're admiralty highlights, dear."

"Well, at least I won't look too young for the job when the day comes."

"Cheer up. Your loyal ship's company has a surprise for you." BB drifted to the door. "Would you care to come to the bridge?"

Osman managed a smile. *"And be it understood, I command a right good crew."*

"Oh, I do so love comic opera. Are you going to give us a tune?"

"No, and you'd thank me for it."

Mal was already on the bridge with Devereaux and Phillips. *Stanley* was a strangely empty ship at the best of times with only six humans on board, but she felt far emptier with Naomi and Vaz deployed to the surface. Mal had placed the cake under a small metal dome that looked suspiciously like part of an environment filter. His hand hovered over it, waiter-style.

"Is that the head of John the Baptist?" Osman asked.

"Not unless he's a Victoria sponge, ma'am." Mal lifted the cover. "Congratulations."

Phillips clapped and handed her a knife. "We'd have brought balloons and party whizzers, but there's a war on. Sort of."

Osman cocked her head as if she was calculating and cut the cake into eighths. It was funny how dividing up a cake could tell BB everything about her. Four portions would have meant she didn't think beyond the crew present on the bridge. Six would have omitted the Huragok. They all ate and made small talk for a few minutes—pay, pensions, how best to preserve Vaz's and Naomi's share of the cake until they returned—and then the chat died away.

"Okay, so where are we now, people?" Osman peeled the gold icing off her portion of cake and put it aside. "Vaz and Naomi—establishing their cover on Venezia. Mal and Dev on standby to relieve them. Primary objective—find *Pious Inquisitor.* Secondary—map the weapons supply routes, which we can roll up with keeping the supplies flowing to 'Telcam."

"I've been listening to 'Telcam's radio chatter overnight," Phillips said. "He's getting more agitated about *Inquisitor.* Piecing it together, I think he's going to hire someone he can trust to track Sav Fel and get the ship back. I wouldn't want to be Fel when he finds him."

"Is that pride or desperation?" Devereaux asked. "I know he's short of vessels, but there have to be easier ways of getting another ship."

"Maybe he wants the data on board. Don't forget *Inquisitor*'s been through a few hands. The Brutes had her when they fought the Sangheili, and then the rebel Sangheili under the Arbiter. There's probably loads of dirt and intel in the computers."

"And he's got to be as worried about asset denial as we are," Osman said. "Okay, keep monitoring that until you get a lead, Evan."

Phillips nodded enthusiastically. "I bet 'Telcam calls in rent-a-crow. It'll take another Kig-Yar to find Fel."

BB could have monitored all the channels simultaneously for Phillips—and did anyway, discreetly, just in case Phillips missed anything in real time—but humans preferred to do things for themselves. Phillips came into his own on the face-to-face interaction, though. He was very persuasive with Sangheili, completely at home with their language and culture, and he wowed them with his skill with an *arum* puzzle ball. It looked like a toy to humans, a sphere of complex, interconnected pieces that had to be moved in a precise sequence to release a stone held at the center. But to Sangheili it was a powerful cultural and political symbol on multiple levels, the embodiment of patience, discipline, and acceptance of the rigid order of society to achieve outcomes. Mastering it made Phillips something of a celebrity to them.

" 'Telcam's due another arms shipment from us in a couple of weeks, Evan," Osman said. "You want to ride along for that?"

Phillips nodded. He never refused an opportunity. "Can I have some more firearms training first, though?"

"You did okay with that plasma pistol back on Sanghelios,"

Mal said. "You could tool up with one of those. It's not like we haven't got a hold full of them, is it?"

He said it innocently, but Phillips flinched. BB made a note of that. Osman either didn't notice or thought it was wise to move on. She finished her slice of cake, checked the level in her coffee cup, and sat down to read through the overnight signals, if night had any meaning 200,000 kilometers off Venezia. BB monitored every scrap of data that came in or left the corvette anyway. In a sense, he *was* the ship.

Phillips went back to the hangar deck, where he'd laid claim to a small compartment as his listening station. Leaks—Leaks Repaired, the other Huragok conscripted into *Port Stanley's* service—had taken to upgrading it whenever he was allowed in. BB still wasn't sure why Phillips had holed up down here when he had an entire corvette to choose from, but Mal had muttered something about the compartment being Phillips's *gardening shed*. BB had had to look that one up.

He followed Phillips, zipping through the decks via relays and conduits for cameras, environmental monitoring, and power controls, a hundred roads for an AI to travel, and projected himself in the doorway.

"I'm going to intrude," BB said. "Are you all right? Please don't keep beating yourself up about Nes'alun. That's what happens in a civil war. The natives kill each other. The ones you save may very well end up killing *you*. So best let nature run its course and stop blaming yourself."

Phillips busied himself with the console. "But we're not doing that. We're throwing arms on the barbecue to keep the war simmering."

"I know. Humans do that. Despite numerous lessons from history that arming third parties who don't like you almost always backfires at some point."

"Oh, you've got a better idea. I see."

"I'd rather launch an all-out biological war of the kind ONI keeps in the freezer in places like Trevelyan. But those backfire quite often as well."

Phillips scratched his scrubby beard. He looked more like a student than a professor. "Actually, I was thinking about Naomi."

"You'll need a ladder. But I admire your pluck."

"I meant how far this might go with her dad."

"Are you asking if ONI plans to terminate him in their signature way?"

"I suppose I am."

"Let's hope it doesn't come to that."

Phillips looked as if he was going to press BB on it but stopped short. He changed tack. "So how are *you* doing? Have you come to terms with your broken fragment yet?"

"As much as any human comes to terms with their own mortality."

"I nearly died once."

"I know. I was there. Thanks for getting me damaged as well."

"No, I mean I nearly drowned myself off Bondi years ago. Being a dick, naturally. And when I really thought that was it, I'd bought it, it was surprising how ordinary it felt. An anticlimax, almost. So I don't worry too much about dying now."

"Oh good. I won't feel too bad about volunteering you for suicide missions, then."

Phillips managed a grin and paused for a moment, listening to the audio in his earpiece. Everyone's routine was slipping back to normal, or at least normal for Kilo-Five. BB did a quick check to locate the crew—Osman on the bridge, Adj and Leaks tinkering with the water reclamation a couple of decks below her, Mal and Devereaux in their respective cabins—but felt frustrated that Naomi and Vaz had gone silent between sitreps. He was used to monitoring them. Not being able to sense them felt like his path was dotted with bottomless black pits. Planned absence of data had never bothered him before he'd reintegrated the fragment of himself that had been damaged on Sanghelios when Phillips was caught in a bomb blast. The data gaps that it left felt like harbingers of rampancy. It was what Devereaux described as the sensation of someone walking on your grave. BB knew exactly how that felt. Without a body, he shouldn't have been able to, but his mind had its foundations in the pathways of a real human brain, donated by an individual man who'd lived and breathed, and its most primal components underpinned his existence. Somehow, he recalled how some things felt.

He could have found out who that donor was, but he'd stopped himself from accessing the data so that he was never tempted to look.

Whoever he was . . . I'm me. A distant relative with a few characteristics in common.

It was a step beyond the measures he'd taken to firewall Osman's data so he never accidentally blurted out something she didn't want to hear. That was *forgotten*. His own data was *not known*. He understood exactly why Naomi was the only Spartan who'd taken up ONI's offer to open their background file.

And look what she's found. Awful, awful pain. No thanks.

Not even Osman had looked into her own past. She'd had ONI clearance to do it for years. BB blocked his recall of the detail, but he remembered how he'd felt when he read her file.

Oddly enough, it had felt like . . . relief.

JARROW CROSSROADS, NEW TYNE, VENEZIA: APRIL 2553

"Naomi, are you okay?"

The vehicle had gone. No matter how long she looked down the road, she couldn't change what she'd just seen. She'd been confident—completely confident—that it wouldn't make any difference to her, but it had.

Naomi-010, Spartan and UNSC Petty Officer, couldn't recall ever being Naomi Sentzke or living on a colony world called Sansar, but she'd just seen the proof drive past her in a truck—her own father, a man she couldn't remember, talking to a Kig-Yar in the passenger seat as the vehicle waited at the stop lights. She recognized him from a photo in an intelligence folder. But it was one thing to look at a photo without feeling anything, and another entirely to see someone in the flesh.

Halsey had convinced Naomi and her fellow conscripts that they were immune to the weaknesses of normal humans, but she'd probably never planned for the unlikely event that a Spartan would come face-to-face with their real family again. A crack had opened in Naomi's world. Her curiosity drove her to peer through it.

For a moment, she wasn't sitting in a Warthog on a potentially hostile planet, and she wasn't operating undercover. She was . . .

She was . . .

She just didn't know. She couldn't remember. She simply *felt,* and it wasn't a feeling she could define or name. She only knew that it made her uncomfortable.

"Naomi, did you hear that?"

She replayed the footage on her datapad. *Look at him. That's me. That's who I take after. That's my father.* She tried to connect the thought to some emotion, but it only triggered a vague sensation of guilt, as if she knew she'd done something wrong but couldn't recall what it was.

"Naomi, I said *did you hear all that?*" Vaz Beloi nudged her with his elbow, almost peering into her face as he leaned over the steering wheel. His finger was pressed against his concealed earpiece. "Did you hear what Spenser said?"

"What?"

"He ID'd the Kig-Yar in the truck as the one who hijacked *Pious Inquisitor.* It's Sav Fel."

"Yes, I *heard,* Vasya." Maybe that was too abrupt. "I keep my comms channel open. I always do."

Poor Vaz: he'd gone out of his way to be kind to her. He'd even read her background file to find out who she'd been before she was abducted and what had happened to her family, because she couldn't face reading it herself. He'd shouldered the burden of deciding what was too harrowing to tell her, the first person she'd truly trusted outside her narrow Spartan circle.

"Okay, no point trying to tail Fel now," he said, as if Staffan Sentzke had never been part of the equation. "We'll pick him up again later."

"Say it."

"Say what?"

"What you'd say if I was Mal." What should she call her father? Sentzke, Staffan, Dad? Every possible name seemed wrong. "You'd speculate about Fel supplying . . . Sentzke with a warship to use against Earth."

Vaz started the Warthog and pulled out of the parking lot to turn onto the main road. "Naomi, every human here has some grudge against Earth. The aliens probably have a grudge against Earth *and* their own governments. Welcome to Venezia. It's Grudgeworld."

Damn: they were less than two days into this op and her personal connection to it was already putting Vaz in an awkward position. She wasn't supposed to let anything get in the way of her mission. But Halsey and Chief Mendez had never taught their Spartans how to deal with friends who felt outrage on their behalf.

"So who's calling this in?" she asked. "You or me?"

"We need to talk to Spenser first."

"Why?"

"You ever wonder why BB had no idea your father was here?" Vaz kept checking the rearview mirror. "I don't know why I didn't ask sooner. Because Spenser hadn't put him on any database that BB could access. He keeps it all on his personal datapad."

"Oversight?"

"Old DCS habit, maybe. Spooks live in a permanent state of paranoia. And he's a *civilian* spook. I bet he keeps intel to himself without even thinking about it."

"But DCS have been reporting to Parangosky since she was a captain."

"Yeah, but *he's* been around since the colonial insurgency."

"We don't tell him everything, either."

"Well, what we do to others, they probably do to us. Never mind. Parangosky allows for that."

Naomi did the math. Spenser must have been sixty or so, then, older than he looked. But she had no reason to mistrust him. Not sharing low-level intel seemed a natural precaution for an agent who lived undercover most of the time. It must have been hard for him to decide which was the real Mike Spenser, the DCS agent or his Mike Amberley persona, electrician and ne'er-do-well ostensibly seeking a quiet and unnoticed life in New Tyne. He spent more hours being the latter.

How had he come across her father? Dad had never been a colonial rebel, not according to her file, so all he'd done was show up here and plot his vengeance against Earth. Had he ever done any more than that? What had he done between leaving Sansar and arriving here? Her file said that Dad had worked out half the story for himself—that his daughter had been abducted and replaced by a short-lived double, that it was all part of some government conspiracy. He just didn't know the rest, or how right he was. It was an impressive feat for a factory worker.

Oh God. I'm thinking of him as Dad. How did that happen?

It caught Naomi off-guard. She shook herself and focused on keeping an eye out for potential trouble. Venezia, untouched by the Covenant, looked strikingly normal to her in a way that few other colony worlds did. *Few? I don't think I've seen any intact. And I don't even remember Sansar.* New Tyne's houses and stores were undamaged, with a patina of sun-fading and lichen that said they'd been there for a long time rather than rebuilt after a Covenant attack. It was a world that had somehow been spared.

She watched a Brute drive past in a small troop carrier, heading south with a Grunt sitting beside him. On the sidewalk, a woman strolled with a shopping basket in one hand and a small boy hanging on tightly to the other. Aliens that had been Naomi's deadly enemies a few months ago were still a sight that made her uneasy, but New Tyne didn't exactly look like a hotbed of insurrection. Spenser said that anyone with a reason to avoid the authorities—human or non-human—could find sanctuary here in Venezia's unique multiculture of shared risk, the common bond of being on the wrong side of something or someone.

Naomi had no idea how long alien fugitives had lived here alongside humans. But given that the rest of the galaxy had only just ended a thirty-year war, even months would have been impressive feat of tolerance.

She hadn't seen any Sangheili, though. She had no illusions about them. Arming their rebels was something she did because she was ordered to, not because she liked the idea. She'd killed thousands and she had no regrets about that at all. Was that wrong? No, she'd seen too many ravaged worlds. She'd been taught to take satisfaction from a necessary job done well.

They deserve what they get.

"Weird, isn't it?" Vaz said.

"What is?"

"All those Covenant aliens, walking around like the war never happened." He glanced at a passing pickup with a couple of Kig-Yar in it. "Did you ever plan for a life outside the service?"

It was the hardest question Naomi had ever been asked. To plan, you had to want something. What did she want? A little voice murmured warnings at the back of her mind, more a vague uneasiness than anything audible or articulated. She was still trying to remember something that just wouldn't crystallize. She hadn't felt that for a long time.

"I didn't know it was even possible," she said. "Or that I'd live long enough to have the luxury of wondering about it."

"Yeah, it's easy to forget there's still a world out there."

"I wonder where Jul 'Mdama is now."

"Well, if he's still alive, he's plotting his revenge." Vaz pulled his dubious expression, wrinkling his nose. "Especially if he's found out his wife's dead."

"I'd still rather deal with him than 'Telcam. At least he tries to kill you to your face."

Vaz laughed, but she wasn't joking. It troubled her when that happened. She felt gauche, as if she'd missed something that normal people understood but that she didn't. She wasn't used to feeling inadequate. She'd only ever been told she was exceptional, mankind's best hope.

"Ah, the mad monk," Vaz said. "But he does speak good English for a hinge-head. Even if he can't say *Phillips.*"

"Do you ever wonder how many ODSTs he's killed?"

Vaz slowed for another set of stoplights. New Tyne seemed to have an awful lot of controlled intersections for a small place. "All the time," he said. "Elites don't have full-time interpreters. He was an *armed* 'terp. When the time comes to kill him, I'll volunteer. And sleep easier."

A shadow fell across the front seat as another vehicle pulled up next to them at the lights. Naomi braced, hand on her sidearm. This was when ambushes happened. She could see the driver out of the corner of her eye, a thickset middle-aged guy in a plaid shirt, but he just glanced at them and looked away again. If he'd seen her, she hadn't reminded him of anyone. The lights changed and the vehicles moved off.

She slid her hand under her coat for the reassurance of her

magnum again, still a little disoriented without her Mjolnir armor. It was about more than just missing the augmentation and electronics. She felt more conspicuous in a drab gray parka and shabby combat pants than she ever did in three hundred kilos of gleaming titanium alloy. The Mjolnir face was who and what she was, the tribal identity she shared with the family she'd spent most of her life with—her fellow Spartans. Her civilian-looking self was flayed, peeled, missing both its protection and its self-image. She took her cap out of her pocket and pulled it down hard on her head. It was a poor substitute for a helmet.

"It's the eyes," Vaz said.

"What is?"

"It's not your hair that makes you look like your dad. It's your eyes."

The arms dealer they'd just sold an MA5B rifle to had definitely recognized a family resemblance. He hadn't said the name Sentzke, but then he hadn't needed to. Naomi had seen the look on his face. She ducked her head to check herself in the wing mirror and saw her father's pale gray eyes blink back at her. Dying her white-blond hair some other color wouldn't change that.

"I need some colored contacts," she said.

Vaz studied her face for a moment as she turned to him. "Adj can whip up a pair. I'll ask BB on the next radio check. He knows all your biometrics, seeing as he's been in your neural interface."

"Yeah, I don't have any secrets," she said. "Except from myself."

She realized that she'd put her hand on the back of her neck, a reflex reaction to cover the external port of the interface at the base of her skull. Adj had remodeled it to reduce the profile. If anyone got too close—closer than she'd tolerate, anyway—all they'd see through her hair would be something that looked like the regular implant that most UNSC personnel had. It supported the simplest of cover stories, that they were Naomi Bakke and Vaz Desny, two deserters looking for a quiet refuge in New Tyne. It was easier to play a soldier with a reason for hiding on Venezia than to try to walk, talk, and behave like a civilian. Some things were hard to conceal.

Her thoughts drifted back to the kid walking along the road with his mother. What was it like to grow up in an outlaw community? It didn't look that different from what she thought of as normal life.

"There." Vaz indicated left and turned down a ramp into the grim concrete housing estate where Spenser lived an outwardly regular Venezian life. "Nobody tailed us, either. So far, so good."

Spenser was making sandwiches in the kitchen, filling the place with the smell of hard-boiled eggs. He was a rumpled-looking, everyday guy with gray hair and a lot of lines, as far from the movie image of a spy as it was possible to get. It made him perfect for the job.

"I've got to go to work," he said, putting the sandwiches in his lunchbox. He did contract maintenance shifts at the local militia base, a testament to what Mal Geffen called his *spook-fu*. Naomi was always impressed by the power of ordinariness. What better place for a spy like him, a civilian used to working in military environments, to infiltrate? He fitted in seamlessly. "So . . . Sav Fel's shown up here. How do you want to play this?"

Vaz didn't look at Naomi. "Our priority's *Pious Inquisitor*. Are we going to have to do this the old-fashioned way?"

"Yeah, we're going to have to tail him. I'll see what I can glean at work, but he's got to have access to a small atmosphere-capable transport, because he's going to have a hard time hiding nearly two kilometers of battlecruiser on the surface. I'm assuming Oz hasn't detected anything that size in orbit."

Naomi wondered if Spenser would still call Osman "Oz" when she became CINCONI. "We'd have heard if she had."

"Okay, so we follow Fel somehow," Vaz said. "Or Sentzke."

"Where do they hang out?"

"Not sure yet. I'm still putting the pieces together on Sentzke." Spenser sealed his lunchbox with a snap. "Some of the locals are known quantities from my DCS days, but he's a new face to me. I've only been here a couple of months, remember. Did I tell you how I pinged him?"

"No," Naomi said. "But I did wonder how you got the photo."

"Sorry. Old spook habit. Sometimes he does maintenance work at the barracks. It's not his main job—I think he does it as a favor. Anyway, you know what they're like for insisting on passes, so I just poked around in the admin filing cabinet one night." He looked at Naomi as if she'd reacted, but she was sure she hadn't. It was still just *words*: father, Staffan, Sansar. "I knew when he went off-planet because getting to and from Venezia is a big logistics job. Think about it. Even if you've got your own small vessel, you need to get a ride with a slipspace-capable ship if you're heading for another planet. The bigger vessels tend to belong to the militia. I overheard someone arranging it. One thing you need to remember about the culture here—it's *cautious*. These people don't trust tech that can be hacked. Nobody's ever created better security than pieces of paper you can burn and conversations you have face-to-face."

Spenser played his cards close to his chest, just like the local population. Naomi wasn't sure if that was simply his ingrained secretiveness or if he was trying to be diplomatic about her father. But she had to ask.

"Do you know where he lives?"

Spenser's expression changed for a moment, as if he'd slipped out of character and was trying to ground himself again.

"Fifteen, Mount Longdon Road—on the south of town, next to the old slate quarry. But I promised Mal Geffen I'd leave him to you. So I haven't been near him yet. Just keeping my ears open." Spenser shrugged, looking embarrassed. "I'm sorry. This must be awkward for you."

"Not at all." Naomi had learned long ago to lock down her

own expression and shut out all external distractions. She was still uneasy, but she couldn't pin it down to whatever her father was doing right now. "If it was, I'd ask Osman to redeploy me."

"Well, I plug into the Kig-Yar bush telegraph. The Jackals get around. If Fel's selling off that warship, I'll get to hear. He definitely isn't hanging out with Sentzke to attack Earth, though. Kig-Yar couldn't give a rat's ass about Earth, not unless we want to buy something."

"No use for a battlecruiser themselves, then."

"Not their style. A big warship isn't much use for a lot of the things they do, and it's goddamn expensive to maintain." Spenser took his jacket off the hook on the back of the door. "I'll leave you to tell Osman. Okay, I have to go now. You've got your map, yeah?"

Vaz tapped his pocket. "All the recommended hot spots."

"Don't forget there's a bounty on your head for offing those Jackals on Reynes."

"They don't know it was us," Vaz said. "We didn't leave any witnesses, did we?"

Spenser chuckled. "I'm glad to see ONI's teaching you something. Did you sell the rifle, by the way?"

"Got eight-seventy-five for it."

"Not too shabby. Remember to secure the house if you go out."

Vaz didn't say anything for a long time after Spenser left. He topped up the coffee machine, humming to himself. He was picking his words. Naomi wanted him to just speak his mind.

"Well, if Sentzke's in the market for a warship, I wonder how he's going to pay for it," he said at last.

"And he'll need a crew. Unless he's got an AI as good as BB."

"Well, that'll take him some time. I bet the Covenant didn't have anything."

"Isn't it time we called this in to Osman?"

"What do you want me to say?"

"That we've spotted Sav Fel, and that he was with my father. That'd be a start, I think." There: she'd done it again. "Sorry. I didn't mean to be abrasive. Okay, I'm going downstairs to call the ship."

Vaz just nodded. He knew she needed to do it herself. She didn't need to explain.

Spenser had set up a mini listening station in the basement, complete with a fridge and a battered sofa. It was probably a lot more comfortable to work in than the disused mine shaft he'd lived in on Reynes while he was monitoring the Sangheili. Naomi opened the secure link to *Port Stanley* and BB responded

"Remember to call Osman *Admiral* now," BB said. "It's official. We baked a cake. We'll send you some on the next resupply run. Anything you need?"

"Cosmetic lenses. Blue, hazel, green—anything to darken my eye color. Just in case anyone spots the resemblance." Words: still just words. But she did feel odd. She was trying to remember and wasn't sure what or why. "We just made a positive ID of Sav Fel in New Tyne. We eyeballed him less than an hour ago. He was in a vehicle with my father."

That even silenced BB for a second. "Oh," he said. "At least that narrows your search area."

"Tell Osman we're going to work on a way to track Sav Fel to *Inquisitor.* Next radio check in two hours."

"Is that all you want to say?" BB asked.

"Yes. Naomi out."

She cut the link and leaned back on the sofa, picking at a rip in the leather while she worked out a search pattern to locate both the truck and Sav Fel.

We need to know when they leave the planet. Dad might be a red herring. He might be involved with Fel for some other reason, but common sense says the ship's the most likely reason. So . . . how do we do this?

Tagging Sav Fel—or her father, if her suspicions were right—

was going to require face-to-face contact anyway. Whatever they did, they'd have to get personal.

Dare I risk that?

And I'm calling him Dad *again.*

She waited for Osman to call back and pull her out because the risk of recognition was too high. But no call came. She looked at a six-pack of sodas on top of the battered gray filing cabinet, debating whether to just go back upstairs and tell Vaz the deed had been done and the sky hadn't fallen in. No, she had to sort out this uneasiness first. Spartan or not, she was human, and the brain always tried to complete the pattern: a gap had now been filled in her memory, the one that said *Father.*

So how about *Mother?* What did that evoke?

Naomi tried to grasp the thought as she poured a soda into the only clean glass she could find. The absence of hostile aliens—obvious, dangerous, lethal—was allowing thoughts that she hadn't been aware of before to surface. She watched the soda bubbles rise and vanish.

Bubbles. They only form a running bead in carbonated liquid when there's dirt on the glass.

For a second the surface of the soda was completely still, a perfect mirror before it shivered and broke up. Now she remembered what she'd wanted. It was the last thing she'd truly longed for, other than wanting to go home to her mom and dad.

She'd been five years old, maybe six. And she'd wanted a doll's house.

FIVE KILOMETERS OUTSIDE NEW TYNE, VENEZIA

Skirmisher Kig-Yar were a lot like birds, Staffan Sentzke reminded himself, and that explained everything he needed to know about dealing with them.

Kig-Yar weren't canine, despite the nickname most humans used—Jackals. Their ancestors were reptiles. Some sub-species still looked very lizard-like to Staffan, but others were more like birds, just the way Earth's lizards had branched off to grow feathers and beaks. The most birdlike were the Skirmishers from T'vao. They liked shiny, glittery things, they squabbled, and they displayed. He suspected it was the legacy of an ancient ancestor that collected blossoms and pebbles to impress prospective mates. As he drove up the track to Sav Fel's grand house, he couldn't help but notice the fragments of brightly colored glass set in the concrete gate posts.

An armed Grunt stood guard. Staffan peered down at him from the truck window.

"I've come to see Shipmaster Fel. Staffan Sentzke."

The Grunt checked a datapad. "Your name's not on the list, and if your name's not on the list, then—"

"Cut the crap and try spelling it with two *F*s," Staffan said.

"Oh. Yeah."

"I didn't think you guys liked Kig-Yar."

"He pays on time."

Staffan took that as a sign that he could mistrust Fel a little less. He'd learned to assume that everyone he dealt with from the time he'd lost his daughter was a liar with an ulterior motive, and that nothing he saw was what it seemed, but there was a spectrum of bastardry. Some bastards were at the shoot-on-sight end of the curve; some were otherwise regular people with occasional but repellent flaws. In the middle lay the wide spread that the world wouldn't miss if they met their deserved fate. Kig-Yar generally scored as less objectionable than many humans because they didn't have ideologies. They liked *stuff,* pure and simple—acquiring it, smuggling it, stealing it, selling it, trading it, possessing it.

It's a game. Shiny stones. Bower bird mentality. But at least they make sense.

Sav Fel made sense too. He had his own agenda that happened to be running in parallel with Staffan's for a while. He wanted what Staffan had a great deal of, and Staffan wanted something that was little direct use to Fel: a warship.

Perfect.

One of the paneled front doors eased open just before he reached out to knock. A beaklike snout poked out of the gap, then the door creaked open fully to let Staffan in.

"He's in the office." The Kig-Yar minion was the more common reptilian kind. He took a few paces toward a corridor and let out a stream of ear-splitting chatter. "Wait here. I'll get him."

The hall wasn't quite as luxurious as Staffan had expected. The whole place smelled slightly of ammonia and what he could only describe as mud. The furniture was an odd mix of styles, but every piece had some gilding or polished metallic detail. Fel had the typical Kig-Yar weakness for glitz. It was echoed in his beaded, studded belt as he emerged from the passage.

Staffan caught a glimpse of another Skirmisher before Fel closed the door behind him, and heard a burst of angry jay-like noises. The shipmaster flinched.

Oh, it's his wife. It has to be his wife. Staffan tried not to give in to a smile. The idea of Shipmaster Fel being squawked at by an angry female was too funny. Staffan kept forgetting their society was matriarchal, because most of what he saw of it was the males toiling for a living. *Henpecked. Literally. Hah . . .*

Fel's minion trotted into the room to be dismissed again with an imperious gesture and a long rattling hiss. Fel might have been doing the Kig-Yar equivalent of kicking the cat, or just reminding his more reptilian cousin of his place in the pecking order. Skirmishers definitely thought they were a cut above other Kig-Yar.

"Welcome." Fel's black head feathers lifted a little. He reminded Staffan of a pterodactyl in the process of turning into a crow, with rows of little teeth set in a long beak. The vertical pupils in his yellow eyes were pure reptile, though. "Were you followed?"

"If I thought I was," Staffan said, "I'd have driven to the grocery store and wasted his time, whoever he was."

"There are spies here, you know."

"There's spies everywhere. But you know they don't last long here." Venezia was a colony of dissenters—and criminals. Strangers were treated with due caution, and a spy would have to be very good indeed to escape Staffan's attention for long. "So you have one at last, do you?"

Fel almost preened. He knew he'd pulled off a coup. "The opportunity presented itself. I seized it."

The Kig-Yar opened another inner door and led Staffan through into the main room. It was full of gilded mirrors that gave the place the feel of a home decor showroom. He could hear other Kig-Yar now, a mix of adult voices with higher-pitched ones in the distant background—children. *Chicks.* Staffan wondered if they were cute and fluffy when they hatched. He settled in the most comfortable-looking seat without being asked, just so that Fel understood who held the power here, and crossed his legs.

"Tell me exactly how you took the ship," he said.

"Don't you believe me?"

"Oh, I believe you. I just want to be sure that this isn't some elaborate setup."

Fel jerked back his head, offended. "The Sangheili are falling apart. They're not capable of scams. Certainly not scams that cost them warships."

"*Everyone*'s capable of scams," Staffan said. "Especially when they're desperate. Although I can't think why the Sangheili would suddenly take an interest in Venezia, unless you've pissed them off some other way."

The Covenant had either never found Venezia during the war or never bothered. The planet was unglassed, untouched, and in pretty good shape, which no doubt irked the Earth authorities. Staffan missed little. He had enough deserters from planetary militias to maintain a pretty good listening station, and pieced together with reports from Kig-Yar ships, the information formed a useful picture.

As useful as you can get now that the Covenant's collapsed, anyway.

"The Sangheili were so used to the San'Shyuum thinking for them that they're still struggling without them," Fel said. "They're in chaos. And the Arbiter certainly isn't uniting them. It's what you call a *free-for-all* when it comes to keeping track of their assets. One of their rebel factions asked me and my crew to transport a warship from one of their yards."

"Which faction?"

"A religious one."

"And you transported it."

"We did."

"Except you didn't transport it to its destination."

"It was a *battle*. I don't like that kind of destination. Not when it isn't my fight, anyway."

"So you just took it. Easy as that."

"Yes. Because, as I'm trying to tell you, the split-faces were too busy fighting each other to come after us."

"Okay."

"I thought it would come in useful for a customer. It is, as you say, a planet killer. A battlecruiser with a ventral beam. *Pious Inquisitor.*"

Staffan hated those sanctimonious Covenant names, albeit in a theoretical kind of way. The Covenant had never troubled Venezia. Earth was the only power that had ever done that. He hated some UNSC ships' names a lot more; they were about ferocity and bravery, when all he could see was an imperial power that didn't do much for its empire except bleed it dry and leave it to save itself when the Covenant came.

I got out of Sansar in time. Millions didn't.

"That name . . ."

"The Sangheili are very upset at losing her," Fel said. "Apart from hulls being at a premium in these uncertain times, I understand she has quite a history."

"Is this making the Sangheili extra-pissed off?"

"I wouldn't risk offering her to the Arbiter."

"Very wise."

"But I did check the stored data in the navigation computer, and this ship has deployed to Earth in the recent past, so given your interest in acquiring a more compact warship and your relationship with Earth . . . I thought of you immediately."

Staffan tried to recall if he'd heard the ship's name before. "Have you ever seen a planet after it's been glassed by one of those beams?"

"Of course I have. I used to serve the Covenant."

"I mean one of your *own*."

"No. But *you* have—yes, yes, I know all that. Just tell me who you might use this ship against."

"None of your customers, Fel."

"Humans, then."

"I may have scores to settle with the Covenant, but those with my own species come first."

"Because you know—"

"Yes. Glassed cities are cities that can't do business. Glass a city and you glass the merchandise. Don't glass the customer. I get it."

Only a Kig-Yar would turn down the chance of keeping a battlecruiser that could reduce the surface of a planet to molten slag. But it wasn't morality. Kig-Yar simply didn't fight that way, not if they had a choice. Staffan tried to recall any human culture that had abandoned an empire before over-expansion and hostile subjects brought it to its natural and inevitable end, but he couldn't. Yet the Kig-Yar had done just that. It was hard to think like them. They progressed, they expanded, and then they reverted to their tribal, piratical, scavenging selves.

No ideology. No manifest destiny. No mission to civilize or enlighten or save souls. No obsession with dominance. They just do it because they're good at it, and they actually enjoy the acquiring and winning more than they enjoy what they've taken.

Staffan needed to understand motives. If he knew why someone did something—an individual or an entire culture—then they rarely caught him out. Kig-Yar didn't need big capital ships because they didn't want to invade or destroy worlds, and most warships weren't built for raiding and slipping away. Kig-Yar preferred to be free and agile. They preferred to travel light. Even a relatively modest warship like *Pious Inquisitor* was a little too big for that.

That's what they do. Strike, peck, collect, fly. Carrion rather than prey. Opportunists. They're turning into birds. Vultures.

No, magpies. And magpies can be nasty little bastards.

The universe made perfect sense again. Staffan knew that it would if he thought about it long enough.

"So what will you pay for it?" Fel asked.

Staffan stared him out. "I'll tell you when I see it."

"I need particle beam rifles, dropships, and plasma pistols."

"Plenty of pistols and dropships, but the rifles are temporarily in short supply."

"*Temporarily?* You're one of the biggest arms dealers on Venezia."

"Meaning I'll see what I can do. I need to see the ship first."

"That means a trip to . . . another system."

"Fine. I didn't think you'd park it in your yard. And I want to test the ventral beam, so let's find a quiet backwater where we can do that."

"I shall. There's something else. It's extra."

"What is?"

"I'll show you when you see the ship."

Fel looked almost excited. Kig-Yar didn't have any facial expressions in common with humans, but they did have little gestures that gave a lot away if you knew how to look. Staffan did. There was a little back-and-forth jerk of the head, almost imperceptible. Most Kig-Yar males displayed color changes when their moods shifted, but Staffan had never seen any real change in Skirmishers at all. Sometimes he thought he caught something, but it was simply iridescence on their feathers.

"If this is a bait and switch, Fel," Staffan said, "ask your compatriots what happens to business associates who try that on with me. You told me you had a ship with a ventral beam. That's all I want. Don't try palming me off with anything else."

He hoped Fel would ask around. Venezia had its laws, whether people believed that or not, but it was fairly relaxed about how its residents settled disputes. It didn't need a police force.

"Wait to hear from me," Fel said. "What are you going to do about crewing this vessel?"

"I can find plenty of willing hands," Staffan said. "I'll let you know if I have recruiting issues."

As he drove back into town, Staffan racked his brains to remember the name. *Pious Inquisitor.* He'd have to look it up. He wanted as much information as he could get on the vessel, not just the sales brochure detail that Fel would peddle. He checked his mirrors for vehicles that might be following, because Fel had a point about spies. Tribal rivalries, business feuds, and even foolhardy outsiders employed by some Earth or colonial agency weren't unknown here, and the one thing Venezia didn't have and didn't want was a border patrol recording who went in and out. It was a safe haven for people who couldn't show a passport anywhere else. Small ships were almost impossible to control anyway.

But Staffan took comfort from the fact that the border was almost self-policing. If someone wanted to get to Venezia, they couldn't exactly catch a scheduled flight. They'd have to pay someone with a ship to bring them in, or they'd need the kind of money to have a ship of their own. And sooner or later, unless they wanted to live like a hermit on a diet of grass and mice, they'd have to come into town. Eventually, they'd be spotted.

And then we remove them. Permanently.

Edvin was sitting in the garden with Kerstin when Staffan got home. She rushed up to him, excited and giggling. "Grandpa! Grandpa! I've been drawing!"

"That's my clever girl." He gave Edvin a look: *you haven't mentioned the doll's house, have you?* Edvin just blinked slowly to indicate that he hadn't. "Grandpa's got to do some work first, but I'll come and look, okay?"

There was a little bit of Naomi in Kerstin, Staffan was sure. It was the long blond hair. If she'd been any more like her, though, that would have been too painful.

When do you let go? When is it time to close the book and move on?

Staffan asked himself that once in a while, and the answer was always the same: never. This had to be done. The question had to be answered, and the price had to be paid. It had just taken a lifetime to reach the stage where he had the power to demand an answer with the only kind of persuasion that Earth understood—a warship.

Kerstin picked up a toy bucket and trowel and began digging holes in the flower border. She liked to keep busy. Edvin got up and walked slowly out of earshot with his father.

"Well?" Edvin asked. "Was it true?"

"Yes. We may have a battlecruiser."

"Wow."

"I still have to check it out and make the payment. But this thing exists. Imagine it—the mighty Sangheili, losing a battle-cruiser to the Kig-Yar."

"Fel's a cheeky old crow, isn't he?"

"*Pious Inquisitor.* That's the ship."

Edvin stared into the mid-distance for a few moments, then put on his concerned face. "Are you sure this is what you want, Dad?"

"What, to have the clout to get some respect from Earth?"

"I meant are you sure that you shouldn't just hand the ship over to the militia. Isn't that what we all want? Some justice for all Earth's done to the colonies over the years?"

"When I'm done with the ship, I will," Staffan said. "But I need answers. And I'm doing it for Remo, too. If it hadn't been for him, I'd have signed myself into a mental hospital long ago."

"Okay," Edvin said. "I know you won't do anything dumb. Just trying to put things in perspective."

"Son, I've had thirty-five years of perspective. Whatever I do won't be rash."

It was too late for Remo, but at least he'd died knowing that someone else would continue the search for information on what really happened to his son. Staffan wanted something that few people would ever get. He wanted the government—somebody's government, anyway—to tell him the truth.

And if that meant reducing Sydney or some other major city to glass, he'd do it.

THREE

A SLIGHT AGAINST ONE KIG-YAR IS A SLIGHT AGAINST ALL
KIG-YAR, BUT FORTUNATELY THEY'RE STILL FIGHTING EACH
OTHER OVER WHAT THEY SHOULD DO ABOUT IT.

—SANGHEILI SAYING

MYUR CITY, T'VAO, Y'DEIO SYSTEM: APRIL 2553 IN THE HUMAN CALENDAR

"He's too young to understand," Ais said, barely looking up from her data module. She squatted on cushions in the shade of the fruit trees, reading something. "And he's a male. Don't waste your time. Just toughen him up."

The chick—Laik—scuttled around the yard after Chol Von, mouth wide open. He'd pursued her all morning, first with begging peeps and whistles, but now that he was getting genuinely hungry his calls had become urgent squawks. For a moment he gave up on his mother and turned to his grandmother. Chol held up a warning hand.

"He's learning self-control, Mama," Chol said. "Don't feed him."

Ais spread her arms. "I have nothing for him anyway. When are you going to hatch some daughters?"

Chol dug her claws into her palms. This was the worst thing about the end of the war. She no longer had a ship to command, and her mother had descended on her to help out with the children. Vek had gone off at short notice with his comrades to look for tantalum deposits on Reynes, the coward. He might at least have had the decency to stay and give her moral support. If she met a better mate while he was away, he could forget about coming back and expecting to find a place at her table. She was T'vaoan, for goodness' sake. She could take any mate she pleased.

"I would rather have smaller broods and better children," Chol said carefully.

"Hah. You'd rather have *no* brood and be an empress." Ais ran a claw down the screen and let out a long, rattling sigh. "I wish you'd stop it."

"Stop what?"

"This talk of building a national fleet. A united army. It's unhealthy. People are gossiping about you."

"Cooperation made us a spacefaring species. Otherwise we'd still be stuck on Eayn, robbing one another and sinking each other's boats."

Ais glossed over the point with her usual speed. "Strength lies in a big clan, my dear, in a lot of people who owe you allegiance based on kinship. Not in politics and treaties."

"Strength also lies in firepower. We've relied on avoidance. The next threat might not be avoidable."

It was a cloudless, baking-hot day in Myur and the only shade in the yard was under the trees. Beyond the wattle and daub wall, constructed in the same way that Chol would make her own nest, screeching laughter and shouts told her that the youngsters from last year's brood, three males, were squabbling over something they'd found. The strongest would take it even if the weakest found it. She kept trying to teach them that cooperation would mean more for all of them. Robbing fellow Kig-Yar simply made everyone poorer. The Covenant had handed them that lesson on a plate.

"I don't want to be an empress or any damn thing, Mama,"

Chol said. "But I do know that we couldn't stand up to the Covenant when they invaded, and now we're free of them for the first time in . . . how long? A thousand years?"

"They never managed to subdue us like they did the rest."

"We were never free to do as we liked, either."

"And now they're gone. So? The crisis has passed."

"Or it's the perfect time to make sure it never happens again. We have weapons, the Covenant kindly perfected our combat skills, and there are ships around for the taking. Am I the only person who sees the obvious opportunity there?"

"We *have* ships."

"But we don't have the *right* ships. We need the kind that would make any invader think twice about crossing us. And the organization to deploy them effectively."

"Privateering not good enough for you, then?"

"Mama, I would prefer the Kig-Yar to be feared because we can exact revenge on entire worlds. Not because we steal the silverware."

Chol sidestepped Laik again. He squawked angrily and executed a tight turn, claws scrabbling on the paving stones. He'd get fed, and with the very best meat she could afford, but he needed to learn to put off immediate gratification for a greater reward later. She'd read about that in the computer library of a captured human ship. The flat-faces had done tests with their own young. The human chicks who could resist eating sweet food put in front of them for a set period of time were more successful later in life than those who ignored the instruction and ate it right away. It was a small detail that spoke volumes to Chol. She wasn't sure if the self-control was something inborn or taught, but if it could be taught, then it might achieve the same result. When Laik had learned to wait, he could progress to resisting temptation. Chol wanted to make a thinker of him, a planner, a shipmaster capable of seeing a much bigger picture.

She thought her mother had given up on the argument, but

after a long pause, Ais looked up from her data module. "The Covenant didn't turn us into indoctrinated cannon fodder like the Sangheili because we're scattered," she said. "Because we're anarchic. Because we're a rabble. That's our *strength*. Not a weakness. Central control of any kind will be the death of us."

"Then we need to be a rabble with warships," Chol said.

Laik crashed into Chol's legs, arms flailing. His brown fledgling down, the coat of fluffy feather that would gradually molt and give way to scales and plumage, made him almost irresistible. But she had to stand firm. Eventually his squawks became more plaintive. He stood staring up at her, mouth still open, making little hiccuping noises, all squawked out.

"Go find your brothers," she said. He was old enough to understand even if he could manage few actual words yet. "Go on. Go find your brothers and bring them back here. Then you'll all be fed, and you'll learn something."

Laik gazed at her expectantly for a few more seconds, then trotted away behind the house, crestfallen. Chol felt guilty. She was only doing it for his own good. She wanted more for him than life as a scavenger fighting lower-status scavengers for scraps. Why prey on your own people? Nobody benefited from that. It was hard to think that and look at her mother's accusing face, though. Ais radiated disappointment, one eye half-shut.

"So when are you going to this assembly?" Ais asked. "I came all this way to look after the children so you could go on your little jaunt. Seeing as your latest useless mate isn't around to help."

"After I've fed Laik," Chol said. "Then you can pretend you're in charge for a whole day."

Chol envied other avian species. Some would drive an old female out of the roost. In others, the parent drove off the chicks to make them find an independent territory of their own. They'd obviously worked out something about family dynamics that the Kig-Yar hadn't.

We're becoming birds. There's a lot we can learn from them.

The three older boys came rushing into the yard, Kij and Gon chasing the biggest—Hiiq. He was clutching a handmade catapult in one fist. Chol couldn't recall any of them having one before, so it had probably been stolen from another roost's youngsters. Hiiq stood against the wall with his prize held above his head, batting away his smaller brothers. Laik came trotting some way behind, tripping over the tree roots.

"Mama, it's not fair!" Gon said. "Make him give it back, Mama!"

"If you can't take it," she said carefully, "then nobody's going to give it to you. How about you all agreeing to share it? Equal time. Then you all get to use it, and you all improve your aim, and then you can defend yourselves better."

They looked at her as if she was insane. Then Gon sank his teeth into Hiiq's arm and a brawl broke out. Chol waded in, cuffed them all, and forced them apart. They stood at a reluctant distance, all eyeing the catapult which now lay on the ground.

"Save that for *outsiders*," she rasped. "Here's your choice. Accept that Hiiq won, or reach an agreement. Or carry on behaving like some ignorant Unggoy, and then I'll feed you to your brothers."

Heads hung. "Yes, Mama."

"No more of this nonsense. I have to leave now. If I hear you've given Grandmama any problems, there'll be *consequences*."

They disappeared into the house, leaving only a silence broken by buzzing insects. Laik sat at Chol's feet, gazing up at her, mouth closed this time.

"Very well." She pointed at the ground. "Stay there while I fetch you something."

She wasn't expecting him to obey, but when she opened the door to the pantry and looked around, he wasn't at her heels. It was a start. She took some soft berries and chopped up a small piece of *uoi* steak with a little enzyme powder. Laik was past the stage of needing puréed food.

"Here," she said. Instead of dropping it into his mouth, she put the small bowl on the ground where he could reach it himself. Her mother tutted dismissively. "Can you wait? Can you wait until I count to ten?"

She wasn't sure he understood numbers yet, but he could recognize words. She leaned over. Her shadow fell on him.

"One . . . two . . ."

"You really should regurgitate for him," Ais said. "I don't think it's good for them to be plate-fed."

". . . five, six . . ."

"I regurgitated food for *you* until you shed your down."

". . . nine . . . *ten*."

Laik pounced on the food. He had to dip his head, scoop up the meat, and flip it back down his throat, but he ate on his own.

And he'd *waited*. Chol was ecstatic with pride. "My clever boy! My clever, *patient* boy." She nuzzled him and groomed his down with her teeth while he made little get-off-it's-all-mine noises at the back of his throat. "See, Mama? I shall make a prince of him."

Ais said nothing. Chol took that as conceding defeat and set off for Dal'koth, a short hop from T'vao among the belt of small moons and asteroids orbiting Y'Deio. She savored being back at the helm of a ship again. She'd laid claim to her last command—*Joyous Discovery*, a missionary vessel whose name she'd changed immediately to *Paragon*—when the Covenant was too busy with its own civil war to notice, but this Phantom was her personal transport, seized from a Sangheili who made the mistake of underestimating those near the bottom of the pecking order. It had taken her weeks to get the smell of rotting meat out of the cockpit. Chol thought the pilot should have simply handed it over in gratitude for cycles of far more loyal service than his kind deserved, but the fool decided to put up a fight, and he didn't win.

And still some Kig-Yar choose to serve them. What do the humans say? "They got religion." Traitors, all of them. Weak-minded children who want to believe in magic.

The gathering on Dal'koth was no more than an informal get-together. To call a meeting at a specific time required organization, something Kig-Yar mistrusted almost as much as cash on delivery, so Chol had simply responded to word passed around the clans to get together to swap intelligence on the state of the postwar galaxy.

And also what's happened to all that hardware. We should have moved faster. We should have grabbed more when we started to see the cracks. The Sangheili shipmasters have commandeered far too much.

There was still a substantial navy out there somewhere, even with all the vessels lost in battle. Sangheili elders had seized ships for themselves and taken them back to their keeps. All Chol was doing was applying the same common sense as they had.

She swaggered around the airfield, looking for familiar hulls. It was fascinating to see how many dropships and small fighters had been liberated from the Covenant fleet, but there were also UNSC Pelicans. They had their uses. The UNSC might now be in the market for used parts. When she went into the hangar, the vaulted cavern was full of Kig-Yar trading carbines and other small arms. One of the males turned to look at her, abandoned his haggling, and came trotting over to greet her. She took a few moments to recognize him. It was Zim, a scout she'd employed on several missions some time ago. The seasons didn't seem to have treated him well. He looked thin and bedraggled.

"Well, nothing like a breaking branch to shower those beneath with fruit," he said, brandishing a human rifle with some satisfaction. "What brings you here, Shipmistress?"

"Curiosity and the need to escape my mother."

"Oh. Not the news of an interesting contract, then."

"How interesting?"

"I don't know, but it seems to be of great amusement to Mistress Isk." Zim cocked his head in the direction of a dais made out of ammunition crates stamped with the UNSC emblem. Chol found it interesting that they chose a bird as their totemic symbol. The few humans she'd had contact with seemed to think birds were for eating or hunting, not revering. "She's promised to address that matter first before opening the floor to ship trading."

Isk was too old to do much traveling now, but she was still fond of brokering deals and taking her cut. She clambered up on the dais and called for attention. It took her a little while to get it because of the busy trading over the sudden glut of weapons. Zim was right. There was always some capital to be made out of someone else's disaster, in this case the Covenant's.

"I have mixed feelings about what I'm going to tell you," said Isk. She paused, head bobbing as if she was trying not to laugh. "It seems that Sav Fel has disappeared with one of the Sangheili's more significant vessels."

A loud chorus of cheering interrupted her. She held up one hand.

"He took the battlecruiser *Pious Inquisitor*," she went on. There were sarcastic oohs and aahs. "Or at least he failed to deliver it in the middle of a battle, which, might I say, is a most prudent thing to do."

"How much did he get for it?" someone yelled.

Chol didn't take note of who'd asked that question. She was much more interested in the name and class of the ship. *A battlecruiser.* It was a capital ship made to scour life from planets, to melt their surfaces to glass.

It was exactly the kind of warship that a united Kig-Yar navy needed.

"Ah, therein lies our dilemma," Isk said. "Fel has disappeared and the ship can't be found. We should applaud him for that alone, but Field Master Avu Med 'Telcam has put out an offer. He'll pay for the return of the ship. I believe he needs it to glass his Sangheili brothers' cities."

"Unless he pressed the wrong button and blew it up," a female said. "That's what happens when you let males drive, you see . . ."

It got another laugh, but Isk had left out the most important detail for the majority of Kig-Yar present.

"How much is he paying?" Zim asked.

"Eighty thousand gekz," Isk replied. "For what that's worth these days. He has few goods to trade at the moment."

It wasn't enough to start a stampede. It wasn't even enough to make it worth stealing the ship, because if it was damaged the repair bill could be a great deal more. Just maintaining a battlecruiser while waiting to find a buyer was too expensive for most Kig-Yar to consider.

Chol didn't want to sell the ship, though. She had other plans for it. This was an opportunity she couldn't afford to ignore. All she needed was a skeleton crew to find it and bring it back. She'd worry about exactly how to do that when she'd secured the contract.

"Where was *Inquisitor* last seen?" she asked.

"All we know is that it isn't in Sangheili space." Isk peered at her from the dais. "Are you interested in this contract?"

What do I have to lose? Nothing. The galaxy was in disarray and a new galactic order would emerge. The choice seemed to be between carrying on as before and hoping for the best, or establishing a stronger position for all Kig-Yar.

"Tell the Sangheili I'll take the contract," Chol said. "How do I contact this 'Telcam? What is he?"

"He'll contact you." Isk still looked dubious. "He's a disciple of the Abiding Truth. Religious lunatics. Are you sure you want this job? It's a very big burden."

Chol was certain now. It was time for the Kig-Yar to remember they'd once done very well without the Covenant to provide for them.

"You're crazy," Zim said. "All that hard graft for eighty thousand? What if he can't pay? *Won't* pay? Currency's worth nothing these days. What are you going to do with a battlecruiser left on your hands? Ah well. I suppose you could strip it for parts."

Chol almost gave him the speech she hadn't given her mother, the one that she'd made too many times in bars, about how Kig-Yar had let themselves be ground down and despised, and that they were nobody's servants any longer. But there was no point in showing her hand yet.

"You lack vision," she said. He looked up at her. She was taller than the average male, being T'vaoan, so she could command physical respect as well as deference to her gender. Just as T'vaoan males had much heavier upper-body plumage than other Kig-Yar, T'vaoan females had a ruff of feathers on the head and neck instead of dull scales, and there was a certain satisfaction to feeling them rise and fan out. It could make any male back down. "You forget the most important thing."

"Which is?"

"We might squabble over garbage heaps now," she said, "but we were an empire once. And we shall be again."

UNSC *PORT STANLEY*, OFF VENEZIA

Up, down, or in front of?

Mal lay facedown on the transparent deck, propped on folded arms, and told his brain that the blue marbled disc of Venezia lay beneath him. If he tried to convince it that the planet was anywhere else, it became too disorienting. He let the ship's generated gravity settle the argument. *Down there. Below. Definitely.* His body confirmed it.

The view was one-way. *Port Stanley* could monitor Venezia,

but Venezia or any passing ship couldn't see *Port Stanley*. The corvette was in stealth mode, cold and silent and invisible. Where would Sav Fel park a CCS-class battlecruiser nearly two kilometers long? It obviously wasn't within *Stanley*'s sensor range, or else they'd have found her by now. Mal could have asked BB to display a chart of features within Venezia's system, but he didn't feel like chatting. He rolled over, took his datapad out of his shirt pocket, and studied the images.

Once we know what the buzzard's using to get on and off the planet we'll have some idea of the range, and that'll give us a clue. Maybe.

Of course, he could always be getting a lift from a buddy with an FTL drive . . . and that still doesn't mean he can't do short hops.

It didn't solve much. *Stanley* had remote sensors in stationary orbit, football-sized spy satellites that could watch a small city like New Tyne, but keeping an eye on the business that went on indoors still came down to getting on the ground and following people. Mal switched to the feed from the sensors and checked to see if there was any traffic entering or leaving Sangheili space. Apart from Venezia's network of monitoring satellites, nothing was moving. It was a backwater planet with a small population that didn't even need to import food on a regular basis. Spotting larger ships in transit should have been easy.

Mal flopped back onto his stomach and went on watching the infinite black, just letting his mind wander, but that was a mistake. Thoughts that he kept trying to shut out wheedled their way back in like pushy insurance salesmen.

So what are you going to do about poor bloody Staffan Sentzke, eh? Just blow him up too, yeah? Poor bastard loses his daughter—twice—and loses his wife, and then loses his mind, and it's all thanks to your employer. Feel good about yourself now, do you? Going to follow orders? Is a lawful order about an unlawful act lawful at all?

It just wouldn't leave him alone.

Staffan Sentzke was an enemy that Earth had made for itself from scratch. The poor sod didn't even know the half of what had happened to his daughter. Mal was trying to weigh the certain knowledge that he would have reacted just like Staffan—worse, probably—against the fact that his job was to defend Earth. He realized he was now agreeing with Vaz. And Vaz had admitted standing outside Halsey's holding cell in *Port Stanley* with his sidearm, on the point of dispensing the justice that the bitch would never face in a court. Only BB's intervention had stopped him.

We need defending against the Catherine Halseys of this world more than the Staffan Sentzkes. But that's not my job, not while I wear this uniform. More's the bloody pity.

It was a circular argument. Mal was close to banging his head on the glass deck to make himself stop when the reflection of a ghostly blue cube drifted into view behind him.

"I'm not even going to ask what you're doing." BB settled on the deck right in Mal's eye line, landing gently like an air balloon. "But you'll never get a decent suntan there."

"Just thinking. Remind me why the jelly boys did this to the deck."

"I asked them nicely."

"Why?"

"Because Naomi's fascinated by astronomy. I thought she'd like it."

"Was your brain donor a bit of a lady's man?"

"I have no idea. Why?"

"Because you're very smarmy with the female crew. And prone to pissing contests with the male ones."

"Which I win." BB could somehow say that with a wink despite the fact that nothing in his avatar changed at all. "But I can see why you'd be envious of my effortless charm."

Mal eased himself off the deck press-up style and knelt back on his heels. "So . . . you really think that Naomi's old man is planning to glass Earth?"

"That's quite an extrapolative leap."

"Yeah. But everyone's making it."

"You feel sorry for him, don't you?"

"Of course I bloody well do. ONI cost him his wife and kid. And now we're going to finish the job. Yay us, as Phyllis would say."

"Oh, we don't know how it's going to turn out yet, do we? You're going to miss the Admiral's briefing." BB buzzed him like a fly. "Chop chop. Move it, Staff. Get some exercise."

"Don't you start. That's all I hear from Vaz."

Mal got to his feet and headed for the bridge, up ladders, through decks, and along passages, a quick jog in a small ship. BB went ahead of him, occasionally doing dice rolls and singing something vaguely nautical to himself that sounded like Gilbert and Sullivan, but Mal could never remember which one was *H.M.S. Pinafore* and which was *Pirates of Penzance*. Were all AIs like this? Mal had never worked with one before, but he knew he'd be disappointed if the next one he met wasn't as good a mate as BB. BB wasn't some user-friendly interface. He was a proper bloke, albeit a posh and educated one. Mal sometimes felt the urge to tell him. The cocky little sod knew, though.

Phillips and Devereaux were chatting to Osman at the navigation console when Mal arrived. Phillips looked up and brandished his datapad like it was going to be the topic of the briefing.

"Staff, there's been a change of plan," Osman said.

Mal parked his backside on the edge of the chart table. Osman could always take a joke. "Bugger me, ma'am, I'm stunned. I've never known that happen before in the entire history of the UNSC."

"Given the extreme interest now in *Pious Inquisitor,* henceforth known as *P.I.* because I'm fed up repeating the name, Parangosky would like us to retrieve her in one piece."

"Shame," Mal said, relieved. He'd imagined a scenario of having to fire a couple of Shivas at Staffan Sentzke and then trying to live with the knowledge that he'd killed a guy who had the moral high ground. "I love big explosions."

Phillips handed him the datapad. It was a transcript in English. "That's our buddy 'Telcam talking about some Kig-Yar. I don't have a name yet, but it's obviously a female because he's referring to her as shipmistress. Quite a courtesy, coming from him. The usual Sangheili term for a female Kig-Yar translates roughly as *overbreeding chicken-bitch*."

"Of course, she might just literally be that," Osman said. "A ship's commanding officer. They trusted them with missionary ships and the odd frigate."

Mal scrolled through the file and picked out a few key words. He noted that 'Telcam was asking the Kig-Yar to find the ship and notify him, not to bring her back. Well, that was academic. If 'Telcam was worried about the buzzards welshing on the deal and holding the ship to ransom, then he wasn't going to be able to enforce the look-don't-touch order unless he had a warship of his own on instant standby. Otherwise the Kig-Yar could hot-wire *Inquisitor* and be light-years away in seconds.

"He's going to follow her, then," Mal said. "Because he wouldn't take a Kig-Yar's word for anything."

Osman shrugged. "Well, we never actually planned to stop him using *P.I.*, remember. He just happened to lose her mid-battle. So no actual harm done if he *does* reclaim her, but we've never recovered a fully functional capital ship intact from the Covenant, let alone one that might have some interesting data in her systems."

"So why can't our Huragok add Covenant gizmos?" Phillips asked. "I thought they all shared data. If they maintained the

Covenant fleet, don't they remember all the blueprints or whatever? If I were Fleet, I'd be asking them to add a ventral beam
or three to *Infinity.*"

"Good point, Phyllis," Mal said. "Maybe the Covenant didn't
want the Engineers swapping trade secrets with the rest of the
fleet, though. We've confined *Infinity*'s Engineers for the same
reason."

"Yeah, Fleet procurement's still bitching about that." Osman
sounded weary. "They wanted a Huragok in every vessel. We
should never have told them we had them, but that's what happens when you have to car-share *Infinity* with CINCFLEET."

"Trust us, we're ONI," Phillips said in a mock-professorial
voice. "We'll make the best use of these little chaps. They're
perfectly safe with us."

Osman didn't volunteer information about plans for ventral
beams or anything else by way of mass destruction, but Mal
was starting to think the ONI way now. If ONI had commis-
sioned a vessel with a ventral beam, it would only mean one
thing: that they were thinking about glassing the Sangheili, and
Admiral Hood was pretty old-fashioned about sticking to the
peace treaty he'd shaken hands on with the Arbiter. Acquiring a
Covenant ship with glassing kit was the politically expedient
alternative. Mal could imagine Parangosky smiling at Hood
and telling him that they were just capturing more Covenant
hulls to reverse-engineer them, same as they'd done with Forerunner technology for years. And he wouldn't believe her, of
course, but he'd back off. Parangosky might well have wielded
more practical power than Hood and she'd undermined Fleet to
help the Sangheili rebels, but she'd avoid an internal civil war.
God bless the old girl. She was all about getting the job done.

"So." Osman stretched out in her seat and meshed her hands
behind her head. "Ideas, people?"

"Assuming we get to *P.I.* first," Devereaux said, "how do six of us seize a ship that size? Not that they'll have a full crew, and they'll only be Kig-Yar, but they're not good odds even for ODSTs."

BB materialized in the middle of the conversation. "Just let me find a carrier wave and I'll be in there like a rat up a drainpipe. They don't have AIs like me. Well, *nobody* does, because I'm unparalleled magnificence, but once I'm in their systems I'll smack down any lockout defenses they might have in the computer, paralyze the ship, and vent the atmosphere. It's hard to fight back when you're sucking vacuum. And once I'm in, I can drive the tub too. Home in time for tea. Splice the main brace and all that."

Phillips smiled fondly. "I'm glad you're on our side, BB."

"Oh, flatterer." BB settled on Phillips's lap. Phillips reached out instinctively and almost patted him like a dog, but it was hard to touch pure light. He looked a bit embarrassed. "You're lucky I'm a paragon of virtue and that I've got a soft spot for you *mucky* little meatbags."

"Okay, I like the sound of that." Osman nodded. "So all we've got to do is find *P.I.* and establish the right kind of comms link."

"I've been trying to place a call, so to speak," BB said. "But wherever she is, she's in radio silence. Very wise."

Mal tossed a crumpled scrap of paper at him. It passed through the hologram and landed in Phillips's lap. "Well, if it was easy, you wouldn't need meatbags, would you?" Mal looked to Osman. "Shall we pull Naomi out, ma'am? One-woman army or not, her father's going to spot her sooner or later."

"She won't welcome that."

"Someone's got to keep 'Telcam busy. And deliver his weapons. Can't leave that to Phyllis, not even if Dev's holding his hand. Or any other part of his anatomy."

Phillips scrunched up the paper pellet to bullet hardness and threw it back at Mal. "True."

"And Parangosky's sure she wants the ship in one piece?" Mal asked.

"Or at least with repairable damage," Osman said. "So it's worth a try."

"Okay. Because it occurs to me that the easiest way to deal with this is to just sit back and see if Staffan takes the ship and heads for Earth. Planetary defenses should be able to handle one battlecruiser. It's not like he's got a fleet."

"It may well come to that."

"So do you still want me to deploy to New Tyne, ma'am?"

If it had been up to Mal, he'd have held Naomi back for the arms run for 'Telcam and never let her near Venezia, no matter how useful she was. She could have inserted into Sydney, Mombasa, or any other big city full of millions of assorted humans, and nobody would have taken much notice of her. But New Tyne was small-town suspicious. For a moment, he wondered if Osman might be using her as bait for her father.

Would she really do that, though? Jesus. I really like the boss as a human being, but she isn't Parangosky's chosen one because she does charity work.

Osman looked like she was thinking it over. "Okay. You and Vaz can focus on Staffan Sentzke. And Spenser can keep tabs on Fel. I'll pull Naomi out to keep an eye on 'Telcam." She spread her hands. "I admit it. I screwed up. I should have pulled her out as soon as we knew Sentzke was there, but now that he's directly involved with the ship, it's pushing things too far. Just because she's a Spartan doesn't mean she's automatically the best choice for the task. I'm sorry."

Mal had a lot of faith in Osman, not because she never made mistakes but because she was ready to admit when she had. He could have told her right from the start that she was taking a gamble for all the wrong reasons. Naomi wanted to be in the thick of everything, and seemed to need to show she could put personal issues aside in tight spots. She'd practically insisted on arresting Halsey to prove she hadn't been too brainwashed into worshipping the old cow to follow ONI's orders. Now she looked like she was making the same point with her father.

"Fair enough, ma'am." Naomi and Vaz had only been in New Tyne a few days, so Naomi could be withdrawn without provoking too many questions. "I'll relieve her. She won't like it, but it's not like she won't have plenty to keep her busy on the Sangheili side."

"And we could do with another dropship, ma'am," Devereaux said. "You can fly dropships, can't you? I'm pretty sure Naomi's qualified too."

"We can always enlist BB to get us up to speed." Osman seemed relaxed about it now. "Anyway, Mal and Vaz have some skills. Isn't that right, Staff? Trained enough to commandeer a Spirit, at least."

Mal shrugged. The Covenant dropship was still on Criterion, maybe even still airworthy, but it wasn't a flight he ever wanted to make again. "I'm not saying it was a perfect landing, ma'am. And it did take three of us to do it. Plus it was a case of fly or die, as I recall."

"Devereaux's got a point, though. There might come a time when we need to be two places at once, and *Stanley*'s not a shuttle. Okay, Dev, talk to Bravo-Six and see what they can drop off within reasonable range, and then Adj and Leaks can modify it. Evan—make contact with 'Telcam and find out where and when he'll take a weapons drop."

"He's still pissed off about us forcibly extracting him from Vadam."

"Lack of gratitude noted. But you've still got something he wants. The translations of the inscriptions at the Ontom temple."

Phillips beamed. "I've never bribed anyone with a bible before. Boy, when I do my lecture tour . . ."

"When this is ever declassified . . ."

"Only joking, Admiral."

"Okay, dismissed. Let's crack on."

Mal went down to the hangar deck with Devereaux while Phillips diverted to his listening station. *Tart-Cart,* the Pelican dropship modded beyond recognition by the two Engineers, sat clamped to the deck. The ship looked the same shape as before, more or less, but she now had a version of *Infinity's* top-end slipspace drive with the hull reinforcement to go with it, instant FTL comms, and even more stealth features than ONI had originally fitted. Mal wondered what would happen if he gave the Engineers a shoebox and a pile of scrap metal and told them to go crazy with it. As long as they had enough raw materials, they seemed to be able to build anything out of anything else. There was a fortune to be made there postwar, he decided. Military hardware was probably the least of their uses.

"I'm going to set myself up as a custom vehicle salesman," he said, hauling himself into *Tart-Cart's* crew bay and sitting on the edge of the folded ramp. He could smell the jasmine air freshener. Whatever you asked an Engineer to install, you got it. "Or an upmarket patisserie shop."

"Kitchen appliances," Devereaux said. "The coffee tastes more like liquid bliss every time they upgrade the galley machine."

"See, who needs instruments of death and destruction?"

"We do, actually." Devereaux climbed in and prodded him with her boot. "You better warn Vaz and Naomi. And arrange an RV point."

"She's not going to be happy."

"I know. She'll think we think she's going soft. Just remind her that if 'Telcam gets stroppy, she's the only one strong enough to punch him out, so she's better deployed there."

"That's a very persuasive argument. You should be a sergeant, Dev."

"I *am,* Staff . . ."

"Okay, let's aim for forty-eight hours. That should give them enough time to tie up any loose ends she's started." Mal dropped down off the ramp. "Where would *you* hide a battlecruiser, Dev?"

Devereaux shrugged. "A distant system. A shipyard, among all the other big ships. Or right under everyone's nose, if I had the stealth kit. Nobody's spotted *Stanley* so far, have they? Or *Tart-Cart*. Which reminds me . . . Leaks? Are you in there? What do you know about Elite armor?"

The Engineer drifted out of the cockpit door, rubbing his tentacles together. Mal had no idea what that meant, but it made the creature look like he was wiping his hands on an oily rag, mechanic-style.

<*No, I am out here now.*> Leaks's artificial voice was deeper and slower than Adj's. He was also ploddingly literal in a way that might actually have been sarcasm. It was hard to tell. <*I know much about Sangheili armor.*>

"That active camo. The invisible stuff. Can you coat a ship in it?"

<*In theory. But* Loose Woman's Transport *already has stealth camouflage. Much more stable.*>

It took Mal a moment to work out that he meant *Tart-Cart.* The translator was a constant source of entertainment.

"I meant big warships." Devereaux held her hands wide apart like an angler bragging about the one that got away. "Battle-cruisers."

<*Some capital ships have stealth measures. But nothing is foolproof.*>

"She'll give herself away sooner or later," Mal said. "Someone's got to go and get her. Someone's got to open the hatches or ditch gash. There's always a trail. We'll find her."

He went back to his cabin and started selecting the clothes, kit, and wallet litter that would make him look like a bloke who'd finally had enough of the UNSC and didn't plan to wait to be discharged.

If he thought about the Sentzke family hard enough, he suspected he might convince even himself that it was true.

NEW TYNE, VENEZIA

Naomi took the news that she'd been retasked without so much as a blink. It was a bad sign. Vaz had noticed signs of a thaw in her, but the freeze was back.

"You had doubts about all this yourself," Vaz said. "Remember?"

"I thought I'd be too conspicuous. Still, I have my orders." She glanced down at herself as if the civilian clothes were getting on her nerves. "Someone's got to deal with 'Telcam. Phillips can't handle that on his own."

Vaz tapped his watch, trying to change the subject. "We've still got time to establish our presence in the bars. When someone starts looking for a crew, UNSC deserters will be part of the scenery and we'll have all the right contacts. Mal can walk in later, and it'll all look fine, like there's a few of us trying to lie low."

"What makes you think my father will recruit a crew?"

Vaz scratched the scar on his jaw. "Look, we don't know if your dad's involved in any of this yet."

"Don't humor me. What else would he be doing with Fel?"

"Okay, if he's bought himself a battlecruiser, it's for humans. He'll want as many humans in the crew as he can get, not Kig-Yar, because he's not stupid. They don't do causes. He'll want people who are committed."

"Kig-Yar know a lot more about crewing Covenant ships than we do."

"But it's not their war. Venezia wants arms to attack Earth—or to defend Venezia, if they think the UNSC's going to resume counter-insurgency operations."

"You think we might?" She seemed to think he was humoring her. But they were both standing there, living proof that the UNSC hadn't forgotten the colonial insurgency at all and was taking steps to preempt a renewal of it—which was also what might start it again anyway. It was a self-fulfilling prophecy, as wars usually were. "Really?"

"Look, we're making judgments based on what *we* know, not what *he* knows. We think this is some payback for abducting you, because we know what happened. He doesn't even know you're still alive. I think he's more worried about Earth attacking New Tyne, and he's got enough reason to contribute a battlecruiser to the cause. Remember that Venezia minded its own business for years. The only thing that kicked it all off again was *Ariadne* showing up and asking for emergency help."

Naomi had now pulled down the shutters completely. She looked right through him, eyes dead and bloodless. Vaz was upset to think he could be shut out so easily, so quickly, but she'd probably had to learn to do that to cope with what had happened to her. He tried to make allowances.

"Well, there's no point speculating," she said. "Let's go out and do the deserter act. Put ourselves about a bit."

It was a very un-Naomi thing to say, a measure of her anxiety. Vaz wondered why he'd ever believed that Spartans were immune to the things that affected everyone else.

They're human. Whatever extras they've got, however messed up their systems are, however indoctrinated they've been— they're human. Just better at hiding it.

He secured the house and they drove off to look for bars on Spenser's list. New Tyne was a very small town, a place where people knew each other by sight if not by name, and they noticed newcomers sooner rather than later. Vaz headed toward the center of town and pointed out a brick-fronted, single-story building with two wide windows obscured by security mesh. The sign read STAVROS MIDDLE EAST ASIAN CUISINE AND BAR.

Naomi made a *huh* noise. "I hope his cooking's better than his geography."

"Spenser says the place is popular with Kig-Yar." A couple of men were standing outside, talking. When the door opened, Vaz could see tables and a long bar inside. "And I admit I have no idea what they serve in there that could be of interest to buzzards, except doner kebab."

They were both on unknown territory, then. Naomi had been fighting aliens for more than twenty-five years but Vaz was sure she'd never encountered them in a social environment any more than he had. They were supposed to be recent deserters, though, so complete ignorance was a tidy fit for their cover story.

Twenty-five years. Damn, she was already on the front line when I was a kid.

Vaz parked close to the building for a quick exit if needed and stopped to look at the menu in the window. The dishes seemed to cover everything east of the Balkans. Maybe Stavros wasn't so navigationally challenged after all.

Naomi scanned the menu, unmoved. "Mal advised me to stay away from pies and anything involving re-formed meat."

"He's from Wolverhampton. Take his advice." He opened the door and walked in, trying to pitch his confidence at the right level—not too aggressive, but not too nervous either. Noise and smells hit him. "Cross between a swimming pool and a chicken shed. And garlic. Good sign."

Everyone glanced their way to check who'd walked in. It was quite an education. Vaz had often wondered how Kig-Yar drank with those long beaklike muzzles. He'd had a mental image of them dipping their beaks into the liquid and tipping their heads back like ducks. And that was exactly what some were doing. Most, though, had opted to drink straight from bottles.

It was hard to tell what they were drinking. For all he knew, alcohol might have been toxic to them. But it seemed like a human social activity the Kig-Yar had adopted to oil the wheels of commerce.

"I know this sounds weird," Naomi said, leaning on the bar, "but have you noticed we've never fought any species with proper lips capable of forming a tight seal?"

She seemed relaxed again. Vaz put a couple of bills on the counter. "Well, there's Grunts. They can pucker up. Kind of."

The bartender, a woman who looked even older than Parangosky, zeroed in on them like a missile. "What can I get you kids?"

Vaz indicated the Kig-Yar with a jerk of his head. "What are they drinking?"

"You don't want that." She pulled a face. "It's sugars and fats, basically. Not liquor. They've got funny digestions."

"Okay, two beers and a plate of mezze to share, then." There was a bowl of bagged snacks on the counter. "And some of these for starters."

The old woman opened a couple of bottles and put them in front of Vaz with two unbreakable glasses. "You're new. What brings you here?"

"A pressing need to avoid the UNSC."

"Looking for work?"

"When the money runs out."

"Engineers?"

"No. But we're combat-trained."

"Pity," the old woman said. "Lot of demand for engineers. And pilots."

Vaz took his beer and Naomi followed him to a table by the window. A guy standing at the bar looked her over for a moment, then turned away sharply. Vaz wasn't sure if it was because she reminded the guy of her father or because Vaz had shot him a hands-off look without even thinking about it.

She'd obviously noticed. "How am I supposed to deal with that?" she whispered, taking Vaz's lead and putting her elbows on the table. "*Leering.*"

Vaz took a pull at his beer. "Avoid eye contact and don't smile. Carry on looking like you'd rip his head off for a bet. It obviously worked."

"I'm reassured."

A group of Kig-Yar at a table on the far side of the room were having a loud debate in a weird mix of Sangheili, English, and something that was probably a Kig-Yar dialect from the pre-Covenant days. Phillips would have been fascinated. One of them was stabbing a claw at his companion, quills raised. Vaz was waiting to see a fight break out, but Kig-Yar always came across as shrill and argumentative whatever the topic. Vaz opened the packet of unidentified snacks and crunched loudly on one. Whatever the snack was made from, it must have scored a nine on the Mohs scale. He was sure he'd broken a tooth. He left the bag on the table between them.

Naomi tried one while she watched the Kig-Yar. "Ow."

"Yeah, Mal would love these. Have you seen what he eats? Those disgusting rendered *pigskin* things."

"How long do we give this?"

"A couple of hours. You've never killed time in a bar, have you?"

"No. I haven't."

"You realize this is the first conversation I've had in months that BB hasn't been able to overhear?"

They just looked at each other. They could now say anything they wanted, but Vaz couldn't think of a single thing that he'd been dying to say without BB overhearing. He automatically censored everything he said anyway, always expecting to be recorded or overheard, whether via a helmet link, the radio net, or simply under the unsleeping vigilance of a ship's AI. Now he was in a bar where the customers would probably put a round through his head if they knew what he was. He had to be careful what he said here, too.

Naomi didn't say anything. The Kig-Yar conversation was probably more interesting anyway. Occasional English words popped out of the jumble of alien language: *fool, delusional, waste, doomed.* Whatever the context, it seemed to really piss off one of them. He slapped both hands down hard on the table to lean over it with his quills raised and beak wide open like an angry starling. The other Kig-Yar half-rose and leaned over the table too, complete with quill display and hissing, and for a moment Vaz waited for feathers to start flying. If they hadn't all been carrying sidearms, it might have looked funny. Then one lowered his quills and pulled back a little. Everyone sat down and went on chattering.

A guy at a nearby table glanced in Naomi's direction. He was mid-forties, with buzz-cut brown hair and the build of someone used to hard physical labor. "Good thing that buzzards don't get drunk," he said.

Vaz found himself suddenly annoyed that the guy had started talking to Naomi. He hadn't realized he was so protective and jealous. Shit, she was a buddy, not his girlfriend; where the hell had *that* come from?

"What's their problem?" Vaz asked.

"Just politics." The man waved it all away with a dismissive hand. "They're arguing about some female of theirs who wants to unite them with a central navy again now that the Covenant's gone. Von or something. It's too much like hard work for most of them. They prefer piracy. Less paperwork."

That was rich coming from a citizen of a rebel world. But Venezia did seem to be organized and orderly, regardless of what some of its residents did for a living. A couple of the Kig-Yar glanced their way. Vaz kept looking at the guy with the buzz-cut in case he started a fight by accident. He'd done that once too often.

"I hear Kig-Yar government is afraid of its masses," Vaz said. "Which is the way it should be."

The guy laughed and drained his glass. "They don't seem to have a functioning government at all. It's a kind of piracy cooperative. What do they want? More stuff. That's about the size of it."

Vaz lowered his voice. "I've never mixed with them socially. Last time I saw one was through my rifle optics."

"I don't think they'll take it personally if your credit's good." The guy seemed to be addressing his answers to Naomi. Vaz couldn't work out if it was because she reminded him of Staffan or if he was planning to hit on her. Vaz braced to step in. He was pretty sure she wouldn't handle that well. "So, you two are new in town, yeah? I'm guessing ex-UNSC, and not the Pay Corps, either."

Word got around faster than expected. "We had creative differences," Vaz said. "You know how it is."

The man stood up and put a small flex card on their table, a slip of bright orange plastic. "You'll be at a premium, then. The militia here always needs recruits. Professionals, I mean. That card's good for a couple of drinks at any bar in town, so when you get bored, show up at the barracks and ask for Nairn."

"That's you, yeah?"

"Yeah."

Naomi suddenly decided to speak. "Are you expecting trouble?"

"Well, the colonies haven't forgotten Earth," Nairn said. "And I'm pretty sure Earth hasn't forgotten the colonies. Now the Covenant's imploded, it won't be long before they remember they had to put Trebuchet on the back burner."

Vaz watched him go. TREBUCHET was the code name for the last counterinsurgency operation against the colonies, before Vaz was even born. *So they've got very long memories here. Or he was one of us once.* It could well have been both, of course.

He turned the flex card over and studied it. "I didn't even

know they still made these." He mimed a flexing action. "They break along the stress lines. Snap one off and spend it."

"In an uncertain world, analog beats digital every time," Naomi said. "Venezia's banking system's never going to be screwed by a power outage."

"This thing might be *enhanced*." Vaz had to consider that it might be a tracking device. "Maybe I should leave it here."

Because that's what we'd do. Because we've tagged every piece of hardware we've supplied to 'Telcam so we can follow it. Neither of us have any idea now if a piece of plastic is a threat or just a free drink.

Look at the world we've created for ourselves.

But they'd made the first contact with the militia, and all they'd had to do was walk into the right bar in a small community. *Either that, or they know what we really are.* They'd find out soon enough. The mezze arrived, a plate of interesting things that might or might not have had a passing acquaintance with Greece, although some of them looked more like dim sum and sushi. Vaz was pretty sure the glistening white lumps were cheese, and the dark green parcels were stuffed vine or cabbage leaves of some kind. The meatballs and small kebab-type things—he'd try one when the beer had stiffened his resolve a little. He decided to pass on the miniature bowls of what he could only think of as a road crash involving baby octopus. Naomi peered at them.

"Well, the sign did warn us," she said. "I'll try the meatballs."

Vaz watched her chewing. "Too risky."

"Pork. I think. What, too scared? And you a Helljumper."

"Diarrhea. Sealed drop pod. They don't mix."

"You think? Try living in your armor."

They burst out laughing but it only lasted a few seconds. Then Naomi's face froze, and for a moment Vaz thought she might burst into tears. But she didn't. She just composed herself and retreated behind her Spartan indifference.

"Should we be worried about a Kig-Yar nationalist?" she asked.

"Like the man said, they enjoy pillage, but paperwork's too much of a pain in the ass."

Vaz would pass the intel on to Osman on the next radio check. He wasn't going to lose any sleep over it. They finished the mezze, spent the flex card on a couple of beers to take out, and wandered down the street, just looking around in the way that any innocent deserters who were new in town would. Vaz activated the recorder on his jacket to capture a few faces that passed, just for BB to run through facial recognition.

But he didn't lose sight of the fact that the most sophisticated intelligence operation in human history had still managed to miss Staffan Sentzke for the usual banal reason: human nature. In a way, it reassured him. Humans could still screw systems. They weren't slaves to any machine.

Naomi went silent again. Somehow it added to the authenticity of their cover, two people who knew each other so well that they hardly had anything new to discuss. When she finally spoke, it made him jump.

"If I'm leaving," she said suddenly, "then there's something I need to do."

"Sure."

She went from quiet to almost inaudible. "Let's take a look at the chart. How close can we get to Mount Longdon Road?"

It took Vaz a moment for the penny to drop. "You want to go look at your dad's house?"

"Observe."

Vaz nearly asked her if she thought that was a good idea. But what harm could it do? If she thought she could take it, if it helped her come to terms with what had been done to her, then he'd go along with it.

"Okay."

Vaz turned around and they walked back to the Warthog. He did a discreet check for explosive devices and bugs with the handheld scanner he used to track tagged weapons before heading south out of town. There was a park. Vaz thought that was the weirdest thing—a park with picnic tables and sports fields on a planet that was the number-one destination for the galaxy's terrorists. But they had kids and families like anyone else. *Except us.* He realized Mal was right: he really did watch too many apocalyptic *GlobeWar* movies. Humans were pretty domestic, even angry humans that wanted to blow other humans up.

He ran the 3-D projection of Venezia on his datapad while they sat in the Hog and watched a bunch of kids playing field hockey. Surreal didn't quite cover it.

The mapping sweep that *Port Stanley's* sensors had compiled from orbit showed one conurbation—New Tyne—with a few scattered settlements in a ten to fifteen kilometer radius, a mix of factories, farms, and all the other processes that needed to stay outside the city limits. Most of Venezia was an uninhabited wilderness. Vaz zoomed in on the network of roads that ran out of New Tyne into the countryside. So if that was the south, then Mount Longdon Road had to be *this* one, and *that* was the old quarry. He zoomed and tilted the projection to check the line of sight from vantage points near the house.

It was the kind of surveillance that BB could have carried out by dropping a tiny surveillance drone to hold position a few hundred meters above the house. But Naomi obviously needed to see this for herself.

"There," Naomi said. She pointed to a hillside covered in bushes that looked like gorse. "We could lay up there, assuming they don't have any surveillance sats of their own that we've missed, or if we pull back to *here* and use a scope, we won't necessarily look suspicious if we're spotted."

She was going to do it anyway. He knew it. All he could say was "Okay."

It was definitely Mount Longdon Road. In that oddly bureaucratic, respectable way that Venezia had, there was a proper road sign of the kind that Vaz would have found in Sydney or St. Petersburg. The nearest place to park the Warthog meant a walk of a couple of hundred meters. It was a nice afternoon, so he took the two bottles of beer to help them pass themselves off as a couple just killing time while they worked out what they were going to do now they were on the run.

Naomi wandered down into the gorse. He lost sight of her for a moment or two, but he could still hear her boots swishing through the grass. When he caught up with her, she was sitting on the ground in a gap between some bushes, hugging her knees and looking down the hill at a sprawling two-story house with a lot of land and outbuildings. It was much closer than Vaz expected, and left him feeling a little exposed. He wasn't sure what to say.

"Is that it?"

Naomi nodded. "If this is making you uncomfortable, just say."

"No. I'm fine." He knew how to keep his position hidden. It was no big deal. He settled down, opened the beers, and passed her one. "You're okay, yeah?"

"I'm not drunk."

"That isn't what I meant."

"If you're asking if I'm going to lose it, I've already seen Dad once today. Twice won't kill me."

But she *did* call him Dad. Vaz was prepared for anything. There were still thousands, maybe millions of displaced people wandering around the inner colonies, refugees from all the worlds that had been glassed in the war, and sometimes he let himself wonder if his father might be one of them, no possessions or ID, not entered into any database, still trying to get home to his son. He hardly remembered his father now. He'd been four when his dad had left Earth for a few weeks to work on a construction project on Lostwithiel, but the Covenant had shown up, and Oleg Beloi had never returned. How would he react if he saw his father now, out of the blue, back from the dead?

He hoped he'd take it calmly like Naomi, but he doubted it.

They sat watching for a couple of hours. Vaz had to take a leak behind a bush, and later Naomi disappeared for a few minutes as well. If they hung around too long he'd miss the next radio check, but he could signal with his personal comms, a brief blip so BB would know they weren't in trouble.

Suddenly Naomi stiffened and leaned forward. "Look."

They were so close to the house and it was so quiet that Vaz felt as if they were sitting on the doorstep. He couldn't see the front door, but he could hear a vehicle coming. A pickup turned into the front yard and parked halfway up the gravel drive, and a man in his late twenties or early thirties—medium-brown hair, medium build—got out of the driver's side to open the passenger door. A little girl with long blond hair and blue dungarees climbed out backward as if she was frightened of falling. The guy scooped her up and sat her on his hip, laughing, as Staffan Sentzke appeared on the porch and held out both arms to the kid.

"Grandpa!" she squealed.

Vaz had no idea what effect that had on Naomi, but it floored him completely. He couldn't look at her. He just watched Staffan with what was obviously the new family he'd built on the wasteland of his old life, and had no idea how to fit that into what he thought he knew about the Sentzkes. Staffan took the little girl and they disappeared into the house, happy and normal.

Maybe Staffan wasn't bent out of shape about Naomi at all.

Vaz risked turning to look at her, and for a second he thought he saw something. But then her expression went completely blank. It always did when things got bad. Vaz knew that by now.

"Well," she said. "Looks like I've got relatives."

FOUR

Mortal Dictata Act: Section 1A/3—Introduction and Overview

1A/3a: A human being shall be defined as a person recognized and accepted by a reasonable layperson as being human on the basis of form, behavior, or external appearance, and no authority shall be permitted to use any element of a genetic profile to exclude a person from that definition.

1A/3b: A human being shall not be restricted, selected, or subjected to discrimination on the basis of their genome or genetic profile, whether altered or unaltered.

1A/3c: A human being shall not be brought into existence with the intent of providing biological material or research data for the use, treatment, or benefit of another.

1A/3d: A human being shall not be subject to any commercial claim, patent, or restriction on the basis of any part of their genome or genetic profile, whether altered or unaltered.

1A/3e: A human being, regardless of any engineering of their genome or introduction of non-human or artificial DNA, shall not cease to be classed as human under any circumstances.

1A/3f: No human being shall be subjected to genetic alteration except with their express and informed consent, or, in the case of a person under 18, with the consent of their legal guardian for the sole purpose of correcting a health defect in that child.

1A/3g: A human being or part thereof may not be owned by any individual or organization.

1A/3h: A human being shall not be cloned.

—BASED ON THE UN GENETIC RIGHTS ACT, EXTENDED TO THE
COLONIES IN 2165 TO PREVENT ABUSES BY GENE TECH
CORPORATIONS CONDUCTING RESEARCH OUTSIDE
EARTH'S LEGAL JURISDICTION

NEW TYNE, VENEZIA: ONE WEEK LATER

The word came from Sav Fel just as Staffan was putting the finishing touches to the chandelier for Kerstin's doll's house.

His phone bleeped at just the wrong moment. Threading the crystal beads was a fiddly job that he couldn't put down until he'd bent a loop in the wire to stop the beads from scattering everywhere. He let the phone bleep a few more times, swearing quietly to himself, then pressed it with his free hand. He never left it on voice activation. It was too much of a risk.

"I can take you to the ship now," Sav Fel said.

Staffan leaned against the edge of the workbench. "With a demonstration?"

"Yes."

"Where are you planning to do that?"

"A barren planet a long way from anyone's monitoring systems."

"Okay, so what are we doing for transport?"

"We meet at the airfield. Once out of Venezia space, a ship will rendezvous with us, we'll transfer, and transit straight to slipspace. Only a short trip. But I don't want to be followed."

"As if I'd have anyone do that."

"I meant my compatriots. I hear the original owner of the ship has hired a shipmistress to recover it."

"So you've got a religious lunatic and an angry hen on your tail now, have you?"

"*Inquisitor* is obviously a very desirable ship."

"If you're trying to hike the price, I'm immune."

"Where will you get another warship with a ventral beam?"

"Where will you hide if your rivals realize you're here?"

Sav Fel went quiet for a moment. He obviously knew a threat when he heard one. "When can we meet?"

"I'm bringing an adviser. It'll have to be tomorrow or the next day."

"Very well."

"I'll call you back as soon as I fix a time."

Staffan ended the call and picked up the chandelier again. He was pleased with himself. He'd now managed to light the entire house by weaving fiber-optic cable through the walls and floors, just like the real thing. With a small power pack and a few transparent caps from a control panel, Kerstin would have lights in every room.

The house—three exterior walls but no roof yet—sat on an old wooden table at one end of Staffan's workshop. He walked around it, scrutinizing it. The wood-burning stove in the kitchen glowed red and orange from two LEPCs, and there was a painted dresser to match the Gustavian-style furniture in the other rooms. The wallpaper was in place, but he still had to source some carpets. Maybe he could find someone to make some tiny rugs for the rooms with floorboards and tiles, too.

It was immensely satisfying work. He liked getting things just right.

Here I am, creating my happy little house. No war, no government, no grief.

He'd known from the moment he started making it that it was more than just a special gift for his granddaughter. He accepted that it was a penance for failing to get one for Naomi, a subconscious motive buried in so shallow a grave that he could see the bones below with little effort. Lately, though, he'd delved a little deeper into his psyche and seen the perfection that couldn't be spoiled, the miniature world that could shut the door on the harsh reality of adult life. Within this doll's house, another reality could be built, a safer and happier one.

In an underground store, he kept salted cabbage, dried mutton, and two thousand ex-CMA rifles, not cutting-edge technology but more than capable of punching through light armor and flesh, along with a dozen crates of plasma weapons favored by Kig-Yar. In the quarry, in a cathedral-like hangar formed by the excavation of sandstone for the city of New Tyne, an assortment of Darters, Albatrosses, Phantoms, Banshees, Hornets, Vultures, and other small craft sat under tarpaulins. Some planets had more sheep than humans, but Venezia nearly had more dropships and small fighters than it had inhabitants. The arms cache built up here—some of it Staffan's, some belonging to other dealers—was enough to mount a coup in a large nation. It was all rather accidental, people had told him when he arrived, just a consequence of various dissident groups ending up here, bringing their equipment with them because they had nowhere else to go, and Venezia had turned that into a revenue-earner. There'd even been UNSC Shortswords on the black market, although acquiring the nukes for them was a tall order, and, as with all the fighters Venezia could lay its collective hands on, they just didn't have trained fighter pilots to make use of it all. But you could acquire pretty well anything in a thirty-year galactic war. Security would never be watertight. Staffan's business depended on it.

A small fleet of armored freighters and small, obsolete frigates and patrol craft were all that Venezia had by way of a navy. But then they'd been thinking in terms of fending off attacks from Earth, not becoming an expeditionary force in their own right.

But now we can have a battlecruiser.

And I'll donate it for the common good—when I've worked out how to use it to get the answers I need.

That was the trouble with opportunities. If they were exceptional, then they had to be seized first and thought through later. He'd never get a chance like this again.

Staffan locked his workshop in case Kerstin visited unannounced and went into the house for lunch. Edvin was helping Laura in the kitchen while his wife, Janey, kept Kerstin occupied reading a book. Janey looked up at him as he walked in and raised her eyebrows. Staffan nodded and put his finger to his lips. It was their code for asking how the doll's house was going and being told it was fine.

"Ed, are you free tomorrow or Wednesday?" Staffan asked. "I need someone to look at a used car with me."

Laura never asked questions or offered an opinion. The euphemism wasn't for her sake but just a good habit to get into with a child around. Edvin squatted to take the casserole out of the oven.

"Just say the word, Dad."

"Might take a day or two. I don't know where the testing ground is until we leave."

"I'll make sure I pack a change of clothes and a few extra ammo clips, then."

"It's a look-see."

"Just give me a time."

"Noon tomorrow, here?"

"Fine."

Edvin farmed and did odd jobs in exchange for favors and food, like most of the adult population. Life was a mix of barter and cash, and everyone was expected to make a contribution to communal projects like roads and schools. For the most part, it worked. It was certainly enforced. If anyone back on Sansar had told Staffan that he'd be ready and willing to put a round through someone's head for robbing a neighbor, he wouldn't

have believed them. But he had: and it seemed entirely reasonable. You didn't prey on your own. There were plenty of real enemies out there, enemies that wanted you dead, both alien and
human. The rule of law had never protected the colonies. It had
certainly never given Staffan any justice.

In the dining room, Kerstin coughed. To Staffan it was just a
cough. But Edvin darted away to check on her. He came back
into the kitchen, looking relieved.

"Just sniffles," he said.

"What else would it be?" Staffan asked.

"She's six."

"Sorry?"

"I'm just cautious, that's all. She's coming up to the age when
you said Naomi got sick."

Edvin was his son, as close to his father as two men could be,
but he still had the capacity to shock the shit out of him. It hurt.
"Kids don't all get sick at that age, Ed."

"I know."

"What's that supposed to mean?"

"Nothing. Really."

"What, you think there really *is* some genetic disease in this
family? Is that it? You don't believe a frigging word I told you?"

"Take it easy, Dad."

"No, you listen to *me*." Staffan wanted to cry rather than rage,
but he was too hurt to let it out. His own son; how could he say
that? How could he not believe him after all these years? "We
never had any genetic disease in the family. Naomi didn't die of it.
Some other kid died. It was all a bullshit cover story, because that
girl who came back was never, *ever* my daughter. Do you hear
me? After all these years, you think I'm some crazy old asshole?
You know damn well I'm not. I wasn't the only one. You *know* it."

"I'm just being an anxious dad. That's all. Of course I believe
you."

Staffan found himself shaking. He wasn't sure if it was from anger or shock. Laura stepped silently between them and gave Edvin a push into the dining room. It was just as well, because Staffan wanted to grab Edvin and shake him. *He doesn't believe me. He still doesn't believe me.* The one thing Staffan held on to was his sanity, handed back to him by an equally broken father called Andy Remo after years of knocking on doors and making calls. If it hadn't been for that one conversation a few years after the poor kid who replaced Naomi had died, Staffan was sure he would have followed Lena and killed himself. Anything that threatened to upend his certainty might plunge him back into those depths, and that would be the end of everything.

"He didn't mean that," Laura whispered. "Come and sit down. You love chicken casserole. I made it specially."

Staffan couldn't get himself back together right then. "I'll be a few minutes," he said. "I need to wash my hands. Don't wait for me to start."

He went into the bathroom, locked the door, and sat down on the toilet with his head in his hands. Not being believed by his own family was the most painful thing he'd ever experienced. He was reliving it right now. His shoulders shook as he fought back tears.

Lena had never believed him, either. She believed the doctors.

Sansar didn't have the best medical facilities in the outer colonies, but the pediatrician at New Stockholm's main hospital had been adamant about why their daughter was dying, and that had convinced Staffan that the child struggling through one illness after the next was *not* Naomi. It was a rare genetic mutation, the doctor said, an extreme metabolic failure that was crippling her with arthritis, making her skin raw and infected, and destroying her lungs and kidneys.

Did they still have any pictures of her? Staffan was sure he'd kept one as evidence, but he'd burned the rest after Lena died. They weren't happy family snaps. He only wanted to keep the ones of Naomi, the real Naomi, and remembering that now made him feel like the impostor child had died twice.

I knew she wasn't ours when we picked her up from the hospital. I knew there was something wrong. She said all those weird things about usually having more doctors around.

She didn't remember the house.

She didn't want to read her books.

She never mentioned the doll's house.

She was sickly from the moment we got her home.

She changed. Quiet, withdrawn . . . a stranger with my girl's face.

And there were never any genetic illnesses in my family or Lena's. We checked. We went back through all the records. We would have known.

Staffan could still feel his fingers gripping the molded plastic of the wheelchair handles as he pushed that frail, paralyzed little girl through the park and tried to make her unhappy life a little easier. She'd had to wear a hat and cover herself up so that her raw skin and distorted body didn't upset passersby. He hated it when people stared at her. He'd hit a guy for that once. He wished he'd killed him.

Staffan knew that she wasn't his, but she was a kid, and she didn't deserve that suffering. Her funeral was a strange new low point in his nightmare existence. He both mourned her and felt relief that she was finally gone. Lena hated him for that; she could see his relief, and she didn't understand his anger and denial. She wanted him to shut up about the girls being switched. She just wanted to believe the doctors. Who wouldn't? Who would choose to believe the crazy idea that the child wasn't Naomi? It hurt more, if such a thing was possible.

Maybe if we'd had another baby, she'd have seen then. She'd have seen the kid was okay, and that I was right. And she'd be here now, helping me look for the real Naomi.

Staffan had been through this cycle of tortured thought so

often over the years that it was like a familiar bus journey. He knew exactly what scenery was coming next, and if it was too awful to watch he could shut his eyes until the bus had passed a certain point. But the journey was always in his head, lurking behind his eyes, and there was no blanking out the image of Lena lying fully clothed in the empty bath, wrists cut, bled out, too house-proud even in death to make a mess on the floor.

He felt the relief again and hated himself for it.

And I wanted to be dead as well. I envied Lena for having the guts to do it.

Staffan hadn't relived it with that intensity for years. Just when he thought he'd come to terms with that part of it, he realized he hadn't. He'd just parked it because it was too much to deal with. He could only focus on what he was able to do.

He took his phone out again and checked through the numbers. Andy Remo's file was still in there. Staffan still couldn't delete it, even after all this time. It would feel like murder, like destroying those pictures of the girl who wasn't Naomi.

What was her real name? Who was she?

"Staffan?" Laura rapped on the door. "Your chicken's getting cold."

Staffan stood up and turned on the tap, making hand-washing noises. He snapped back to being the guy that Remo had made him, the man who didn't give a shit about authority and was ready to spit in its face, not the meek tax-paying citizen who kept his nose clean and thought that obeying the rules would stop his government from picking on him.

"Coming, honey."

Staffan sat down to eat, trying not to let what he'd been thinking leave its awful marks on his face. Edvin got up, stood behind his father's chair, and put his hands on his shoulders.

"Sorry, Dad."

"No problem." Staffan squeezed his arm. How could he be angry with his own son? "When we get back, let's have everyone around here for a barbecue. Then Hedda can eat her *surström-ming* and we won't be trapped with it in a confined space."

"I want to try it," Kerstin said, chin almost level with the table.

"It's horrible," Janey told her. "It's what trolls eat. That's why they have to live under bridges."

Everyone was laughing again. One thing Staffan had learned over the years was that you could make yourself do anything if you needed to badly enough. That night he packed his rucksack and picked his weapons, "tooling up," as Remo used to call it. It had taken Staffan months to work out that this pleasant, serious, unhappy man, another father who believed he'd buried a stranger's child, was actually a criminal, and a very successful one. Nothing too violent, not unless he was backed into a corner: he specialized in fraud and robbery. He'd taught Staffan a lot about breaking the rules and taking care of himself.

"We're not mad, buddy," Staffan said aloud, mimicking Remo's accent. "It's the rest of the bastards—they're the crazy ones for thinking we won't find out."

The next day, he and Edvin did their usual feint to throw off any of Sav Fel's rivals who might have been informed that he was on Venezia and had come to see what they could get out of it. The end of the war had thrown up a fair few newcomers of various species, from Unggoy who wanted a fresh start to humans who needed to disappear now that order and record-keeping was making a return to the inner colonies and Earth itself. Discretion was an automatic precaution. Staffan drove Edvin to the airfield, took a shuttle out to the coast, and met Sav Fel's vessel on Weymouth Island. He was pretty sure he wasn't being tailed, but if they were, then they definitely shook off any tracking when they docked with the Kig-Yar vessel farther out in the Venezia system.

It was a weird-looking thing, something known as a missionary ship, all storage bays and recovery equipment, more like a factory than a vessel designed to carry bibles and earnest men and women intent on bringing the word to the heathen. Missionary work had been the Kig-Yar's sweetener from the Covenant. They'd searched for ancient relics for their masters as long as they were allowed to do a little piracy and appropriation on the side. It had seemed to work.

"Another hull you liberated from the Covenant?" Staffan asked as they docked.

"Now they know that their gods were just an extinct alien race," Fel said, "they don't need to look for holy artifacts any longer, do they?"

Staffan hadn't left Venezia more than a dozen times in the last twenty-odd years. He'd forgotten how rough a slipspace jump could feel. Sav Fel spent the short transit listing what equipment he needed, occasionally glancing at Edvin as if he was worried that he might shoot him, and Staffan was so engrossed in negotiating what weapons and transport he might be willing to part with that he was caught short by the sudden drop out of slipspace. He stood up and went to the viewplate in the forward section.

For a moment, he couldn't see anything except the speckling of stars and the hazy streak of a gas cloud across the dense blackness. Then he spotted a patch of more intense black without the dappling of starlight, and realized he was looking at something solid. It was hard to tell what it was or how close he was to it, only that it was big and irregular. Then the Kig-Yar ship moved, and he found himself looking along a short line of small, dim lights that definitely weren't stars.

Now he got it. He was actually looking at the stern, and the lights were from an open hangar bay door on the starboard side.

"Jesus," Edvin said. "That's big."

"You've seen very few Covenant ships, then," Fel said. "This is quite small by comparison."

Staffan still couldn't see it for what it was. He felt he was staring at one of those optical illusions that someone had to point out to you before something clicked in your brain and your perspective shifted. Fel ushered him to the missionary ship's docking bay and into a six-seater shuttle that slid out of the bay doors and tracked along the length of the black hull.

No, Staffan still couldn't get the scale. *Pious Inquisitor* was just a landscape of curved surfaces, too big to take in as a single object. It was only when the open hangar swallowed the shuttle that he got a sense of being inside a warship. The shuttle maneuvered into a berth that was level with a deck, and Staffan stepped out.

Everything that hit his senses disoriented him. It was cold. The deck tugged at his boots as if the ship was still set to Sanghelios gravity, and the air smelled of chemicals, dog food, and smoke. The light was dim and purple. And everything seemed to be bigger and higher, with the controls set farther up the bulkheads than he was used to.

Sangheili were big. He knew that, but he'd never seen one in person. Just raising his arm to touch a panel by a hatch brought that home to him. He could hear Edvin walking behind him.

Is he thinking what I'm thinking? No. He never saw Sansar. He doesn't remember much before Venezia. He's never seen a devastated world.

In a ship much like this, a crew of Sangheili had calmly pressed controls to incinerate the surface of Staffan's home world and reduce it to molten slag that eventually cooled into a glass lake. It might even have been this very ship that had turned Sansar into glasslands.

But Staffan's world had already been destroyed long before then, while the buildings and trees were still standing. There were times when he wished he'd known the Covenant was coming so that he could have waited for it to end his misery. But he hadn't: and here he was, about to take possession of one of its ships to use against another empire that didn't give a shit who it rolled over.

There were no more than thirty Kig-Yar on board. The ship seemed largely shut down and in darkness, with occasional glimpses of dimly lit control panels in passages leading off the one they were walking along. Staffan had left Sansar on a big mining freighter, but this thing had to be twice its size.

Edvin looked around. "I can see why you want to dispose of it, Fel. It must need a big crew."

Edvin was an old hand at playing backup on his father's business deals, so it might have been part of a ploy to drive down the price, but he did sound like he meant it. Staffan wasn't sure if Fel had heard him. They stepped into an elevator, pressed together more closely than he was comfortable with for a few moments.

"You don't need many," Fel said. "But it depends what you want to do. She can carry an army. She can take out other warships. She has pulse lasers and plasma torpedoes."

"Minimum."

"I appropriated her with a crew of forty or so, and many of the functions are automated."

"Does it have an AI?"

"The Covenant forbade the construction of AIs. Not that they didn't try to make use of human ones they captured. But don't worry. I may be able to offer you a better alternative."

"I'm not paying extra for it."

Fel didn't say a word. The elevator stopped on a deck that was fully lit and Staffan could now hear noise—Kig-Yar noise. He took a guess that they were near a bridge or control room. Fel stood back to let Staffan and Edvin step off the platform.

This had to be the bridge or the command center. A central platform overlooked consoles dotted with holographic displays. A few Kig-Yar were lounging around, apparently checking the status of various systems as if they knew what they were doing. There was another bank of mauve and pink lights to the right of the doors.

Then the mauve lights moved, all at once. A faintly glowing shape glided toward him.

"What's *that*?"

"The alternative," Fel said. "A Huragok. An Engineer, as humans call them."

Staffan had heard Kig-Yar talk about Huragok but he'd never seen one. It was utterly alien despite the long, almost animal face with multiple pairs of small black eyes. It hovered level with him, a translucent bag of gas with bioluminescent patches and wafting tentacles. The blue, pink, and lavender coloring made it look like an oversized toy. Kerstin would love it.

Naomi would have been fascinated, too.

"So this is your alternative, is it?" Staffan asked.

"A Huragok can repair anything. *Improve* anything."

The creature just stared at him. Staffan tried to look it in the eye, opting for the largest pair. "Can it talk?"

"It uses sign language. They can understand us, but it needs a translation unit to answer you. They're artificial. The Forerunners—the aliens, the false gods—made them. Now they replicate themselves."

"Does it have a name?"

"Sometimes Sinks."

"Seriously?"

Fel cocked his head. "All their names have something to do with their buoyancy qualities. Why they've never run out of words to describe that, I have no idea."

"If he's such a wondrous asset, why do you want to sell him?"

"I need weapons and transport more than I need an Engineer. And he can't replicate. He needs other Huragok to do that, and the rest of them disappeared when the San'Shyuum cowards ran away."

"Why not sell it to the Sangheili?"

"They have no money and they have nothing else we want at the moment."

"You mean the Arbiter's people don't trust you enough to

arm you, and if the rebels catch you, you *personally,* they'll kill you."

Sav Fel didn't look fazed. "All those things may well be true. Much better to sell him to you, yes?"

It was a plausible story, but Staffan hadn't survived in the world of arms dealing by taking anything at face value, especially Kig-Yar. "Why do I need him? I just want a ship."

"How will you maintain the ship without him? He absorbs all data he encounters. You need very few special parts for the ship, because he can make almost anything from raw materials."

"Just as well, seeing as the Covenant spares shop is out of business now."

Staffan was still looking for the catch. A lone Huragok wasn't as lucrative as two that could replicate, but it was still a technical edge that no sane man would pass up. If what he'd heard about them from Kig-Yar over the years was true, then they were a fantastically useful toolbox if nothing else. Staffan was a mechanic; all he could see were the possibilities that a Huragok could open up, not just weapons and ships but all kinds of products and processes. Just one of the things, for as long as it lasted, could transform a town.

Kig-Yar didn't think like humans, though. They'd tried imperial culture once and decided it wasn't for them. Maybe they were right: humans were constantly in denial about their ape-sized social circles, always pretending they could think on a global scale when history proved every time that they really couldn't.

The Kig-Yar had space flight and planetary colonies when we still thought tallow candles were the state of the art.

Kig-Yar also robbed, murdered, and shat anywhere they pleased, though, so progress wasn't all it was cracked up to be. Staffan racked his brains to think what angle Fel might be playing to forego a prize like a Huragok. Maybe the price he could get for the thing was worth it in his short-term mindset.

Remember that he might well have a point, too.

"I hear they're a pain in the ass," Staffan bluffed. He'd heard the opposite, that all they wanted to do was work. "More trouble than they're worth."

Fel cocked his head left then right, his hang-on-while-I-think-of-an-objection gesture. "If your ventral beam systems breaks down, how will you fix it?"

"It only has to work once."

"You say that now, but you'll get a taste for it."

"We're not in the business of empire-building," Staffan said. "This is about self-defense. We just want to stay free of Earth."

"In my experience," Fel said, "the humans who talk most loudly about freedom are the ones who think it's so good that nobody else should have any of it."

Fel ambled around, probably hoping the scale of the ship would make the sale for him. Sinks wafted after him at a discreet distance. It was hard to work out if the Huragok was following him like a loyal dog or just keeping an eye on him in case he stole anything.

Staffan was getting cold feet. What the hell was he going to do with this? He could get a crew together, and there were enough ex-Covenant personnel on Venezia to train a human crew if they were paid enough. But this was far bigger than he'd expected, despite the fact that he knew the battlecruiser's dimensions before he set out. It must have cost an arm and a leg to maintain it. He kept finding more reasons why the Kig-Yar wanted to sell it on.

Edvin's right. I can't keep this as a private vengeance machine. I have to give it to the militia.

But not yet.

Edvin leaned in close to him. "We can't call her *Pious Inquisitor*," he murmured. "That's revolting. It's everything we despise. State religion, hierarchies, witch hunts . . . but the name alone is going to get the UNSC's attention."

"I haven't said I'll take her yet." Staffan ambled across the deck to Fel and his cronies. Damn, this thing was *big*. Crossing from one side of the bridge platform to the other was like walking across a ballroom. "Fel? What about the armaments? What else is still on board?"

"Missiles. The larger ordnance that we don't have a market for."

"Yes, it would be a bit of a giveaway trying to sell those on, wouldn't it? Okay, let's see what she can do. Where's that barren planet you promised me?" There was one thing Staffan needed *Inquisitor* to be able to do above all else. "I want to see her glass the surface."

UNSC *TART-CART*, EN ROUTE TO NEW LLANELLI, BRUNEL SYSTEM—KNOWN TO THE SANGHEILI AS LAQIL

Phillips had run out of *arum* puzzles to challenge him. Naomi could tell. As he twisted the sphere in his hands, making it click and rattle, the light had gone out of his eyes.

"You need a new one," she said. "You know all the combinations."

"Okay, I'm hooked. I admit it."

"You could always make your own."

"But I'd know all the solutions. It'd be like trying to tickle yourself."

He fiddled with the polished wooden ball, obviously knowing exactly what was coming next. A small green stone dropped onto the deck.

"I meant you should ask Adj to make you a new one," Naomi said. "BB can help. That'll keep you all busy."

"Yeah, that's a good idea." Phillips released his safety belt to retrieve the stone. "I'm sure BB can come up with something to defeat me."

Naomi waited for BB's ghostly blue-lit box to appear in the cabin to make some cutting remark, but it didn't. The AI was listening, though, either through the real-time FTL comms link to *Port Stanley* or via a fragment of himself that he'd split off and inserted into *Tart-Cart*'s systems. Phillips leaned back in his seat with his helmet in his lap, almost at home in ODST armor now. He put the helmet on and took it off a couple of times as if he was doing a safety drill. He'd been shaken by the cabin fire a few weeks ago. BB, who'd obviously kept an eye on him, said he constantly practiced getting the helmet on and sealed in two seconds.

"I still haven't got the hang of this HUD," he said. He must have felt that she was staring at him. "Like sticking my head inside a busy nightclub when I'm drunk. Too many flashing lights."

Naomi had never seen the interior of a nightclub. She took his word for it. "I disabled half the data feeds for you to make it easier."

"I know. But I tried activating them again. I wanted to see the three-D plot of the approach to Laqil."

"New Llanelli."

"Sorry. Bad habit."

Naomi wasn't sure if he was pumped up about the mission or just talking to avoid straying onto the subject of her estranged family. She knew the others must have talked about it. It was hard to explain to them that it was a theoretical thing for her, underpinned by vague remnants of emotions that had faded years ago, and that she was far more deeply affected by losing fellow Spartans. By any definition, *they* were family. But she knew that what had happened to her and her parents had been criminal, unthinkable, even if time had spared her the capacity to feel just how bad it had been. The rest of the squad was doing that feeling for her.

Her father had another family now. She was glad. He seemed happy. It didn't put anything right, but she felt less guilty for not . . . she didn't know what, but it was *something*. She just felt it was her fault, the same way Osman said that she did, that they both had some responsibility for being the source of so much suffering for their families.

"I'm okay," she said. "Really. Don't tread on eggs, Phyllis."

"You've never called me that before."

"Would you prefer Evan?"

"No. I'll always be Phyllis now, won't I?"

The intercom popped. "Starting descent," Devereaux said. "Stealth measures off. Practice your best smiles for the nice hinge-heads."

Tart-Cart set down near the RV point. Every sign that New Llanelli had been a small agricultural colony had been erased by the near-stellar heat of a Covenant ship's ventral beam seven years ago. When the clouds parted, the sky was incongruously blue, and the reflected glare from the vitrified land gave the cruel illusion of a sunlit ocean in the distance. And that was what a ship just like *Pious Inquisitor* had done.

Naomi put on her helmet and walked a few meters from the ship. As she crunched through a thin layer of glass, she kicked up fragments that sparkled like diamonds in the sunlight, something that would have been magically pretty if she hadn't known how it had happened. Phillips backed the heavily laden Warthog down the ramp and she swung into the passenger seat. The last time she'd seen 'Telcam, he'd been furious because she'd dragged him bodily from the siege of Vadam keep. Maybe he was in a more forgiving frame of mind now. They reached the rendezvous point and waited, watching the horizon until a black dot appeared and grew into a ground transport heading straight for them.

"No fighting," Phillips said, taking off his helmet. "Let me charm him."

'Telcam's transport drew up with a couple of Brutes to unload the weapons. Naomi was mildly surprised that any Brutes had stayed loyal after the last of their buddies on Sanghelios had finally turned on their masters, but even Brutes needed a job. 'Telcam walked up to her, looked her in the visor, and nodded. It was an acknowledgment of a sort. Then he towered over Phillips.

"Scholar *Philliss.*" Sangheili didn't have the anatomy to cope with bilabial sounds like P, even the ones who were as fluent in English as 'Telcam was. The best they could do with their four-way jaws was something like an F or an S, much to the ODSTs' amusement. "Did you bring the translations?"

Phillips reached inside his chest-plate and pulled out a small notebook. He'd taken the time to hand-copy all the Forerunner inscriptions from the Ontom tunnels that he'd recorded on his datapad, adding the Sangheili translation underneath, all written out with painstaking care. The effect was one of a bible copied by a devoted abbot. There was a much more pragmatic reason for it, of course: he couldn't hand over all the images to 'Telcam because he and Osman had decided to redact all the symbols that might give the Sangheili portal locations and other hard data they might not already have. But that wasn't what 'Telcam wanted. He wanted the word of his gods. He wanted them to reassure him that they still existed despite all the evidence to the contrary.

Naomi watched 'Telcam as Phillips handed over what was effectively an album of signage from a garrison complex, basic housekeeping and safety warnings. But these Sangheili would somehow derive deep spiritual meaning from it like some bizarre cargo cult. There was nothing that the *Neru Pe'Odisima*— the Servants of the Abiding Truth—couldn't interpret as a coded message from the gods, even a site maintenance manual for an ancient Forerunner base that had somehow passed into history as a temple. Naomi didn't find it funny. It was actually rather disturbing.

Thou shalt not commit murder. Thou shalt not commit adultery. Thou shalt not allow garbage to accumulate in the communal areas because of the fire hazard.

She wondered if Phillips should have doctored the transcript a little and added a few lines where the gods said humans should be left in peace. 'Telcam took the notebook like a movie Moses accepting the commandments at Sinai.

Naomi was there to make sure nothing went wrong while Phillips made small talk with 'Telcam. She expected them to converse in Sangheili, but 'Telcam stuck to English as if he thought it was more polite with her present. Would he mention that he'd hired Kig-Yar to find his missing warship? It was the kind of thing that allies would share, even uncomfortable ones who didn't much care for each other.

"Did your friend 'Mdama ever show up?" Phillips asked. He was very convincing, sounding as if he was clutching at conversational straws. "You said he vanished."

"No," 'Telcam said. "That remains something of a mystery. But our war is not over, and in dangerous times, warriors are lost."

He couldn't have known how true that was. The last thing Parangosky wanted was for Jul to show up again shooting his mouth off about how ONI had kidnapped him and held him at one of their research stations before he escaped. But if he had, Naomi wondered if 'Telcam could keep it to himself. Maybe he could. The average Sangheili would have confronted Phillips with it, but 'Telcam was a much more subtle individual.

He looked Naomi up and down. "And *you*," he said. "Are you winning your war?"

"That's not for me to decide, Field Master." She hadn't expected him to make small talk with her. Neither of them were equipped for it. "That's one for the historians."

Go on, 'Telcam. Tell me you're so pissed off with Sav Fel that you've put a bounty on him and you've got a Kig-Yar repo team looking for Inquisitor. *You know you have.*

But 'Telcam didn't mention it, and he didn't ask Phillips if Osman had located the ship, either. It was one of the last things she'd said to the monk, that she'd have to find the battlecruiser before it became a problem for anyone else. It was a natural thing to discuss.

Maybe he'd already worked out that Osman had no intention of handing *Inquisitor* back if she got to the ship before he did.

"I think 'Mdama is dead," 'Telcam said suddenly. "If he could have returned, he would have."

Phillips took over the conversation. He was good at this verbal fencing. "You think the Arbiter's forces caught him?"

"Perhaps. He has nothing useful to tell them, though. Or perhaps he ran across *your* troops. The ones who don't know what you do to thwart them."

"We haven't heard anything. If I do, I'll let you know. Just as well Sangheili children grow up in a communal environment. What with 'Mdama's wife dead as well."

"You remembered."

"I just thought it was really sad for their kids to have both parents gone at the same time. Not that they know who their father is, I suppose, but they'd miss anyone they thought was an uncle, wouldn't they?"

"It has been hard for them."

That sounded as if 'Telcam had stayed in touch with the Bekan keep. His English was too precise for that to be a slip of the tongue. Who would be the clan elder now, then? Naomi realized she knew nothing about the Sangheili laws of inheritance within keeps.

"Are you still looking for *Pious Inquisitor*?" 'Telcam asked suddenly. "And has this Shipmistress Lahz shown up again?"

Phillips didn't look at Naomi. He just shook his head. "Still searching. If the ship ends up in the hands of *our* rebels, we've got problems."

He hadn't told 'Telcam any more than he already knew or could work out for himself. Shipmistress Lahz was never going to make another appearance, though, not unless BB decided to resurrect her. When BB did a spot of misinformation and spoofed a ship, he really made a thorough job of it—not just false transponder codes, but a false commander, too, one that had even convinced Kig-Yar. Naomi had to keep reminding herself that Lahz didn't actually exist.

"So how long are you going to sit it out here?" Phillips asked.

"Until we persuade more keeps to join the rebellion, or we acquire enough ships to destroy all those who refuse," 'Telcam said. "It's an equation. As you say, a numbers game. And it would help if your Admiral Hood would stay out of Sangheili affairs and withdraw support for the Arbiter."

"I wasn't aware we were giving him assistance anymore."

"Maybe not practical support, but the legitimacy it confers is provocative."

"But it's just words. Not weapons." Phillips was impressively relaxed. Naomi had to admire his nerve. "And Sangheili don't care what humans think, do they?"

Port Stanley had left remotes in orbit around Sanghelios to transmit real-time surveillance. A stalemate was exactly what ONI had set out to achieve, a finely balanced and long-running civil war that would eat what was left of Sangheili military capability while Earth sneaked out the back door to strengthen its position. But they were only months into this. They needed to keep it going for years, and arming factions in civil wars had much the same success rate as buying lotto tickets. Naomi wondered if the Sangheili might ever think of playing exactly the same game with Earth and Venezia.

"Well, let us know if *Inquisitor* shows up." Phillips paused a beat, almost as if he was waiting for 'Telcam to come clean. "Or your friend 'Mdama. Like you, I hate mysteries."

'Telcam did that little sway of the head that Naomi interpreted as regret. He was clutching the notebook of Forerunner translations to his chest in a way that made him look like he was living up to the nickname that Phillips had first given him—the Bishop.

"I should have sent his wife back to her keep rather than enter a combat zone," 'Telcam said. "Her sons would have a mother now. I should have known better. So the elder boy, Dural, wishes to fight and avenge his mother, and I've agreed to take him into my service. An apprentice, I think you would call it. A cadet. Have I chosen the right word?"

"Sounds about right." It was a guilty moment. Phillips had been as responsible as anyone in ONI for the fate of Jul 'Mdama, the fierce Sangheili nationalist who wanted his people to reclaim their former glories. "I know I shouldn't ask if that's actually Jul's son, but it's not as if I'm going to break the taboo and tell him."

'Telcam just tilted his head. Sangheili males were never allowed to know who their fathers were. It was a secret kept by the females to give all youngsters an equal start in life. Naomi assumed they managed bloodlines to prevent inbreeding.

"Is he bitter?" Phillips asked.

"As only a grieving son can be." 'Telcam lowered his head and took a couple of steps toward his transport. The meeting was over. "Or a grieving parent. They're the surest enemies, those we deprive of their loved ones."

'Telcam couldn't have known that he'd described both Naomi's father and Dural 'Mdama, just two in a list of angry, vengeful victims that ONI left in its wake. Phillips said nothing. Naomi waited for the Brutes to remove the last crate before she went back to sit in the Warthog's driver's seat. Phillips took a few moments to say good-bye to 'Telcam before he headed back to the vehicle and 'Telcam's party went on its way.

"Sometimes I think he's psychic," Phillips said. "Or maybe he just states the crushingly obvious."

"What, how we make enemies?"

"Something like that."

"He never mentioned that he's hired the Kig-Yar."

"He's still the enemy. Why would he tell us everything?"

"I thought you liked them."

"There's respect and there's being on their side. I never said I was the latter."

She'd never heard Phillips openly call them the enemy before, however implicit it was the work he now did. His whole career was built on the Sangheili. He was probably Earth's foremost expert on them, and he'd been genuinely upset by the deaths of the females and their children in Nes'alun. But he lived and worked with people who had every reason to hate them. It seemed to have tempered his enthusiasm for his area of expertise.

"Tell me something," he said. "Would you want to know exactly who glassed Sansar? Would you want to know if it was him?"

Naomi made every effort not to wonder. It didn't matter. Whatever she knew and felt had to be kept in check so that it didn't get in the way of the job. Not knowing things like that was the best way to handle it.

"No, I wouldn't," she said. "Because then I'd have to ask the Huragok if they'd maintained ventral beams, and then I'd have to ask which ships. Pretty soon the whole thing comes unraveled."

That was what had happened to her father. She couldn't argue with the logic or sense of justice. *Unraveled.* Yes, there were unfortunate doors that opened and couldn't be closed again. It was best not to open them in the first place.

FORMER COVENANT BATTLECRUISER *PIOUS INQUISITOR*, APPROACHING SHAPS' STAR

The deck shivered. Staffan felt like he was in an elevator that had suddenly accelerated. His first reaction was to check his watch—less than two hours' transit time—and his next was to look to Edvin for his best guess as to where *Inquisitor* had dropped out of slipspace.

"So where are we?"

Edvin studied his datapad. "Well, pick one of two star systems. Cordoba or Shaps. They're both in range."

Fel huddled in an alcove on the control room deck with a dozen of his crew plus his two lieutenants, Dhak and Eith, and there seemed to be a debate going on. Staffan had picked up a few words in various Kig-Yar dialects over the years. He made sure nobody knew how much he actually understood, though. Ignorance might not have been bliss, but the appearance of being a stupid flat-face was a great negotiating advantage.

He strained to eavesdrop, expecting this to be something about how they were going to disguise *Inquisitor*'s lack of capacity or some other defect, but a few words leaped out at him. *Home. Pay. Late. Enough trouble.* Fel's crew just wanted to close the deal, get paid, and lie low.

That was useful to know. Fel had to be under pressure from all sides. He was stuck with stolen property that he needed to off-load before his crew got too restless and before an angry Sangheili tracked him down. He'd be flexible on price. Kig-Yar thought they'd written the book on piracy and sharp practice, but Staffan had been taught his trade by a genuine, fully-qualified, twenty-four-carat gangster. Fel had surrendered control of the transaction the minute he decided to stroll off with a warship with very few potential buyers he could sell it to.

"Where are we, Fel?" Staffan asked. "Cordoba or Shaps?"

He hoped Edvin was right about the system. He usually was. Intelligence ran in the family. Fel's huddle broke up and the shipmaster stalked across the deck, doing a good impression of someone who was in control of his crew.

"Shaps' Star," Fel said. "Very good. Shaps Three is a wasteland. Just ancient ruins, and nobody's going to notice the energy spike out here."

"So what's your plan?"

"We'll be in position shortly. We'll make this fast, just to be prudent." The Kig-Yar trotted over to the far end of the command console. "I've launched a remote to sit on the surface and send back images. Then we can see how effective the beam is. Actually, *beams*. There are two."

"You haven't tested it, then."

Fel looked over his shoulder at Staffan as if he was mad. He could turn his head a disturbingly long way, almost like an owl. "Of course not. Vaporizing the surface of a planet is inclined to attract attention."

"I meant on Sanghelios."

"Glassing would have been extra. We were paid to *transport*."

Staffan sometimes wondered if Fel was joking or simply playing up to the Kig-Yar stereotype. But he looked at the mad little yellow eyes with their slit pupils, and decided that the bastard meant every word.

Good. Makes life easier.

Staffan could communicate with Edvin like a card cheat. A glance here, a breath there, and his son knew where he was heading with a deal, and Staffan knew what Edvin thought as well. They watched Fel tapping in coordinates. Then the bridge doors parted and the Huragok floated in. He was moving pretty fast, as if he had urgent news. Staffan was distracted for a moment, fascinated by the engineering feat of making a fairly heavy creature like that buoyant and mobile simply with gas sacs.

"What do you want?" Fel asked irritably, not even looking up from the controls. "We're about to deploy the beam."

Sometimes Sinks hovered right next to him. How did Fel understand it? The Huragok appeared to understand him, but its responses were all flurries of tentacles, a kind of sign language. If the Huragok came with the ship, then Staffan was going to need a better interface than that.

"What do you mean, *no*?" Fel said suddenly.

Sinks backed off a little, but his tentacles were going crazy like a bookmaker at a racetrack.

"It's got to be done," Fel said. "Go away."

The Huragok appeared to be getting increasingly distressed. Staffan couldn't tell what the bioluminescence meant, but when the Huragok put one tentacle on Fel's arm, it was hard not to see the gesture as an attempt to stop the ventral beams from being fired.

"What's up with him?" Edvin asked.

Fel put out a bony arm to steer the Huragok away. "Artifacts. He says we can't destroy the artifacts down there."

"Are they important?"

"Just Forerunner ruins. The false gods. If they were useful—like portals—we would have made use of them by now. Some of those still function, you know. It's simply that you have no guarantee where the wormhole terminates, because they haven't been maintained for thousands of years."

Fel stepped back from the console as if he'd given up on the idea, then turned toward the doors. Sinks followed him. The door parted, the two of them disappeared down the passage, and Staffan waited. The Kig-Yar on the bridge glanced over their shoulders as if this was a regular delay in their day. It was only when Fel came back some time later without the Huragok that Staffan wondered if Fel had shot the creature.

No. They're too valuable. He's still trying to sell him to me.

"I locked him in the brig," Fel said. "But he might reconfigure the locks."

"I thought they were supposed to be obedient," Edvin said. He shot Staffan a glance. "How do you control them?"

"They have one purpose in life," Fel said. "To be engineers. To build, maintain, and repair. That's how the Forerunners made them, to ensure that they'd always be happy and willing workers. Sometimes they can be very insistent about looking after inanimate objects, but despite their strength, they're not aggressive. Just *annoying.*"

Fel walked back to the console and started switching between cam feeds. Staffan could now see multiple holographic views of Shaps 3 and the keel of the ship, including the surface of the planet from ground level, showing a cluster of extraordinary buildings in the distance.

"Are those the Forerunner ruins?" he asked.

Fel adjusted the controls. "Yes."

"They're astonishing." Staffan had never seen anything like it. "How long ago did they abandon them?"

"Millennia." Fel was unmoved. He was used to seeing this, but Staffan definitely wasn't. "Don't worry. I doubt they'll return to file a complaint."

It was no time to worry about cultural vandalism. Staffan still felt uneasy about it, though, like nuking the pyramids at Giza. He put it out of his mind. Buildings weren't people, no matter how fascinating and awe-inspiring they might be. Lives came first.

Another camera gave him an aerial view of the planet with a magnification that looked like an altitude of ten thousand meters. When the beam fired, he'd see exactly what it did from every angle.

And this is what they did to Sansar.

He had to put some emotional distance between that and what he was seeing now. He'd left Sansar behind long before the place was glassed. But it was hard not to remember the house, the neighbors, and the forests, and calmly accept that they'd all been vaporized without mercy or warning. He looked at Fel.

But Fel didn't press that button. And Fel didn't take my daughter.

When it was impossible to tell whose hands were clean in this world, getting through the day was a matter of deciding who you hated least. Staffan concentrated on the cam feed projections and took a couple of steps toward Edvin. His son was watching Fel too.

"Did they say prayers?" Edvin asked.

Fel's head flicked from side to side as he stared down at the controls. The ruff of black feathers made him look even more raven-like. "What?"

"Did the bastards say prayers before they pressed the button? You know. To sanctify the act or some voodoo bullshit like that."

"I have no idea." Fel seemed to take the comment as a shared dislike of the Sangheili, not the thinly veiled insult to an entire Covenant that included him. "I was never present for such a thing. Is everyone ready?"

"Do it," Staffan said.

He was already thinking which city he might target in due course, and how he'd feel when he was in Fel's position. It made him feel slightly sick. He wondered if the Sangheili who gave the order to fire had any misgivings, but then reminded himself that the entire Covenant war was about maximum collateral damage. It was genocide.

And if I use this as a bargaining chip, then I have to be prepared to do the same.

It didn't matter. Whatever question he asked would be heard more loudly with a battlecruiser to back him up, even if he left it berthed in some shipyard.

"It's fully powered." Eith leaned closer to a control panel and scrutinized it with a beady red eye. He didn't seem to bother with formal commands and responses. He gave Staffan the impression that he thought all that military discipline was nonsense. "You may activate it, Shipmaster."

"Watch," Fel said. The Kig-Yar spread his claws and pressed his palm on a large disc-shaped control. "Make sure you watch, Sentzke."

A faint, tickling vibration climbed through the soles of Staffan's boots. He didn't dare take his eyes off the screens, but the back of his tongue started to itch, an irritation that made him want to scratch deep inside his ears. In the hull cam view, a pinpoint of white-hot light fringed with violet expanded into a swirling ball of energy in seconds.

The projection dimmed slightly. The deck shivered and the sensation in Staffan's ears became so intense that he jammed his fingers into them to try to relieve it. Then all he could see for a painful second was blinding, blue-white light.

When he blinked again, he was looking down a long, narrow beam of fire apparently connected to the surface of Shaps 3, and a heartbeat later a white-hot ball spread like a bursting dam and turned red-hot in seconds. The beam vanished. The red area roiled like the surface of the sun, broken up by an undulating black mesh.

Molten rock. Smoke. Oh God.

A strange wailing, keening sound, desperately animal, suddenly filled the bridge. Staffan's gut lurched: the hair rose on his nape. It sounded like souls in torment, and for a moment he let himself be swallowed by something stupid and irrational.

It's not the dead. Look for the explanation. You're a rational man, for God's sake.

But Staffan still thought the unthinkable. He hoped whoever had snatched Naomi had taken her off-planet. He couldn't bear to think of her dying like that.

Fel made an angry rasping noise. "Dhak, go and shut that thing up." He turned to Staffan. "The Huragok's managed to access the ship's broadcast system. That's him, whining. He's upset about useless Forerunner ruins."

Dhak went trotting off to sort out Sometimes Sinks. Knowing what the noise was didn't make Staffan feel any more comfortable, but he composed himself to look at the ground view of the strike. Edvin asked for it to be replayed a few times. Each seemed freshly shocking, especially the ground-level view. One moment the horizon was low hills and cliffs with a cluster of ancient, gigantic, thoroughly alien ruins, and the next it was just pure white light, followed seconds later by what looked like an instant red ocean that lit the sky like a sunset behind dense black clouds. There was nothing left but heat and smoke. Even the geological features seemed to have vanished. The terrain was now almost completely flat.

"At least you wouldn't feel anything," Edvin said. "Not unless you were a few kilometers outside the area. Then you'd know a *lot* more about it."

Staffan was speechless. He was also stunned that the beam had erased the entire Forerunner site. He thought he could still pick out a few stumps of the foundations, but that was all. His scalp prickled.

Get a grip. This is a war. Not a conservation project.

He'd have to calculate the blast radius of the strikes. He didn't even know if he could vary the output. But the Huragok would, and presumably it wouldn't care about what happened to Earth any more than it had cared about the colonies.

"So this is the Huragok's ship, then," Staffan said, trying to look unimpressed. "I mean that he's the resident engineer."

"No, we salvaged him from a wreck we found drifting. He was stranded." Fel looked toward the doors as Sinks drifted in, still making sad little *oooo-oooh* sounds. The shipmaster strode up to him, feathers raised. "It's just crumbling stone, you idiot. Shut up. Do you hear me? It's nothing important."

Edvin moved closer to Staffan and gave him a discreet nudge to indicate he'd ask some questions to shake Fel down. "If these Huragok are so brilliant, how come he was stuck in a wreck?" he asked. "Why didn't he repair it, or rebuild the hull, or whatever?"

Fel shrugged. "I don't know. Maybe he was damaged by whatever destroyed the ship. Maybe all his comrades were killed so there was nobody left to maintain him. But he's still useful."

Sometimes Sinks floated toward Staffan. It was hard to see the creature as a machine. He peered into Staffan's face, which might have been an appeal for moral support or an accusation. It was impossible to tell. Then he made a flurry of signs with his tentacles, none of which meant anything to Staffan, but if the speed and the increased bioluminescence were anything to go by, it was a long and impassioned monologue. None of the Kig-Yar took any notice.

"You really need to get this thing a translator, Fel," Staffan said. "He might be telling us something important, like the power's about to overload or something."

Fel glanced at the Huragok. "He isn't. He's just complaining and telling us we're doing bad things to the ruins." The Kig-Yar shrugged. "They don't normally express opinions. Maybe his last ship dumped him to get some peace."

Edvin checked that the power levels had returned to ready status. There was no point buying a battlecruiser that had fired its only shot.

"I want to try it," Staffan said.

He half-expected Fel to make some excuse to avoid it, but the shipmaster seemed relaxed. "Go ahead."

Fel indicated the controls. They were surprisingly simple for such an apocalyptic weapon—a power readout, a simple palm-sized button, and a nav display like others he'd seen in Covenant ships. He wasn't entirely sure how to change the aim. Sometimes Sinks hovered at his side, making odd noises. Staffan could only see him as a distressed child, desperate to stop the grown-ups from doing something upsetting.

"Okay, *you* tell me where to aim, then," Staffan said. He looked into the Huragok's face, trying to connect with him. "I know. It upsets you. We don't have to hit the ruins."

Sinks moved to tap the controls. The views on the various displays changed. He seemed to have shifted the ship by about fifty kilometers.

"Okay now?" Staffan asked. The Huragok moved away, lights reduced to a gentle glow. "I understand. It's not nice to see historic buildings destroyed."

It didn't take a genius to work out that the creature was desperate to avoid damage to the artifacts. The Forerunners had made the Huragok: it made sense that they'd still be programmed to protect company property. There was no harm in humoring the thing, especially as he would be essential to keep this ship running.

"Okay." Staffan reached out and held his hand above the button. It felt unreal. "Firing now."

He'd tested some interesting weapons in his time, everything from carbines to grenade launchers and railguns, and they'd all given him a sense of destructive power either from noise or recoil or both. But this was so silent, so distant, so purely and utterly *white*, that he almost understood why the Covenant called it cleansing, even if their meaning was a perversion of the reality.

He leaned on the button rather than pressed it. A tingling hollowness filled his ears. For a few seconds, every shadow vanished from the world.

Let there be light.

Yeah, I bet you felt like gods, you assholes.

He closed his eyes and tried to imagine which bastard he wanted to see at the focus of that energy beam, but there was no face, and that was the most frustrating thing of all. He had no idea who was responsible for taking Naomi.

The light died down. "Better make that the last test in case we're blipping long-range sensors somewhere," Edvin said.

Staffan shook off the emotional chaos that was threatening to surface and reminded himself that he was here to buy a warship. He needed to stay sharp. He tried to ignore Sinks and focus on Fel.

"Okay, I'll take the risk," he said. "Twenty fighters, twelve Phantoms, and one shipping container of small arms."

"But this is a battlecruiser."

"Yeah, I admit I'm getting cold feet. I'm not sure we can afford to operate her."

Fel lowered his chin, either puzzled or gearing up for a fight. "I thought you were in the market for a capital ship. That was why *Inquisitor* suggested herself to me as a solution for your needs."

"She might end up being of no use to us if we can't arm and crew her."

"She was, as you call it, *a special order* . . ."

"Think what you can do with all those fighters and dropships."

"What about the Huragok?"

"I'll give you a Darter for him."

"Two."

"*One.* If he's so useful, keep him. Everybody wants a Huragok, surely."

Fel cocked his head. He obviously wanted this ship off his hands as soon as possible so he could disappear and stay out of 'Telcam's way. He needed those small vessels, too.

The Huragok . . . well, maybe he couldn't sell him after all. They weren't on anyone's side. The creature would probably download every bit of data he'd absorbed while he was in the ship and hand it over to the first person who asked him for it. Sinks must have known every location and datalink that Fel and his crew had used, and Fel was obviously more afraid of Sangheili wrath than he was of Venezia's.

Staffan waited. He really wasn't sure if *Inquisitor* was a psyops asset, a saber to be rattled, or something Venezia might use in earnest.

Once we use it—we'd have to finish the job. Or the UNSC would be back to finish us.

Still, better to have an asset than not. Same for the Huragok.

Edvin said nothing. He walked across the bridge to lean on the console. On the projections, the surface of Shaps 3 was still a blast furnace.

"Well?" Staffan said, trying not to look.

Fel didn't move a muscle. "I accept."

"Good. We'll do the handover a little closer to Venezia. Establish an RV point, and we'll have everything ready by the end of this week." Staffan watched Sinks. The unlucky Huragok seemed pacified. His lights had dimmed and he was floating just above the deck. *Ah. That's where he got his name, then. He sinks. Sometimes.* "Leave me the manual for that guy, too. Has he got some translation device? How safe are they to handle?"

"He can make a device," Fel said. "Just remember that they tinker with everything they see, that's all."

"Sounds familiar." Edvin gave his father a knowing smile. "Better keep him out of your workshop."

As they left the bridge, Staffan had to pass Sinks. The Huragok reached out a tentacle and laid it on his wrist. Staffan's instinct was to jerk it back, but the touch was cool and velvety, and it was clear that the creature wasn't trying to stop him from leaving. It was a friendly gesture. It felt like a thank-you.

Was he attributing emotions to the Huragok that it didn't have? No, Sinks had feelings, all right. Anyone with an engineering background could understand that, because emotions were simply chemical controls to make animals do what was best for their survival. Life was a mechanism. Sinks had those controls too. He certainly got upset and anxious, and now he seemed to be grateful.

"You're welcome," Staffan said. "You're chief engineer now. It's going to be interesting working with you."

Edvin nudged him in the back. "You've got a new friend there."

"Won't he get lonely and bored on his own?" Staffan tried to understand Sinks's motivation in the same way he did the Kig-Yar. Huragok liked being busy, people said, and little else. "I better find him something to do."

The last thing Staffan saw as the bridge deck elevator doors closed was Sinks drifting in the doorway, lights firing much more slowly this time. He didn't quite wave good-bye, but it was tempting to think he had.

When they arrived back on Venezia, Laura seemed surprised

to see them. She stood at the front door while they unloaded the pickup.

"Something wrong?" she asked. "I thought you'd be gone a day or two."

"Easy negotiation," Staffan said.

Edvin slung his rucksack over one shoulder and waited for Laura to be out of earshot. "And you're going to talk to the Militia Council about this, aren't you? Promise me. This is too big for a private war."

"I promise," Staffan said. "Hey, how about giving Sinks an old Calypso to play with? He can service the slipspace drive. Or fit it into another vessel."

"He's not a pet, Dad." Edvin paused. "Or a kid."

"No, but he's intelligent and stuck on his own. No buddies to work with. And I need him happy."

"Okay. We'll find some stuff to amuse him when we take possession of the ship."

Staffan would have to pick his words carefully when he told Laura what they'd just acquired. She never wanted to know more than she had to, which was a wonderful quality, but he needed her to know about this. It was about Naomi so she had to be told sooner or later.

It was hard for a family to live with ghosts. But it was even harder for him to live with the thought that Naomi was still among the living, and that he might die before he knew for sure. *Pious Inquisitor* would get some questions answered. Edvin was right, though: it was a shitty name, replete with everything he hated. What did guys do when they bought a sailing yacht? They gave it a relevant name. He'd known a man who called his fishing boat *Susannah,* after his wife.

It was obvious, really. There was only one name he could choose for a warship like that.

He'd call her *Naomi.*

CHAPTER

WE CAN, SO WE WILL.

UNOFFICIAL MOTTO OF THE DEPARTMENT FOR COLONIAL
SECURITY, REGARDING THEIR USE OF POWERS
IN THE COLONIES

NEAR AP'OT FLOATING DOCK, Y'DEIO SYSTEM

"So you were a shipmistress before the Prophets fled. I thought your particular kind preferred to be infantry."

Chol made sure she took the call from Avu Med 'Telcam in her Phantom, drifting in the asteroid belt. If he could trace her—and she was pretty sure he couldn't—then she didn't want to give away the position of her clan's roosts. He'd be in a vengeful mood if she pulled this off successfully.

"Skirmishers have many skills, Field Master," she said. "I happen to excel in naval engagements. Are you providing a ship with this contract?"

"No. We're only having this conversation because the last Kig-Yar I entrusted with a ship *stole* it. I believe the humans have a saying—throwing good money after bad."

"But Fel made off with your vessel some time ago, didn't he? The trail's very cold. No doubt you've already searched for yourself."

"I can't put an entire rebellion on hold while I search for one ship. Which is why I thought a Kig-Yar could handle the task."

Chol let the insult roll off her. There was no face to be lost when dealing with the Sangheili. They set great store by their imagined honor, but that was part of their problem and what had now brought them down, she decided. It was all about appearance and ritual, thinking that it translated directly into reality beneath the surface. If they'd had the sense to put results first and swallow a little pride to get the job done, then they wouldn't have been tearing each other apart now. All Kig-Yar had to do was go through the motions of compliance in public and then do as they pleased when the idiots' backs were turned.

They really are all about rules. Cogs within cogs. Things happening in their allotted way because something else has been done according to rules farther up the line. Everything in its place, and no room for deviation. Dogma getting in the way of winning battles.

"If I take this contract, you'll need to share much more information with me about Fel, then," Chol said. "Because I'll be risking my own ship for a paltry fee. Which is why you didn't have a crowd of my cousins clamoring for his job."

"Why are *you* so anxious to do it, then?"

"It's a personal matter regarding Fel." Chol had no idea who Sav Fel was and certainly had no grievance with his clan, but Sangheili happily swallowed any nonsense about Kig-Yar tribal feuds, and Fel was in no position to tell 'Telcam otherwise. "Do you know who else was in his crew? And how many?"

'Telcam seemed to be considering the question. "I believe he had thirty or forty. I recall him mentioning only two names—Dhak and Eith. I will enquire. Does this matter? Do you have issues with them too?"

"I doubt it. I'm simply working out the mindset of the crew to narrow down where they took your ship. If I know who he's with, I may well have a better idea of the why and the where."

The principle was simple. Chol wasn't going to explain it to 'Telcam if he couldn't work it out for himself. If you stole something, even on a moment's whim, then you had a plan, however vague it might be. You would need somewhere to hide what you'd stolen, and probably yourself as well if your identity was known.

And Sav Fel's is. He must have known he'd be hunted the second he decided to make a run for it. So he must have had a customer waiting.

There was always the chance that he'd had the same idea as her and was setting up his own united Kig-Yar navy, but she doubted it. Most Kig-Yar who stole a ship planned to sell it or use it. Collecting gems and trinkets was a habit, a nest egg for the future, or a display of desirability to impress a mate, and they cost nothing to keep except the price of a strong lock. A battle-cruiser, though—that was another matter entirely. They needed to be berthed somewhere and they needed maintenance. Whatever other species might do, a Kig-Yar wouldn't keep it as a ludicrous trophy.

Who'd buy the ship from him?

That was all she really needed to know.

"Has he sold the ship to the Arbiter?" Chol scratched the back of her neck thoughtfully. "Maybe you wouldn't know until one of your keeps was reduced to a pool of lava."

'Telcam clamped all four jaws together. Even on this screen, grainy and in need of servicing, she spotted the flecks of spittle. She'd never seen a Sangheili completely close his mouth before. It made his face look as if it had collapsed in the center. Human faces were flat and disturbing, as if something vital had been lopped off, but this was even stranger. Then 'Telcam relaxed his mouth and his face became the familiar jagged maw fringed with fangs again.

"If he'd been foolish enough to do that," he said, "he'd be dead by now. Where do you plan to begin your search?"

Chol wondered who else would be in the market for a battlecruiser, but decided to keep the speculation to herself. She wasn't being paid to do an analysis for the Sangheili. If 'Telcam hadn't volunteered the information, then he didn't know, and if he wanted to know, then he could pay for her expertise like anyone else. It was irrelevant anyway. She wanted the ship. All her decisions and actions would flow from that.

"I'll find out where his allies are," she said.

"I could do that myself."

"You'd be hard-pressed to find any Kig-Yar willing to tell you what they'd tell me."

But he must have realized that to invite pitches for the contract. He had little interest in finding out what Kig-Yar thought, just like the rest of his kind, or else he might have heard about her views on acquiring navies and worked out that she might not have been the most trustworthy contractor for this job. But Sangheili had never understood Kig-Yar or even tried to. Their cultural arrogance blinded them. Feuding apart, Kig-Yar rarely betrayed their own to aliens; they simply liked to look as if they might, because it was good for business, and Sangheili were comfortable seeing them as a race of thieves. That made deceiving them much easier.

And four-jaws always had to have the last word. She let him have it.

"Forty thousand gekz will be transferred to an account of your choice," 'Telcam said. There was no *yes, very well,* or even *okay.* Nor did he ask any awkward questions about the ship she'd use to pursue Fel, because a Phantom clearly wasn't going to be doing any slipspace jumps. "The remaining forty will be payable when you succeed and I regain control of the ship."

Chol thought that still seemed a little trusting. She would have done it for less, for the fueling costs alone, but she had to feign indignation to keep her motives hidden. "That hardly covers my up-front costs. How do I know you'll pay the rest?"

"How do I know you won't simply do a deal with Sav Fel when you find him?"

"Because if we were that friendly, I wouldn't be sitting here. I'd be splitting the proceeds of the sale with him." But at least the four-jaws was talking in terms of *when* she found Fel, not *if.* That was almost approval coming from one of the arrogant bastards. She leaned forward and tapped the console. "Send the payment to this account. I'll make preparations as soon as I receive it. In the meantime, send me any other information that you remember."

Chol cut the link and powered up the Phantom's drive to head for Ap'ot Port. She now needed a crew large enough to take *Pious Inquisitor* from Fel, and that was more than was necessary simply to move *Paragon.* But nobody would read anything into it. They'd expect her to do a little collecting and salvaging along the way to make the trip pay for itself.

She headed for Ap'ot, planning her next move. The port was a spidery collection of long jetties and booms arranged along a central spine, with each spine connected to the central hub. When Chol turned to make the approach to the main bay, she passed a row of ex-Covenant frigates and corvettes, and scanned along them anxiously to make sure that *Paragon* was still on her moorings. There she was: the missionary ship looked an odd little thing next to the more traditionally designed warships, half the size of a corvette and dwarfed by the hulls either side of her. Most Kig-Yar commanders had taken the opportunity to claim their vessels when the Great Schism started, and why not? The Covenant had had its use of the Kig-Yar, and now the Kig-Yar would balance the books.

Berths were at a premium in every dock and shipyard in the system, which meant space was tight. The port was, as the flat-faces would have called it, a very crowded parking lot. And it now cost her a hundred credits to berth the Phantom for a day. *Outrageous. Criminal. Profiteering.* She watched the transaction flash on her screen automatically as soon as the Phantom's nav system engaged with the port's computer. That was sheer robbery on top of the fees she paid for *Paragon.* She was furious. When *Paragon* was ready to slip, she'd put the dropship in the hangar and pay nothing.

Chol powered down the Phantom, set the intruder countermeasures, and stalked down the docking tunnel on her way to the hub. She bristled. Her hackles rose. As soon as the inner airlock opened, she ran into a drab brown male who took one look at her glistening black ruff and jumped back. She was a fearsome sight. His instincts told him to back off.

That made her feel better. She was still a commander, Covenant or no Covenant.

Zim was already waiting for her, squatting against a bulkhead near the main port administration office and reading a data module. His eyes darted back and forth. He was too absorbed to see her coming.

"Looking for another job already?" she said.

He jumped to his feet. "Checking, Mistress. For who might be where, so to speak. Do we have a contract?"

"We do." She held out her hand for the module. Zim handed it over obediently. It was a list of ships seeking crews, complete with names of those who'd enlisted. "You'll go far."

Zim looked bashful. His light-brown neck quills flushed blood-red. "To be more exact, it's about who's *not* on the list."

"Let me hazard a guess." She skimmed through the names. This was as near to central organization as Kig-Yar liked to come—a clearing house of employment, one degree more advanced than rounding up a ship's company by word of mouth and clan connections. "Dhak and Eith, to name two."

"Do you know them?"

"No, but the four-jaw recalled the names."

"But not the *clan* names."

"He doesn't understand all that. He just uses the first syllable."

"Well, Dhak is more common a name in the Gei clan, so I think Fel still calls on his old allies with roots on Eayn."

A few more males passed, clawed boots clattering along the passage, and turned to take a sly look at Chol.

"Are you looking for work?" she demanded.

The two males froze in their tracks. "We're already contracted to a ship, Mistress."

"I'm recruiting," she said. "It's a short mission that requires frontline combat experience. Tell all your friends. I'll be here tomorrow at the same time to take names."

They dipped their heads and trotted off. With any luck, she'd find a crew who hadn't heard of her eccentricities and wouldn't start squawking in the bars before *Paragon* set off.

"So what now, Mistress?" Zim asked. "Other than finding a platoon in a matter of two days."

All Chol wanted was enough names to form a pattern, some clue to work out which clans might be involved so that she knew where to start looking. Sav Fel had a battlecruiser with a slipspace drive. That meant he could now be anywhere in the galaxy within a spherical search area that was getting potentially bigger with every passing second. Hunting someone confined to the ground by working out from the point of origin was relatively simple. Finding someone who could travel in any plane in three dimensions was near impossible. It had to be done by educated guesses and predictions.

And by persuasion.

"Just find me enough males to crew *Paragon* and take *Inquisitor* by force if need be. Unless Fel has picked up reinforcements for some reason, he has a crew of fewer than forty. In the meantime, let's find out who might know Dhak and Eith, and perhaps find Fel's clan."

Zim cocked his head in surprise. "Why warn them?"

"I wasn't planning to *warn* them," she said. "I was planning to spy on them." She handed back his data module and wondered if she could still find some of her old crew from the days when *Paragon* had been *Joyous Discovery*. "If they know where Fel is, they'll call him as soon as they know we're hunting him. If they don't, then we may learn what he sees as a viable customer."

"Who would want a battlecruiser, other than the four-jaws?" Zim asked.

"Brutes, perhaps." *Me, of course. But I won't tell you that until we're under way.* "Unggoy—never. The minor races—where are they now? Gone home. Gone back to resume their lives."

"There's always the humans. But what would the flat-faces want with a battlecruiser? I hear they have new ships now, *astonishing* ships. I hear one bombarded Sanghelios to support the Arbiter."

Chol shook her head, bemused. And humans thought Kig-Yar were amoral opportunists with no sense of loyalty? "What short memories they have."

"No, you're right," Zim said. "What use would humans have for a ventral beam now?"

STAVROS'S BAR, NEW TYNE, VENEZIA

"I used to dream about this," Mal said. It was the first time he'd been in a bar in months, even if this wasn't strictly social. "Getting paid to drink on UNSC time. Who'd have thought it?"

Vaz wasn't paying attention. He was watching the door, looking even more surly than usual. Mal tossed one of the rock-hard snack things across the table at him and it landed in his beer with a small splash. That finally snapped him out of his fog.

"Nairn's late." Vaz fished around in the glass and dredged up the snack, which didn't seem any softer for a soaking. "We do the business with him, then we go find Spenser. Yes?"

It had been a few days since Naomi had returned to *Port Stanley*. Mal wasn't entirely sure why they needed to go through the motions of gaining acceptance in the local militia, because they now knew exactly who they were looking for, but it would make access easier. Space was a bloody big place to hide a warship.

Every clue counted. The dedicated remote had picked up Staffan Sentzke leaving his house; another remote had detected the signature of a slipspace jump in Venezia's system, but even if they'd positively ID'd it as Staffan's vessel, they couldn't follow it. There were a lot of puzzle pieces to guess about and maybe reach entirely the wrong conclusion.

In the meantime, it was relatively easy to play a marine on the run, and Mal made the most of it.

"Yeah." It was funny how a big galaxy had now shrunk to a relatively small circle of people. Maybe that was a measure of just how many had died. "Mike can keep an eye on his Kig-Yar mates. He's definitely got a way with poultry. Maybe he was a chicken-farmer in a previous life."

"Nice try."

"What?"

"You're right. I'm worried about Naomi."

"I wasn't prying." Mal was careful what he discussed in bars. "You're sure that was who she thought it was?"

"I'm sure."

"It's just getting weirder by the day."

"Well, we're here, so we must think it's true, mustn't we?"

Mal crunched his way through the packet of snacks. He still had no idea what they were. Considering Venezia was Desperado HQ, he felt safer here than he did in some bars on Earth. There was no hobby violence and nobody trying to make a name for themselves on the gangster circuit. If he got a thumping here, it would be serious, delivered by people who did it as part of a rough job, not because they were bored delinquents who couldn't handle their drink. In its own awful way, it was comforting.

Vaz shuffled on his chair, instantly alert. "Heads up. Here he is."

Nairn walked in, looking exactly as Mal expected him to, with razor-cut brown hair and a fair bit of meat on him. He recognized Vaz and headed for the table.

"This is my buddy, Mal," Vaz said, introducing them. "He's been a naughty marine and he needs a fresh start."

Nairn shook Mal's hand. "How naughty?"

The lie tripped off Mal's tongue easily. "A gentlemen's disagreement over a lady." But then it wasn't so much a lie as ancient history. Mike Spenser's crash course in amateur spook-fu for the relatively innocent had been worth its weight in gold: if you weren't a trained liar, it helped to stick to lies you knew something about, nothing over-detailed, just salted with authenticity. "It's okay. The bloke made a full recovery. It's amazing what surgeons can do these days."

"So, skills?"

"Point me at something and I can usually kill it."

"Ship handling?"

"I've never crashed a dropship. Yet."

"But you're familiar with big ships."

"Yeah. Corvettes. Frigates. I've had some experience with Covenant ships and hardware, too."

"Really?"

"Yes." *And what I don't know, BB can ride along and prompt me with, like he did for Phillips.* "Vaz and I nicked a Spirit once. Didn't we, mate?"

"How are you with aliens?" Nairn looked him over cautiously. "We're a little irregular here. We tend to get on with them. Or at least we don't shoot them on sight."

"If they don't bother me, I don't bother them." There was such a thing as seeming too trusting. Mal had to stay in character. "What are you looking for, exactly? And why?"

"Two main areas," Nairn said. "Defense of New Tyne, which is basically responding to attacks on the ground, or crewing ships if we need to do anything off-planet. Which could be anything from seeing off a nosey UNSC vessel to retrieving something or somebody."

"Can do," Mal said. "What's your background?"

"Corporal, Reach militia."

Mal tilted his head slightly to indicate a lone Brute sitting in the corner of the bar. "So no hard feelings about some of our big hairy chums, then?"

"I left years before the Covenant trashed Reach. But that's not to say I'd behave myself if I ran into an Elite. I left a lot of friends behind."

Mal wondered whether to ask Nairn why he'd banged out of Reach, but decided that polite Venezian society might frown on delving into people's dodgy pasts. For all he knew, Nairn might have had a lot of debts or an angry ex-wife. He'd find out soon enough. All that mattered was getting Nairn to let him join the militia, where he and Vaz would be perfectly placed to volunteer to serve in a Covenant battlecruiser if one happened to show up.

Maybe it really will be that simple. Get on board and let BB slip a fragment into their systems. Job done.

Who was he kidding? Nothing ever went that smoothly. It just went *fast*. It wasn't the same thing at all.

Vaz got a round of drinks at the bar while Nairn continued sizing up Mal. "So what happened to his girlfriend?" Nairn asked. "The blonde with the legs?"

Mal wasn't sure if Vaz had mentioned Naomi's name. That was another problem with lying. "I never ask too many questions where those two are concerned. She might be back. Who knows?"

Nairn seemed to take it as simple unwillingness to gossip to a stranger. He nodded and looked around the bar like he was checking who was in tonight. After a second or two of feeling pleased with himself, Mal decided he didn't like being able to lie that easily. It was too seductive. He'd have to make sure he left that persona behind when the job was done.

"So how did you end up here?" Nairn asked.

Get the aliases right. At some point, someone might follow them to Spenser's place anyway. *And keep the cover story as low-maintenance as possible.* "Friend of a friend of a friend of Mike Amberley."

"Well, I'm glad we're getting some UNSC know-how," Nairn said. "The military expertise here is mostly ex-militia and aging insurgents. It's a shame to have all this equipment and not make the most of it."

"So this place is built on the arms trade, then."

"Hell, no. Tantalum mining. What do you think we're here for? We're not building an evil empire. We just want to be left alone. Now that Earth's finished with the Covenant, someone's going to remember that we've got all this lovely metal and that folks also have grudges against us."

It was sobering to see Earth from a colonial perspective. Mal had long since given up thinking in terms of good guys and bad guys, at least among humans, but he had a vague childhood recollection of how the grown-ups hated all colonial bastards for setting off terrorist bombs on Earth. Now there was a whole generation that didn't remember the daily threat and actually felt sorry for them.

Never mind. There'll be another batch of bastards along soon.

Vaz came back with three bottles of beer and sat down in silence, looking like a wet weekend in Grimsby.

"So who did you sell the tantalum to?" Mal asked.

"Kig-Yar, mostly," Nairn said. "Traded for arms and ships."

Vaz wiped the mouth of the bottle with his palm. "At least they couldn't use them to kill us, then."

"So what's the UNSC going to do now it hasn't got a war to fight?"

Mal shook his head. "No idea. So am I in, or do I have to learn how to do a proper job? I don't know anything about tantalum or farming."

"I'm sure we can find you something to do," Nairn said. "Report to the barracks tomorrow evening, eighteen-hundred."

Mal clinked his bottle against Nairn's. "Done."

So they were home and dry. It was that simple. They didn't have to pretend that they didn't know one end of a rifle from another, and they didn't have to pretend they didn't know Spenser, either. They'd be the first to hear about planet-killing warships being added to the arsenal.

Nairn was still studying him, though. Mal could see it on his face. "We don't get that many UNSC guys out here," Nairn said. "You might be useful in other ways, too. It's always handy to have someone who can pass for an insider."

Mal's blood braked to a halt in his veins. *Oh shit.* "Meaning?"

"If we need to infiltrate the UNSC, you two could be really helpful."

Vaz was still gazing mournfully at his beer. "They'd probably shoot us on sight."

"I was thinking more in terms of intel. There'll come a time when guys like you could be the edge we need. If you've got any disgruntled buddies, tell them to get in touch."

Mal breathed again and hoped Nairn forgot what a great idea that had seemed. They finished their beer, made small talk about fifty-year-old rifles still being as effective as ever, and left. Mal and Vaz ambled back along the road, in no real hurry now, heading out to the parking lot. There was a wonderful aroma of woodsmoke and grass on the air, a hopeful kind of smell as if summer was on its way, although there was no reason to assume Venezia had anything like Earth seasons. The setting sun was just low enough on the horizon to make the evening hazy and luminous.

"Jesus H. Christ," Mal said. "I wasn't expecting that. All this double agent stuff does my head in."

"It must be our cheeky faces."

"You think he knows what we are?"

"I can't see how."

"Better do our homework on CCS-class battlecruisers, though."

"Is there any detailed intel on them?"

"Not a lot beyond 'heard a loud noise, looked up, got fried,' I suspect."

"How about Adj and Leaks? If they share all their data, some Engineer must have worked on those ships, so Adj is bound to have that stored somewhere in his little jelly brain."

"You know how hard it is to get information out of them unless you ask the right question in exactly the right way. It's like Freedom of Information requests."

"BB can come up with something." BB always had an answer. It was hard to imagine running operations like this without him. "You know the way he worked with Phyllis on Sanghelios? He can do that again."

"He doesn't need meatbags like us at all, does he?"

"Well, he does if he wants to go for a walk."

"You think he misses that, Mal?"

"How? He said AIs haven't got their donor's memories. Or their personality."

"I mean his matrix. It's based on the architecture of a human brain, and brains expect to plug into limbs and organs. Remember he said that there's an AI based on a brain from one of Halsey's own clones."

"Yeah, it makes me wake up screaming some nights."

"He says the AI was really devoted to her Spartan."

"Oh, that's just all wrong." Mal held up both hands to make it all stop. He could cope with ONI as long as it was just about normal dirty tricks like assassinations and destabilizing allies. Once it got into needles, experiments, and brains in jars, he couldn't stand it. "The poor sod gets a stalker plugged straight into his brain. Terrific."

"I meant that smart AIs are a lot more human than BB admits. They're nothing like their donors, like he says, because I can't imagine Halsey being devoted to anybody, but they still seem to hold on to something from their past."

"Christ, Vaz. You hang out with Phyllis too much."

"Mark my words. BB's got emotions from a previous life. Emotional memory's stored separately from factual recall. Even dementia sufferers can remember how they felt if—"

"That's it. Enough. I'm not going there." For a second or two, Mal wondered if the spysat remotes that BB deployed could pick up voices as well as keep an eye on the ground. He hadn't picked up ambient sound on Sanghelios, not even explosions, but Mal was still uneasy. "What's started all this? Naomi?"

Vaz kicked a stone ahead of him every few strides, hands in his pockets. "Of course it is." The stone finally vanished down a drain and he walked on. The Warthog was in sight now, parked on its own in the middle of a big, empty lot. "You said her father had a right to know."

Shit, I did. "Yeah. I still think he has."

"Before or after he's in custody?" Vaz had his grim disapproval face on. "What did you have in mind? Tell him before he ships out to glass Sydney, or after we've detained him? Or just before we shoot him, so he has some closure before he dies?"

"You need to take it out on Halsey, mate. Not me."

"Sorry."

"I know it's a mess. It always is. And we're the ones who have to mop up the shit."

"Nobody ever has an exit strategy. Do you think Halsey planned for this?"

"Of course not. Scientists never see the big picture."

Mal wondered what she'd had in mind for Spartans who made it to old age. Maybe she never thought any of them would survive that long. They were expendable weapons, after all. He approached the Warthog with the required caution, checking for anything odd—fingermarks on the dusty bodywork, anything dangling underneath the chassis, small bits of debris or footprints around it—and ran his key-sized scanner over it to sniff for explosives. It came up clean. It was only when he started the engine and headed for the exit that he saw two Kig-Yar pull across the gate. They had a Warthog too, or at least something that had been a Hog before they'd welded a cargo box on to it. Everybody liked Warthogs—even Kig-Yar—because they could run on water, and even on piss if they had to.

"They can't possibly know who we are," Vaz murmured, sliding his magnum out of his jacket. "Even if Nairn does."

There was still a contract out on both of them, in theory. But nobody could ID them. All the Kig-Yar knew about the firefight on Reynes was that some unknown humans had killed a bunch of their mates. It didn't necessarily make them any safer, though.

"If you don't know which human did it," Mal said, "maybe any human will do."

"Come on, any Kig-Yar could have jumped me in the bar a few days ago. Or shot any human in New Tyne."

"No, any human with a UNSC neural implant. That's their proof of a kill, remember?"

"Oh."

"Yeah."

Vaz nodded. "I'll just smile, then."

"There's always a first time for everything."

Mal could drive a Warthog with one hand. He had to. His right hand gripped his own sidearm, and the Kig-Yar vehicle didn't look like it was planning to move. Did he ram them, or stop and chat?

He stopped but kept the engine running. At least they could hear him without him needing to get out of the vehicle.

"Evening, gents." He could see Vaz out of the corner of his eye. He'd drop the driver the second he saw him reach for anything. Christ, another run-in with the Kig-Yar was the last thing they needed right now. "Did you want us for something? Because we're heading home."

Mal was expecting trouble. He always did, and he wasn't wrong all that often. The driver, sporting a big, studded Sam Browne–type belt and bedraggled plumage, gave Mal that weird sideways leer that they seemed to have. It was probably something to do with focusing on him. Whatever it was, it came under the heading of *looking at me funny,* and Mal didn't warm to it.

You don't know what I did. And I'm not going to react like I did it.

"You want to sell any handguns?" the driver asked.

The situation flipped from being spotted as a bounty to being mugged for their bloody magnums. Only a Kig-Yar would be daft enough to do that.

Vaz raised his, almost in the safety position, but angled so that it was clear he might conceivably use it. Mal was convinced. Vaz did have a temper. That was how it had all kicked off on Reynes to start with.

"I can't sell you this," Vaz said calmly, "but if you can pay, I'll see if I can get you one."

"Is it as accurate as they say?"

He must have meant the KFA-2 sight. Vaz shook his head.

"No use to you, comrade," Vaz said. "The scope's linked to armor systems. It's just a regular thirty-mill handgun without all that."

"We still *like,*" the Kig-Yar said. "You get some, come and find us at Stavros's place."

And then he drove off. Mal hated to admit it, but his heart was pounding. It was simply not being able to do what he was trained to do and blow the buzzard's head off that stressed him.

"Phew," he said.

Vaz holstered his magnum. "See? I can be diplomatic."

Mal turned onto the road and headed back to Spenser's place. He was counting the event as a good result until he thought it through a little, and then the reality dawned on him. Two strangers had identified them as ex-UNSC and decided that where there was UNSC, there were magnums. That meant their faces were getting known.

They couldn't blend in. They'd have to brazen it out, and Staffan Sentzke was going to find out that they were here. Even if he hadn't worked out all the details about Naomi, he certainly had no love for Earth.

He might assume they didn't, either. Mal wasn't sure if that was good news or bad.

MOUNT LONGDON ROAD, NEW TYNE

Peter Moritz never arrived at Staffan's house without a bottle or two. Staffan looked up from his bench to see the man leaning against the door frame, dangling a string bag that clinked enticingly.

"Shochu," Peter said. "That sweet potato glut we had last year. It's mellowed a little."

"Grab a seat. There's some glasses on the shelf."

Staffan carried on painting the tiny gilt mirror. It took a pair of forceps and a steady hand. He couldn't look away, but he heard Peter twist the top off a bottle and then there was the comforting *glug-glug-glug* of liquid slopping into a glass. He wasn't sure where Peter had learned to make shochu, but it was a pleasant, fragrant drink that didn't leave him wrecked later.

"That looks like a labor of love." Peter put a glass on the bench, just within reach. "When's the birthday?"

Staffan put down the brush and reached for a miniature clamp to hold the frame while it dried. "Next month. Plenty of time." He sat back and took a sip of the shochu. "Damn, that's good."

They laughed and toasted the progress of the doll's house, walking around it as it sat on the table and inspecting it like building surveyors.

"I hope it dismantles," Peter said. "Or else you're going to have a damn hard time moving it."

Staffan nodded. "Yeah. I'm a pro, remember."

"So . . . you said you had something to discuss."

The more Staffan thought about it, the less concrete his plan became. Edvin was right. *Inquisitor*—or *Naomi*—was too big an asset to be wielded without a lot of thought, and she had to be deployed intelligently to achieve the desired result. What did he want? Did he want to lash out blindly, still not knowing which authority had taken his child, or did he want answers?

But without answers, there could be no target to lash out at.

He had to put the impotent, bitter anger aside and channel it. He'd waited more than thirty years for this. He could wait a little longer. Was he losing it? He'd always been careful, always a meticulous planner, a man taught by his carpenter father to measure twice and cut once, and the sudden urge to vent his pain in indiscriminate destruction caught him off guard.

Is that me? Is that really me?

It just wasn't every day that a small country—a city-state, nothing more—was handed a warship that could worry an empire.

Staffan drained his glass and held it out for a refill. "I've acquired something. Something that'll change the game if Earth decides to pick up where it left off with the colonies."

"Well, everyone's wondering what's going to happen now the other war's over."

It was always that *other* war, not *the* war. Staffan knew Venezia was lucky to avoid the Covenant, and that the Sangheili would have glassed New Tyne regardless of whether the humans there were loyal to Earth or happy to see it burn. But that didn't change history. It didn't change how Earth had used its proxies in the colonies to kill its own people. You could keep a lot quiet if it happened light-years from home. Everyone here knew what had happened to Far Isle. How many on Earth knew, though? Did they know the UNSC had used nukes to put down the insurrection?

That's what we're dealing with. Don't forget it.

There were assholes in the colonies, of course. He knew that. He knew how many "freedom fighters" were criminals, opportunists, psychiatric cases, or just social inadequates who embraced a cause because it was convenient, profitable, or gave their pitiful existences some meaning. He'd met them. He wasn't going to glorify them by calling them patriots. He'd studied Earth history and seen the inevitable cycle of thugs acquiring respectability through time and myth and ending up as heads of state. An asshole was an asshole, regardless of passport or species.

But he'd also met too many guys like himself, crushed under the wheels of politics, robbed of family or livelihood or both, who wanted to hit back or just go someplace else where it would never happen again. He was somewhere between the two. On any given day, he might find himself at one end of that spectrum or the other. It depended how tired he was and how many nightmares had kept him awake.

Today, though, he needed to be on an even keel. He needed to *plan.*

Peter topped up his glass again. It was only a shot glass and shochu wasn't full-proof liquor. It wouldn't affect his judgment and make him say something he'd regret later.

"I've got a battlecruiser," he said.

Peter looked at him for a moment, frowned, then glanced at the doll's house. Staffan could see the thought form and crumble: Peter was still thinking in terms of toys for kids, and then suddenly he wasn't. He studied his glass for a few seconds, blinking.

"You want to flesh that out a little, Staffan?"

"I've lined up a CCS-class Covenant battlecruiser in working order and almost fully armed."

Peter stopped blinking. "I'm not good on tech specs, but I'm assuming that's fairly big."

"Eighteen hundred meters. At the smaller end of the Covenant fleet. Ventral beam, plasma cannon, laser close-in defense."

Peter looked as if he was holding his breath. It took him a few moments to even move.

"Jesus," he said, shaking his head. "Jesus, Jesus, *Jesus*."

"I'm glad that's finally sunk in."

"Where the hell did you get it? How?"

"Fallout from the Sangheili civil war. Some buzzard who was transporting the ship for the rebels decided it wasn't his war."

"They passed on a *battlecruiser*?"

"What use is it to them? They're tribal. It's a nation's asset. It's designed for big objectives, not piracy. Besides, it's expensive to operate." Staffan was starting to feel a little more like he'd done a prudent thing rather than squandered serviceable small ships on a white elephant. "It cost me some fighters and a few dropships."

"Shit."

"Well?"

"Well what?"

"There's something I want, something I have to do or I'll die crazy. But a battlecruiser puts us on a more level playing field with Earth. I can't start a war just to get what I want and not think beyond that."

"What are we talking about exactly?"

"Naomi."

Peter looked lost for a moment and then his face changed. He remembered. Staffan didn't talk about her outside the family these days, but he'd known Peter for a long time, ever since Remo had introduced them, and he'd felt no shame in telling him a story that made others smile nervously, nod, and walk away.

I am not insane. I know I'm not.

"Why are you so sure?" Peter asked.

"Because it happened to Remo too. You *know* it did. You know he lost his son. His *gifted* son. His son who kept getting visits from educational psychologists. Same time period, same scenario. Same unexplained genetic illness. Same death. And he managed to pull all the colonial police files for that period, all the reports of missing kids, all the death certificates from the CAA, all the school records. That's what you can do if you're a gangster with cops and city hall in your pocket."

"You can make patterns out of anything."

It had taken Staffan and Remo years to pull it all together, and most of the leads were dead ends. But they'd found enough. What they couldn't work out was why. Who would want to abduct exceptional kids? All Staffan could think of was a government eugenics program. It wasn't unknown. Earth's history was peppered with schemes that had taken children from their parents to be raised by others, usually based on some racial ideology of improving the species. There was nothing crazier than reality.

"I need to know the truth, Pete," Staffan said. "When wars end, all the shit comes tumbling out. People talk, point fingers at each other, reveal things they've kept quiet for years. I know we've lost pretty well all the colonial records, but Naomi disappeared long before the Covenant showed up. I can't pass up the chance to ask what's in the UEG's records. But now I can ask those questions from a position of strength."

"What, hold a gun to their head? The *ship*? Are you serious?"

"Okay, okay, I know the politics are more complicated than that. But you know where I'm going with this."

Peter put his hand out to locate the chair behind him without looking. He was definitely shocked. Who wouldn't have been? Even in Staffan's world, where arms deals were daily routine, acquiring a planet-killer was in a different league.

"Why are you telling me this?" Peter asked.

"Because we're the nearest thing that New Tyne has to a legitimate government, and I suppose that makes you as near as damn it the head of state. Whatever I do with that ship affects everyone here. I know I can do as I please with it, but one thing I know I can't do is head for Earth, aim the ventral beam at Sydney, and demand answers from—well, who, exactly? Who actually runs Earth? It isn't the goddamn civilian government. Not that they were any great loss."

"You've got *one* warship. A serious one, yes, but what do we do if they come after us with a whole fleet? We'll be charcoal."

"Well, gee, that's fighting talk, Pete." Staffan was the same age as this guy. They both remembered the galaxy when it was just human-on-human violence. "Weren't you the one planting bombs and hijacking ships around the inner colonies? You obviously had more balls in those days."

"We weren't a fixed target then."

"Hey, I'm not the one who managed to piss off the UNSC a few months ago by refusing to help a ship with a reactor going critical."

"You know that could have been a ploy to insert UNSC personnel."

"We're on their list already. Maybe if they thought there'd be consequences if they pissed around with us, they'd think again. You know how you do that? You treat a battlecruiser like a submarine. You keep it out there, hidden, moving around, ready to launch a strike if anything happens to the home country. We can do that now. It changes everything. You don't need an entire navy to make that work."

Staffan had been sure he was doing the right thing. Edvin had convinced him that this was an asset for Venezia, not a private war. Now Peter Moritz, firebrand and insurgent, a man who'd sworn to overthrow Earth control by any means necessary, was pissing his pants and worrying what Earth would think of them.

They all want to be statesmen in the end. Respectable and comfortable.

I just want to know what happened to my little girl.

"So where's this ship at the moment?" Peter asked.

"I'm keeping everything on a need-to-know basis because of the Kig-Yar." Staffan meant that, because they'd steal whatever they could if there was a buck in it. Now he was worried that Peter would muscle in. "If a rival clan decides to seize it, they could end up selling it to Earth, and no prizes for guessing where the UNSC would test the ventral beam."

Peter was looking slightly past him in defocus. "I think the phrase is *poisoned chalice.*"

"Not quite," Staffan said. "Having the ship brings a lot of tough choices. But *not* having it gives us no choice at all. Letting someone else have it puts us at risk." He drained his glass. "So I'm going to hang on to it, and not do anything dumb. I'm not planning to rush out and glass Earth next week. But I have a big military advantage that could also be Venezia's."

"What do you want from me?"

"Nothing. I was just telling you."

"Jesus, Staffan, are you okay with this thing?"

"I told you. I'm not mad. And I'm not going to do anything rash. But I have it, and now I need a plan."

Peter got up and refilled their glasses. "I've got to hand it to you. Nothing's too big for you to take on, is it?"

"Not where my daughter's concerned, no. I've come halfway across the galaxy to find out what happened to her."

"What will you do for a crew?"

"It won't be Kig-Yar, for a start. I'll find humans. Maybe some Grunts to make up numbers." Staffan wondered if he should mention the Huragok. He decided not to for the time being. It was too complicated a distraction and he'd be under pressure to use it for all kinds of unrelated things. "But there'll be ex-Covenant aliens willing to train us on those systems."

"Nairn says we've got UNSC deserters showing up."

"See? This is where it all starts spilling out, like I said."

"They've got some experience. Anyway, we've signed them up for the militia."

"Do they know anything about Covenant ships?"

"Nairn says they do."

There was nothing more to discuss without going into detail that Staffan wasn't willing to risk sharing. Peter was a friend, not a guy looking to stiff him at the first opportunity, but Staffan could see that he didn't trust him not to use the ship in a fit of anger and bring down the wrath of the UNSC on the whole planet.

Like I said. I've waited thirty-odd years. I need my answers first. But if the UNSC wanted to nuke us, they would have done that when we wouldn't save their warship.

Missiles had been fired both ways. But all the UNSC had done was take out an anti-air battery. Maybe they had their reasons for restraint.

Peter left the shochu on the bench and they parted with slaps on the back, as if nothing had happened and there'd been no talk of battlecruisers glassing Earth. Staffan picked up the clamp and touched his fingertip against the gilt paint of the tiny mirror frame. It was already dry. Now he could add the reflective panel, plastic in place of glass for safety.

UNSC deserters? Venezia didn't get hundreds, but it wasn't unknown. They were the first for a few years, though. It would do no harm to debrief them.

CHAPTER

IT WAS A LONG SHOT, REALLY. I WASN'T EVEN LOOKING FOR
CONSPIRACIES. I WAS SO BLIND WITH GRIEF THAT I LET MY-
SELF GET TALKED INTO GOING TO A SUPPORT GROUP FOR
BEREAVED PARENTS. I EVEN MET SOME FOLKS WHO BE-
LIEVED THEIR KID HAD BEEN SWAPPED FOR A CHANGELING,
BUT IT WASN'T UNTIL I MET A COUPLE WHOSE KID HAD BEEN
KIDNAPPED YEARS BEFORE THAT I TRIED THE MISSING CHILD
CHARITIES. I FOUND ONE THAT LINKED PARENTS FROM DIF-
FERENT COLONY WORLDS WHO WERE LOOKING FOR AB-
DUCTED KIDS. AND THAT WAS HOW I EVENTUALLY MET ANDY
REMO, A GUY FROM HERSCHEL, AND WE COMPARED NOTES.
THEN I KNEW I WASN'T MAD. OR ALONE.

—STAFFAN SENTZKE, TALKING ABOUT HIS SEARCH FOR THE
TRUTH ABOUT HIS DAUGHTER

TILU CITY, EAYN: Y'DEIO SYSTEM

"It's been days, and we're still here," Zim said. He followed Chol
through the crowded street, making impatient clicks. "Mistress,
we're losing time. I could take a ship and start searching the—"

"You will *not*," Chol said. "Time spent here will save time
wasted going around in circles. Fel may well be anywhere, but
he had to *start* somewhere, and he has to *stop* somewhere. And
we look for his crew, not him. Because that's what we call *not
attracting attention*."

Barbed comments never seemed to ruffle Zim's feathers. "I

can't find a record of him living in the system anyway. Not even in his clan home."

"He might use an alias. It'll prolong his life expectancy."

"You're sure he has a customer?"

"You said it yourself. A warship that size is no use to him. It's just a giant beacon summoning 'Telcam to kill him."

"True. Only an idiot would want to keep it."

Maybe she *was* an idiot. She'd be the owner of that kill-me beacon herself before long. But that wasn't reason enough to change her mind and hand the prize over to 'Telcam, and it was far easier to take a battlecruiser from a small force of Kig-Yar than to try to seize a fully crewed one from the Sangheili.

Central Tilu was all nooks and crannies, a little like the aster- oid belt. They were both ideal places to hide things. The ancient city was one of the cradles of Kig-Yar civilization, but the little streets and alleyways that had been designed for small carts were now an annoyance for a modern-day shipmistress in a hurry. The streets were so narrow that it was impossible to get a vehicle through them. It had its advantages, though. It was easy to melt into the crowd and lose anyone who might be tailing her.

Trust was a carefully stacked nest of boxes. Chol preferred to take her chances with a fellow Kig-Yar than with another spe- cies, but among Kig-Yar she could only trust T'vaoan, and among T'vaoan she could only really trust her own clan, none of the others. The humans had a phrase for it; the devil you knew was preferable to the devil you didn't. But the humans had a won- derful phrase for everything, then proceeded to ignore the wis- dom in all of them.

"There's nobody following us," Zim said. He wasn't T'vaoan, but he was scared of her and probably thought he had a chance of mating with her if he behaved deferentially enough. That cre- ated its own loyalty. "I'd have noticed."

"The world is full of carrion eaters." Just as humans said they saw their own core selves in apes, Chol looked to her distant cousins in the wild birds of Eayn as a guide to their shared fundamental instincts. "Vultures always follow hawks in the hope of stealing their kill."

"But they still get clawed if they get too close."

"Perhaps we should end the analogy before we get on to feather mites."

"Yes. Sorry."

Word would be out now that she'd taken 'Telcam's contract, and other clans would keep an eye on her to see if they could follow her and move in at the last moment after she'd done all the hard work and spent all the resources. But any fool trying to muscle in on her quarry now would definitely feel more than her claws. They'd get a plasma pistol in the face.

She tried to dodge the street merchants shoving ornaments and brightly colored leathers at her. But once she sidestepped those, she found herself cornered by snack vendors, yelling their prices in hoarse voices—half a gez for neatly coiled roast snake, one for a loop of small rodents threaded like a bead necklace, and two for wafers of an air-dried and unknown meat packed so tightly onto a central skewer that it looked like a bottle brush. The smell of spice, sizzling fat, and charcoal was overwhelming, but she ignored the temptation and pushed past. Behind her, Zim's footsteps stopped. Chol carried on struggling against the tide of bodies, but eventually she stopped to look back.

Zim had stopped to buy something to eat. He dodged through the crowd, trying to catch up with her.

"Apologies, mistress." He held out a paper wrapper full of snake coils as if he was offering her one. "I haven't eaten this morning."

"No thanks. I don't trust their hygiene here."

"Germs build your immune system."

"They also give you *jha-sig*."

"True." Zim uncoiled one of the snakes, holding it carefully over the sheet of paper, and bit off the head. "How do they keep them flexible once they're cooked?"

"Marinade," Chol said.

"I never thought to ask before."

"Didn't your clan mother cook them for you?"

"No. She said they were vulgar."

"Very true."

"So we just wait for Eith to show up again? The ship will be long gone."

"I'm not waiting for him," Chol said. "How many times do I have to explain this? I'm narrowing down the number of places he might have gone."

"Yes, mistress." Zim put a section of snake between his teeth and pulled, stripping off the meat to leave a ragged zip of vertebrae. "Sorry, mistress."

"Eat the bones." Chol hoped her mother was making sure the boys ate theirs while she was away. "Calcium's good for you."

It was a big galaxy, but most of it was cold, hostile, and transparent, and there actually weren't as many places to go as Zim seemed to think—not if you were trying to hide a warship, anyway. Sav Fel had fewer planets to flee to than ever because so many worlds had been reduced to rubble, and those that hadn't generally had populations that would either turn on him or turn him in. He had to sell that vessel to somebody. This wasn't like offloading a dropship or a few rifles. *Inquisitor* was still a capital ship, even if she wasn't the biggest, but her only purpose was destruction and invasion. Apart from the Sangheili who still intent on wiping each other out, there were few people left in the business of galactic-scale warfare.

Chol would find Fel. Intelligence would answer the question of *where*, because it would tell her *who*.

"There," she said. Up ahead, a woven arch of vines thicker than her waist formed the entrance to a teahouse that had been in business since before the Covenant ever came to the Y'Deio system. That was the story put about by those who wanted to lure big-spending visitors to Tilu, anyway. It certainly looked ancient. "You wait here. If I need you, I'll call."

Zim wiped his hands on the crumpled wrapper and tossed it into the gutter. "Nobody knows me. I could slip in there anonymously and simply enquire after Fel."

"It's not going to be that simple. This requires an oblique approach."

She kept walking. Zim peeled off and disappeared around the corner of the block. As she stepped through the vine arch, the noise and smells of the street were suddenly gone, shut out by thick mud-brick walls and a line of ornamental trees smothered in bright orange flowers with the scent of honey gum. It was like walking through a Forerunner portal to another world. In the shade of the trees, elderly matriarchs sipped from sequin-studded porcelain bowls while a couple of males—quite well off, judging by their waistcoats—tried to catch the eye of some younger females by preening their forearm plumage. If you had a little wealth, or wanted to latch on to someone else's, this was a good place to be seen. It was such an upmarket and genteel venue that there was even a separate latrine some distance from the building, not just a scrape by the front door.

It was also a place where shipmistresses and masters did business, at least for high value expeditions. Chol thought it was worth the price of a bowl of tea. She strutted into the building and was swallowed up by deep, cool shade. An artificial breeze rustled through wreaths of dried tea fronds hanging from the beams, filling the room with a smoky sweetness.

"Tea, your best fermentation," she said to the waiter, sitting down at a table. "Is there any shipping business being done here today?"

"In the back room, mistress."

"I'll take my tea in there, then."

She got up and wandered into the room, pushing aside the heavy tapestry curtain across the arch. There were no automatic doors or holographic displays here, just the simple decor and utensils that her ancestors a thousand summers ago would have recognized. That was remarkably relaxing. When she sat down, nothing vibrated or hummed on the threshold of her hearing. A ship was a noisy, confining thing, not like true flight at all, just a box in motion, and however central spaceflight was to all their lives, it was good to be reminded that there was such a thing as a quiet roost.

The ship commanders hunched around the table looked across the room at her.

"I'm looking for Eith Mor," she said. "I want to offer him a position. Does anyone know where I might find him? This is his clan's territory, isn't it?"

One of the shipmistresses was making notes on a data module or tallying a price. It was hard to tell from here. She took a few moments to finish and look up.

"I hear he's waiting for payment from a previous trip. He'll be back next week when that's concluded. Can I send him a message?"

That was news Chol didn't want to hear. It might have meant the handover had already taken place, so there might be a new owner to separate from his or her purchase. If *Inquisitor* had been bought by Brutes, then that was going to be a challenge. But she wasn't giving up before she'd even spooled up her drives.

"Tell him to contact my lieutenant." Chol handed Zim's comms code to the shipmistress on a slip of paper. Unless Eith was an idiot, he'd check who was looking for him, and it was too easy to find out that she'd been hired by 'Telcam. There was no documentation to link Zim to the mission yet, though. "The sooner the better. I need to pick up a cargo in a fairly volatile sector, so there'll be a bonus. Depending on where he is, he could join my ship en route."

"I'll pass that on." The shipmistress squinted at the comms code and cocked her head. "You could ask his cousins on the other side of town, too, in case he's made contact. Huz Mor-Kha, I think it is. He processes scrap metal at a place out on the Riran highway."

"Very helpful," Chol said. "Thank you."

She'd go and lean on the cousin. She drained her bowl of tea and left. Zim was squatting in the alley at the side of the teahouse, snatching at beetles in flight and crunching them.

"Have you got tapeworms?" Chol said. "I've never seen anyone eat so much."

"I try to eat natural foods." Zim dusted off his pants and stood up. "Any luck?"

"You might get a call from Eith. I gave a shipmistress your code to pass on. Just a scam telling him I've got work for him, so we can trace the comms nodes and work their route backward." She headed back to the business district, the modern expansion of Tilu that had been tacked on outside its southern city wall. "But I have details of a cousin who might be more helpful."

She'd rented a ground vehicle to cover her tracks, an ugly thing called a Mongoose. The humans had no sense of design. They did churn the machines out in large numbers, though, and they were prone to lose them the hard way on the battlefield, so there was a market for them in places like this. Zim always wanted to drive. This time she let him and clung to the rack on the rear, directing him to the Riran highway.

The wealth map of Tilu and its neighboring towns was like a set of concentric target rings. The money was at the old heart, and the farther out you went, the poorer the clans became. Huz was a scrap metal dealer. He should have been able to make a very good living at that, but there he was, in what humans called the *buttock* part of town. Or at least she thought that was the term: sometimes Brutes lost a lot in translating conversations.

"I see it, mistress." Zim took one hand off the controls to point across toward the lush green forest. "What a mess."

He turned the Mongoose into an approach road and bounced the vehicle across soil rutted and scarred with burned tree stumps. Huz looked as if he was expanding the site, so business couldn't have been so bad. Chol slid off the rear rack and went into the yard to look for him. This time, Zim followed her with his hand resting on his sidearm, which was touchingly protective under the circumstances.

Chol followed the hiss, thump, and creak of a metal press in a workshop on the far side of the compound. The path to the door was a canyon of pallets and containers, all loaded with reclaimed metals and sorted by type. By the time she got to the workshop doorway, Huz had emerged from the gloom and stood there in a leather apron, wiping his hands.

"You tripped the alarm," he said. "What do you want, mistress?"

"I need to contact a cousin of yours. Eith. I know he's going to be back soon, but I need to call him urgently."

Huz cocked his head on one side and considered Zim, then her, then Zim again.

"Why? What's he done now? Whatever you think he's got, he paid for it. He always does. He's a good boy."

Chol held up an imperious hand for silence. "I need to talk to him to see if he can do an urgent job for me."

Huz just stood there, as if she'd get bored and go away if he did it long enough. Zim moved up beside her. Huz gave in.

"Very well." He took out a comms device and turned his back on them. "I'll see what I can do."

He was routing a message. That was all Chol needed, really: a clue to where Eith was, which would filter a hundred possible locations down to perhaps half a dozen. If Eith was traveling on his own budget, he'd take the most direct and economical route home. Chol debated whether to interrupt the call and seize the device as soon as Huz appeared to get a response, or wait for him to finish and then grab it.

Or just ask him, of course. It's worked well so far.

She waited. Zim moved in. Huz talked in hushed tones, head bent over the device, then ended the call and turned to her.

"He says he'll be back in a few days."

"Where is he now?"

"Why do you want to know?"

"Because if he's on the other side of Covenant space, it'll be too late."

Huz looked resigned. "He's at the Station of Constant Sustenance."

Chol had to look interested in anything except establishing Eith's route. "Is that still functioning?" It was a former Covenant resupply station, one of a network that had spanned the galaxy. "I'm surprised he's found any of them left."

"It's much depleted, mistress. They're stripping it of cable and metal sheeting. No point passing up an opportunity, after all. But he's traveling alone, so he's arranging passage at the moment."

If he was alone and arranging passage, that meant Sav Fel had split the crew and everyone had scattered. At least that might take her nearer to the location of his customer.

Zim was poring over his data module. "That's near the Korfo system."

Huz looked uneasy. He turned away and looked like he was reaching under his apron, and that was when Zim sprang at him and knocked him to the ground. He slashed at Huz with his clawed feet, leaving a big rip in the leather apron, a blow that would have disemboweled the scrap dealer if he hadn't been wearing it. Then Zim shoved the pistol in his face.

Chol had never seen Zim fight, not like that. It was a dirty move, a real street brawler's reaction. Her admiration for him shot up a few points.

"Were you thinking of drawing a weapon on my mistress?" he rasped, looming over Huz. "She asked you a polite question."

Huz drew up his knees, arms almost crossed as if he wasn't planning to surrender but to pick the right moment to slash back. "You just want to muscle in on my supplier."

"We're not interested in your supplier." Chol stood over him. If Zim didn't stomp some sense into him, she would. Maybe it was time to simply drop the pretense. "We don't care what he supplies. We're not even looking for Eith. I just need to know where he is. Where he's been."

"See? I knew it."

"Start making sense before I kick you. I'm not looking for your trade secrets." She squatted over Huz. Zim still held the pistol on him. "I'm looking for someone that Eith's been with. If you give me a location, I won't share it with your rivals. But if you make me beat it out of you, I will. I might even shoot you anyway. Do we have an understanding?"

Huz looked defeated. Then he nodded, and she let him stand up. A change of tack sometimes worked with males. She took off the pendant she happened to be wearing today, nothing of any great sentimental value, just a faceted yellow beryl that a previous mate had wooed her with, and dangled it in front of Huz's face.

"If you were to give this to a prospective mate, I'm sure she'd be impressed enough to give you the time of day," she said. Huz's eyes followed the glittering stone. "I'm not asking you to sell your grandmother to a human pervert. Just tell me if you know where Eith went. Where he's been."

"He took a contract to deliver a ship."

"Where?"

"I don't know."

"Who hired him?" It was a circular question, more to test Huz's willingness to be honest than anything. "I need a name."

"Fel."

Now she was getting somewhere—she hoped. "And where's Fel right now?"

"He's probably gone home to his family."

"Do you remember what I said?"

Huz held out his hands. "He lives on a pebble in the middle of nowhere. I only know it as Fen-Es-Ya. It's not even on the charts. I've never been there. They trade ore and arms."

Kig-Yar pilots weren't good at pooling navigation knowledge; who wanted their rivals to show up when they'd found a private source of minerals or metals? But the Covenant had been much more keen on record-keeping, and insisted on a database for each world visited. She had Korfo, then, and now she had Fen-Es-Ya. It was part of the puzzle.

Zim consulted his module. "No Fen-Es-Ya in the Covenant records."

"Try the human records, then," Huz said. "Fel trades with the flat-faces as well."

Humans.

Chol hadn't really factored them into this. What would they want a battlecruiser for, when they'd won the war and were now stronger than the Elites? She was hearing gossip coming back from the civil war on Sanghelios, stories from Kig-Yar pilots about a massive new human warship. Why would they want a ship like *Pious Inquisitor*?

Whatever their motive, they were probably the only faction left that Fel could sell to without risking discovery by 'Telcam, apart from the Brutes. It was worth pursuing.

"Do humans have different clans?" she asked. "Warring tribes?"

"Oh, yes," Huz said. "They had a civil war too. Doesn't everyone?"

"Zim, find me their records." Chol handed Huz the pendant. He seemed quite satisfied for someone who'd just been threatened and knocked down, but net profit was the only measure of happiness on any given day. "Find me the flat-faces' history."

NEW TYNE, VENEZIA

"Damn, I must be getting old." Spenser fumbled inside his jacket for his security pass as his Warthog approached the barracks gate. "It took me more than two weeks to infiltrate this place. You guys managed it in what, three days? Four?"

"Right place, right skills, right time," Vaz said. He'd left all his incriminating kit at the house, including the scanner that checked weapons for the micro-tags they'd inserted to track 'Telcam's supply routes. If they searched him, they wouldn't find anything awkward to explain. "Either that, or they already know who we really are, and they're going to cut our throats the second the door's closed."

"Optimism gets you through the day, huh, Vaz?"

"Pessimism keeps me alive."

Mal, sitting behind him in the back of the Warthog, snorted with amusement. "Don't deprive him of his hobbies. Watching ice hockey and being a misery-guts."

"Makes my day," Vaz said.

"Oh, and falling for hopelessly unsuitable women. Let's not forget that."

Vaz knew it was meant kindly, but it still stung a little. "That's only when the hockey season's over."

It made Spenser laugh, anyway. Like all humor, there was an uncomfortable element of truth in it. Vaz went back to studying his forged ID pass, the antique plastic colonial kind that said he was now Vasily Desny, and wondered why he hadn't found that odd before. If he'd just deserted, why wouldn't he have a UNSC pass instead? Ah, now he finally understood the convoluted thinking. Nobody would desert without fixing some moderately obvious forged credentials. You couldn't get to Venezia without a guy who knew someone who knew someone else who could eventually find you some guy who would help you get to Venezia for the contents of your wallet. It all made sense.

I just can't think like a spook. Mal's right. It's another universe.

Spenser was pretending to be the real thing, a guy on the run for embezzling funds from the CAA. Vaz decided that you either had to have an astonishing memory or the ability to forget who you really were in this business. Maybe he really had lifted a few roubles in his time, though. It was impossible to tell.

Mal whistled tunelessly. "We're just shaking hands and answering questions today, right?"

"I still think we over-rehearsed this," Vaz said. "We won't sound spontaneous."

"Just think like a deserter." Spenser slowed to a crawl behind a small delivery truck. "They'll expect you to be reluctant to reveal things. You're guilty men."

Mal twanged his pass with his finger. "I'm in the role already. I've got my motivation."

"Got your transponder? If you end up taken away for questioning—"

Vaz patted his pocket. Spenser kept on about the tracking units. "Yeah. We got it. We've got our implants, too."

"No use if they transport you out of range," Spenser said. "Or if your head gets separated from the rest of you."

The guard on the gate looked them over. He obviously knew Spenser and exchanged nods, but spent some time scrutinizing Mal's pass. Then he looked at Vaz's. Vaz scrutinized him in return and decided the guy had never been properly trained, even if he looked completely at ease with a rifle. Would anyone know how to tell if they were genuine UNSC or not? Well, if he could tell the difference between a civvie and a soldier in civilian clothes, then it probably worked the other way around as well. The guy didn't ask them to surrender their sidearms. Either they'd passed muster or else asking a New Tyne citizen to hand over his weapon was like asking him to take off his pants. You just didn't do it.

"Nairn's waiting for you," the guard said, waving them through. "Drill hall, Mike."

Mal waited for the Warthog to pull away and didn't look back. "Jesus, do they really drill? That's a bit serious. I haven't had a proper parade inspection for years."

"Yes, you did," Vaz said. "Voi. A few weeks ago. We turned out for the Voi memorial service."

"Okay, apart from that. Remind me which side is my left."

The complex was a collection of brick, concrete block, and assorted composite buildings on what looked like a factory site, tidy but not *military* tidy. It was much bigger than Vaz had expected, though, and everyone he saw on site was human.

"No aliens, then?" he asked.

Spenser shook his head. "You can only trust your own, can't you? Getting along together doesn't mean they'd stand and fight with us if push came to shove."

"Us?" Mal said. "You're really into your role, then, mate."

"I meant humans."

"Busy place for a part-time army."

"Full-time core. Everyone does their time. And this is one of the main armories, too. Don't you listen to anything I tell you?"

"Of course I do," Mal said. "Just commenting. We could wheedle our way in here full time, Vaz. It'll be just like home."

Spenser dropped them off on the far side of a big open tarmac square. "You're on your own now, guys. If I hear sustained fire, I'll assume they've rumbled you. Which means I'll be next."

"Don't worry, we're ONI," Mal said. "We've got the adqual in lying like a hairy egg."

"Son," Spenser said kindly, "it's one thing lying to your CO about who started the brawl in Murphy's Drink-o-Rama. It's quite another fooling a population of career fugitives."

Nairn was waiting at the open hangar door, rifle slung over one shoulder. He beckoned to them. Vaz broke into a jog automatically with Mal behind him. All they had to do was behave like ODSTs and pretend that the only thing they knew about Venezia was that it was a place where bad boys could hide.

"So you made it." Nairn ushered them inside. "That's what I like about guys who've served. Discipline and punctuality."

When Vaz's eyes adjusted to the light, he could see that the hangar housed an indoor range with pop-up targets, nothing high tech or fancy. A couple of men and a woman in the usual militia rig of mismatched camo pants, tactical vests, and plain T-shirts were wandering around as if they were waiting for them. Vaz was pretty sure he recognized one of the guys. It really was a small world here.

"See the dark-haired guy?" he said to Mal. "I sold him a rifle."

"Let's hope he was a satisfied customer."

Nairn must have heard them. "That's Gareth. He's our resident small arms expert. But you've obviously met." He called out. "Gareth? Guy says he knows you. This is Vaz and Mal. Let's see if the UNSC trains their people right."

Gareth gave him a big grin. "Ah, our Russian buddy," he said, slapping him on the back. "Where's your friend? The blonde who looked like Staffan Sentzke."

Mal didn't say a word. It confirmed Vaz's worst fears. But there was only one right answer to the question, and it wasn't his excuse about Naomi moving on and getting a ride with a freighter. The name shouldn't have meant anything to Vaz. He tried to look credible. Suspicious worked better than innocent. He could manage that.

"Who's Staffan Sentzke?" he asked.

"Arms dealer," Gareth said. "But if you had those kinds of connections, you wouldn't have had to desert and sell your stuff, would you?"

"True."

"Don't ask me for my CO's assessment," Mal said. The two other militia were just watching from the sidelines. "I think he's still getting over my good-bye note."

"No, you just show us how good you are. We know what we're looking for." A row of ammo crates stood along the right-hand wall, each with a Covenant or human weapon on it like a buffet table of destruction. "Show us what you can do with each of those."

It really wasn't that hard. There was an M45 shotgun, MA5B and BR55 rifles, a plasma pistol, a plasma rifle, a sniper rifle, and an M41 Jackhammer. Vaz and Mal browsed along the line.

"I assume you'd like us to take the Jackhammer outside," Mal said, hefting the rocket launcher with a wistful smile as if he'd really missed the thing. "Or you won't have a range left."

Gareth nodded. "In your own time."

Vaz really wasn't sure if they were checking for competence or just confirming that they were UNSC-trained to substantiate their story. He did it by the book anyway. He started with the MA5B, checking the weapon and demonstrating safe loading before firing both prone and standing, then handed it off to Mal. The targets had to be checked and replaced each time. It was a slow and deafeningly noisy progression until he got to the plasma pistol. His expertise in that consisted of grabbing one from a dead enemy when he was out of ammo and using it against whatever got in his way. If there was a safety drill for energy weapons, he'd never seen one. He simply aimed it at the ground, checked the charge indicator, and made sure he wasn't discharging it near anything flammable.

The green energy bolt cracked and sizzled against the target, filling the range with the smell of burned wood and plastic. Mal seemed to be doing okay with the plasma rifle. He made a big mess of a target and grinned like a delighted kid.

Gareth called a halt. "Okay, stop. Safeties on. We've seen all we need to."

"I don't get to play with the M-Forty-one?" Mal said. "Oh. Bugger."

"We just wanted to be sure that you really were frontline UNSC and not the Catering Corps."

Vaz was pretty sure that neither of them looked like cooks. He indicated the scar along his jaw. "I didn't get this opening a can of beans."

"Yeah, I know, I know." Gareth held out his hands in mock submission. "We're just cautious. People try to sneak in here to spy from time to time, but we always suss them in the end. You can always tell if someone handles firearms for a living or if they only use them as a last resort."

Vaz wasn't convinced by the logic, but he wasn't going to argue with it. They were in; that was all that mattered. Nairn showed them around the barracks and signed them on to the payroll, which obliged them to serve two days a week and be on standby for emergencies. He counted out a pile of bills for both of them and gave them a copy of the duty roster for the next three months, plus personal comms units for militia use only.

Spenser was doing his night shift now, so they had to make their own way back. Vaz ambled out of the security gate, counting his money. Real physical currency was a novelty. He was still getting used to the idea of handing over actual tokens instead of just being billed via his comms chip. Damn, when had he ever handled money on Earth? His gran had given him three antique silver coins as a kid. They hadn't been legal currency for centuries, but he'd kept them as a lucky charm, still sealed in an old tobacco tin with the rest of his personal effects in storage in Sydney. They weren't going to bring him much luck there.

It was a long walk back to Spenser's place, unaccustomed exercise that they used to take in their stride. Vaz wondered whether to volunteer to organize some fitness training for the

militia just to stop himself from going soft. It was pretty harmless activity that wouldn't turn the locals into a better fighting
force than the UNSC wanted.

Mal took the power pack out of his comms set and motioned
to Vaz. "Better disable these until Spenser gets back and checks
them for bugs and stuff. In case they're doing to us what we're
doing to them."

"Humans. Nasty things, aren't we?"

"At least we don't eat our young."

"Who does? Sangheili?"

"Phyllis says they don't seem to have any weak, sickly kids."

"Maybe they're just a healthy species. If anyone eats their
imperfect offspring, it'll be the Kig-Yar."

"I bet they say the same about us. Everyone lies about the
enemy."

It was a discussion for the bar, and preferably not within the
earshot of any resident aliens. But there was a limit to how much
time they could devote to slowly killing their livers, so they spent
the evening in Spenser's basement ops center, watching the feed
from the remote sats. The cams showed them little activity around
Sentzke's place except a vehicle pulling in and leaving again an
hour or so later. Then it got too dark to see anything, and the
infrared kicked in. It was the first time Vaz had realized how
many small animals were on the prowl on the edges of the city.
They showed up as little ghostly shapes wandering around or
suddenly running like hell to escape or chase something.

"That Gareth bloke spotted Naomi right away, didn't he?"
Mal said, eating beans out of a can. He propped his boots on
the chair opposite. "But it's probably better this way."

"You think her father would recognize her now?" Vaz kept
having doubts. "There's lots of cases of parents needing a DNA
test to confirm if a kid's theirs when they've been separated for
a long time."

Mal just looked at him, one eyebrow raised. "Gareth made

the connection. It doesn't matter if Staffan doesn't. We'd still be stuffed."

Spenser returned from his shift at 5:00 A.M. and checked the comms units for recording software. "I ran into one of my Kig-Yar chums last night," he said. "He says Sav Fel's strutting around all pleased with himself about something, but very tight-lipped. Or tight-beaked. I think he's sold the ship. Which means I'd bet my pension on Staffan Sentzke being the proud new owner now."

Vaz realized he'd still been hoping it was all a misunderstanding, and that Staffan was just an angry old guy with a lot of maps and grudges but no way of delivering on them beyond handing passing insurgents a free rifle and a chart showing Earth's location. Now he was looking like a very patient man with a plan.

There's no law against a colony buying ships. It might just be a precaution.

As soon as Vaz thought it, he felt like a fool for making excuses and bargaining with himself. Mal went back down to the basement to call *Port Stanley* on the secure net. Vaz followed him and flopped onto the old sofa to listen in.

"We've taken the militia's shilling, ma'am," Mal said. "Any chance of shaking down Adj and Leaks for technical tips on battlecruisers? Spenser says it looks like Fel's handed over the ship, so we've got to assume Sentzke's got the keys now."

"I'll get BB on it," Osman said. "Are you listening, BB? Silly question."

BB didn't pass comment on the Sentzke angle. "I've got everything you need on the class. What do you want, tire pressures? How to check the oil level?"

"Things that a Sangheili crew would be aware of. Known problems. What to watch out for when you're the helmsman. Just in case we need some insider skills to impress people with our knowledge on steering and bombing the shit out of things. We need an invitation to take a look at her. We've got to get access to her comms node somehow to let you in via the back-door, haven't we?"

"I'll see what tips I can extract from our Huragok shipmates."

Osman cut back in. "Are you two okay?"

"Hoofing, ma'am," Mal said. He looked at Vaz, daring him to say otherwise. "Never better."

Mal ended the call and leaned on the back of the sofa, drumming his fingers on the peeling leather.

"With any luck," Mal said, "we can nick the ship, nobody gets hurt, and Staffan carries on as before, only a little out of pocket."

"Really?"

"Yeah."

"We've both said he's got the right to know about Naomi."

"Easier said than done."

"Most things are."

"I didn't say I was enjoying this."

"Why do we always have these conversations?" Vaz asked. "I have moral objections, you say it's the way of world, and I end up agreeing with you, doing nothing, and feeling like shit about it."

"Would you feel any better now if you'd shot Halsey when you had the chance?"

"Yes. And I'd still feel obliged to set things straight for Staffan Sentzke, too."

"Except you'd be in jail awaiting a special ONI court martial behind closed doors, the kind where they start with 'March in the guilty bastard.' If you got a hearing at all, that is."

"Without the ship, he's not a threat. He's a nuisance. And if he knows about the Spartan project, so what? Who's going to care? Who's he going to tell?"

"We've been down this path about a hundred times, Vaz. Let's play it by ear."

They killed the rest of the day walking around the center of town and being seen, acting like normal guys starting a new life. Spenser had lectured them on how that was the way to succeed at undercover work, to melt into local society instead of hiding behind the shutters all day and prompting neighbors to ask questions. But Vaz found himself checking faces as he watched people going about their business. He noted every man in his thirties who looked vaguely like Staffan's son—or son-in-law, because he still wasn't sure—and every woman with a kid who could have been that little blond granddaughter. He caught Mal watching him with a look somewhere between exasperation and sympathy.

"You'll know the right thing to do when it happens," Mal said. "That's why I never make decisions in advance. I trust my gut. It's a spur-of-the-moment kind of organ."

He had a point. Vaz always thought he knew what he was going to do and then often ended up not doing it. Maybe Mal felt better about himself because he didn't set himself ultimatums that he later failed to keep.

They reported for duty at the militia barracks the next day, ready to listen and learn while they set up some training exercises. Clearing buildings was always a good place to start. Mal said it was real enough to look as if they were serious about their new role, but wouldn't make Venezia a significantly more efficient enemy if push came to shove. Vaz was busy sketching out plans for how they could turn one of the vacant office buildings into a mock-up of a house when he heard the door open behind him. Mal looked up.

"So you're our marines, are you?" said a voice.

Vaz turned around. Staffan Sentzke stood in the doorway, a familiar face that should have been a stranger. Vaz felt his gut tighten. It wasn't the adrenaline of finding himself at a critical moment in maintaining a lie, but a terrible guilt. There was only one thing he wanted to say, and couldn't.

Your daughter isn't dead. I could tell you that right now. You've got a right to know.

Staffan didn't look quite as obsessed and dangerous up close as Spenser's mug shot of him. That had been cropped from a larger picture, probably a wedding photo, and maybe the guy just didn't like posing for the camera. He had those very pale eyes, just like Naomi.

"That's us. Helljumpers." Vaz looked into Staffan's face. The need to tell him how sorry he was almost overwhelmed him. "I'm Vaz Desny. This is my buddy, Mal."

"Staffan Sentzke." He held out his hand for shaking and looked them over, not particularly monstrous at all. "I do odd jobs here when they need things fixed. But I'm mainly an armaments man. I hear you've got some experience of Covenant systems."

Vaz tried to separate his assessment of the man from what he knew about the injustice done to him. It was impossible. "Yeah. We have."

"Ground forces, or ships as well?"

Mal nodded. "Mainly ground, but you can't separate Covenant ground assaults from their fleet."

"So you've been on the receiving end of ship bombardments."

"Yeah. Too many."

"And you know how to counter Covenant warships. Or at least the procedures."

Mal nodded. "You think we won the war?"

"I don't know. Did you?"

"No. The Covenant lost it. It ripped itself apart with some help from us. The UNSC did some bloody amazing things to save Earth, but we didn't beat the Covenant to a standstill."

Staffan studied Mal for a moment. Vaz had no idea where this was going, but it had to be about *Inquisitor*.

"I've got a project," Staffan said. "Covenant hardware. Not something I want to bring to the attention of our non-human residents."

"Very wise." Mal nodded. "It's still a very uncertain galaxy."

Staffan nodded and swung his arms. "Okay, want to come and look at it?"

"What is it?" Mal was doing a pretty good job of playing dumb. "Is it in the hangar?"

"Not exactly. It's a ship."

"Oh. Okay."

Vaz felt a moment of relief. It was all going to work out after all. They could call Osman back at the house, get BB to piggy-back a fragment of himself on the channel, and they'd be set up to visit *Inquisitor* and get him into the system to take control of the ship. They wouldn't even need to kill any Kig-Yar to do it now. It'd be quiet and bloodless, and when the dust had settled, Staffan could be told what had happened to his daughter. It was nowhere close to happy ever after, but it made Vaz feel better than the idea of assassinating Staffan for being a victim who wasn't conveniently dead.

"Well, come on, then." Staffan indicated the door. "It's okay. I've cleared it with Nairn."

"Now?" Vaz asked. *No. I need to get BB's fragment down-loaded first. We need to get him on board.* "Right away?"

"Yes, it'll only take a few hours." Staffan beckoned to them. "Come on. Let me show you the good ship *Naomi*."

If Vaz had any questions left at all about where Staffan Sentzke was heading with all this, they'd just been answered. *Naomi*. It didn't have the same martial ring as *Invincible*, but it might as well have been *Vengeance*.

NEW TYNE AIRFIELD

"Bloody hell." Mal didn't have to feign surprise. The Calypso-class recovery dropship sitting in the dappled shadow of a cam-ouflage net looked like it was one of the first airframes off the production line. "I thought these had been scrapped when Nelson was a boy."

"Still does the job," Staffan said. "What are they, thirty years old? No age at all for a ship. Perfect for quick transfers."

Mal didn't ask how he'd acquired it. He was trying to work out how he'd keep tabs on their movement, because Calypsos had slipspace drives—not big ones like warships, but useful enough to get you out of a tight spot, or make it hard for you to guess where you were if the pilot wasn't saying. His neural implant, his personal transponder to avoid friendly fire or just help someone to locate his corpse, was already well outside of *Stanley's* range.

Well, we might not have BB's fragment, but we do have a transponder. . . .

He glanced at Vaz. He'd served with the bloke for six or seven years now, as good as a lifetime in a war, and he knew every thought in his head. It worked both ways. Vaz caught his eye as they climbed into the Calypso.

Next time. We'll have BB on board then. Meanwhile, improvise.

Vaz just nodded at him. Mal hoped he'd said yes to the right unspoken question.

"Aren't we going to suit up?" Mal asked.

"Six emergency suits rated for one hour. In the aft locker." Staffan didn't seem to be bothered about putting one on. "But we're not going far."

Far wasn't so much the point as *airworthy* and *hull integrity*. An hour was forty-five minutes better than they had with regular ODST armor, anyway. Mal tried to look on the bright side and wondered if he could still get an emergency suit on and sealed in twenty-five seconds like he used to. As they slid into the crew bay behind Staffan, he saw another man sitting on one of the bench seats along the bulkhead, thirty or so, with medium-brown hair and pale eyes he'd definitely seen before. He had to be Staffan's son.

"Edvin, this is Vaz and Mal," Staffan said. "Guys, this is my son."

Mal took comfort from guessing that right. His detachment kicked in as he focused on 1700 meters of metal and composite that he needed to retrieve or destroy. But now he was looking at Naomi's half brother. The root of all this trouble was a simple but bloody horrific explanation that he could have given them right then, on the spot.

And what would Staffan say? Oh, thanks, Mal, glad we cleared that up. So my girl was kidnapped and subjected to hideous medical procedures to turn her into a child soldier, you say? So I wasn't imagining it all? Well, no hard feelings. Have a cup of tea.

Mal clenched one hand and dug his fingernails into his palm to force himself to change tack. Edvin moved along the bench to make room.

"You okay?" he asked. "You don't throw up, do you?"

"Fine," Mal said. "Really. "

Vaz settled down slipped his hand in his pocket, but Mal didn't even catch him placing the palm-sized transponder. He just saw him fumble at the side of his seat to secure the safety restraints, spending a second longer doing it than he needed to. Then he looked up at Mal with a faint smile. Maybe it would have enough range, and maybe it wouldn't, but they could try.

Vaz craned his neck to look forward to the cockpit, all innocence. "No pilot yet?"

Edvin leaned across to a repeated panel and pressed it. "We normally use the AI."

"I could fly this," Mal lied. He could probably guess his way through it, though, and all he really needed was sight of the nav screen so he could see the position. Calypsos were less complex than a Pelican and designed to be more forgiving of a pilot under fire. He tried his best cheeky grin. "No union restrictions, are there?"

"No need," Staffan said, sitting down opposite Mal and buckling in. "Let's talk."

The hatch closed and the drive started up, a familiar low grumble that rose into a whine and peaked off the scale of human hearing, leaving an itch in the back of Mal's throat. The ship lifted off.

But it's got a maximum range. Calypsos don't have the power for big jumps. Wherever Inquisitor *is, she's within a tight radius. That's something.*

Staffan leaned forward. "Why didn't you desert during the war? Seems to be the smartest time to do it, rather than wait until it's over. The UNSC has time to hunt you down now."

"We don't abandon our mates in the middle of a fight," Mal said. He found himself on that borderline between knowing he was acting but feeling genuinely offended by the idea that he'd run out on fellow marines. "We're just a bit naughty. Not cowardly arseholes."

That seemed to go down well with Staffan. He smiled. Mal almost wished he hadn't. He found himself wanting to like the guy, still unsure if that was based on sound instinct or colored by his friendship with Naomi.

"So what's special about this ship?" Mal asked. "I hear a large chunk of the Covenant secondhand fleet ends up being part-exchanged through New Tyne anyway."

Staffan nodded. "Have you heard of *Pious Inquisitor*?"

"Shit, yes." *No need to lie there. Authentic distress. See?* "She glassed Earth. Well, a bit of it. But she was only trying to be helpful, at least the second time around."

"Well, I've acquired her. To level the playing field."

"You think you're going to need to?"

"Trebuchet was only suspended. Not terminated, as far as I know."

"But that was thirty years ago."

"Indeed." Staffan looked distracted for a moment. "But in case we need to defend ourselves, it's wise to be ready."

"Mind me asking if the hinge-heads are going to be looking for her?"

"I bought her from a Kig-Yar and didn't ask too many questions about provenance, if that's what you mean."

"You better give her a really convincing re-spray and change the plates, then."

It was almost too good to be true. No, it *was* too good to be true. They'd come here to spend months working their way into the organization with the objective of finding *Inquisitor,* and here they were being taken straight to the ship. Vaz glanced at Mal. Maybe their cover was blown already and there was a nasty surprise waiting at the other end. Mal sized up the crew bay to work out who he'd take out first if things went pear-shaped. Vaz just half-closed his eyes for a second: *I know, I'm working that out too.* Their relative positions made Staffan the natural target for Mal.

Sorry, Naomi. After all that shit, I shot your old man.

No, it's not going to end like that. Not if I can help it.

It was just Edvin and Staffan. Mal was damn sure he and Vaz could take them, but that would leave Spenser in a difficult spot if he wasn't compromised already.

"How long have you lived in New Tyne?" Mal asked, trying to work out what was normal conversation for deserters.

"Over twenty years. Have you got family?"

"Not anymore."

"Me neither," said Vaz.

"Well, you should make it a priority to get one." Staffan nodded to himself. "And keep it."

Mal was wondering just what meaning he'd have taken from Staffan's conversations if he hadn't already known too much about him when the Calypso's deck shuddered. The dropship was spooling up for slipspace. Mal had hardly noticed jumping to slip in a bigger vessel, but Calypsos were fifty meters and de-signed to get forces out of a tight spot fast, not in comfort. For a second or two, his chest felt like it had been emptied of all his organs before someone dumped them back inside. He wasn't even sure which way up he was until he focused on the opposite bulkhead again. If that was what Osman felt every time *Stanley* jumped, he felt sorry for her. She was a notoriously wobbly sailor. But as Devereaux said, if seasickness didn't crimp Nelson, then the twenty-sixth-century equivalent wouldn't crimp Osman.

Osman. Does she ever have time for a bloke? Where does she live? Does she get someone to water her houseplants while she's off destabilizing the galaxy?

She had the same emotional baggage as Naomi, except she seemed a lot more normal. The thought that ONI was a more nurturing environment for a teen than Halsey's Spartan train-ing was disturbing on too many levels for Mal to think about. He checked his watch and timed the transit, collecting whatever data he could for BB to crunch later.

"You don't ask many questions," Edvin said.

Vaz looked up. "We're marines," he said. "We don't expect to get any answers."

"Yeah, the lack of planning and communication is what makes the Corps so much fun," Mal added. "Like a mystery tour."

Nine minutes later, his viscera deserted him again and the deck rolled. They were back in normal space. It was hardly worth warming up the drives to do a small jump like that. Maybe it was the ship's limitations, but it was probably just some sensible opsec to prevent anyone tailing them.

"Here we are," Staffan released his belt and squeezed through the cockpit hatch. "The battlecruiser *Naomi*."

Mal got up and took a look through the forward viewscreen. It was hard to pick out a ship in space until something illumi-nated it, but he could see the black void where stars should have been, and then the regularity of a line of tiny white lights gave it away. It didn't have the heart-stopping scale of running into *Infinity,* but it was still the stuff of which loss of bowel control was made.

Maybe it was the shape. It was curved and organic, the kind of outline that made him think of earwigs and parasites, not slab-sided and industrial in the manly, honest way that UNSC ships delivered their kick up the arse to the enemy.

Yeah, that's emotional and makes no sense. I'm fine with that.

And Mal had to ask an increasingly obvious question if Vaz didn't. It was just too weird for an innocent person *not* to ask, seeing as Staffan had now said it twice.

"Why did you call her *Naomi?* Apart from *Pious Inquisitor* being a bit dickish for humans."

"My daughter," Staffan said. "From my first marriage. She was abducted."

"Oh. Sorry, mate."

Mal caught Edvin's expression. *Pained.* That was what he'd have called it. Mal wasn't sure if it was embarrassment because Edvin didn't believe his father's story—if Staffan had even told him the details—or if it was just unhappiness about one of those family wounds that had never healed.

And we could set it straight in a second. Not put it right— way too late for that. But every time I don't say something, it gets worse. If and when we tell him . . . he's going to wonder what kind of bastards we are to sit here and say nothing.

And Staffan was now a bastard who could glass Earth. When you were a hammer, as Mal accepted he was, then everything looked like a nail. It did no harm to start testing the waters to see if there was a different solution.

"Can I call you Staffan, or do you prefer Mr. Sentzke?" Mal asked.

"Staffan will do fine."

"Just so I don't say the wrong thing at the wrong time, is there anything you want to tell me before we go any further?"

"Should there be?"

"If you've called that thing after your daughter, I'm assuming there isn't already another ship called *Naomi*. So a battlecruiser isn't your average tribute to someone you've lost."

Staffan looked into Mal's face so intently that it felt like having brain surgery. Mal was sure the man could see every thought and memory scrolling on his retinas like some confessional head-up display. The very pale, boiled-looking eyes didn't help one bit.

"That's a damn good question," Staffan said. "I'll explain when I've got my own head straight about it. Let's talk after we dock."

He leaned back into the empty cockpit, pressed something on the console, and the ship powered up again to move steadily toward the stern of *Pious Inquisitor*—no, *Naomi*. That name was going to cause some confusion for radio procedure, Mal decided, but that was the least of their problems. He'd stick to *Inquisitor*. Inserting the word *Naomi* into most of the ship-handling phrases they used was just too freaky for him.

He couldn't tell that the dropship had maneuvered through the aft port shuttle bay doors until the light levels changed. Some muffled clangs and thuds shuddered through his boots, and then the air pressure changed enough to make him swallow.

Vaz jumped out as soon as the hatch opened, one hand on his magnum. Staffan raised an eyebrow.

"There's only one member of crew on board," he said. "I promise."

"Fine." Vaz was still checking out the hangar. Mal could tell he wasn't putting on an act. They were on the actual deck, not in one of the upper berths that held vessels in place with a gravity anchor. "But my paranoia often comes in useful."

Staffan led the way through the bay into a curved passage, Mal at his heels. The space felt empty in a way that a six-kilometer ship like *Infinity* didn't. It was something about the stark design, devoid of notices on the bulkheads, firefighting equipment, chevron hazard markings, and all the other visual clutter that made Mal feel at home in a UNSC vessel. It was also very *purple*, the kind of purple that would have looked equally at home in a bishop's office or a hooker's boudoir. Mal settled on the religious image. The ship was architectural, like a cathedral. It seemed to want to live up to the holy war that the ship was designed to wage.

Actually, no, not a cathedral: it was more like a nightclub after hours with the cleaning lights on, except there were no mystery stains or gum on the carpet.

"I gather she's passed through a few hands," Staffan said. "Trying to invade Earth one minute and trying to save you from the Flood the next."

Mal kept walking. Vaz's boots echoed behind him. "You've checked her out pretty thoroughly, then."

"I had to ask ex-Covenant personnel. The UNSC helpline was busy."

"Well, the Brutes used her to attack the Sangheili during the civil war. The Great Schism. Then she was part of the Arbiter's Fleet of Retribution. Then the Sangheili rebels got her back. So she's had a few careless owners. Stop me if I'm getting boring."

"No, I'm riveted," Staffan said, raising an eyebrow. "Feel free to give us the guided tour, then."

Mal decided he'd sold himself and Vaz as useful additions. The air in the ship smelled slightly stale, a blend of chemicals, the estuary mudflat scent of Kig-Yar, and hot metal from the Calypso's maneuvering thrusters. Once they were in the elevator, the aroma changed again to something more industrial. Edvin said nothing. He just watched like a patient cat. Mal got the impression that he'd take betrayal very badly.

"So how did you guys counter these ships?" Staffan asked as the lift climbed.

"Fire everything you've got at them, or board them and destroy the command and control systems," Vaz said. "They don't glide well."

Mal decided that his and Vaz's real value to Staffan was their knowledge of how the UNSC would deal with *Inquisitor* if she showed up near Earth. They knew a little more about this particular class than anyone on Venezia—anyone he'd trust, anyway— but you could pay a Kig-Yar to get you the operating manual for anything.

"We've boarded them," Mal said. "They're not invincible or impregnable. On the other hand, if you're just looking to defend Venezia from attack by giving visiting ships a big hello, they've got lots of lovely laser turrets and plasma torpedos."

Vaz didn't offer an opinion. Maybe he thought that Mal was being too helpful, but what these cruisers could do was bloody obvious to anyone who'd watched even a few seconds of news in the last thirty years.

The elevator doors opened, spilling them out onto a deck that was probably the CIC suite. So they were now midships, then, because that was where hinge-heads put their CIC, in a citadel like any sensible navy did. Mal had never fought his way quite this far through a Covenant cruiser. The sight of it almost distracted him from his current task.

"Hinge-heads haven't got any taste, have they?" he said, hands in pockets as he gazed around, trying to look a lot less interested than he was. "It's like a tacky nightclub. Purple, purple, purple. All they need is a mirror ball in the deckhead and they can rent this out for downmarket corporate functions."

This was a ghost ship. The emptiness was overwhelming. But it was a ghost ship with all its main systems running, and that meant that it had a nav display somewhere, something that would tell Mal exactly where they were, with a comms node for BB.

And now I know exactly what information I should have asked BB to get. Ah well. We'll just have to improvise again.

Vaz jumped down from the platform and walked across the

deck, inspecting the various workstations. "Don't worry, I'm not going to press anything," he murmured. "Just fascinated. A little . . . sobering to see the world as they saw it. The bastards." He leaned over a display and peered closely at it. "Is this nav display off? You don't want it calling home."

Edvin rushed down the ramp from the platform and went to fiddle with the display. "We're still working through the manual, kind of. But I think that's off."

"Sure?" Vaz prodded it a few times. Mal leaned on the rail and watched the display switch between scales. "What's this, then?"

"Venezia."

"Sure it's not Sanghelios?"

"No, look." Edvin toggled between the scales, zooming through tens of light-years at a time. "Because that's Korfo. I read enough Covenant script to recognize that."

Vaz was taking his time over it, frowning. *Memorizing. Or maybe he's got a minicam running.* The crafty little sod was reading off the ship's coordinates from the projection. *One problem down, one to go. Sorted.* If the transponder didn't work, they still had a good idea of where the ship was. Mal was impressed to see that Mr. Earnest'n'Honest could be sneaky when he needed to be.

"Let's ask the expert," Staffan said. "Sinks? Come here, Sinks."

Staffan clapped his hands and looked around like he'd lost someone. It didn't occur to Mal that Sinks wouldn't be human or Kig-Yar. It was only when a blur of pink and violet light flashed in the corner of his eye that he turned and saw an Engineer drifting in their direction.

"This is Sometimes Sinks," Staffan said. "A Huragok. Have you come across them before?"

"Oh yeah." He'd have all the ship's data in his brain. But if BB got into the system, Sinks would be all over him, too. "Well, that solves most of your problems."

"I don't need to explain them to you, then."

"No, we've met a few."

Vaz beckoned to Sinks. The creature's mum must have warned him not to talk to strange Russians, because he gave Vaz a wide berth and drifted up to the command platform. "You're lucky to find one these days. Most of them disappeared when the Covenant fell."

"The Kig-Yar who supplied the ship said they found Sinks in a wreck. He's not part of the original complement." Staffan pointed to the nav display. "Sinks, is that nav system transmitting any signal to the Sangheili?"

Sinks drifted down to the deck level and examined the display with fluttering tentacles. *<No.>* His translation collar gave him a plaintive little male voice like a bullied clerk. *<I disabled the link as you requested.>*

"Thanks, Sinks."

<Tell the new one not to destroy anything.>

"You mean Vaz? It's okay. Vaz works for us. So does Mal here. They're not going to destroy anything."

<Wrong. All wrong. What will the masters say? So much destroyed.>

"Don't worry about us, Sinks," Mal said. "We'll behave."

Engineers all had their funny little ways. Sinks's lights were flicking on and off, the Huragok equivalent of getting a bit red in the face. He definitely wasn't a happy jellyfish.

"Is he always like that?" Mal asked.

"I'm getting used to him," Staffan said. Sinks rose from the deck and circled Mal, head jerking back and forth suspiciously, then moved in to hang next to Staffan as if he was hiding behind him. "He understands me fine, but I'm not sure I always understand him."

<The Kig-Yar destroyed the work of the Forerunners,> Sinks said. *<It's wrong. It must be stopped.>*

"They're not going to destroy anything, Sinks. It's okay."

<The masters will return, and they'll blame us.>

"It's okay." Staffan gave Mal and Vaz a look as if he was making excuses for a dotty old aunt who'd started rambling. "The Kig-Yar glassed a Forerunner site as a demo. You know about the Forerunners?"

Mal was starting to realize how much knowledge he took for granted that the civilian world didn't have or regarded as an amazing novelty. "Got the T-shirt," he said. "I've even got a mate who can read their language."

"Oh. We're a little behind the curve, then."

"It's what the whole war was about."

"Really?"

"Don't worry, someone will write it all up one day and you'll be able to watch endless documentaries on it." Mal had Staffan's attention now. "Anyway, you're right, Huragok are very touchy about damage to Forerunner artifacts."

"He got pretty upset. He keeps going on about it."

"Yeah, they don't like anyone doing that," Mal said. *Shit. The ventral beams still work, then.* "They're very protective of anything the Forerunners left behind. Bit sad, really. Have you told him they're never coming back?"

"I think you just did."

"Oops." Mal looked at Sinks. "Sorry, mate. I've got a mouth like the dockyard gates."

"Do they eat? Do they recharge or something?"

"Didn't the Kig-Yar tell you?" Mal decided to score a few points, hoping that his dismay about the ventral beam didn't show. "They *can* recharge, but they like a nutrient sludge. It's a mix of nutritional yeast protein, sugars, and fat. I can help you make some."

"Oh God, he must be starving." Staffan looked mortified and patted his pockets, a real granddad's gesture, and pulled out a handful of brightly wrapped sweets. "I'm sorry, Sinks. I didn't understand. Here. Have this while we get something fixed for you."

Mal wished Staffan hadn't done that. It was hard to see a man as a threat to civilization when he was distracted by a creature in distress. Staffan unwrapped a sweet and held it out to Sinks, who fondled it in a blur of cilia for a moment, probably checking its chemical composition. Then his tongue shot out and he started licking it.

"They like sweet stuff," Vaz said. "You've got a friend for life now."

Edvin was leaning on the rail at the edge of the command platform, shaking his head and smiling. "That's so cute. Better not let Kerstin see it. She'll want one."

"Granddaughter," Staffan said. "She'll love the pink lights, too."

Sinks seemed to be demolishing the chunk of hard-boiled sugar pretty fast, a pretty impressive feat without any teeth. His rasping tongue dissolved it down to the last sliver. Then he licked his tentacles and waited patiently.

<What are my instructions?> he asked. <The ship is repaired. I have improved the dropship, too. I have no more work.>

Staffan gave him another unwrapped sweet. "Just look after the place while I find something else for you to repair. Protect the ship in case anyone shows up and tries to seize it. Got that?"

<I understand.> Sinks slurped happily. The poor little bugger was probably just knackered and in need of a sugar boost. <Are any means forbidden to me?>

"Well, avoid using the weapons except as a last resort. Just keep intruders out. And remember the drill. If we miss a scheduled signal to you, you know what to do."

Do what? Glass Sydney? Call the militia? Bloody hell.

Mal had never thought of giving Engineers access to weapons systems. But they were like an AI in their way, and if they could rebuild systems, then they could almost certainly use them, and there was bugger all you could do to keep a Huragok out of a system anyway. It was a scary thought. Mal had taken their quiet obedience for granted.

But Sinks obviously liked Staffan. It seemed to be mutual. Maybe it was some kind of bond between mechanics, or just a response to a bit of kindness from a grieving man who'd never set out to be an arms dealer.

"There doesn't seem to be anything he can't do," Staffan said, almost proud. "He's like a fantastically clever kid."

That really stung. Mal caught Vaz's eye and got a faint hint of a reaction. It was tempting to jump to some amateur psychological conclusion about Sinks filling a gap that another very smart kid had left in Staffan's life. On the other hand, maybe he was just stating the obvious.

Venezia now had the use of a battlecruiser, and a man with a grudge had control of it, but how that all slotted together into a threat Mal could define was still a mystery.

"I said I'd explain to you about my daughter," Staffan said suddenly. "In case the UNSC told all you boys that the colonies were hotbeds of terrorism for no good reason. My little girl was abducted, and I think some Earth authority was responsible. I've spent my life looking for truth."

Mal searched for exactly the right words, scared that he wouldn't find them. He had one shot at getting this right and gaining Staffan's trust so he could get a comms channel set up to backdoor BB onto the ship. It was a knife-edge moment.

"If you find out, what will you do?" he asked.

Staffan gave Sinks another sweet. The Huragok slurped at it, watching Mal with six suspicious, beady black eyes.

"The guilty will be punished," Staffan said. "I'll have my revenge."

Mal opted for a silent nod. This definitely wasn't the time to tell Staffan Sentzke that what had been done to his daughter was probably worse than he could have imagined.

CHAPTER
SEVEN

IS ONI ONE HAPPY FAMILY? OH, PLEASE. WE'VE GOT FOUR DIVISIONS, OFFICIALLY, AND ONLY ONE OF THEM KNOWS THAT WE'VE ACTUALLY GOT MORE THAN THAT. THERE'S SECTION TWO—MADE UP OF PSYOPS AND PR, WHO EACH KID THEMSELVES THEY'RE NOT LIKE THE OTHER AT ALL— WHICH TELLS THE LIES; SECTION ZERO, WHICH THINKS IT SPIES ON EVERYONE ELSE, TELLS LIES TO SECTION TWO, AND *THINKS* IT TELLS LIES TO SECTIONS ONE AND THREE; SECTION ONE DOES STUFF WE CAN *ALMOST* TALK ABOUT, THE INTERFACE WITH OTHER BRANCHES; AND SECTION THREE DOES THE STUFF WE CAN'T TALK ABOUT OR ELSE IT WOULD HAVE TO KILL EVERYONE IN FASCINATING AND GROUNDBREAKING NEW WAYS. TECHNICALLY, YOU'RE NOT A NUMBERED SECTION AT ALL. YOU'RE THE PRAETORIAN GUARD FOR CINCONI, IN A WAY, AND WE JUST CALL CIN-CONI'S STAFF CORE FOUR, ALTHOUGH IT'S ACTUALLY IN CORE FIVE OF BRAVO-6, AND DCS REPORTS DIRECTLY TO IT. YOU'LL NOTE I DIDN'T MENTION HIGHCOM, AND THAT'S BE-CAUSE ALL ONI SECTIONS LIE TO HIGHCOM AND TELL IT THAT IT'S THE MOST POWERFUL BODY ON EARTH, WHICH GENERALLY WORKS WELL AT KEEPING THE OLD BUFFERS CONVINCED THAT *THEY* MAKE THE DECISIONS. NOW, ARE YOU CONFUSED? I CERTAINLY HOPE SO, BECAUSE THAT'S MY MISSION.

—BB, EXPLAINING THE PERCEIVED STRUCTURE OF ONI TO THE REST OF KILO-FIVE, AND ONLY PARTLY JOKING

CAPTAIN'S DAY CABIN, UNSC *PORT STANLEY*: OFF VENEZIA, FOUR HOURS AFTER LAST SCHEDULED RADIO CHECK

Mal and Vaz had now missed two radio checks.

Osman wouldn't have worried about one going adrift, but two was cause for concern. If it went to three, she'd have to mount a rescue operation. First, though, there was still Mike Spenser to ask for enlightenment. She checked the local time to see if she'd get an instant response.

Damn. The analog clock display set in the bulkhead read 1830, and it was Wednesday. He'd be at work. Secure calls went to his house because he couldn't risk carrying personal comms that might compromise him if he was searched, so the best she could do was leave a message. It hardly seemed the stuff that espionage was made of.

"What do they do in *Undercover* when this happens, BB?" she asked.

BB popped up on the desk and nestled between *The Admiralty Manual of Seamanship Vol. II* and the spill-proof coffeepot. "Well, their secret agents always rush out of restaurants without paying, never use the bathroom, and have shootouts in the street in front of passersby who never seem to take their picture and splash it all over the public net. So are you sure you want to use the worlds' worst TV drama as a training manual for real-world intelligence work?"

"I see you're not a fan."

"People believe it all, you know."

"I was actually planning to call Spenser and check before going to action stations."

"I'm sure Devereaux can punch her way through a locked door, and Phillips would throw himself into it with endearing but inappropriate courage, but you'd still have to send in Naomi in the end."

"If we need to pull out Mal and Vaz, then our cover's blown anyway. And Spenser's."

"This is why I should go on all missions."

"It didn't help on Sanghelios, did it?"

"Hardware problem. We were doing fine otherwise."

"Whatever medium we put you in, it'll be subject to damage that could disable you."

Osman knew she was capable of doing this herself. She'd been a field agent for a few years, and not just operating against the Covenant. In every war, long or short, there'd always been humans who undermined their own war effort, not by being active traitors but doing their own special damage through profiteering, corruption, strikes, and all the other shitty little antisocial things that made life unnecessarily tough for everyone else. A species under threat of extinction should have been too public-spirited to stab itself in the back. But it wasn't. She still hated those human assholes even more than she hated the Covenant. They should have known better, *done* better.

If I could cope with working undercover in the arms industry or trade unions, I can handle Venezia.

"I've been keeping an ear on the comms chatter," BB said. "But there really isn't much coming out of New Tyne. Just their ATC clearing freighters. They've learned to be tight lipped."

"Or maybe they've got some snazzy tech."

"No, I suspect they're just good at keeping their mouths shut. No technology can crack silence. Not even me."

"Okay." Osman slapped her palms on her thighs. "I'll leave a message for Spenser on the spook-o-phone, and if we don't get an OPSNORMAL from Mal and Vaz at their next scheduled check, we start search and retrieval."

She keyed in Spenser's secure code and call sign—Kilo-Three-Nine—and waited for the system to handshake. BB's box dimmed and darkened for a moment as if he was fading.

"Mike? It's Oz. No calls from the lads today. Is everything all right? Let me know." Even on a secure channel, Osman was happier keeping things short and vague. She ended the call and looked for something to keep her busy while she waited for the next window. "So how are we doing with the extra dropship?"

"Fleet Auxiliary's dropping off a Pelican and an old Calypso drive at Anchor Ten tomorrow by eighteen hundred," BB said. "I'd suggest that Devereaux and Naomi go to pick it up and take Adj with them. Then he can fit and upgrade the slipspace drive and Naomi can fly it back. Better than taking *Stanley* off station to collect it."

"Okay. Naomi's happy with that, is she?"

"I've offered to have my fragment ride shotgun in her neural implant if she doubts her piloting skills."

"So we have to write off those two for twenty-four hours."

"Subject to Mal and Vaz not needing extraction."

"Fine. We'll decide that after the next radio check."

Waiting for that was worse than watching paint dry. Osman killed some time by reading Phillips's transcripts of the intercepted voice chatter and watching the live feed from the Sanghelios remotes. The feed was a little miracle she was rapidly starting to take for granted, and without Halsey, they wouldn't have had it. If the bitch hadn't pulled that stunt to hide out on Onyx, then ONI would never have discovered the Forerunner technology stored there, like the precision slipspace navigation, the improved propulsion, and the instant FTL comms, plus a team of original Huragok to incorporate the refinements into UNSC hardware.

So even a stopped clock is right twice a day. That doesn't vindicate her.

Just thinking about Halsey made Osman bristle. The woman was phenomenally productive, but as Vaz had pointed out, that was a bit like saying the war opened up lots of opportunities for new architectural talent, what with all those bombed cities to replace.

When I'm CINCONI, will I have the sense to put a bullet through her head, or will I go on being too scared of losing her skills? She's not the only genius in the world. And one day, she'll be dead anyway. We'll learn to live without her.

Yes, Halsey had played the you-can't-afford-to-lose-me card once too often. The Huragok could do pretty much everything that she could, they were team players, and kidnapping, illegal experimentation, and fraud would never have crossed their minds. They were better company, too. They could even bake cakes.

Damn, how much longer was this going to take? Osman switched to the ship schematic to see where everyone was. Naomi and Devereaux showed up as moving blue dots in the hangar bay, located by their neural implants. Three other icons wandered around the hangar as well, the green dot of Phillips's comms unit and the two yellow dots of the Huragok translation devices. Assigning them different colors had helped. It had been hard to tell Phillips from the Huragok until one of the lights drifted up a shaft between decks.

They all appeared to be hanging out together. It was either a positive sign of team bonding or an all-hands emergency that they hadn't chosen to share with her. She switched off the display, feeling slightly guilty and intrusive for keeping an eye on them, but that was what the system was for—to locate personnel and objects when necessary. The ship was too big for her to get up and search for a handful of people every time she needed something. But it still had that chess-piece feeling that she hated. The lights were units, stripped of personhood into deployable assets.

She didn't want to get used to doing things this way. Once that distance between herself and subordinates was established, it became a process of othering, of *not like me,* and then she might feel entitled to use them much as Catherine Halsey might have done. They would be relegated to assets, just means to an end.

People. People, *even if some of them are Huragok. If we fought to save humanity, then the word ought to have some meaning.*

She'd jogged around the decks, burned an hour in the gym, and made herself two pots of ONI's finest Blue Mountain by the time her radio alerted her to an incoming message from Spenser. She took it in the galley.

"Hi, Oz." Spenser always called her that. He'd first met her when she was sixteen, a cadet on a study attachment to ONI as far as the official record was concerned. The name had stuck. "I just got back. They haven't called in, then?"

"Nothing."

"Well, don't panic just yet. It's their first honest day's work at the militia HQ. But Vaz had a transponder with him. I've checked the log and it went from the airfield to the jump point, then disappeared. My guess is that they went somewhere in a slipspace vessel."

"Or blew their cover, and got taken away and dumped out of an airlock." Osman checked the time display on the radio. "Okay, can you send me that transponder link? I'll track it from here as well."

"It's no trouble, Oz."

"You know I like to worry personally."

"Okay. Sending now. I'm monitoring some local channels for chatter, too, just to be sure."

Spenser didn't pass any comment about the wisdom or otherwise of asking frontline marines to do undercover work. Osman went back to the bridge and settled in to watch for the transponder signal on the monitor, not sure what it might mean if it reappeared. It all depended on where Vaz had put it.

A little later, Phillips came bouncing through the doors, put an *arum* in her hands without saying a word, and left. BB must have suggested that she was in need of some substantial distraction. Those puzzle balls definitely provided that. Within minutes she was so mesmerized by the thing that some time later, while she was wrestling with a sequence that she was certain she hadn't tried before, the monitoring system chirped and she had to make herself put the *arum* down. A three-dimensional holographic image of the Venezia sector popped up in front of her just above the console, flashing a small point of yellow light.

"Any idea what that is, BB?" she asked.

He didn't appear. He was just a disembodied voice. "Not yet. If it's going to land at the airfield, I'll move a remote to watch it."

The vessel, which might or might not have contained Vaz and Mal, emerged near the inner slipspace limit, the closest point to Venezia that a small vessel could make a jump or drop out of slip. The holographic plot scaled down until it took in Venezia itself and then zoomed into the surface, showing the vessel coming to a dead stop. It had landed. That was the only way she could interpret it. But it was another hour, a tense hour that even the *arum* couldn't make pass any less stressfully, before the comms console came to life and Mal's voice filled the bridge.

"Daytripper to *Port Stanley,* over."

Osman savored the relief. "Go ahead, Staff. Where the hell have you been?"

"Sorry we missed the last couple of checks, ma'am. But we've got a fantastic excuse for staying out late. Is Naomi listening?"

"No. I can guess what's coming next, then."

"Maybe not. We were inspecting a ship."

"A ship, or *the* ship?"

"It was definitely *Inquisitor.* And we didn't even have to blow a hole in the hull. Staffan let us scramble all over her. In fact, he insisted. One fully serviced, cannoned-up, fully fueled HMS *Bastard.*"

"Where is she?"

"Did you pick up the signal? You should have her coordinates."

"Probably out of range, but I'll check again."

"Never mind. Vaz used the transponder, so it'll be on the log somewhere. He worked it out by hand too. BB, stand by for the position now, just in case we don't get the chance to call in again."

Osman was almost afraid to get her hopes up. It was going so smoothly that it felt like a setup. But Mal and Vaz were too smart to fall for anything like that. "What about the comms channel for BB?"

"We did try to extract a comms frequency, but pushing it might have made them suspicious."

"Sorry. I'm being ungracious. Well done, both of you. Good result."

"Staffan's got some kind of radio check system going with the ship. We could try intercepting that signal. Which brings us on to the bad news."

"Y'know, Staff, I feel oddly happier knowing that there *is* some."

"He's got an Engineer on board. Mad little bugger called Sometimes Sinks."

"We can handle that. Can't we, BB?"

BB appeared immediately and spun on one of his corners with a sparkly effect. "Piece of cake, ma'am. Mad buggers my specialty."

"And," Mal said, "Staffan's renamed the ship."

Osman repeated that to herself. "I've obviously missed something here."

"He's called her *Naomi*."

Mal didn't have to explain further. Osman wasn't surprised, just dismayed that they hadn't overestimated how fixated Staffan Sentzke was. "Well, at least we know how his mind's working. Has he said anything about it?"

"Yeah. We had a brief chat." Mal took a long breath, his cue that he was about to say something that he wished he didn't have to. "He's spent his life looking for her. He's a clever bloke, ma'am. *Very* clever. Very persistent. You can see who Naomi takes after."

Mal ground to a halt. Osman could fill in the rest for herself. Mal, Vaz, and Devereaux had been picked for Kilo-Five for specific qualities on top of their soldiering skills. They were honest and loyal, with a strong moral compass. Parangosky had given Osman a Praetorian Guard, as BB liked to call it. They'd watch her back but never be bootlickers. Within the rules of command, they'd argue. They'd challenge her. Being CINCONI was a lonely job, and it was a healthy brake on megalomania to have a close circle that wasn't afraid to tell you that your plan sucked.

Well, she'd definitely got that with Kilo-Five. Mal had made it clear that he didn't think ONI were the good guys this time.

"I know you're not happy with this, Staff," she said. "But the best thing we can do for him is to stop him from using that ship against Earth in any way."

"I never said it wasn't. Anything else for us?"

That could have easily been my father. Does that mean I ought to be more detached from this crap, or less?

"No, go and get a beer," she said. "You've earned it."

"What about BB? We still haven't identified an entry vector for him."

"Are you scheduled to visit the ship again?"

"Nothing planned, but can BB send a fragment down the line so that we're ready if we do?"

"Patch in via your personal comms," BB said.

"Okay—there. We're connected. Got it?"

"I'm in. I love slumming it."

"I'll make sure I keep you in my arse pocket, then. If there's nothing else then, ma'am—next radio check in six hours."

Whatever Mal and Vaz felt, they'd do their jobs. Osman was sure of it. "Keep your head down, Staff," she said. "And tell Vaz well done."

Osman stood at the bridge viewscreen for a while, wondering how she was going to break this to Naomi. Blurt it out, no frills? Temper it a little? It was hard to judge. *How would I react if someone stopped me in the street and told me who I really was, with all the detail about my family?* Naomi had consented to being told, but that didn't change a damn thing about how she might feel.

"Want me to brief the others, Admiral?" BB asked.

Osman watched the reflection of his ghostly blue cube track across the bridge and come to a halt next to her. The viewscreen, an unbroken sheet of glass from deck to deckhead, had become her thinking spot, the place where she could let her mind rove and come up with solutions. The view was never a blank sheet. It was black and infinite, but it was also speckled with the luminous proof that humanity was a small, transient detail that the universe would blink and miss, and that she was an even tinier fraction of that irrelevance. Rather than making her feel helpless, it told her that all things were possible. If she took a risk, then it wouldn't knock creation out of balance. There was a sense of freedom in that.

"It looks bad if I don't do it, BB," she said. "But thanks."

"They're loafing around on the hangar deck. They usually do. It's like the mall for ninjas."

"I better head on down, then."

"Call me if you need me."

"You'll be lurking anyway."

"Only because my entire existence is one giant lurk, dear. Just remember that the trick is to go as your guts guide you. Over-thinking, expectations, what will the neighbors think—*pah*. Do what you think is *right*. Start rebuilding the ONI you want it to be."

If anyone had told Osman a year ago that she would have adored an AI and regarded him as her best friend, she would have laughed at them. One day, all too soon, it would break her heart to lose him.

"Were you a saint in a previous life?" she asked.

BB usually had a glittering riposte for every comment, but he paused for a moment before answering. A second's pause for BB was an hour's careful consideration for a human.

"I have the feeling that I wasn't very nice at all," he said. "But I'm perfect now, so that's all right, isn't it?"

"Yes," she said. "I think it is."

MIKE SPENSER'S HOUSE, NEW TYNE, VENEZIA

"You could have done this from the start, you know," BB said. "And I'd have *Inquisitor* halfway to Trevelyan by now."

Mike Spenser leaned into his field of view. "Oh, it's you. I know that voice. The blue box."

"*Black*-Box."

"Well, make yourself at home, buddy. You can't project your avatar from there, then?"

"No. I'm incognito."

Spenser laughed loudly and sat down, arms folded on a tabletop. BB worked out that they were in the kitchen. Mal's personal radio, BB's temporary home, sat on the table with the camera facing the back door, looking across a landscape of sauce bottles, a jug of juice, a pile of toast, and a steel coffeepot. Without access to any other sensors like Naomi's helmet filter or environmental monitors, he was reduced to two senses, just sight and hearing. He couldn't smell anything even though he could see the frying pan on the stove coughing up little flecks of fat from time to time.

"Damn, if I'd had a guy like you in my gear when I was on Reynes, I might not have gone crazy," Spenser said. "You know, if you don't talk for long enough, you forget how to. I used to talk to myself a lot to stop that from happening."

"It's a strange life, being someone else."

"It's even stranger trying to recalibrate yourself to being you again. I'm not sure I'm the me that I used to be." Spenser felt in his pocket and pulled out a packet of cigarettes. The fingertips of his right hand were stained with nicotine, so his smokes were the real thing. "Still, peons like me wouldn't get issued with top-end AIs. You're a big budget item."

"Handmade by craftsmen, dear boy. And the right brains don't grow on trees."

"Donor, right? Actual volunteer, I mean. Not just harvesting brains postmortem."

"Well, yes. Halsey grew her own, but that's another matter."

"Is she still officially dead? I was kind of hoping for a show trial."

"It'll take a stake through the heart to finish her off. I'm maintaining the volunteer list for that. Want me to put you on it?"

Spenser laughed again, then got up to prod the contents of the frying pan. BB saw a shriveled strip of bacon flip over. Judging by the densely amber color of the juice, it was carrot, not orange, and the toast was whole grain. BB decided Spenser was a man who believed in balancing the healthy eating books.

"Okay, BB." Spenser tipped the bacon onto a plate. "I'm going to check out the radio and telecomms network around town to see which transmitter Sentzke would use to contact the ship. If it's any distance away, he'll have to relay it the orbital node that the Kig-Yar stationed just past the jump point anyway. But I think our best bet is to get you in at the transmitter."

"You can do that, can you?"

"I'm the barracks electrician. They expect me to fix anything with plugs and a power supply. Mostly, I can."

He settled down at the table and assembled the bacon and toast into sandwiches, liberally glued together with bottled brown sauce. BB could hear Mal and Vaz talking in another room. The murmur of conversation grew louder and they walked into the kitchen.

"Ah, bacon sarnies," Mal said, inhaling like he'd caught a whiff of some luscious perfume. He rummaged in the fridge and took out a paper-wrapped wad of rashers. *"Proper* breakfast. Want some, Vaz?"

Vaz grabbed a slice of toast and buttered it. "Ninety percent of your food triangle is some form of dead pig."

"Not true. I had a vegetable last week. A tomato, I think."

"You two sound chipper." Spenser gulped down his juice. "I'm off now. Note that I haven't had any sleep. I've told them I'm doing an extra shift to sort out the comms in the barracks. Which means I get to look at the landline and satellite plans for the whole town."

Spenser left for work and BB sat watching the ODSTs going through a fascinating morning ritual. Mal flipped his bacon like a pancake.

"I hope Staffan calls the ship more than once a month," he said. "Or else this is going to get bloody tedious."

"Didn't you ask him how often?" BB said.

"Let's just say it didn't flow naturally." Mal piled the bacon between two slices of bread. "There's such a thing as being too curious on a first date."

Now that they knew where *Pious Inquisitor* was, they could have simply cut their way into the ship and boarded her the hard way, but there was a Huragok on board, and while they were busy hacking away at metal, he could have deployed any number of countermeasures. BB's experience of Huragok was the two passive little chaps that *Stanley* had acquired. But if the ship was venting atmosphere, they'd rush to do something about it. So would Sinks.

Far better to sneak in via the computer and just sort it out quietly. No damage, no fuss, no casualties.

"So is this going to work?" Vaz asked. "Once you're in, what are you going to do, exactly?"

"You want the full explanation, or a meatbag's guide?"

"Meatbag version, please. I can't cope with technobabble in the morning."

"I get into the ship's central computer, lock Sinks out of the power supply in case he thinks it's a glitch and tries to fix it, and neutralize the ship's defenses."

"Terminate him. Or her."

"Just isolate the decision-making process. It's just a very dumb AI, Vaz. Not a self-aware personality. No him or her. The Covenant weren't into that."

"Oh, wow, the relativism . . ."

"Then I move in and take over power and navigation. Do you want the Huragok alive?"

"I think ONI would like that. He'll be chock full of lovely data."

"Okay, then I take over life support as well. Then I lay in a course for Trevelyan, kick the old tub into slipspace, then sit back and scarf all the peanuts and cocktails during the flight. *Voilà*. I hope there's a good movie."

Mal gave him a knowing grin. Sometimes BB had to remind himself that Mal was responding to a small piece of electronics the size of a bar of soap. He seemed to have superimposed a person on top of that. Everyone did.

"Well, we're due on watch the day after tomorrow, so how are we going to use this time fruitfully?" Mal asked.

"Show me around town. I want to see the place. Analyze some data. Remember that I pick up more than you do."

There was a practical purpose to it, but BB also quite liked the idea of exploring this place. He'd enjoyed wandering around Sanghelios with Phillips. Provided there was some link or carrier wave that he could access, and he had an interface to be his senses, he could have traveled anywhere in the galaxy and experienced the universe in more ways than a human ever could, seeing wavelengths beyond their limited eyes and hearing what they could never hear. But accompanying a human was somehow a lot more fun. They reacted. You could compare notes. You could *do* stuff with them.

"Okay, we'll take you to the pub, then," Mal said. "Because that's what blokes do."

"Oh, I'm a *bloke*. How splendid."

"We'll take you to the place where the Kig-Yar hang out. That'll be fun." Mal held the radio up to his face and peered at the camera. "Now, you know what happened last time you went on a trip with Phyllis. We're going to maintain a link to *Stanley,* so if things get hairy, you transmit yourself back to base the second we're compromised. Got it? You bang out, up the line, and call the cavalry. No hanging around getting caught. Because the first thing they'll do is grab our comms. Oh, and warn Spenser right away, because if we're burned, he's next."

"Got it, Staff."

"Promise?"

"Scout's honor."

Vaz drove them around town in the old Warthog, pointing out the sights while BB took in the view from his vantage point in Mal's top pocket. BB recorded everything—all intel came in useful sooner or later—and agreed with their assessment: New Tyne was shockingly normal. The bar, Stavros's, was a little more wild and entertaining, though, full of squabbling Kig-Yar who were speaking a fascinating patois that would keep Phillips enthralled for days. BB could filter out each separate conversation and analyze it. He couldn't translate it all because he didn't have access to all his databases back on the ship in this fragment form, but on the next radio check, he'd sync up with himself and transfer all the data. There were lots of names being bandied around, places and events, all of which would be useful to store and slot into intelligence gaps at a later date.

And damn it, he heard 'Telcam. He was sure of it. But the dialect defeated him. They were speculating about a shipmistress called Von. It all seemed to be part of the same discussion.

"BB," Mal whispered, "what language are they speaking? I keep hearing English bits."

"Pidgin? Ha. See what I did there? Oh, never mind. We'll unpick it later. It's mostly their own dialect. But I think I heard a familiar name."

"Keep listening."

After a couple of hours, Mal got a call from Spenser. BB found it an odd sensation to be lodged in a radio that was picked up and answered. The whole room skewed in his field of view and brought back memories of his fragment, damaged and confused, exploring the Forerunner tunnels under the temple at Ontom with Phillips.

"Got it," Spenser said. "I need to pay a visit somewhere and plug in something, but we should be able to detect comms traffic and work out a timetable for you."

"I *think* I understand all that."

"See you back at the house in an hour."

BB rather admired Spenser's technical expertise. He was a comms man who'd spent most of his career listening to enemy voice traffic in some lonely and dangerous places, starting with colonial insurgents and coming full circle via some remote listening stations in the heart of Covenant space. When they got back to the house, he was in the basement, tinkering with some equipment that looked as if it dated back to the early Insurrection.

"Ah, just in time for me to dazzle you," Spenser said. "It doesn't have to be cutting edge to do the job."

"Bean cans and string." Mal bent over the device. It looked like an ancient radio with jack plugs hanging out everywhere like a Gorgon's head. "Not exactly Forerunner tech, is it?"

"You haven't spent enough time in the colonies, son. It's not all rich and snazzy like Reach. The backwaters had to keep obsolete tech going for a long, *long* time."

BB was fascinated. "Can someone patch me through to *Stanley*? I need to sync myself and access the database. Come on, Mal. Chop chop. Make yourself useful."

Mal took out his radio and tapped at the fascia to connect

with *Port Stanley*'s systems. For a moment, BB had a view of his chin pressed into his chest as he looked down, frowning while he entered the code, and then BB was looking at the basement room again, sitting at table height as Mal set the radio down on its base.

"There you go," Mal said.

BB merged his fragment with his matrix and became one entity again. It was an interesting sensation that he tried to analyze in human terms, because Phillips would ask him to describe it. What did it feel like to reintegrate his fragments? When it went smoothly, BB thought, it must have been a lot like a human waking up—that second or two of blank disorientation while they remembered where they were, what had happened the night before, and what they had to do today. Time and life made sense again. That was pretty much what reintegration felt like as long as the fragment hadn't been damaged. When he split off the fragment again to store part of himself in Mal's radio, he had the shared knowledge of what both fragment and matrix had been up to while he was separated.

"So," Spenser said. "I've got all Staffan's numbers and origin codes. There's what they call a cabinet on the south side of town—a comms junction box that routes outgoing signals to the orbital node. It's actually got some Covenant tech inside, so it's capable of slipspace comms. You plug this box of tricks into the cabinet and it tells you which calls are coming from where, and when they happen. We leave this in place for a day and see what falls out."

"That simple?" Vaz asked.

"The hard bit is plugging it in discreetly."

"We can do that," Vaz said.

"No, I'll do it. I'm not senile yet." Spenser beckoned. "Watch and learn."

They had to wait until dusk to crack open the cabinet. For BB, that was a lifetime to fill, so he spent some of it wandering around *Port Stanley*'s systems to see what Phillips was making of the material he'd recorded in New Tyne. Phillips was translating the Kig-Yar conversations, pausing while he tested unknown words against patterns and context to gauge their meaning. One thing was clear, though: they'd been talking about 'Telcam, and it confirmed that the name of the shipmistress he'd hired to find *Inquisitor* was Chol Von.

Well, she was a popular gal right now. That was the same name that BB had heard being discussed in the bar.

Spenser made his move just before midnight. Mal drove him out to the woods on the south side of town, where the comms cabinet was situated on the hillside to align with the satellite. The area was deserted, about a kilometer from the nearest house, and the hardest part was getting the locked cabinet open. Spenser, always full of surprises, picked the lock as burglars had done for centuries, with a straightened piece of wire and a thin file. The door swung open and revealed the cabinet's innards.

It should have been in a museum. BB had never seen so many wired circuits and plugs in his life. Spenser connected the scanner, wedged it into the free space in the cabinet, and checked that it was transmitting.

"Now all we do is wait a day," he said, closing the door again.

Mal and Vaz spent the next twenty hours sitting in the basement, watching movies and playing darts while they kept an eye on the remote readout from the scanner and waited for the critical set of originating numbers that would identify calls being made by Staffan. They were still studying it when Spenser came back from the barracks.

He checked through the readout. "I think that's the code," he said. "He's calling the ship every eight hours."

"What if it's not the ship?" Vaz asked.

"Then BB can just look around and come back. Stroll out there just before seven tomorrow morning and plug into the cabinet, and BB can jump aboard and ride the signal."

"Arrrrr." BB projected a pirate hat complete with skull and crossbones. "We be ready for boardin', matey."

"You enjoy your work, don't you?" Spenser said. "I was like you once."

"Pure genius? An endless fount of *bons mots* and wisdom?"

"That's one way of putting it."

Mal was up at five, and BB with him. Vaz drove them out to the hillside, parked the Warthog under cover, and the two of them crawled through the undergrowth to access the cabinet. It was about the size of a domestic stove and provided useful cover.

"Ready, BB?" Vaz asked.

"I'm cammed up and I have the knife between my teeth," BB said. He felt himself flow into a river of data as Vaz connected Mal's radio to Spenser's device, bridging BB with the comms uplink. "Figuratively speaking."

"Okay, you're waiting for the signal coming from code eight zero zero six three six one."

BB cast around, waiting for the sequence of numbers to run past him, ready to insert his code into the signal. The best way he could describe it—and he knew Vaz would ask him later—was that it was a lot like stepping onto a moving walkway while still holding on to the static rail, letting one arm stretch to infinity behind him. *How do I know what that's like?* He just did. He had to move sideways and forward and lean into the direction of movement. He had to feel the carrier wave and ride it to the receiver at the other end, into the ship herself, without letting go of the rail receding into the infinite distance behind him. He had to be a bridge. He had to be an inchworm. He had to be—oh, he'd think of a good analogy for the humans sooner or later.

There. There it was.

He just had to *jump.*

When he slipped into the wave, the debris of the voice signal swirled around him, a slow, meandering river by an AI's standards, giving him time to think and refine his plan. Once within the hull, he'd sink into the comms, then cross via the power conduits into the main data system, where he'd overwhelm the computer with a flurry of commands that would send it into a loop while he took over the entire ship.

There wasn't even a crew to pacify. There was just an obliging Huragok.

Bang.

BB hit the satellite relay that directed the signal through a slipspace link. It was like the impact from a dive into deep water, a moment of weightlessness. *Is that a real memory?* And then he was off again, riding the carrier, and—

Bang.

That wasn't supposed to happen.

For a moment he stared into a void. He couldn't move forward. There was something missing, a gap he couldn't leap. He couldn't even control what happened next. The slipspace node pulled him back and then, *slap,* he was back where he'd started, in Mal's radio.

"I can't get in," he said, indignant.

Mal's voice was a whisper. "What happened?"

"I'm shut out. It's that little bastard Sinks."

"Oh, shit."

"That's never happened before."

"Can you try again?"

BB scanned for the signal, but it was gone. "No, he's finished the call."

Vaz's voice interrupted. "Never mind. What other options do we have now?"

"You'll need to get me on a data chip and physically insert me into the system."

"No problem. We can do that. We can talk our way on board again."

"I'm sorry. I didn't make allowance for the fact that he'd filter incoming signals."

Mal disconnected Spenser's equipment and dragged it back into the trees, shuffling backward on his knees. "He's a smart little sod, that Engineer," he said. "I hope he isn't going to be a pain in the arse."

"You think he thought that up on his own, BB?" Vaz asked. "What if Staffan's already got this worked out?"

As Mal had said, Naomi got her brains and resourcefulness from somewhere. If her dad was that much like her, then they'd taken on a formidable enemy.

And he had a Huragok. This wasn't going to be the usual piece of cake.

"He's smart," BB said. "But I'm the Eighth Wonder of the World. I'll crack this one way or another."

KIG-YAR INDEPENDENT VESSEL *PARAGON*, APPROACHING COVENANT RESUPPLY FACILITY, STATION OF CONSTANT SUSTENANCE, KORFO SYSTEM

There was an etiquette even in pillage. Kig-Yar didn't spoil what they didn't need.

Chol was satisfied to see that the courtesy was still being observed without the heavy hand of the Covenant to enforce it. She sat at her command position, watching the display as the navigator and helmsman brought *Paragon* into alignment to dock at Constant Sustenance. The supply station—a long spindle of a structure, all long curves and spines—hung in the blackness, abandoned by the Covenant but still illuminated and functioning. A pattern of navigation lights still flashed on its docking ring. The berths that would secure ships were still intact. And Chol knew the gravity generator would still be functioning.

It was the responsible, polite thing to do. If you were salvaging and reclaiming, then you didn't pluck out the essential structures before others had had a chance to remove smaller prizes.

Without the power supplies and other big machinery, it would be much harder or even impossible for other vessels to dock and strip out what they needed. Chol didn't relish the idea of hanging around to see the free-for-all when all that was left of the station was the bulky, high-value machinery, because that *would* be fought over, but nothing would be wasted by foolish, hasty greed.

"Shall we send out a reclamation team to find parts, mistress?" Zim asked. *Paragon* shook slightly as the docking clamps secured her. "We might as well make the voyage pay for itself. Parts and ration packs."

"If you can find any." Chol stood up and checked her pistol. "But no hanging around. I've come to find Eith Mor, and we can't afford to lose any time. For all we know, *Inquisitor* could be fully crewed by now."

Zim hopped onto the command seat. Chol was leaving him to look after *Paragon* while she searched the station, in case she'd misjudged any of the hired crew and they decided to make off with her ship.

"Is that our problem?" he asked. "All we agreed to do was find her. Not retake her."

Chol had nearly let her real plan slip out. For all she knew, the crew might have been enthusiastic about her politics, but there was no point risking a walkout mid-mission.

"The fewer excuses I give 'Telcam to renege on paying the rest of the fee, the better," she said. "Now I've got to find Eith and see how helpful he's willing to be." She gestured to her two biggest, most aggressive crewmen to follow her. "Nulm, Bakz—with me."

The moment she stepped out of the hatch and jumped down onto the walkway connecting the berth to the hub of the station, she could see how much material had already been stripped out of the structure. The metal covers to the control panels, worth a fair sum when melted down, had already gone, along with every decorative detail. The controls were reduced to their bare bones, just touch pads and movement sensors, and even the covers of the light fittings had been taken, leaving a harsh blue-white light that cast stark shadows. The station was on the edge of Covenant space, a depot for lone ships traveling without the fleet replenishment support of an agricultural ship. It was a comfort to have it there just in case of emergency, but times were hard and the resources were needed here and now.

Besides—if they left it, someone else would strip it, probably the Unggoy, and that was unacceptable.

The doors to the hub floor opened and a tidal wave of noise rolled out. Kig-Yar were moving pallets loaded with sheet metal, crates, and coils of cable. One Unggoy tottered past her carrying a single chair over his head. The place was being dismantled from the inside out.

But the environment controls were still working, as she expected. She reached out and grabbed a small male Kig-Yar by his shoulder-belt.

"You," she said. "Have you seen Eith Mor? Do you know him?"

"No, mistress."

She didn't even know what he looked like. That wasn't necessarily a problem, though. There were other ways to identify someone. "Where are the public address controls?"

"The next deck down. What's this Eith done, then?"

"Nothing." Chol cocked her head at Nulm and Bakz. For all she knew, this *was* Eith. "Search everyone before they leave this deck. Check that they *are* who they claim to be. I'm going to flush out Eith."

"We will, mistress."

"You may well see someone rush for the doors when he hears my announcement."

"Don't worry. He won't get past us."

Nulm and Bakz went back to the exit to guard the doors,

hands on their holsters. Chol headed for the next level down, the flight controller's center, which was much less busy than the hub deck. As she passed the signs directing her to the office, she noticed salvage seals daubed on walls and doors. Everyone seemed to have staked their claim to the contents, with names, dates, and details of what they intended to return for scrawled in indelible paint. When she got to the controller's office, the only creature in it was a miserable-looking Unggoy sucking on a tube of infusion.

"I want to use the public address system," she said.

The Unggoy went on sucking his narcotic and just held out his hand for payment. It was strictly tokens only now. The Covenant was gone, and with it all its treasury clerks and their minutely detailed systems. Chol slapped a fifty-gezk chip in his palm, and the Unggoy pointed to the console at the back of the control room.

She debated whether to flush Eith out by panicking him or luring him. Maybe he'd already fled. If his cousin had managed to warn him that she was looking for him, then he might have been working out his price for the information. But this was her best lead, and she had to follow it.

She leaned over the controls and pressed the transmit key. "Eith Mor of Eayn," she said. "Eith Mor of Eayn, a ship from home is ready to offer you passage in exchange for assistance. If you want to make a deal, go to the ship *Paragon* at the docking level." She paused. "And if Eith Mor has already departed, I'll pay a reward for information on his whereabouts."

She switched off the microphone. As she went to leave, the Unggoy looked up at her, tube still clamped between his teeth.

"I could tell you when he arrived," the Unggoy said. "But that'd be another fifty."

Chol wanted to cuff him around the head and beat the information out of him, but it was quicker to play his game. "I'm not interested in when he arrived, but whether he left."

The Unggoy held out his hand again. She paid up.

"The master of *Distant Beacon* agreed to transport him in

exchange for some of his acquisitions. The ship's still here. Berth five-zero."

"Did you see Eith? And I expect that answer to be included in the price."

"Yes."

"Describe him."

"Within the price?"

"Yes."

"He has a bright blue vest and unusually light coloring. And a few missing teeth."

"Thank you."

That was all she needed to know. She'd work through every Kig-Yar on the station to find him. When she got back to the docking level, Nulm and Bakz were still by the exit, scrutinizing everyone who went in and out.

"He's here," she said. "Look for someone very pale skinned, wearing bright blue. That should narrow it down. He may try to leave with *Distant Beacon*."

Nulm nodded. "I'll check that he's not already aboard, mistress."

There was always the chance that Eith had anticipated this and paid the Unggoy to mislead anyone looking for him. Chol prowled the four main decks, peering into compartments and checking behind stacks of crates, hoping that he'd have the sense to take her offer and not force her to do anything unpleasant. He wasn't from an allied clan. He had no political protection from her.

Her communicator alerted her as she walked past the cold store for the third time in an hour. She stopped to answer the call. It was Bakz.

"I've just seen him," he said. "On the gantry above the docking deck. Do you want me to pursue him?"

Chol visualized where she was in relation to the ladder leading down from the gantry. "Leave Nulm on the door. I'm going to approach Eith from the deck above. Drive him along the gantry, and we'll grab him."

It was a long time since she'd hunted like this instead of simply sitting in a comfortable seat and opening fire from within a ship. It was exhilarating. She sprinted along the deck, scattering a gaggle of juvenile Kig-Yar, and burst through the doors. Eith was leaning on the safety rail, watching the activity on the deck below.

He hadn't seen Bakz, then. But Chol could see him, slowly climbing the near-vertical perforated metal steps up to the gantry. She closed the gap. Eith had only one escape route. He'd have to jump.

But that's crazy. He'll break his legs from that height.

Eith looked left, then right, and appeared to realize he had a problem.

He could have just stopped and talked, of course, and got a ride home at the end of the mission. But he didn't. He scrambled over the rail and dangled there for a moment before launching himself onto a heap of sacks that must have looked like a soft landing from this angle.

It broke his fall, but he struggled to stand up again. Chol didn't even think before she launched herself after him. T'vaoans were bigger, tougher, and stronger than their ordinary cousins, and she was willing to risk a few bruises to get Eith. She hit the pile of sacks, felt it rip out some plumage on her left arm, and rolled onto the deck. Momentum kept her going. She crashed into the limping Eith a few seconds before Nulm rushed from the doors to pin him down for her. Bakz caught up with them a few moments later.

Everyone on the deck simply stood back to let them sort out their issues. They probably thought it was a squabble over a disputed piece of salvage. Nobody wanted to intervene in those.

"You didn't need to run," she said, hauling Eith to his feet. A streak of purple blood trickled from one of his nostrils. "But seeing as you did, it makes me curious."

"I don't like being cornered." Eith fluffed up his quills, indignant. "You look like criminals."

"Really. You heard my broadcast?"

"Yes."

"I just want some information."

"That'll cost you."

"You don't know what it is yet. When you do, you might just be grateful that I don't kill you."

The rest of the Kig-Yar had resumed their looting. Nobody cared what was happening to Eith. He probably realized that.

"What do you want?"

"Tell me what you did with the ship."

"What ship?"

Bakz leaned over him as Chol tightened her grip. "You know damned well which ship. The one you were supposed to deliver to the crazy four-jaws. Where is it?"

"I don't know."

Chol balled her fist and punched him hard in the side of the head. He squealed. A couple of Kig-Yar looked his way, then went on dismantling a chest-high metal tank with a laser cutter. It was none of their business.

"Where is it?" Chol demanded.

"I don't know. I *really* don't know. I know where it was. But—" Eith stopped. "It was moved."

"Fel's starting his own navy, is he? What would you pathetic flea-catchers do with a battlecruiser?"

"Ah. You know about Fel."

Chol gave him some credit for not offering up his shipmaster right away. "Of course I do."

"Well, there's no point going after him, because he hasn't got it, either."

"You sold it."

"Wouldn't you?"

Chol grabbed him, both hands tight around his neck, and dug in her claws. "Enough. Where's the ship? Where's Fel? Who did he sell it to?"

Eith flailed and choked. Chol hung on for a few seconds until he got the idea and started to go limp in her grasp. Then she let go.

"You'd side with the four-jaws against your own kind?" he gasped.

"No, I just want to know where the ship is. I have nothing against Fel. Where's Fen-Es-Ya?"

Eith looked puzzled for a second. "If you know where he is, why pick on me? Ask him. He's the one with the big ideas."

An elderly Kig-Yar with a lot of scars ambled over to peer at them. "*Ven-etz-ee-ya,*" he said. "It's Venezia. Mostly humans. One town, basically. They do business with some of the clans."

Chol straightened up. "I've never heard of it."

"It orbits Qab. That's about all I know. Like I say—one town and a lot of nothing."

He walked off again. Chol let go of Eith. "So Fel likes the flat-faces, does he? Has he sold the ship to a human?"

"He's my shipmaster. I can't betray him."

"Forget Fel. Where did you last see the ship?"

"Shaps. Shaps Three. I doubt it's still there now."

Chol had everything she needed. She could find Fel now. She didn't want to get involved with humans if she didn't have to, because other humans would pitch in, it would become a conspicuous feud, and 'Telcam would notice. She just needed to find *Inquisitor* and seize the ship very, very quietly.

The opportunity might have passed by now, but she'd come this far. She had to press on. She gestured to Bakz and Nulm to get back to the ship.

"Let's go," she said. "Make sure we have everyone embarked. I saw some of the crew liberating a few items."

She half-expected Eith to come scuttling after her, asking if he could have passage back to Eayn, but he dusted himself down and disappeared into the maze of corridors leading off the deck. Maybe he thought traveling with her was too risky.

Zim vacated the command chair as she swept onto the bridge. "Successful?" he asked.

"Lay in a course for Qab," she said. "Fel's living on Venezia. A human colony. It all makes sense now."

"But where's the ship?"

"Eith doesn't know, but it was off Shaps Three at one point, and if Fel's on Venezia, and he's fond of the company of humans, then *Inquisitor* can't be far from there. Let's pay him a visit."

Chol almost lost her nerve on the slipspace jump to the Qab system. She'd lost too much time already. *Inquisitor* was almost certainly in the hands of the humans, but were they an isolated colony or a military base? She wasn't suicidal. The Kig-Yar needed their own defense force, but taking on a navy of that size without the weight of the Covenant to back her up would be a very brief battle, and she would certainly lose within minutes. This had to be done stealthily. She needed to find the ship, assess how much of a fight the crew could put up, and then make her decision.

Do humans even know how to operate a battlecruiser?

Perhaps they could learn very fast. She had to face the prospect of shelving her plans and simply locating the ship for 'Telcam. Then it would be his problem to deal with the humans.

But when will I ever get another opportunity to take a ship like that?

Probably never.

Venezia wasn't what she expected at all. It was, as the veteran shipmaster had said, one town and a lot of nothing. She asked for permission to land—although if she hadn't, she wasn't sure how they would have detected a ship, let alone prevented it from landing—and took one of *Paragon*'s shuttles to the surface, accompanied by Bakz and Nulm again. At the airfield, the vessels parked up were from every era, human and Covenant, and there were even Kig-Yar wandering around talking to humans. It was the most unnatural thing she'd ever seen.

And there were freight shuttles. That explained Huz's reaction. This was a cozy little market for some clans, and they wanted to keep it to themselves.

"Who'd have imagined this?" Bakz said. "To think we'd have enough in common to live here with them."

Chol stood by the shuttle, working out where she'd need to go to get information. Then one of the Kig-Yar trotted over to intercept them.

"What's your business?" he asked, no sign of deference to her standing whatsoever. He must have picked up some insolent human ways. "Do you have a meeting here?"

It was worth a try. She feigned casual indifference. "I'm looking for Sav Fel."

"He has an estate out on the western side of town. Follow the road to where the buildings end, then look for the bridge across the river. You can't miss it."

"Thank you."

He trotted off. She checked the nav display. "Let's pay Fel a visit and see what he can tell us."

"An *estate*?" Bakz said. "He's made a princeling of himself. Business must be good here."

The signs said this place was called New Tyne. Chol had seen bigger middens than this. It was square and tidy, like all human settlements, a grid of roads with rules and regulations written on boards everywhere. No wonder the flat-faces had clashed with the Covenant. They were much the same, bureaucratic and always seeking to spread and overwhelm. They had no idea how to just fit into the easy spaces that any fool could find. The town was so small that they located Fel's estate in minutes and set down by the gates, which were wide open. The place had thick walls and every indication of being a fortress, but she was able to walk right in.

It was early evening, a very pleasant spring day by the look of the trees. Maybe Fel wasn't at home. As she walked up the path, she noted the lavish decoration set in the gate posts and the very human style of the building. And the front doors were open as well: what was going on?

Then a T'vaoan male trotted out of the doors and went to a vehicle parked near the steps, a human-style truck with tires. That explained why the gates were open.

Chol called out. "Sav Fel?"

He looked up. T'vaoans were a minority, so he should at least have been interested to see one of his own kind. But he simply looked puzzled and a little preoccupied.

"I was just leaving," he said. "I have business at the mines. Who are you? You'll have to make an appointment."

She looked at Bakz. He nodded. She could hear the sounds of chicks and juveniles from behind an inner courtyard wall, squawking and squabbling while adults tried to break up a fight, so whoever was in the house was probably distracted. Fel needed to know she meant business, too, and it had nothing to do with mining. Bakz and Nulm approached him and grabbed his arms, flattening him against the Warthog just as she shoved her pistol in his face.

She put one claw to the tip of her nose: *be quiet.* Fel froze.

"I'm sure you can fit me in to your busy schedule," she said. "Come with us, Fel. We're going to take a little trip. It's a lovely evening for it."

**YOU ONLY NOTICE WHAT WE DO WHEN WE'RE NO LONGER
THERE TO DO IT.**

—SOMETIMES SINKS, RESIDENT HURAGOK OF THE
INDEPENDENT BATTLECRUISER *NAOMI*

MOUNT LONGDON ROAD, NEW TYNE

"Finished." Staffan applied the last coat of matt lacquer to the tile-print paper covering the roof of the doll's house, then took a couple of steps back to admire it. "Damn, I'm talking to myself now. What a senile old bastard."

He washed the brush and dried it on a piece of rag while he walked around the table, studying the roofless structure. The house stood in the center of the workshop like a mansion on a private island. When he knelt down, chin resting on his folded arms on the tabletop, he began to understand the fascination it held for a child. You really had to see it from their physical perspective to get a sense of the wonder of it. He reached out and closed the front wall, and it became even more absorbing. The little paneled front door opened to reveal a tantalizing glimpse of a staircase and a hall table. Light shone golden and inviting from the downstairs windows. He felt for a moment that he could almost step into the house and live the untroubled, unchanging life of the dolls who would take up residence: no pain, no aging, no weariness, and no grief.

It was for Kerstin, but somehow it was also for Naomi.

It had taken him thirty-five years to fulfill his unspoken promise to her. How long had it taken to make this house? A couple
of months. He could have made one in time, before she died—no,
he couldn't have. The child who died wasn't Naomi. Why did he
keep thinking in loops like this? She *wasn't* Naomi, and that
meant the little planetarium lamp, the one he'd kept and trea-
sured, the one that had given that dying child so much comfort
in her final days, was something the real Naomi had never seen.

The star lamp, a battered leather briefcase full of essential
documents and photos—all hard copy—and a few precious manual tools like his antique Vernier scale were all he'd taken with
him when he left Sansar. The keepsakes you rescued in a disaster, Staffan decided, told you who you really were. He'd already
lost everything that truly mattered long before the Covenant
glassed the planet.

He pushed open the tiny front door a few times with his fingertip and let it swing almost shut. Damn, he was proud of
those miniature hinges. Closing the door required use of his
fingernails, but Kerstin's little hands would cope with that easily.
It wasn't so much a toy as an expression of everything he was
and everything he held dear. If she broke it or got bored with it,
his heart would be broken too.

But that's not how you give.

*When you give, you give the person what they want. Then
you let go.*

He dabbed the roof cautiously with his fingertip. The water-
based lacquer was already dry. He'd have to dismantle the whole
house to move it, but for the moment it was finished and perfect,
every tiny item of furniture in its place. He locked the workshop
and went into the house for dinner.

Laura was in the kitchen. "Just got to check in with the ship,
sweetheart," he said, leaning around the door. "Time to call the
Huragok."

"Damn, do you have conversations with it?" she asked. "Poor thing. Stuck there all on its own. I hope it doesn't go stir-crazy."

"It's all they want to do, apparently—work. I don't think they sleep."

"Wow. We could do with a few more of those."

"Yeah, he was a bonus I didn't expect."

"So how long is this going to go on? Where are you going to keep it? What do you do with those big ships, keep them in orbit? Land them? Kind of hard to hide if the UNSC shows up again."

Staffan shrugged. "It's going to take us years to build any kind of orbital dock, so she just has to stay in a stable orbit somewhere for the meantime. Security's a matter of getting a watch crew together. Better still, finding some way to lock her down so that she can't move if anyone boards her. The Huragok's the best bet at the moment."

"You think someone could do that? Cut their way in or something?"

"UNSC troops boarded Covenant warships a few times. They didn't knock first."

"Damn. You can't even garage it."

"That's why I'm relying on a Huragok night watchman. If anything happens to me and he doesn't get a scheduled call—from me, my voice, not some code that anyone could fake—he's got instructions to trigger a slipspace jump to coordinates that I gave him. He doesn't like the Kig-Yar much by the look of it."

Laura looked slightly dismayed. For her, that was the equivalent of a fainting fit. "What do you mean, if something happens to you?"

"The original owner might come looking for it. Or another Kig-Yar might fancy his chances." He winked at her. "I don't want to frighten you, sweetie, but there's a lot of riffraff in the galaxy. Fortunately, I was trained by someone even worse. Or better. Depends on your moral prism, I suppose."

Staffan tapped in the code and got the comms tone. Yes, it really was a little weird to phone the Huragok babysitter to check that everything was okay. The sudden click and then silence told him that Sinks had opened the comms channel on the bridge. Huragok were smart, but they didn't seem able to master the concept of saying "Hello" or "Sinks receiving." Staffan always had to speak first.

"Hi, Sinks," he said. "It's me. Confirm you can identify my voice."

<It is you, and you are well.>

"Yes, I'm fine. Any problems? Malfunctions?" Staffan was learning the art of questioning a Huragok. They didn't seem to volunteer anything, or at least this one didn't. It was like wording your three wishes to a genie. "Are all the readouts normal?"

<An intrusion was blocked. That's all.>

Staffan wasn't sure he'd heard that right. His stomach flipped. "What kind of intrusion?"

<An attempt to breach the ship's computer systems. A signal exploiting your comms channel. It didn't get past my firewall. I added more security protocols. You told me to make sure nobody accessed the ship, so I improved security on all points of access.>

"When? When was the attempted breach?" Staffan was close to panicking. How many people knew the ship existed? Of those, how many knew how to access its comms channel? The last thing he needed was an angry Sangheili complete with a warship paying a visit here. "Who did it?"

<I only know the origin was Venezia.>

Staffan could think of only one person who had the knowledge to mess around with the ship, but he couldn't think why the buzzard would do it.

Fel, you asshole. What are you playing at?

"It's okay, Sinks. You did well. Just don't let anyone into the ship. Only me and anyone I bring with me, until I tell you otherwise. If you think the ship's compromised, execute the jump as we agreed."

<I understand. I will continue my work now.>

Staffan decided it was time to pay Fel a visit. The idiot was asking for it. He couldn't imagine why the Kig-Yar would try to pull a scam on him, seeing as his family lived here now and his customers knew where to find him, but buzzards were no smarter than humans when they got greedy.

"Sweetheart, can you keep my dinner warm in the oven, please?" Staffan checked his pistol and picked up the truck keys. "I'm going to sort out a misunderstanding."

Laura looked him over. "You're not a kid anymore, Staffan. Whatever it is, you need to take Edvin with you."

"I can handle it. I'm going to see Sav Fel. I'll call Ed on the way."

Not many wives would tolerate their old man ruining dinner to go and shoot someone. He had a gem in Laura. But maybe Fel had a good explanation and it wouldn't come to discharging weapons. Staffan got on the radio and let Edvin know where he was heading.

"You should wait, Dad," Edvin said.

"I'm quite capable of dealing with Fel."

"Even so, I'll drive over. Don't start kneecapping him until I get there."

This was a normal day's business. Staffan whistled to himself as he drove across town, more angry than worried. Sinks had done his job: he'd thwarted whatever security intrusion had been attempted. What if it wasn't Fel, though? Would Peter Moritz have tried something? He was uneasy about Staffan having the ship. It was technology that Staffan wasn't familiar with, so he had to follow hunches based on human—and alien—nature. Technology changed, but base motives were as old as time.

Never let them piss you around. Andy Remo's advice was still as fresh in his memory as it had been decades ago. *No sec-*

ond chances. *If you catch them trying to screw you and don't make an example of them, they'll do it again, and so will everyone else. Start as you mean to go on.*

Fel had stolen the ship once. That meant he could—would—do it again if the disincentive wasn't strong enough. *Why am I surprised?* It was like a man who left his wife for a girlfriend. The girlfriend always seemed shocked when he did the same to her in due course. How did she think she got him in the first place?

Maybe I should just get a few of the guys together and break Fel's fingers.

Remo had taught Staffan everything he knew: how to handle a firearm, how to hit a guy so that he stayed down, how to cover his tracks, and how to make money. But the most important lesson had been that rules didn't exist. You made your own and enforced them. Following all the rules and being an obedient citizen hadn't done Staffan a damned bit of good. The more he complied, the more the system crapped on him. It didn't care what had happened to Naomi. The cops hadn't given a shit about it. The school authority hadn't either, or the hospital, or his CAA representative, or anyone whose job it was to listen to him and see that his concerns were taken seriously. They hadn't much cared about Lena, either.

That was the deal, wasn't it? You obeyed society's rules, and those same rules would be there to protect you when you needed it. But all he saw around him was that the more you gave the finger to doing what was right, the more you got away with. Then he met Remo, and Remo took him one step beyond that, to the unthinkable place where you could become the person who obeyed no rules at all and dared the rest of the bastards to come and get you.

It wasn't Staffan's nature, but anger and grief made the transition far easier. What had he got to lose? Remo had done more to get him through the wasteland of his life than all the useless assholes in officialdom. That was all the proof Staffan needed about right and wrong.

If I met Naomi again, would she even recognize me? How would she feel about her daddy being an arms dealer?

She'd be middle-aged now. She'd understand necessity, that you had to do things sometimes that you didn't intend or choose. Staffan turned down the road that led to Fel's compound, ready to do what he had to.

The first thing he noticed was that the gates were open and there were more vehicles inside than the last time he'd called. Maybe Fel was shipping out, then. Good idea: Staffan would wring his chicken neck when he got hold of him. He parked just outside the gates to avoid being trapped if anything went wrong, slipped his pistol into the back of his waistband, and walked into the front courtyard.

Something wasn't right. There wasn't always a guard on the gate, not unless Fel wanted to impress someone for a deal, but Staffan didn't usually walk in unnoticed. A gaggle of Kig-Yar were milling around, arguing and looking agitated. Then they spotted Staffan and fluffed up their quills.

He didn't wait to be questioned or greeted. "Where's Fel? I need to talk to him."

Staffan stood with his hands on his hips, ready to draw his weapon. Kig-Yar reacted to that body language much the same way a human did. They paused, sizing him up. Then a female pushed through the males and stalked toward him, looking murderous. In the sudden silence, Staffan could hear the distant noise of chicks somewhere in the house.

"Where is my mate?" she demanded. "Is this your doing? Have you come for a ransom? I'll slit your throat. I'll—"

"Hold on a moment, ma'am." This had to be the current Mrs. Fel, the female Skirmisher he'd seen on the first visit. "Are you telling me your husband's missing?"

She looked manic, but then they all did. It was the eyes.

"Don't play innocent with me, flat-face. What have you done with him?"

Okay, Remo time. "Actually, I came to kick the crap out of the thieving jackal," he snapped. "Has someone beaten me to it?"

One of the males finally spoke. "Fel disappeared last night."

"What do you mean, *disappeared*? Has he done something he needs to disappear for, then? Because I've got a bone to pick with him about my goddamn ship."

Mrs. Fel hopped from foot to foot, head jerking this way and that. "Feathers," she said. She ducked back inside the house for a moment and came out clutching a handful of shiny black feathers. When she held them out, Staffan could see that the shaft and vanes were broken, like they'd been yanked out with some force. Some of the quill ends even looked a bit purple and bloody, so they hadn't been shed naturally or plucked from a dead body.

"Look," she said. "I found these on the ground. Someone abducted him. I *know* it. He went outside to put something in his vehicle and then he was gone. Just *gone*. Nobody's heard from him. Nobody knows where he is. He didn't meet up with a customer as planned last night and he didn't return. He *always* comes back. He knows I'll kill him if he doesn't."

She could have been lying, of course. Staffan didn't have any illusions about Kig-Yar. Maybe she was just doing what a human would have done and standing by her man.

"If you've got any suspects," Staffan said, "I'll go have a word with them. I'm anxious to see him too."

"If we had any suspects, we would have run them down already."

The Kig-Yar flock instinct kicked in when they were under stress. They hunted and fought in packs. This bunch certainly didn't seem to be acting now.

"You think the Sangheili caught up with him?" Staffan asked.

One of the males cocked a suspicious head. "The four-jaws

would have slaughtered everyone before taking him, if they needed him for any purpose. If they didn't need him—we would have found his body in pieces. So we suspect *humans*."

"Or your own kind. Or Brutes. So if you think he's been abducted by humans, maybe you should look at who he's been doing business with lately other than me."

It seemed to stump them. The buzzard had a point about the Sangheili. Staffan had heard they weren't subtle about prisoners, so even if they'd managed to find Venezia and land without attracting attention, this didn't look like their handiwork.

"You'll ask your associates," Mrs. Fel said. She probably thought he'd obey because he was a mere male. "I want him back."

Staffan stood his ground. "And you ask yours. And tell me what you find."

He headed back to the truck, holding his radio discreetly so that the shiny side would reflect anyone coming up behind him. He really didn't like turning his back on Kig-Yar when they were that fired up.

If anyone had snatched Fel for an unpaid debt, they wouldn't keep it quiet for long. That was the whole point. It was what passed for law enforcement here. If nobody knew that retribution quickly followed wrongdoing, then nobody else learned to behave. Staffan drove back along the eastbound road into town and saw Edvin's pickup coming the other way. He slowed down and pulled over. Edvin passed him to do a U-turn, drove up behind him, and parked.

He jumped down from the cab. "Jesus, Dad, you had me worried. What happened?"

"Fel's gone missing."

"Legged it, or been snatched?"

"Sounds more like snatched."

"Sangheili?"

"They'd have left a pile of hamburger and taken the ship by now. Well, if he's pissed off someone here, we'll hear about it fast."

"Who'd kidnap Fel in his own front yard?"

Staffan's gut told him this was all connected with the attempt to hack the ship's systems, but he couldn't see how yet. It was a crystal-clear evening, not quite dark, and buzzing with insects in the trees.

"Connect the dots," he said, leaning on the hood of Edvin's pickup. "Someone tries to breach the ship's computer. From *here*. Via my comms signal. Someone knows me, the ship, and Fel. Would Peter do this? Nairn?"

Edvin shrugged. "Who's new in town?"

It hadn't crossed Staffan's mind before. "Our two marines. They're certainly pros. But you think they're up to this kind of stuff?"

"Well, we don't see many UNSC deserters for years, and then three come along all at once."

"Three?"

"The Russian guy had a woman with him when he arrived, but she shot through for some reason."

Staffan wondered what had happened to her. But it was impossible to keep tabs on everyone who came and went. "Well, when it comes to gift horses," he said, "a thorough dental examination is always a good idea. Shall we go and have a chat with them?"

"I think it would be sensible. Either it's them, or they've got a different set of skills to help us find who's done it."

"But how would they know about accessing the ship's comms?"

"How do *we* find out stuff? Someone always lets something drop."

Staffan hadn't made up his mind whether Mal and Vaz were a problem, a blessing, or just two guys who'd picked the place farthest off the UNSC's radar to lie low for a while. But his main asset was a battlecruiser, and he had to do everything in his power to hang on to it. Sinks would stop any attempt to take the ship. That bought him some time.

Start as you mean to go on.

If it was one of his own going behind his back, a friend like Peter or Nairn, then he'd have to act. A man in his trade couldn't afford to show weakness or else he'd be eaten alive. If it was these two new guys—well, he'd deal with them and that would send a message to Earth and the UNSC that they couldn't walk in and threaten a colony any more easily now than they could thirty years ago.

"Let's go and have a chat with Mal and Vaz," he said. "They're usually in one of the bars, right?"

Edvin nodded. "I'll call some backup. You're dealing with marines now, Dad. They make the Kig-Yar look like love-birds."

STAVROS'S BAR, NEW TYNE

"When I'm too old to wrestle hinge-heads," Mal said, "I think I'm going to retire here and open a Black Country restaurant. I'm going to serve gray peas and bacon, chitterlings, brawn . . ."

"This is all about offal again, isn't it?" Vaz seemed to have lost interest in his beer. "Viscera. Organs."

Mal kept an eye on the entrance while Vaz faced the other way and watched the back door that led to the bathrooms. He would have felt better sitting near the door for a rapid exfil, but the tables were all occupied with people who didn't look inclined to move anytime soon.

"Not the peas," Mal said. "Or the bacon."

"But everything else."

"Pretty well, yeah."

"Will there be a wine list?"

"I was thinking blue fizzy pop and pints of the local bitter."

"What's a pint?"

"Just over half a liter. Do try to keep up."

"You realize Wolverhampton isn't technically *in* the Black Country, don't you?"

"Why are you pissing on my dreams, Vaz?" Mal tossed a RHSU—Rock Hard Snack, Unidentified—in the air and caught it in his mouth while he filtered the conversations floating around the bar. "A lad's got to plan for his future."

Mal carried on eavesdropping. He'd never understand enough Sangheili or the dialect that some of the Kig-Yar spoke, but he could spot names in the gibberish. BB could do the rest. The AI was still lodged in Mal's radio, monitoring and occasionally passing a whispered comment via his earpiece. Most people here seemed to wear really old models that obviously still worked fine, so Mal didn't feel too conspicuous. If it hadn't been for the Kig-Yar and occasionally a Grunt or Brute wandering in, this could have been any bar on Earth in his granddad's day.

"We should get a pack of cards," Vaz said. "Or a chess set."

"Or play I Spy."

Mal hadn't had to make so much innocuous small talk with Vaz in years. They knew everything about each other by now and the stuff they really wanted to gossip about was off-limits in public, so it was a struggle. This spook business was a lot more tedious than it looked.

Never mind; all they had to do was wait for the next opportunity to get on board *Pious Inquisitor,* then hand it over to BB. It was slow but straightforward. The only complication was getting to the ship before whoever 'Telcam had sent to find it.

Mal lowered his chin to his chest and whispered, "How are you doing, BB?"

"Sorry, wasn't listening. I was just cracking an obscure Kig-Yar dialect unknown to humans. It's nothing. Only as groundbreaking as solving the translation of Linear B. You carry on discussing edible offal. I'm sure it's riveting."

"You're a cheeky little gobshite."

Vaz frowned at him. "Peasant."

"Not you. *Him.* Our favorite box of tricks."

"Oh."

A shadow fell across the frosted glass panels in the front doors, two figures silhouetted by the fading light outside. Staffan Sentzke and his son walked in. Mal should have been used to that face by now, but it had the same impact on him every time.

"Heads up, Vaz. Staffan and Edvin."

Staffan wandered up to the bar, taking in everything with a casual glance that Mal decided was anything but. Maybe that slight delay before he showed signs of recognizing them was a finely calculated response. This was Naomi's dad, after all: he might have been over seventy, but he was the raw material from which she was made, and he'd survived in an industry that wasn't known for its sentimentality. Mal couldn't afford to lose sight of that.

Vaz nodded acknowledgment at Staffan. "Here they come."

It was all perfectly normal. Two guys who knew two other guys decided to join them because they happened to run into each other in the same bar. New Tyne was small enough for them to cross the path of everyone in Staffan's circle in the course of a week, even if they didn't want to. Two marines still had a novelty value for the Sentzkes. Mal was determined to use it while it lasted.

"Chol," BB's voice said suddenly, right inside his ear, just as Staffan sat down. "It's Chol Von. 'Telcam's definitely hired Chol Von."

"I can't multitask, mate," Mal whispered. He hoped Staffan thought he was ending a conversation with Vaz. "How are you two doing today, then?"

"Oh, you know." Edvin shrugged. "It's like any business. Enforcing contracts. Dealing with faulty purchases."

Staffan helped himself to one of Mal's RHSUs and proved that even in the most forgotten and backward colonies, people still had their own teeth. He sounded as if he was crunching bone.

"The buzzard who sold me the ship," he said. "He's gone missing."

Oh. That's not good. Whatever the reason . . . that's trouble.

Vaz did the talking this time. "Because you're going to find the ship's got engine problems?"

"Well, if he's stiffed me, he knows escape would be a sensible precaution."

"Maybe his previous credit record with the Sangheili finally caught up with him."

"To the best of my knowledge, Vaz, no Sangheili has ever landed here. I'm not sure they've even noticed the place."

Mal pushed the bag of granite chips across the table to Staffan. "Well, the Kig-Yar have, and a secret's a secret until you tell someone else, isn't it?" A little deference never did any harm. Neither did a lie. "So your buzzard got nervous and skipped town. Doesn't mean anyone actually knows where he is."

Staffan looked at him for a few seconds too long, just the way Naomi often did. "I mean he was *kidnapped*. Signs of a struggle. Blood and feathers. Family abandoned. They don't abandon their nests, you see. The females hop from male to male, but the males generally stick around as long as they're tolerated. Mrs. Fel's squawking her head off about it, demanding that I help her find him."

"Are you making a connection between that and your business with him?" Vaz asked. "The way I see it, you're not his only customer. He deals in stolen goods. There'll probably be a ransom demand soon."

Staffan looked at Edvin for a moment and shrugged, as if he was inviting a comment on Fel's customer satisfaction rating. "I'd have thought that too—if I hadn't just done a substantial deal with him, and if there hadn't been an attempt to hack into the ship's systems shortly before he disappeared. You see, I'm very thorough when it comes to separating coincidence from cause and effect. I learned it looking for my little girl."

Mal couldn't look at Vaz. He wasn't sure what the normal reaction of an innocent person would be to that kind of news. Bewilderment was always a good option, and Staffan might even take it for embarrassment. Anything would do as long as it didn't look like guilt.

A sudden voice in his ear made him flinch. *"Chol Von."* Minus his avatar, BB could startle you like the voice of God out of nowhere telling you to stop that disgusting behavior *at once,* or your conscience, or delusional mutterings in your head. Mal kept forgetting the bugger was in his radio, listening and watching. "'Telcam's hired Chol Von to locate *Inquisitor.* And Chol Von is the nationalist who wants a united chicken navy. Shall I draw you a picture?"

BB distracted him completely. He hoped it just looked like he was a baffled marine. A theory formed in his head like a little trailer for a movie: *Fel hot-wires the ship, Chol tracks him down, he won't tell her where the ship is, and she beats it out of him. Oh shit. Well, as long as Staffan doesn't work out who tried to hack the system. If he doesn't get to keep a battlecruiser, then maybe we can all go home and leave him be.*

But Parangosky wanted that ship. Mal had his orders. "So you want us to help you find him."

"That'd be a start. Have you dealt with Kig-Yar much?"

"We've shot a few. Actually, quite a lot. But we're better with Sangheili. They're pretty consistent. If they'd found Fel or whatever his name is, they'd have left a bloody big smoking crater. No house, no wife, and no fluffy chicks."

Vaz nodded, impressively calm. He really did look like he hadn't any idea about that nasty hacking business. "Does Fel know where the ship is now? Any sane criminal would do a deal and let someone have the ship in exchange for not telling the Sangheili where he is."

"But they can't get in. Sinks will see to that. Complete lock-down."

Noted. Thanks for the warning. Mal hoped BB was relaying all this back to *Stanley,* and then maybe Phillips could intervene at the Sangheili end and pull some flanker on 'Telcam. Osman had the ship's position. Suddenly it didn't seem clear at all. The priority was to get the ship out of Staffan's hands, because even if he didn't use it, someone else on Venezia would. A lot of the factions from the insurgency had ended up here. But would it be a bigger loss to ONI? The data on board might be priceless, as would a working ventral beam, but stopping Venezia from using the ship against Earth had to be the top priority now. If 'Telcam got it back, they weren't any worse off than they'd been a few weeks ago.

But they want it all. Even the nice officers. They want you to do it all. Get the bad guy, bring the WMD back in one piece, and save the cat. Okay. That's our job. But screw the cat.

"If you think Fel can't resist a friendly question from his captors for long," Vaz said, "why don't we just go and move the ship? Okay, you still have a problem. You still have someone who can link the theft to this place, and you don't want a visit from the hinge-heads. But to keep the ship, you need to move her now. You want help? We're free."

Staffan chewed it over, unreadable. Edvin never said a bloody word, which rattled Mal almost as much as Staffan swinging between chatty sociability and expressionless ice. Vaz had seized a natural opportunity. Mal went with it.

"Okay, let's do that." Staffan nodded at Edvin. "Come on. We'll take my truck."

He got up and motioned to Mal and Vaz with a jerk of his head. It was starting to feel too easy. Mal tapped his fingernail against his radio, a warning to BB to stand by. Outside, it was a balmy night with insects clouding around the streetlights and the sound of chatter and laughter wafting from open doors. Edvin walked on ahead. Staffan hung back almost level with Mal, with Vaz slightly behind them. They'd fallen instantly into patrol mode. Beer and handshakes or not, this was behind enemy lines, and Mal was ready for an ambush.

He glanced over his shoulder at Vaz. He got a discreet nod back.

"I'm relaying all this," BB said. "Osman's tracking your position."

Once on board *Inquisitor,* Mal's priority was to find a port for BB to plug into. He had a compatible connector, courtesy of Adj. After that, though, he'd play it by ear. They might get off the ship again in one piece, with Staffan none the wiser until BB hijacked the ship later. Or it might end in a shoot-out. For the first time in years, he felt a moment of real panic.

"Relax," BB whispered. He could detect Mal's pulse rate. "You can take those two any time."

But ODSTs are expendable. Remember that? That's my bloody job. Christ, I've got a short memory. They drop us onto the battlefield and if we survive, it's a bonus. When did I start thinking I was special, that I had a right and expectation to come out of all this alive?

"So where did you park?" Mal asked.

Staffan turned around like a tail man, walking backward. "Next junction."

Mal heard a car behind them. He turned, pure reflex. Vaz turned too. It was a small delivery truck, lights dimmed, and it wasn't going particularly fast. Suddenly it was right behind Vaz, about ten meters away, moving at walking pace.

All Mal could do was grunt and hope BB read all the right

meanings into that. Of course he did. The AI was the cleverest thing in the universe, and sneaky with it. He'd be ready to flash Spenser a warning, bang out up the channel, and wipe the radio's memory behind him.

"Oh dear," BB said.

"Go. *Go.*"

Mal walked on, hand ready to draw his magnum. His earpiece went dead. BB had followed orders for a change. Had he left some tracking running in the radio? As Mal glanced back over his shoulder again, Vaz stopped and reached for his weapon, and that was when every muscle in Mal's body went haywire.

The pain was incredible. He couldn't breathe. He could hear himself making a strangled animal noise as he hit the concrete path. Normally he'd run through injuries like any marine, but he had no control over his body whatsoever and the paralyzing pain just kept coming. He'd been tasered once in training. He knew bloody well what had happened now. He should have been able to hear Vaz, but his own agonized howls drowned out everything. Then five or six blokes—he thought six, but he was in no position to count—pinned him down, put cuffs on him, and hauled him into the truck.

He knew it was the vehicle that had been following them because his face was pressed against the molded metal floor of the cargo space, and he could see Vaz facedown on the floor as well. The metal vibrated as the truck drove off.

Staffan's boots were level with his face. Now that Mal's eyes were adjusting to the light and his disorientation was ebbing, he noted that Staffan had come mob-handed to deal with them. There were seven, maybe eight men crammed into the space as well as Edvin.

"Sorry about that," Staffan said, squatting with one hand against the wall of the compartment to steady himself. "But I need you boys to tell me the truth. I'm really big on the truth, you see. I've been looking for it for thirty-five years."

UNSC REPAIR AND REFIT STATION ANCHOR 10, NEAR DRYAD

Naomi should have known that the arrival of a lone Pelican with no visible support from a ship would make Anchor 10's crew curious.

That was putting it mildly. Nobody had seen a Pelican with a slipspace drive before. As Devereaux maneuvered *Tart-Cart* into the hangar and the bay doors sealed, six civilian dock marshals emerged from alcoves and doors in the bulkheads to take a look. There was usually only one on duty per hangar.

"There was a time," Devereaux said, powering down the thrusters, "when guys would line up to look at me, not the ship. Ah well. Let's go impress on them the need for discretion."

Naomi put on her helmet and jumped down from the hatch behind Devereaux, motioning to Adj to stay inside for the moment. As soon as Devereaux walked up to the ladder, five of the marshals disappeared. The duty marshal slid down the ladder from the gantry and touched the peak of his hardhat.

"All monitors disabled, ma'am, and observation panels shuttered. As per ONI instructions. You know you're breaking about a dozen health and safety regulations by not having a hangar crew present, don't you?"

"I won't tell if you won't," Devereaux said. "Our Engineer's a little shy."

He glanced at the patches on her flight suit—the 10th Battalion ODST death's head, her pilot's brevet, and the all-seeing cyclops pyramid emblem of ONI. Even if you were a top secret unit, the rest of the Navy had to know you existed before they could fear you properly, or so Osman said. Naomi could see the logic in that.

Then the marshal looked up at her. "Damn," he said. "You're a Spartan, aren't you?"

"Either that, or I ate all my greens." Naomi knew all the right things to say most of the time, but she never felt she connected with people like Mal or Phillips did. "Yes, sir. I'm a Spartan."

He grinned and held his hand out for shaking. That took her aback. She found herself gripping it, trying not to squeeze too hard.

"You're bloody heroes, ma'am," he said. "Thank you. We wouldn't be here without you."

What could she say to that? She wasn't even sure it was true. She had an urge to take off her helmet so he could look her in the eye and see her for what she was, but she suspected that would ruin the moment for him. He needed to see the Spartan from the ONI public affairs posters, a mirrored visor that brooked no intrusion, no knowledge of the man or woman behind it, the invincible warrior untouched by petty human concerns like pain and fatigue. Spartans were icons. They didn't have fathers, uncertainties, or fears. They slew monsters.

But I was created to fight humans. People like my father. How's that for certainty?

"You're welcome," she said.

The marshal hesitated for a few seconds, then climbed back up to the gantry and dogged the hatch shut behind him. Five meters to *Tart-Cart*'s starboard side, hatch aligned with hatch, another Pelican sat awaiting Adj's rapid upgrade. Adj could work in peace now. Few personnel in the UNSC knew that ONI had acquired Huragok.

"You can come out now, Adj." Devereaux climbed into the crew bay to coax him out. "Nobody's watching. We'll give you a hand."

<I have no objection to being observed.> Adj drifted out and made a bee-line for the Calypso drive. *<I can do this without help. Occupy yourselves.>*

"You sound just like my uncle," she said. "He never liked anyone breathing down his neck while he worked."

Naomi had rarely heard Devereaux mention her family.

Nobody in Kilo-Five had one—all dead, estranged, or unknown—which was part of the selection criteria; they could disappear for long periods without explanation, without disruption to a wider domestic circle or distraction from the job in hand. There were no relatives to demand inquiries when the bad news reached them.

Except me. I now have a family. And I'm distracted, and I shouldn't be.

Naomi felt obliged to help Adj move the large drive parts. Huragok were much stronger than they looked, or else they wouldn't have been able to do the heavy maintenance work they'd been designed for, but she had power-assisted armor. It seemed churlish not to lend a hand. Adj was a natural-born foreman. He bossed her around in his quiet little artificial voice—put that there, don't touch that, hold this—and labored at a breakneck speed, more like a potter shaping clay on a wheel. He worked at the molecular level, remaking materials from the ground up with the fringes of tiny cilia on the ends of his tentacles.

Sometimes it looked as if he was melting the metal and composite and re-forming it, strengthening the Pelican's airframe to accommodate the weight of the drive and the extra stresses that slipspace acceleration would place on it. It wasn't the kind of metalworking that her father would have recognized.

Metalworker. I remembered Dad was a metalworker. Always building things. A mechanic, too. Did I really remember that? Or did I just remember it from the file?

There was no sawing or hammering. Apart from a clang of metal when Adj offered up a part to housing, all Naomi could hear was the occasional sigh, as if he wished he was somewhere else.

But he wasn't. He was a Huragok, designed and bred to love his task obsessively to the exclusion of all else.

Like me.

She hadn't thought about it much before, or if she had, she'd made herself stop. *Have I got free will? Has Adj? If I'm that in-doctrinated, that programmed, am I still human, or an organic machine like him?* Now she knew why she avoided the issue. Surrounded by other Spartans, her world and purpose was defined and reinforced daily. She had a destiny, a mission, a duty to save humanity, and Spartans were its only hope. Catherine Halsey had told them so. It was the one message that had dominated Naomi's life from the moment she arrived on Reach as a terrified, confused child who just wanted to go home to her parents.

Your mission is critical for the fate of all humanity.

Halsey had said it. She repeated it lots of different ways, from the simple explanation to a six-year-old child that they would stop people from killing each other, right through the years until her motivational speech when she declared that *you* Spartans—you—were all that stood between humanity and its extinction.

And if I didn't step up to the challenge, or if I didn't succeed, that extinction would be all my fault.

Naomi wasn't sure if Halsey or Chief Mendez had ever put it in those terms, but the subtext was painfully clear. For a moment, she was angry. The intensity of it caught her by surprise.

For the last few months, that reinforcement of unquestioning Spartan dedication hadn't been there, though. Osman was openly hostile to the SPARTAN-II program in ways that only a Spartan could be. Mal, Vaz, and Devereaux were highly disciplined and courageous to the point of being suicidal, but also cheerfully anarchic and cynical about the UNSC, as if they'd once been like her but were now a lot older and wiser, no longer buying into any of this noble mission stuff. Phillips was a civilian, and an academic, but absolutely nothing like Halsey: the culture he brought with him was oblique, with savage wars over the most trivial and abstract things, and he ridiculed it. And then there was BB. BB was the essence of iconoclasm, not just thinking the unthinkable but saying it loudly.

Kilo-Five was subversive. They were subverting her, too. Humans could be indoctrinated until some habits stayed with them for life, but they normed as well. They behaved like the humans around them. Naomi knew all that. Experiencing it was very different. Kilo-Five was eroding her, wearing away the rock to reveal layers she'd never known were buried.

"I've got to go collect a parcel," Devereaux said, snapping Naomi out of her thoughts. "You want to come along? Explore the station?"

Naomi really didn't feel like it. "What parcel?"

"Candied ginger. From Parangosky. For Osman's nausea."

"Why doesn't she just get medication for that?"

"What would you rather receive from your boss? A memo with a prescription, or a fancy gift box with a nice bow on it?"

The psychology of it intrigued Naomi. There was a strong streak of penance in there somewhere, Parangosky's need for forgiveness from Osman or maybe all the Spartan-IIs. Naomi sometimes wondered if that had influenced the recruitment of Kilo-Five, too. They were all very off-message, not ideologues at all. Either Parangosky thought that dissenting voices were healthier for the organization, or she was quietly sticking pins in ONI to make herself feel better about what she'd let it become.

It got the job done. That was all that mattered. Halsey had said so.

"Okay, I'll come with you," Naomi said. It was purely to be sociable to Devereaux. "Adj is okay. BB can keep an eye on him. If anyone tries to breach security, he'll fry them."

BB had been abnormally quiet on the transit. Now his voice filled her helmet. "Can I come too? Don't leave me here alone with Adj."

"You're *always* with Adj. And everyone else. You're always *everywhere* in some form or another."

"Oh, go on. Plug me into your neural interface. Please please please please *please*."

"But you'll leave a fragment in *Tart-Cart,* right?"

"Oh, of course. But . . . please. Don't make me beg. You're going to need me plugged in for the flight home anyway."

When BB was downloaded to a chip and inserted in her interface, he linked directly to her brain. He saw and felt what she did exactly the way that she experienced it, not through a range of sensors. He could also beef up her responses so that she was temporarily even faster and stronger, as well as providing her with data and direction. She'd plugged him in once for an opposed ship boarding—naval understatementese for fighting your way into an enemy vessel—and it had felt a little like being a horse with a jockey. BB hadn't manipulated her brain in any way, but she'd still had a sense of being . . . being . . . no, she didn't have a word for it. Not *ridden* or *steered*: just under a close scrutiny that was almost sentimental, like someone holding her hand in a dark and dangerous place.

BB had enjoyed the outing, though. For all his bitchy comments about his fellow AIs being *wannabe humans* because they all chose avatars that looked like people, he definitely got something out of experiencing the world as flesh and blood.

"Okay, then, mount up." Naomi climbed back into the cockpit and removed the chip from the console. Now that her interface had been filed down by Adj, it was easier to put the chip in the helmet first and then press it home by pulling her helmet down hard on her head. "So how many fragments have you got on the prowl at the moment? You know what happened last time you overstretched yourself."

She felt him merge with her. It was an odd sensation, like shutting yourself in a closet with someone, muffled and stifling, and then slightly embarrassing. *Did I ever do that?* And she was sure that she could feel something of his state of mind. No wonder he made all those snarky remarks about Cortana.

Poor John. I thought he'd survive us all.

"I'm *never* overstretched, dear." BB's voice wasn't outside, like the helmet audio. It was both silent and in her head, almost a thought she wasn't thinking for herself. "It's just fairer on the world to share myself with as many people as possible. Let's see . . . I'm in *Port Stanley,* and I'm in Bravo-Six giving that ghastly harpy Harriet the runaround, and I'm *sort of* in a number of remotes stationed off Sanghelios and Venezia . . . oh, and Mal's radio. That's why I've been quiet. We're in a pub. He's telling Vaz all about the utterly *disgusting* local recipes from his home area. I don't know if he uses a cookbook or a copy of *Gray's Anatomy,* to be honest."

Naomi strode across the hangar deck and followed Devereaux up to the gantry. They passed through a security door and then a blast barrier. "Can I listen in?"

"Do you want to? Heart, liver . . . and . . . oh my god, *peritoneal fat membranes.*"

"Cooked?"

"Are you talking to yourself, Naomi?" Devereaux asked.

"BB's relaying Mal's recipes. The ones with all the minced organs."

Devereaux laughed. "If you think a French-Chinese Canadian's squeamish about *any* food, think again." They were on the main admin deck of Core 3 now, getting looks from everyone. It was hard to tell what got the crew's attention, a Spartan in full rig or pilot with both an ODST and ONI patch. "My father loved *tripes à la mode de Caen.* Mom liked it steamed with garlic sauce and spring onions. Have you ever tried it?"

"Not even Spartans are willing to take on tripe."

BB did a wonderfully theatrical intake of horrified breath. "Oh dear. I've just accessed the culinary database. They make Mal's favorite dish out of *testicles,* too. Oh, so many jokes, so little time."

"Fine. I'm going to have a cheese sandwich." Naomi could actually feel BB's sheer delight at whatever was going on in the bar. He'd probably hiked her dopamine without meaning to. "*Soya* cheese."

"There's nothing I can't eat," Devereaux said.

"Then you haven't tried *surströmming*. You need Viking blood to—"

Where the hell did that come from?

Naomi almost stopped in her tracks. She could smell that awful, pungent, eye-watering, fermented herring. The memory was vivid, instant, and gone again. She shook herself and carried on walking, unsure whether to pursue the memory or let it sink without trace.

"Your heart rate's jumped," BB said. "Adrenaline's up, too. What's wrong? Do you remember that from your childhood?"

It didn't happen often. She knew why, at least in neurological terms. *Infantile amnesia caused by neurogenesis.* The more you learned as a very young child, the more new neurons formed in the hippocampus, and the more long-term memory was displaced. Kids generally forgot most of the first four or five years of their lives. There was only so much storage space in the human memory. And Spartan kids had learned an awful lot right at the end of that period.

And that's without all the cognitive enhancement they gave us.

"Probably," she said, trying to pass it off as irrelevant. But it was hard to lie when BB was monitoring her brain chemistry and physical responses. "Decomposing herring must rank as a significant childhood trauma."

As soon as she said it, she felt something pop in her brain again. It was precisely that—a physical sensation like a small bubble bursting. There was a certain irony to forgetting that you'd forgotten. Her memories began to take on a more permanent form around the age of six, a few hazy nightmares of loneliness, fear, and pain followed by patchy recall far better than an ordinary human's, but still frustratingly incomplete at times.

"This is great training for having kids," Devereaux said. "You're talking to your imaginary friend again."

"Oops—spike," BB muttered. "Would you like me to turn that adrenaline down?"

Naomi couldn't even identify the emotion that had suddenly made her scalp crawl. It had something to do with children. She wasn't even going to try to guess. "I'll be okay, BB. Let's get on with it."

Devereaux went into the UNSC Fleet Mail office while Naomi waited outside, arms folded across her chest while she read the notices on the bulkhead. They were a window to a world she'd never seen. They exhorted personnel to WRAP IT RIGHT OR LOSE IT, because badly packed parcels sent to loved ones back home got damaged or lost, or to MAKE SURE IT'S DAC-FREE, listing dangerous air cargo and banned materials that families were prohibited from sending in gift packages, or that UNSC personnel couldn't ship home, like trophy weapons or alien plants and animals. Naomi smiled to herself as she thought of Phillips and his plasma pistol, now displayed in *Stanley*'s wardroom behind the bar. The list of average transit and delivery times—Earth to colonies, Earth to deployed ships, base to base, ship to ship, and all permutations thereof—carried warnings about perishable and urgent items.

All these people out there, worrying and caring and thinking about someone. All their friends and families. All the shared anxiety. What must it be like when they get home after a long deployment?

Naomi had heard about homecomings over the years and seen calendars on cabin bulkheads counting down the days to the end of a tour of duty, called *chuff charts* for reasons she had yet to discover. It was a strange and exotic thing to a Spartan. She was lost in thought when BB said, "Stand by, Naomi—problem."

Problem jerked her back to the here and now.

"What is it, BB? Come on."

He was silent for nearly thirty seconds. That was hours—even days—for an AI. She could feel the urgency flood her. She couldn't tell if it was simply her response to what he said or if his connection to her brain had mirrored his emergency reaction in her neurochemistry.

"Mal and Vaz have been compromised," he said suddenly. "I've had to sever contact with them."

"How compromised?"

"I'd make a guess that your father and his associates have taken them for interrogation. The last thing I saw was what looked like the beginning of an ambush, then Mal told me to ex-fil. I've alerted Spenser. He's clearing his comms room and making a run for it."

My father. My comrades.

And *Tart-Cart* was here. Who the hell was going to rescue them? Naomi strode into the office and found Devereaux. "Got to go," she said. "Mal and Vaz are in trouble."

Devereaux grabbed the parcel off the counter. The clerk frowned at her and tapped his screen angrily. "Form eight-three-alpha," he said. "You've got to complete it."

Devereaux tapped the patch on her arm. "ONI," she said. "*We* decide what forms we fill in."

They sprinted back to the hangar. Anchor 10 wasn't as busy as it had been at the height of the war, but it was still a slalom course of bodies to dodge and weave through.

"BB, tell Adj to drop what he's doing and prep *Tart-Cart* for a fast exit," Devereaux said. "We'll come back for the spare later."

BB paused. Naomi heard him rather than felt his response this time. He was using her helmet audio.

"Adj says he'll be finished in eight minutes and that you need two gunships if you're going to extract from multiple locations."

Naomi gave up waiting for the elevator and crashed through the doors to the ladders. "So he's tactical now, is he?"

"He's right."

"I'm sorry, Dev," Naomi said. It was a reflex. She felt personally responsible. If Earth had fallen to the Covenant, it would have been her fault, nobody else's, despite a UNSC force of several million personnel. Now her father had apparently seized two of her friends, and she wasn't there to deal with it right away. "Sorry."

"Why?" They had just one deck to go. "We had to pick up the Pelican sooner or later, and now's the time we need it."

"It's my dad. It looks like my dad ambushed them."

"Jesus, Naomi, that's not your fault."

If only I hadn't . . . hadn't . . .

Hadn't what?

She'd done something thirty-five years ago, and if she hadn't done it, then she wouldn't have been abducted by Halsey's snatch squad. But she couldn't recall what it was. She only knew that it had been a stupid thing to do, and that something else had happened that had left her feeling terrible for a long time. Adj scooted out of her way as she ran across the hangar deck and scrambled into the Pelican's cockpit.

It had been some time since she'd flown anything, let alone a gunship. And the paint wasn't even dry on this one. She put her faith in Huragok obsession and BB's skills.

"Your heart rate's one-eighty," BB said. "They'll be fine. Phillips survived, didn't he? And bless him, he's very keen and gutsy, but he's not an ODST."

"Liaise with the dockmaster, BB." Naomi scanned the instruments, checking pressures and status readings. It all came back to her, possibly with extra help from BB. She felt that little pop again somewhere deep in her brain. "Dev? Ready?"

"Follow me out," Devereaux said. "Show her, BB."

"Course laid in."

Naomi took a breath and activated the maneuvering thrusters. The outer doors peeled back and the Pelican was free of Anchor 10, powering up to reach the minimum safe distance before jumping to slip.

Eight thousand . . . nine thousand . . . ten thousand . . .

"It's just a glorified heavily armed bus, dear." BB was putting a brave face on it, and it showed. No, she could *feel* it. It translated into a hollow in the pit of her stomach. It wasn't like pre-mission nerves at all, but something much more profound and disturbing. "Piece of cake. Safe point acquired . . . spooled up . . . and *hit it.*"

Naomi pressed the paired controls hard forward, listening to the rising whine jump off the scale as the stars vanished from the viewscreen. It could have been a simple switch or button, but it was harder to activate two slides by accident. Adj really did do miracles. Now it was her turn.

Yes, she was personally responsible for Mal and Vaz. Without her, there would be no angry Staffan Sentzke. And without Staffan Sentzke, Venezia might not have had a battlecruiser. She was back on Reach again, digesting the reality of being all that stood between victory and annihilation, and wondering when someone was coming to save *her.*

It was a lot for a six-year-old to swallow.

I HAVE NOT HEARD FROM YOU IN SOME DAYS. WHERE ARE
YOU? MORE TO THE POINT—WHERE IS MY SHIP? DO I HAVE
TO COME AND HUNT YOU DOWN AS WELL?
—SIGNAL FROM AVU MED 'TELCAM TO KIG-YAR VESSEL,
INTERCEPTED BY EVAN PHILLIPS

**STUTTGART ARMORY, NEW TYNE: THREE HOURS AFTER THE
DISAPPEARANCE OF VASILY BELOI AND MALCOLM GEFFEN**

It was a lot easier being captured by the Covenant.

Vaz waited for the door to slam shut, then spat the blood out
of his mouth. He had no idea where he was, and—worse—he
didn't know what they'd done with Mal. He listened, eyes shut,
but he couldn't hear a thing.

If this had been a Sangheili cell, his choices would have been
simple and limited. The Sangheili wouldn't have captured him
to check his credentials and let him go; they wouldn't have taken
him hostage for a prisoner swap; and they wouldn't have held
him as a prisoner of war in accordance with international laws
on the humane treatment of enemy combatants. If they took
him—and they generally didn't bother with prisoners—then he
was already dead. The only question was how long it would
take and how much it would hurt. As the outcome was a fore-
gone conclusion, the sane thing was to do something that would
get you killed immediately—fight back, fling yourself off a
ledge, or make a suicidal run for it, knowing they'd cut you

down in seconds. It was worth trying *anything* to get it over
with.

There was always the chance that your buddies would manage to rescue you. But the hinge-heads would only keep you
alive to ask you questions, so if there was likely to be more than
half an hour's delay before you were extracted, death was probably the better option.

Vaz's best guess was that he was being held in a warehouse
or weapons store. When they'd bundled him out of the truck
with Mal, the vehicle was already in a hangar. But when they
were frog-marched through the passages, Vaz spotted the kind of
blast doors usually installed in munitions depots. There were the
familiar smells of a military establishment—fuel, lube oil, soap,
sweat—but he drew more clues from the fact that there were so
many lockable doors and yet it didn't look like a prison. The other
buildings where security would be paramount had to be defense-
related, like the barracks, a computer center, or somewhere full
of stuff that needed controlling even in a town where illegal possession and use of firearms was probably an essential qualifica-
tion to be let in.

An armory. He was pretty sure that he was in an armory or
munitions store.

Right now all he knew for certain was that he was in a small,
dimly lit room with no windows—not shuttered, just absent, so
maybe a basement—and tied to a metal-framed chair in the center
of a painted concrete floor. There was no grimy, fly-spattered
lightbulb hanging from a single cable from the ceiling, just a single
overhead strip, the kind they used in offices. On the surface, there
was nothing remotely intimidating about it, like most of New Tyne.

Where's Mal?

Nairn had taken Vaz's jacket, magnum, and the contents of
his pockets. They were probably going through his wallet and
radio chip.

What are they going to do to me next?

He took slow, deep breaths and tried to recall everything he'd been taught about resisting interrogation. ODSTs worked behind enemy lines; interrogation training had been routine since the colonial wars. It hurt more than he ever thought possible, but he knew that the instructors didn't want to do him permanent damage or kill him, and that they'd stop if things got out of hand. He didn't have that reassurance now.

Fear of what's coming next. That's what they rely on. So accept the fear and get on with it.

But maybe this wasn't real at all.

It was hard to tell if Staffan's circle knew they'd been infiltrated, or if this was part of the usual security clearance to test newcomers who might need to be trusted with serious assets like battlecruisers. Until Vaz could work that out, he didn't know whether to try to escape or keep up his cover story. If he guessed wrong and made a run for it only to find they were just checking him out the hard way, putting him through a very real exercise for a war they felt was coming sooner or later, then he'd blown the whole mission.

If ONI issued suicide pills, would I even know when to take the damn thing? When do you decide you've had enough if you think you can still talk your way out?

And Mal. Where's Mal?

There was nothing Vaz could do at that moment other than wait and observe. He looked around the room as far as he could by craning his neck, then tried shuffling the chair around to check behind him. There was a stack of identical metal framed chairs standing against the wall, very old with faded canvas seats, and a filing cabinet. He couldn't see any sign that this was used regularly as a holding cell. He inhaled to test the air again and picked up only the musty scent of a room that wasn't used or aired. There was no smell of sweat or urine.

Vaz could have constructed a hundred scenarios to explain everything he saw and didn't see as a positive sign or a negative one. He had to stop this. He needed to concentrate on the physical here and now, to look for unlocked doors and guards who weren't paying attention.

Keep your mind occupied. Don't do their job for them by imagining the worst.

And Mal. He's here somewhere. I've got to find him.

Did Spenser get away?

Vaz shut his eyes again to listen. He almost expected to hear muffled screaming. But there was just the occasional creak of footsteps on a floor somewhere above him and the thump of a door closing a long way away.

BB knows where we were when they grabbed us. Can he track the radios? Osman's going to come for us. It's not like trying to find us on Earth or Reach.

Vaz started to feel the need to pee. He tried to take his mind off it by counting seconds so that he had some idea of how long he'd been here, and then he heard footsteps coming down a flight of stairs. The door rattled, unlocked from the outside, and swung open. Staffan and Nairn walked in and stood looking at him.

What did he say? What did someone wrongly accused say? What did he say when nobody had actually accused him of anything yet?

"Hi, Vaz." Staffan walked behind Vaz and the metal chairs clattered. He put one in front of him and sat down. "Believe me, I'm not fond of theatrics. But we do need to talk."

Nairn stood to one side of Staffan. Then he took three steps up to Vaz and hit him in the face, without threat, warning, or explanation.

The force of it blinded Vaz for a couple of seconds. Christ, it *hurt*. The chair rocked. He'd been hit in brawls before, and been hit a lot harder. But it was one thing to be pumped up on adrenaline and trading punches, and quite another to sit there and take a blow in the face.

Well, that was one thing out of the way, then. This *was* going to be violent. Somehow it was marginally less frightening than waiting to be hit. He stopped himself thinking how it would escalate. And he simply stopped thinking of the man sitting in front of him as Naomi's father. It just happened. This was simply the guy who might kill him, or worse.

"I don't imagine you scare easily," Staffan said. "Whoever you are."

"Where's Mal?" Vaz asked. "What's all this shit about?"

"I've just been chatting to him. He's not dead yet, if that's what you're asking."

Staffan went quiet and just looked at him. They sat staring at each other for a very long time. Vaz counted at least thirty-five seconds. He knew he wasn't doing this right, but he still didn't know if this was a test.

"Who are you working for, kid?" Staffan asked. "No bullshit, please."

Don't try to be clever. Don't engage. Don't . . . No, that was for a different kind of captor. Staffan obviously still had doubts. Vaz just went with his gut.

"You think I'm from some gang? Some business rival?"

"I don't know for sure," Staffan said. "But you're not right. You and Mal. There's something not quite right about you two. I've got a good instinct for that kind of thing."

Halsey's substitute for Naomi hadn't fooled him, either. This was a man who saw what he saw, not what he expected to see. Vaz suspected he didn't fall for card tricks.

"I don't work for any gang."

"What did you do with Fel?"

"I don't even know Fel. I haven't touched him. I don't even know where he lives."

"Well, you're definitely a marine—or some kind of military professional. But that's all I'm sure about."

"Yeah. I told you the truth."

"Why did you come here?"

"So the UNSC couldn't find me."

"How long have you been in?"

"Eight years, in all." Vaz would have stuck to name, rank, and number if he hadn't still been trying to look like a real deserter with nothing to hide—not from Venezia, at least. "Nearly nine."

"How'd you get the scar?"

"Hand to hand with a hinge-head."

"Nairn's going to have to try a lot harder, then."

"Depends what you want to hear."

Staffan fished in his pockets and took out Vaz's radio, wallet, and a few odds and ends. There was an art to assembling the right "pocket litter," the bits that everyone collected without thinking and that provided a lot of information about identity. The carefully chosen contents of Vaz's pockets were the obviously forged plastic ID chip, colonial credit bills, a suitably dated PX receipt from Diego Garcia, and his Warthog key. Nairn wandered around the room, arms folded, looking down at the floor. Staffan held up his radio.

"You don't store many codes. None, in fact. Completely purged."

Vaz shrugged as best he could. He really needed to pee. "It's UNSC property. If I get caught, I don't want my buddies traced, do I?"

"Is your name really Vaz Desny?"

Think like a deserter. "Who'd desert and use their real name?"

"You realize," Staffan said, "that if I was testing you to see if you were any goddamn use to us as an operative, you'd have failed by now? Didn't the Corps ever teach you to keep your mouth shut? I think they did. So you're playing a game with me, and I don't appreciate it."

Vaz was waiting for the next punch from Nairn. Staffan probably didn't have anything concrete, but he didn't need it. Suspicion was enough here. In his position, Vaz would have done the same.

"Why did you try to hack into the ship?" Staffan leaned a little closer. "This is my problem, you see. You show up with some impressive skills just when we need them. I invite you to check over my ship, and the next thing I know is that someone tries to hack in and my supplier's kidnapped. Probably dead. If this was a big city on Earth, I'd buy statistical chances. But this is a small town in a wilderness on a ball of rock at the ass-end of the galaxy. Are you with me so far?"

"Why do we need Fel if you've already taken us to the ship? Why do we need to hack in when we could have done it from *inside* the ship?"

"Or . . . I'm wondering if you didn't desert. That you're still on the UNSC payroll. Checking us out."

"You think the UNSC would send in two grunts when they could simply show up with a small fleet and trash New Tyne?"

"True. They nuked Far Isle just to stop a few rebels, after all. No squeamishness about collateral damage there." Staffan looked up at the light fitting for a few moments. "Anyway, maybe there's more than two of you. It's hard to seal the borders on a planet like this, but we're pretty good at what we do. There's quite a few people here who remember how you guys operated in the old days."

Staffan just looked at him as if he could absorb information from Vaz's brain simply by staring. Then he stood up and jerked his head at Nairn. Vaz thought he was calling him to heel, but Nairn moved in as Staffan opened the door.

"I'm going to find Gareth. Talk to Vaz. Ask him about the woman." Staffan glanced back at Vaz. "I might just hand you over to the Kig-Yar and tell them you took Fel. I bet you know more about what Kig-Yar do to prisoners than I do."

Nairn shut the door. The worst guys weren't the ones who looked like psychos, but professionals who just did it out of necessity.

"Nothing personal, Vaz," he said.

He pushed the chair over and Vaz crashed onto his side. That hurt like hell, too. He hit his head on the concrete. Then he got a kick in the face. At least Nairn hadn't gone straight for a knife or bolt cutters or anything. But the next kick was right on the shin, and that was off the scale. He shrieked.

It was hard to kick the shit out of someone when they were already doubled up in a sitting position, but Nairn managed to make the most of it. All Vaz could think about was when it was going to stop. Then he concentrated on the pain building in his bladder, which was actually worse. He was going to piss his pants. He found himself debating whether to hang on because it kept his mind diverted enough from the pain of being kicked, or to let go and focus on one set of pain at a time.

In the end, his body made the decision for him. For a moment, a brief moment worth grabbing, it was almost bliss. There was no relief quite like emptying your bladder. So the room *was* going to smell like a cell from now on. *Fine.* It felt like a small victory. He hadn't peed himself out of fear, but from too many beers, so that was okay.

"I'm glad you understand the seriousness of your situation," Nairn said. He sounded out of breath. "I ought to use you to mop that up, you filthy bastard. So where's the woman?"

"Ram it up your ass." Vaz sounded coherent to himself. "Told you. She left. Didn't like the place."

"And Mike? Where did Mike go?"

"Christ knows. No frigging idea."

Nairn sounded as if he'd sighed, as if he regarded this as a tedious job and that he wanted it over with. Vaz found he wasn't embarrassed to yell his head off. It helped. But once he decided he was going to die, then—instantly—things became simple: he wasn't going to tell Nairn anything because that would mean that he'd wasted his time dying. He wanted to thwart the bastard. Nairn could go screw himself if he thought he was getting an answer out of him, even today's date. Vaz focused on beating him. Every time he didn't tell Nairn anything, he scored a point. The longer it went on, the more he felt he had to hang on to his score. Maybe he'd hit his head harder than he thought. The pain shifted suddenly from real, screaming, unbearable pain to an awareness of damage, still pain but somehow happening on a different level.

That wasn't a good sign, though. He remembered that much.

No wonder Nairn had opted for kicking him. He didn't want to damage his hands. Punching someone repeatedly made a mess of your knuckles and hurt the joints. But he wasn't trying hard, because if he was, he wouldn't have left Vaz tied to the chair—a crappy position to land a kick, no use at all—and he wasn't aiming for his head now. He didn't want Vaz dead, then, not yet.

Why am I thinking all this shit?

Because I can. Look at me. I haven't told him anything. But it won't save me if I do.

Where's Mal?

Vaz could have said anything to get some respite, but then it'd just start again. As long as he kept thinking, *thinking*, thinking about anything, he kept enough of a barrier between the pain and his mind to stop himself from breaking.

This is okay. Really, it is. No blades, no cattle prods, no plastic bags, nothing weird.

This asshole wouldn't last five minutes in St. Petersburg. Really.

Nairn paused to get his breath and squatted to peer at him. Vaz found himself straining to see where the puddle of urine had spread. There was no carpet to absorb it. He hoped the floor was perfectly level and that it wasn't creeping toward his head.

"Personally, I didn't think she looked like Staffan at all," Nairn said. "But Gareth always says stuff like that. Staffan's probably more pissed off with him than he is with you. You know. The business about his daughter."

It was a card to play, but Vaz had no idea if it was going to save him or kill him. *Naomi.* In an ideal world, Vaz would reveal that she was alive and well, Staffan would weep with joy, and then he'd renounce his insurgent ways. A happy family reunion would follow. But that was never going to happen. And Vaz's sole purpose now was to remove that battlecruiser from insurgent hands.

Which I can't do unless I survive.

His brain was now doing some really weird shit. For a moment, he knew what it was to be BB, with fragments busy everywhere, little mirrored versions of himself each doing different things yet all aware of each other and making sense both individually and as a whole. One piece of Vaz was hanging on to the inevitability of death, because that meant not telling Nairn a damn thing was a final, satisfying, soul-preserving spit in his eye. Another part was saying that it was all very well, but completely pointless, because he had to get out of here to take down *Pious Inquisitor.* Yet another slice of him was busy being aware of how much damage had been done to his body without registering the pain, another was scared, five years old, and wanted his *babushka* to make it all better, and another was waiting for the first chance to get loose and gouge Nairn's eyes out.

If nothing else, I have to get Mal out of here. Yeah. Focus on that.

It wasn't what he'd been trained to do, which was to complete the mission regardless. But what held an army together was the instinct to fight for your buddies. ONI knew where the ship was. They could save Earth by just blowing up the goddamn thing.

They didn't *need* it in one piece. They didn't need it as much as they needed Mal.

Mal. Sorry, Admiral. Mal comes first.

"You believe the story. His daughter."

Nairn frowned. "Speak up."

Vaz thought he sounded normal. *Am I mumbling, then?* "His daughter. Naomi. He thinks she was kidnapped by the government. Replaced by a clone."

"If it gets him through the day to think that, fine by me."

"You think he's crazy."

"Grieving. He's just *grieving*." No, that sounded like *crazy* to Vaz. And that was what he needed. Now he had a wedge to drive between Staffan and his cronies. It was all he had, and he'd use it. "Did he tell you about the double, then? Because normally, he leaves that bit out." Nairn's frown had vanished. He looked completely wide-eyed for a moment, as if a lightbulb had switched on over his head. "He stopped telling people that years ago. Least of all complete strangers. And personally, I've never heard him say *clone*."

Vaz had the feeling he'd slipped up. Had Staffan mentioned that? Shit, he couldn't remember.

No, he hadn't. These people watched detail like that. He used to, once, but he was dazed, in pain, and just a little crazy himself.

And soaked in piss. Not my finest hour.

"I think Staffan needs another chat with you," Nairn said.

Vaz had just one shot at this. "Mal," he said. "I want to see Mal. Let me see he's all right. Let him go, and I'll talk to Staffan all he wants."

Vaz watched Nairn's boots as the man walked out and slammed the door behind him. He wasn't sure if he'd simply caved in like a coward after a moderate to serious kicking—no ruptured organs as far as he could tell, no excuse for weakness—or if he'd taken a daring gamble and grabbed what few advantages he had left to save his best friend and maybe complete the mission.

He'd find out soon enough.

The pool of pee was spreading away from his face. At least that was something to feel positive about.

INDEPENDENT KIG-YAR SHIP *PARAGON*, SOMEWHERE OFF VENEZIA

"I don't want your fee for this, Fel, whatever it is," Chol said. "Keep it. Use it to hide from your four-jaw friends. But I *will* have the warship. Where is it?"

Fel fixed her with a defiant yellow eye, head tilted away from her. "What about my chicks? My mate? My customer will kill them."

"If you don't tell me," she said, "then *I'll* kill them. Because I know exactly where they are, and 'Telcam doesn't seem to know that Venezia even exists."

She let him think about that. He sat in the middle of the hangar deck, well away from any sharp objects or access to comms. He was missing a few feathers and a little bruised, but that was because he'd struggled when they'd seized him and needed restraining. She preferred to get results by offering a choice. Torture and violence were a hobby for the humans, a substitute for intelligent questions for the short-tempered four-jaws, but a last resort from a Kig-Yar. It often yielded unreliable information.

"What have I ever done to you, cousin?" Fel asked.

"I never said this was personal."

"You're the one who preaches a united Kig-Yar to defend our kind against the savages."

"And I need a ship to begin that process. Where is it?"

"He might have moved it by now."

"Then tell me the last coordinates you were at."

"He'll kill me. He's very clever. He's also very patient. He can wait years to put a knife through your back."

"Tell me his name, then." *In case a rival locates him and uses him to get to the ship. I'm so close now. I can smell it.* "Who is he? What does he want a battlecruiser for? The humans now have more of a navy than the Covenant. This is a warlord with scores to settle, by the sound of it. Tell him he'll achieve a great deal more by small bites from many angles than he ever will by one great act of destruction."

"Before or after he slices my head off? Flat-faces talk about *eating* us, you know. We're just large food animals to them. *Chi-kens.* And stuffing. I have had threats of being *stuffed.* Which involves *disemboweling.*"

"Fel, you might well be more afraid of your customers, but they're not here. I am."

It was bad form to treat a fellow T'vaoan like that in front of common Kig-Yar, but this was about her dominance almost as much as finding *Pious Inquisitor.* If she could do this to one of her own ethnic group, then she could exact far worse revenge on a wayward crew or anyone who tried to cheat her. But Fel had appearances to keep up as well. This was going to be slow.

And 'Telcam was getting impatient. He'd send another search party when he could afford one, and then he'd add her to his vengeance list as well. But she had Fel. That was her best treasure map to *Inquisitor.* The ideal one was a human, but that might have been one step too far even for her.

"Just tell me this," Fel said. "*If* I tell you where the ship is, on account of it being no use to me and having been paid, what do I do after that? Do I go home? How will my customer *not* know I was responsible?"

"Do you care nothing for the security of all Kig-Yar?"

"I care for continuing to breathe, along with all my clan."

"There's no better time to do this. We take advantage of the four-jaws squabbling among themselves with their Prophet masters gone. We arm ourselves to make sure they don't come back and think they can swallow us up again. They were part of the High Council, Fel. You all forget that too soon. They weren't drudges like us. *They made the decisions with the San'Shyuum.* They'll want to make them again one day."

Fel was still looking at her with one eye. "Lovely manifesto. I don't disagree with a word of it. But I'm still the one who'll have to pay for this." He turned to face her full-on and dipped his head as if he was sharing gossip with her. "Give me a way to let you have this information without looking responsible for it, and you can have the location *and* the entry codes."

Did his human customer even know Fel was missing yet? Chol thought that through for two seconds before deciding that the rest of the Kig-Yar community on Venezia would know, and so would whoever Fel was due to meet that evening, and his human customer did business with Kig-Yar. He would get to hear sooner or later. Even if she dusted Fel down and took him home, the deed was done.

"How about *half* a lie?" she asked. "They work better than complete ones. We say that 'Telcam managed to track the ship by some devious technological device, because humans will believe any nonsense like that, and sent us to find you while he decided how best to reclaim his ship. You managed to escape. You end up back on Venezia and raise the alarm . . . once we've gone."

"How did I escape?"

"You bribed one of my crew."

Fel nodded. "Ah. Good."

"I expect you to do just that. I hope you have gezk to pay for it. Tokens. More credible as a bribe."

"Outrageous."

"Better than dead. Who is this human, anyway? What does he want a battlecruiser for?"

Fel poked around in his vest pockets for tokens. "To glass other humans."

"I realize that. They're always at war. I meant specifically."

"I have no idea, other than that he understands that glassing customers is counterproductive. Anyway, if the humans resume their civil wars, we have a new market."

Fel handed over the gezk. All in all, Chol felt it was a good outcome, a deal that met the needs of both sides. A one-sided deal forced on someone simply bred resentment and a festering urge for revenge. It was rarely a victory.

"So you'll return me now?"

"First let's see that the ship is where you say it is."

Fel didn't look troubled at all now. "Very well."

Chol went back to the bridge and wondered whether to contact her roost to make sure that her mother was taking care of the children. But it was probably safer to keep signals to an essential minimum, just in case 'Telcam was smarter than she gave him credit for. The ship jumped to slipspace for a very short transit, hardly worth the strain on *Paragon*'s drives, and then the detailed navigation began. Bakz and Nulm were playing a round of *shaks* by the doors, ready to step in if Fel needed physical encouragement to behave himself. He seemed very relaxed, though. He obviously expected to find *Inquisitor* where he'd left her. The human should have thought that through a little better if he knew Fel that well.

So *he* might have moved the ship, whoever *he* was. If the ship wasn't where Fel said it was, then she would become much more insistent.

Suddenly Skal, the navigator, got very excited.

"Found her," he said. "There she is. Shall we let 'Telcam know?"

Fel gave Chol a sly look. She hadn't told him that her crew weren't fully briefed on her intentions.

"No, absolutely not," she said. "Now we board her."

"But we've *found* her, mistress," Zim said. "We let 'Telcam know, and we get paid. That's all we agreed to do."

"*No.* I want absolute secrecy on this. *I'm* paying you. Not him." Chol loomed over him, then stalked around the bridge with her hand on her holster to make her point. "Not one word. Not even a call home to say you're due back. Comms are now locked down. See to it, Bakz."

There were a dozen crew on the bridge now, all looking puzzled and impatient. Skal opened his mouth to say something but shut it again when she glared at him.

"What, you have pressing deadlines?" she demanded. "You have music recitals to attend? A meeting with your bankers?"

"Mistress, we just want to know why the plans have changed," Zim said, head lowered slightly in a submissive gesture. "Are you going to up the price on the four-jaws? That's very risky."

"My plans haven't changed. I just never revealed them to you, for operational reasons."

It was a very human phrase. She was picking up a lot of those. Humans were brilliantly dishonest, so convoluted and sly that even a Kig-Yar could learn tactics from them. They'd stolen hundreds of worlds across the galaxy, after all, with no thought for the life-forms already living there. It was admirable in its way. State piracy was condoned while individual enterprise was suppressed, though, so if they wanted to survive as long as the Kig-Yar as a galactic presence then they'd have to rethink that strategy.

"What might those be?" Zim asked.

"I'm going to take the ship. There's no crew on board, so all we have to do is dock and stroll in."

"But—"

"You'll be paid. In fact, I'll pay you your balance now, all of you."

Chol made a big flourishing gesture with her module. She could commit payment immediately. As soon as the signals reached the crew's individual devices, then that was as good as hard currency. Her bank would pay and then expect her to cover the sum. If she couldn't, then they would hire a debt collector to remove her property to that value, or seize her whole roost if the debt was big enough. If she turned out to have nothing of value to seize, they'd shoot her. Banking worked very simply and efficiently in Kig-Yar society. Payments didn't *bounce,* as humans called it, or at least not very often. Wasn't that a lot more civilized? She thought so. It made things stable. She scribbled on the screen with her claw.

"There. Consult your devices."

There was a synchronized rustle of quills, the tapping of composite screens, and a collective murmur of approval. They had their money. Now they'd obey.

"There's a cargo on board, isn't there?" Skal asked. "Clever. But 'Telcam's going to be very upset with you. He doesn't know who *we* are, of course, but you're fairly easy to find."

Truth to tell, she was feeling a little nervous, even queasy, as if she'd taken on slightly more than she'd bargained for. Ah, ridiculous: what good was anything easy, anything that didn't make you push yourself past the lazy, fat, comfortable limit of what you'd always done and succeeded at? How did you know what you could do until you failed? It was as good a time to tell the crew as any.

"I doubt 'Telcam will want to pursue me if I have a battle-cruiser and knowledge of where his camp is." She'd heard rumors from a Jiralhanae that he'd found a bolt-hole somewhere in the Narumad system. Finding the actual planet would be a lot simpler with all the sophisticated sensors of a capital ship. "In fact, if he has any sense, he'll hide from *me.*"

Skal looked at Zim, then back at Chol. "You're not going to strip it and sell it on?"

"No," she said. "It's more use to me. And to all Kig-Yar."

She watched Skal's head droop a fraction. "Oh. No rumor, then?"

"What rumor?"

"This talk of your rebuilding a Kig-Yar navy, mistress."

"I don't have to explain myself to you."

"No, mistress."

"A position of strength does us no harm as a people," she said. "If your clan was threatened by Brutes or even the four-jaws, would you be relieved to see my ship appear to support you, or not?"

Skal just nodded. Zim was the only one who looked concerned. But they'd all been paid and there was no battle to fight. All they had to do was get *Pious Inquisitor* home and hide her among the asteroids.

"If you were paying for the vessel's upkeep," Skal said, "I'd probably be very happy indeed."

It got a round of laughter, which was a good sign. "Very well, prepare for docking."

Fel sidled up to her. "May I leave now?"

"I'll send you home when we're sure we have control of the vessel and the drives are working."

Fel rolled his head, a resigned gesture, then went to sit with Nulm and play *shaks,* letting the pieces drop and roll on the deck. All that remained was the simple act of launching a shuttle, aligning with the bay doors and exchanging codes so that the doors opened and the shuttle linked to the ship's computer to be guided to its assigned berth. In a few minutes, Chol would dock, step through the hatch, and head for the bridge, situated forward of the shuttle bay. Then she'd take command of her own battlecruiser.

It was a wonderful thought. She would savor that moment.

Skal stood over the helmsman, checking the telemetry, and Chol moved to the viewport so that she could watch the final approach. *Pious Inquisitor* now filled her field of view like an infinite black cliff face. She gazed at it for a moment, completely satisfied, then headed for the hangar to board the shuttle. Skal went with her.

"This is going to be very expensive," he murmured. "I hope you have some profitable trips planned for the future."

The shuttle was now hanging level with the aft bay on the port side. Skal flashed the recognition code from the console, waited, then flashed it again.

The bay doors remained shut. "This *is* the right code, mistress. Isn't it?"

"It's what Fel gave me." Chol had been sure he was telling the truth. She must have been slipping, too distracted in her haste. "The lying scum tricked us. I shall break every bone in his body."

"Why? He knew we'd find out as soon as we got here. He's not suicidal."

Something had made the codes invalid. Maybe there was a simple explanation, some periodic refreshing of codes for security reasons that Fel didn't seem aware of. She watched Skal trying to get the ship to accept the entry code, but he didn't even seem to be able to connect with the computer now. "We're locked out, then."

"Sorry, mistress. It looks as if we are."

A minor inconvenience like that wasn't going to stop her. This was basic piracy, the skills that any Kig-Yar captain had to have simply to ply her trade. Ships didn't present themselves for boarding. They had to be taken.

Paragon had exactly the tool for the job. It would just take a little time, that was all, and Chol was in no hurry now. There wasn't even a crew in there ready to defend the ship. Fel had at least led her to the right coordinates, so she'd be gracious about this lapse.

"No matter," she said. "Prepare the umbilical. We'll cut through the hull. And Fel can wait longer to go home, as a lesson for being careless."

STUTTGART ARMORY, NEW TYNE

Mal didn't much like Gareth. He couldn't decide if he'd start by breaking his nose or knocking out a few teeth, but either way, he was going to have that bastard the first chance he got.

"Are your buddies tracking you?" Gareth stood over him as Mal rested his forehead on the table. It was an awkward position to be in with his arms cuffed behind his back. "The buzzards say you all have neural chips. Where's yours?"

"Up my arse."

Thud. Gareth's fist hit the back of his head and his nose cracked against the table again. Mal took a breath and tried not to anticipate the next blow. It only made it worse. There was a lot of sticky blood on the plastic surface, but blood always looked more scary than the actual injury. Yeah, that was it. Noses and lips bled a lot. He wasn't hemorrhaging. He was still okay.

And as long as he had his head down, at least he wasn't looking at the power drill sitting on the table in the corner.

"I don't mind digging around in a few other places before I try your skull, funny boy." Gareth leaned over him. Mal could see his shadow across the table. "What range has it got?"

Mal was still calculating his escape. If he could get his hands free, he knew he could drop Gareth and take his sidearm, even in his current battered state. He couldn't hear Vaz, though. He had no idea where he was or even if he was still alive. He needed a clue so that he knew where to head once he'd taught this prick a lesson.

"If you don't know, why did you grab me?" Mal mumbled. His lip was split and he was pretty sure his nose was broken, but he still had all his teeth. He checked for gaps and movement with his tongue. *No, all there.* Gareth was right over him now, almost breathing down his neck, looking for the small opening in Mal's scalp, just inside the hairline at his nape. "Anyway, it keeps going even when I'm dead. Like a flight recorder. Tamper-proof. Think about it. Has to be, eh?"

"You've got a mouth with a death wish."

It wasn't a good idea to stoke up an interrogator by talking back. Mal knew all that, but he couldn't help himself. It just made him feel better. And he was *angry*. Anger was useful. He tried to keep its fire fed, and it wasn't hard.

"I could tell you what you want to know. But then my mates would have to kill you."

Mal was quite pleased with that one. He felt the movement of air as Gareth pulled away then walked across the room. A switch clicked. The drill revved.

So . . . can I stick that into him before he sticks it into me?

He's just psyching me out first.

I'm trained and he's not.

And I'm frigging angry.

Mal was handcuffed, too, but he wasn't going to let that get in the way of his logic.

"Let's see how tamper-proof this thing is, then," Gareth said.

The implant wasn't a fancy neural net like Naomi's. It was just a transponder, no conspicuous interface protruding through the skin like a commander's or a Spartan's to plug stuff in. Mal had the monkey model version that located and identified you to friendly forces. It still functioned after you were dead, and nobody could hack it or insert it into someone else. Gareth was looking for it, reluctant to touch Mal for some reason, which was weird considering that he didn't mind punching the shit out of him.

Mal could feel his breath as he leaned right over him. The drill was whining next to his ear.

But it also meant the bastard's face must have been right in line with the back of Mal's head.

Why not? I might not get another chance.

Sod it. Three . . . two . . .

Mal snapped his head back, hard and fast, *crack,* and smashed into Gareth's face. The drill went flying, buzzing angrily for a second before it went dead. As Mal jumped up, his chair tipped to the side and he swung around to do as much damage as a bloke could with his hands tied. It was pure animal rage. He lunged. He didn't think of the pistol or anything else for a second, just the prospect of ripping into the little shit who'd spent the last hour or two causing him pain.

The last thing he saw before they both crashed to the floor was Gareth's stunned face, blood everywhere, then Mal was right on top of him, bloody nose to bloody nose. Gareth was yelling for help. He raised his arm to defend himself and Mal went for it. He sank his teeth deep into the muscle.

Christ, didn't that bastard *scream.*

It only made Mal clamp down harder. He bit as deep and hard as he could, making a *nnrrrggghhh* noise that drowned out Gareth's shrieks for help, grinding down to the bone in the forearm. Mal couldn't see anything but the contorted, bloodstained face and the wide open mouth screaming for someone to get this crazy bastard off him. Why hadn't Gareth gone for his pistol?

Tosser. He can't reach it. It's in the back of his belt. Or he put it down somewhere. Or he's a frigging amateur. And this feels great. And I'll be dead in a minute or two, probably, or he might be.

Mal wasn't expecting his jaws to start aching so soon. Holding a serious bite took a lot more effort than he thought. For the first time he realized how strong and raw everything smelled, especially the blood.

Human teeth. Full of germs. Worst infection possible. Nerve damage as well. Play tennis, do you, you dickhead? How's your forehand now?

Mal heard scuffling feet through the screaming and yelling and growling, and then pain exploded in his head and back almost simultaneously. He didn't know if he'd been shot, stabbed, or kicked. But he didn't let go, not even when someone grabbed his hair and tried to pull him off. He hung on, jaws clamped, until he couldn't hold the bite any longer. Then someone dragged him off and almost threw him against the wall.

"Look what he's done! Look what he's goddamn done!" Gareth was still shrieking, nursing his mangled arm. "I'm going to kill that bastard!"

"What, *now* you think of that?" Nairn pulled Gareth to his feet. "You can't cope with a handcuffed prisoner? How the hell did you let him do that? Wow, that's a mess. You better clean that up."

"He's a goddamn head case. Get me some disinfectant, quick."

Staffan filled the doorway, looking around in disbelief. Then he shoved Vaz into the room—battered, bleeding, limping. Mal could smell urine. Christ, this was a pathetic way to go. He really hadn't expected them to end their days at the hands of other humans, pissing their pants and savaging blokes like dogs. It didn't seem right. Mal added it to the pointless list of things he hadn't signed up for.

"Right," Staffan barked. "Gareth—*out*. Nairn—*out*." He dragged two chairs to the center of the room, about two meters apart, and hauled Mal onto one. "Vaz—sit down."

Mal hurt pretty well all over now. He looked at Vaz. It was a lot worse to see your mate injured like that. "You okay?"

"Yeah. Is that your blood or his?"

"Dunno."

"Savage."

Nairn hung around. "I don't think it's a good idea to be in here with them alone."

"Oh, for Chrissakes." Staffan held up his sidearm. "What do you think this does? You're going soft. I want to talk to these guys and I don't want you butting in. Just get out."

Mal was mildly pleased with the thought that armed men were scared of two unarmed and handcuffed ODSTs. At least the hard-core reputation of the Corps was intact. Staffan closed the door and leaned against it.

"Vaz told Nairn an interesting thing, Mal," he said. "About my daughter. I don't recall telling either of you that I thought she'd been replaced. And not by a clone."

Mal almost shot Vaz a disappointed look but kept his eyes fixed on Staffan. Vaz must have talked. Maybe that explained the pee. His pants still looked damp. Well, you couldn't blame the bloke. Nobody knew what their breaking point was until they met it. He'd just thought Vaz was harder than him.

"Vaz, keep your mouth shut," Mal said.

"Too late."

"See, I'm not sure about something," Staffan said. "I don't know if this is just some stalling exercise while you wait for your buddies to find you. You know how it works. Like a clairvoyant. They pick up odds and ends, gauge some poor sap's anxieties, and put it all together so they sound like they're talking with the dead. Vaz, you're right on the border between what a smart boy could guess and what a UNSC insider might know. So you've got a few minutes to level with me. If you know anything about what really happened to my daughter, tell me something convincing." He held his pistol to Mal's head. "Or I'll shoot your buddy. You care about him even if you don't care what happens to yourself. Don't you?"

The weird thing was that Mal wasn't afraid of dying but of what Vaz was going to say. Oddly enough, the bugger did look like he was in control. There was no reaction on his face. He was back in ODST mode, so maybe he had a plan after all.

"I have a file," Vaz said. Mal was now just the spectator, with no idea of what Vaz was up to. He was too smart to cave in like this. He had to be negotiating. "Like I told you."

Staffan didn't blink. "I haven't heard anything yet to persuade me."

Vaz usually had a good memory. Mal hoped he could remember

what was in that bloody file. Still, getting shot was better than a drill through the brain. Mal had something to look forward to.

"You picked up your daughter from New Stockholm hospital," Vaz said. "Pediatrician—Dr. Kelvin."

That got a reaction. Mal saw Staffan's left hand slowly close and clench against his side, not an angry balled fist but the gesture of a man on the edge trying to keep it together.

"Really. Keep talking."

"She'd been missing all night. They found her—well, a girl they thought was her—at a bus stop just outside New Stockholm."

The door swung open and Edvin burst in. For a moment, Mal was distracted from his escape plan and his assorted pains. Vaz had really hit some raw nerves. Staffan had suddenly changed from a genuinely controlled kind of bloke to a man who was trying very hard not to react. Mal watched the tendons in his throat tighten like steel cables.

"Just stop this, Dad," Edvin snapped. "Don't let him do this to you. He's got access to the records, that's all. The hospital. The police report. It's just a goddamn mind game." He shoved past his father and grabbed Vaz by the collar. "Just shut up, or I'll shut you up. *Permanently.* Stop torturing him. He's had enough."

"That's *my* line." Vaz looked past him. Mal gave him full marks for icy indifference, considering the battering he must have taken. "Staffan, would the records tell me what Naomi asked for after she was taken? Would they?"

"Enough." Edvin drew his pistol. "*Shut it.* Just shut up."

"Egg sandwiches with mayonnaise and dill," Vaz said. "Cut into triangles."

"That's *it*—"

"And she told the psychologist she wanted a doll's house."

Staffan stepped forward and grabbed Edvin's arm, abandoning Mal. He looked like he was shaking.

"Leave us, Ed."

"For Chrissakes, Dad, can't you see what he's doing?"

"Please. Go. You don't understand."

"Dad—"

"Out. *Now.*"

Edvin looked like he was going to have to be dragged away. But after a few seconds' glowering, he holstered his pistol and stormed out. Staffan closed the door again and locked it, not fully turning his back on either of them for one second. He stood with his arms at his side with his finger inside the pistol's trigger guard, which Mal thought was a really bad idea for a bloke getting edgier by the second.

"Now that's an interesting detail." Staffan put his free hand to his nose for a second to brush his top lip. It looked like a nervous gesture. "Tell me why you used the word *clone.*"

"I think you know."

"Don't dick me around. I'm not a tolerant man when it comes to my daughter."

"Sansar was glassed. How would I be able to see the colonial admin records?"

"So this wasn't the CAA," Staffan said. Mal expected a flash of temper from him. What he actually saw was a weird kind of relief. "Well, I get more right every time, don't I?"

Mal wasn't sure if Vaz had now blown the mission or not. But maybe he'd seen the warning signs in his friend and hadn't taken enough notice. Vaz was disgusted by Halsey and was set on shooting her. He'd even cornered Mendez, the Spartans' training sergeant, and had a go at him for taking part in the SPARTAN-II program. Vaz didn't mince his words. He thought they were monsters, the worst kind of scum, Nazis, war criminals. Maybe it hadn't been a good idea to let him get this close to Staffan Sentzke.

Now is this a maneuver to get out of here, a seriously big mistake, a moral stand, or is he just forgetting he's a bloody marine?

But I was the one who said we ought to tell Staffan that his daughter was alive, that the poor bastard had a right to know.

Yeah, Mal still thought that. But it was the worst possible time to do it. They were prisoners, and a Covenant battlecruiser was still out there waiting to glass Earth. Mal needed to get word to Osman to just go and lob a few Shivas at the thing while they still had a location. Parangosky would have to find another ventral beam elsewhere.

And Vaz had orders, just as he had. This wasn't *right*. You thought on your feet, yes, and you improvised, *yes,* but you didn't reveal classified information, because you had no idea what else the enemy knew. You didn't know how many pieces of the puzzle they had, or even what else you didn't know and never would. Command ballsed things up and played stupid internal politics, and withheld things you needed to know; blokes died because of vanity and incompetence upstairs as often as bad luck, superior firepower, and their own bad judgment. But that didn't make the basic rules wrong or optional. Orders were what gave you the best chance of staying alive—or winning, for which staying alive didn't necessarily matter.

Stop it, Vaz.

Mal looked at him. "I think it's time for you to shut up, mate."

"Your men think you're a bit crazy, Staffan," Vaz said quietly, ignoring him. "A tin-foiler. A conspiracy theorist. But I know you're perfectly sane."

Mal realized he'd often underestimated Vaz. He seemed to have learned a lot from Phillips. Phillips was *really* good at this kind of shit, like when he'd interrogated Jul 'Mdama and conned him into revealing all kinds of stuff without laying a finger on him, and in an alien language, too. Now *that* was spook-fu. Vaz—clear-cut, in your face, moral, uncompromising—was definitely playing that game now.

Maybe he played it even better because his grim, earnest honesty showed on his face. Phillips was a smiling charmer. Vaz was the blunt but decent soldier. If push came to shove, you'd take Vaz's word over Phillips's.

"You do, do you?" Staffan said. Mal kept an eye on the pistol. "Then tell me this. *Why my kid?*"

Oh God. No. Please, Vaz, no.

"Because she was one in billions," Vaz said. "She had exceptional skills that Earth needed."

Staffan almost tottered. *Holy shit. Nerve, contact, ouch.* It was hard to judge if it was cruel or kind, but as Mal had spent the last two hours getting tortured, he wasn't going to be picky. Vaz had Staffan's attention for the moment and he was making the most of it.

"*Had,*" Staffan said. He wanted to know if she was still alive. What father wouldn't? "Had. Past tense."

Mal wondered why he didn't just ask the question straight out. Perhaps he was scared to hear the answer "no" after so many years of living on hope. Mal made a note of that as an indicator of a crack in the facade.

"Sorry, Staffan," Vaz looked like he was in a lot of pain. "We want to stay alive like anyone else. We're just better at accepting we might not and dealing with it, that's all." He let out a long breath. "Now you know that we know a lot more than you do. But not all the answers can be beaten out of us. You're going to have to negotiate."

Staffan looked at Vaz for a long time. Mal would have felt a bit better if he'd just put that sodding pistol back in his holster. "So why did you come here? To hunt me down?"

"No." Vaz half-closed his eyes for a moment, like he was going to pass out. "It was nothing to do with you. You just got in the way."

Staffan didn't make them a cup of tea and apologize, but he didn't put rounds through their heads, either. He just left. The door closed—quietly, no slamming—and the lock clicked. Mal sat glaring at Vaz, not sure whether to go ballistic at him or not. He was furious. He also felt guilty. Vaz had done it all for him—the moral act and the clever mind games. They suddenly had more value alive than dead, so Vaz had probably saved his life.

But Parangosky would have Vaz's arse if Osman didn't. He wouldn't have to worry about a court martial now. ONI was very informal about discipline, but also very emphatic.

Shit.

There was a good chance this conversation was being monitored. Mal couldn't undo what had been said. All that was left was to reinforce the idea that they'd been cornered and reluctantly forced into a deal.

"Well, whatever happened to name, rank, and number only, you daft bastard?" Mal asked.

Vaz did his dead-eyed gangsterish look. It was even more convincing with the black eye and split lip. "You're welcome. Glad they didn't drill your brain out to trash your chip."

"Why the hell did you blurt all that out?"

"I didn't *blurt.*"

"We're buggered. And the mission's buggered. Why tell him?"

"He had to be told."

"He doesn't believe you."

"He does."

"Ahhh, *shit.*" Mal had to ask. "Did you piss yourself? You stink like a public urinal."

"It was the beers. I couldn't hold it in any longer."

"Animal."

Vaz mouthed at him. *Bought some time.*

They were both pretty good at lip-reading now. It was the only way of not being overheard by BB, as long as you avoided cameras. It was a shame that BB wasn't here now. He'd hijack all the systems and pull off some amazing stunt. Osman would be searching for them, but that was no use if *Inquisitor* moved again. They might never find her.

Don't know where we are, Mal mouthed back.

Vaz nodded. *BB will.* Then it looked like he said *omniscient.* That was a tough one to read.

Mal shrugged. *Damage?*

Minor I think. Vaz stretched out his left leg with difficulty. *You?*

Mal's head felt like a throbbing, burning spike was being twisted through every cell. *It's only pain.*

Vaz almost smiled, but not quite. That was asking too much. *Mad bastard. Cannibal. You'll eat anything.*

Mal clung to the satisfaction of at least putting up a hoofing fight. The taste in his mouth was disgusting. All he could smell now was blood and piss. He hoped Gareth was being overrun by virulent Wolverhampton-evolved germs that would rot the colonial bastard from the arm up and make his arse fall out.

For starters.

It was good to stay vengeful.

Other than that, they were still alive. And a pair of live ODSTs, trussed up and battered or not, were still capable of turning a battle around.

CHAPTER
TEN

IN A WAY, WE STRUCK LUCKY WITH THE COVENANT. IF THEY
HADN'T SHOWN UP, THEN ALL THE SPARTANS WOULD BE
REMEMBERED FOR WOULD BE KIDNAPPING AND ASSASSI-
NATING COLONIAL SEPARATISTS. HUMANS JUST LIKE US.
IT'S NOT SUCH TERRIFIC, CLEAR-CUT PR AS SLAYING IN-
VADING GENOCIDAL ALIENS. JUST POINT TO THE HEROIC
POSTER AND HOPE NOBODY CHECKS THE DATES. HISTO-
RY'S A GREAT AIRBRUSH, ISN'T IT?

—PROFESSOR EVAN PHILLIPS, ONI XENOANALYST, FROM HIS
INTRODUCTORY LECTURE TO ONI OFFICER CANDIDATES
APPLYING FOR ATTACHMENTS TO SECTION TWO,
PUBLIC AFFAIRS AND PSYOPS

UNSC *PORT STANLEY*, OFF VENEZIA

"I think Parangosky should ask for her money back," Osman
said. "How am I going to run ONI if I can't even manage to have
a pilot on standby when we need one?"

She braced her hands on the edge of the chart table and studied the enhanced holographic image of New Tyne, constantly
rebuilding itself slice by slice in real time via the tiny sensor sats
that BB had deployed above Venezia. It was at times like this
that she really appreciated Forerunner technology. This chart
was a direct result of the 100,000-year-old tech found in Onyx,
a way to blend lidar, camera feeds, and all the other sensors
available to *Stanley* to create a continuously updated and ultra-

accurate image of the surface down to street level. This was as good as a live 3-D image of the entire city that she could zoom into, rotate, or fly through at will.

She could even enter buildings via the extended frequency mapping. It was night in New Tyne, but the chart effectively saw the town in permanent daylight with most of the doors wide open. It was worth taking the risk of being detected to get the data.

The EF mapping wasn't good at seeing soft tissue inside structures, but that was where neural implants came in. Down there somewhere—she hoped—Mal and Vaz were still alive. Leaks was busy building remote implant trackers to sweep for transponder codes. The remotes had to enter the atmosphere to get within range, but Leaks took that requirement in his stride.

If she hadn't been preoccupied with getting her people back, then she might have marveled more at what was happening in the maintenance section. Between them, BB and the two Huragok were developing extraordinary devices. They were coming up with battlefield solutions on the fly, as soldiers had always done throughout history, modding kit to deal with the problems that nobody in Procurement had foreseen. The one drawback was that Huragok didn't document anything. They just presented little works of genius without explanation. Osman didn't get any sense of trade secrecy from them, just complete incomprehension as to why anyone would want to know exactly how Huragok did something when all you had to do was ask them to do it.

I'll worry about the long-term issues later. Right now, I don't care how you do it as long as you help me find Mal and Vaz.

It was hard not to imagine the worst. To most people in New Tyne, the UNSC weren't the heroes who saved the galaxy from the Covenant. They were the bastards who shot their fathers and granddads. They were the brutal regime that put down colonial rebellions and nuked Far Isle. Mal and Vaz would bear the brunt of that hatred.

Even I thought the Far Isle bombing was rebel propaganda until I saw the file. But then the rebels nuked civilian targets too. We're all dirty, all of us.

She focused on the search again. Sentzke wasn't stupid. He might not have been fully aware of UNSC technology, but he'd assume they might be able to track more than he was aware of, so he'd take as many precautions as he could. Maybe he'd even move Mal and Vaz to a deep mine, where no sensor could follow them. The implants were detectable under layers of rubble and rock, but they weren't reliable meters underground.

But they're ODSTs. They'll have a plan to dig their way out with a teaspoon and steal a ship. They're survivors.

"Are you talking to me, Admiral, or just berating yourself out loud?" Phillips leaned on the table opposite her, mirroring her position. "Look, we *need* two Pelicans. There'd never be a good time to pick one up. If you had just one now, you'd still have a problem, just a different kind."

"Actually, I'd have Naomi and Dev, and a means of extracting two guys I can't afford to lose. Three, if we count Spenser as a temporary secondment."

"And you'd also have the dilemma of whether to focus on retrieving them or grabbing *Pious Inquisitor*. And you'd go for the ship and spend the rest of your life drowning in guilt if Mal and Vaz died."

"You're learning the joy of life in a blue suit. Not bad for a few months at sea."

Phillips squinted theatrically at her, looking her up and down. "It's black, I think, and we're in space."

"Well, that's the modern Navy for you. We cling to centuries-old traditions and language so that we don't get mistaken for the Air Force." Osman straightened up, arms folded. "BB, have we got an ETA for *Tart-Cart* and whatever the new tub's called?"

"Two hours." BB appeared just above the nav console. "And it's *Bogof.*"

"Some obscure Russian hero?" Phillips asked.

"Buy One, Get One Free."

"Ah. Nothing like a dose of gravitas."

BB sidled up to Osman. "First trackers ready to launch. Permission to deploy?"

"Tell Leaks he's a genius. So are you, for scoping it out. Do it."

"Assuming the remotes survive atmospheric entry, I'll need to move them across New Tyne via the roofs so that curious local brigands don't spot them." BB paused. "If they've moved Mal and Vaz out of town, though, it's going to be a long, slow job."

"There isn't much *out of town* on Venezia. We know where all the remote sites are. Farms, quarries, factories, mines."

"And any number of random holes in the ground that we can't necessarily pick up on a satellite. They probably know our chaps are chipped. The Kig-Yar certainly do. Assume that anything the buzzards know, the humans know too."

Osman fully expected someone to try disabling Mal's and Vaz's implants. If Sentzke's people were dumb enough to do that—assuming they wanted the marines alive—then the ODSTs were already dead. It was a surgical procedure. The implants would still transmit, though. She'd find them. And if she found the worst, she decided she'd have no qualms returning with *Pious Inquisitor* to test the ventral beam.

Collateral damage, but there's a lot of other bastards down there with long terrorist records too, so maybe I'll have to show them that human shields don't wash with me.

"Good work, BB." She looked up at Phillips. "Evan, next time we pass somewhere with a neuro facility, you need to get chipped. I've managed to misplace three out of five personnel in a matter of months."

"Sure." Phillips nodded. He said yes to everything. She wondered what he'd actually refuse. "Why don't they have longer ranges?"

"Some do, but the ODSTs have the basic version. That's all troops usually need. It's just to stop friendly fire."

"Or to find the bodies."

"Yes, thanks, Evan."

"Sorry."

The tracker was another thing Osman felt she should have addressed before. She'd been too reliant on secure radio, armor-mounted devices, and other sophisticated but easily lost comms to track her people. *I should have learned my lesson after we lost Phillips in Ontom, shouldn't I?* And she should have known better than to expect ODSTs to slot straight into undercover work without more training, too. Covert ops weren't the same thing. Experienced agents got burned all the time. It had been too big a risk.

Even the one guy born and bred for it was in trouble. Mike Spenser had gone to ground somewhere, and all she could do was wait for him to call for extraction.

"Ma'am, remember you can keep a comms link open to *Tart-Cart* if you like," BB said. "*Bogof*'s online too."

"Are you monitoring my respiration rate, BB?"

"I am, and I'm a great believer in the reassuring power of the human voice."

"Okay, if Dev and Naomi don't find it distracting, go ahead. How's Naomi doing?"

"Well, she hasn't mastered parallel parking yet, but she has a fabulous driving instructor."

Naomi's channel popped. "No problems, ma'am. Any update?"

"'Fraid not. Can you receive holographics yet? We've got a functional real-time chart of New Tyne."

"Adj is on board. Send it and he'll adapt the display at this end. I can use the time to familiarize myself before I go in."

Well, she seemed to have tasked herself. Osman wondered whether to remind her whose job it was to make the decisions, but thought better of it. Naomi was only doing what Osman had encouraged Kilo-Five to do—to speak their minds and tell her when she needed telling. There was no point pissing off an elite special forces team with years of frontline experience by pretending she knew what she didn't. What was the point of having Spartans if you made them wait for orders? They just needed a clear objective. So did the ODSTs. How they achieved it was up to them.

"So you're volunteering to infiltrate New Tyne," Osman said.

"I'm best equipped to do that, ma'am. Seeing as we can forget about fitting in seamlessly now."

"Okay, we'll have remotes on the surface soon, so we'll relay the signal when we get it. If you're taking New Tyne, then I'll divert to *P.I.*" Osman had no idea what she was going to encounter when she found the ship. "If she looks like an immediate threat that we can't take control of, then we have to deny her to the enemy. And only *Stanley* can ruin her day with a few well-placed Shivas. But if you have a tough exfil from Venezia or Mal and Vaz need medical assistance, you'll want a ship to dock with pronto."

Nobody pointed out that Osman was an admiral, and slightly rusty when it came to vessel interdiction. But she couldn't sit on her backside staring into space from the bridge viewscreen and leave it all to Dev and Naomi when she knew she was capable.

"We could jump straight to your location if you went after *Inquisitor* with *Stanley*," Dev said.

"What if you sustain damage and can't slip fast enough? No, I'll wait until you dock."

"There's no perfect solution to this, ma'am. But Pelicans were designed for extractions and *Stanley* can make holes in big ships. So that seems as sane a plan as any."

"The key thing is to at least track the ship. The moment Sentzke thinks she's compromised, he'll try to move her. If he hasn't already."

"He seemed pretty confident that his neurotic Huragok can keep the ship locked down," BB said. "Although I can't see how it would deal with an armed boarding. Can openers ready, ladies."

Phillips looked up. "What do you mean by neurotic?"

"Mal said the Huragok went into meltdown when the Kig-Yar glassed a Forerunner site as a sales demo. He's called Sometimes Sinks. And he does. He sinks."

"Malfunctioning? Unwell? In need of maintenance? Mad as a box of frogs?"

"Who knows? They've all got their funny little ways. They do have an instinct to defend technology, though."

"Forerunner tech."

"Where do you draw the line between that and a Covenant ship, though? Their purpose in life is to keep the lights on, after all. Maybe I should ask Leaks."

Osman wasn't sure how significant that was. The question was not what the Huragok thought, but whether Sentzke felt the creature was capable of holding the ship, or if he'd now try to hide her.

"Are we sure that Chol Von is going after the ship, BB?"

"I'd bet Phyllis's pension on it, Admiral. And if she kidnapped Fel, then we have to assume she's there right now."

Osman rubbed her eyes, thinking the sequences through. *Take* Bogof *as soon as the Pelicans are back, tag* Inquisitor, *and go after her later when Mal and Vaz are retrieved. Can we send a remote to monitor her? No, too far, too slow. Mini slipspace portal end to end? Can Leaks build one? No, even if he can, it's easier to use a Pelican. So . . .* Stanley *or* Bogof.

"Okay," she said. There were a lot of assumptions. The only certainty she had was that Mal and Vaz were in trouble, and time wasn't on anyone's side. She'd have to go with her best guess, hoping that she hadn't unknowingly steered everyone to her own wrong conclusion. "As soon as everyone's back on board, I take *Stanley* and deal with *Inquisitor.* Mike Spenser's still awaiting extraction too, as far as we know, but he's got to let us know where he is. Naomi, Dev—grab the boys first, then go get Spenser. If the situation on the ground isn't how it looks now, then play it by ear. The ODSTs have to be our priority."

Spenser could sit it out longer than Mal and Vaz. Osman could always have a second bite at extracting him, provided he was still alive. He was used to operating in insurgent territory, and he knew this particular enemy a lot better than Kilo-Five.

Except Naomi, of course. She's neutralized a few rebels in her time.

"Got it, ma'am," Dev said. "Any restriction on weapons?"

"It's Venezia," Osman said. "Do whatever you have to."

The two Pelicans would reach Venezia in ninety minutes. Osman remembered when that was too short a time to get anything done, but now it stretched like a life sentence. She studied the chart, working out how she would have accessed and breached the armory if she'd been in Naomi's position. Getting in was often easier than getting out, especially in an urban area.

We should have moved in when we first had the coordinates. I should never have waited for a chance to get BB on board. Even if we didn't want to destroy the ship, we could have tried tagging her and hoped the Huragok didn't detect the signal.

Could have, should have, ought. Didn't.

Phillips took a seat at the comms console and plugged in his earpiece, eyes flickering as he listened to one of the intercepted channels. "'Telcam's getting very pissed off about Chol Von," he said, not looking away from the screen. "She hasn't called him for days. He's contacting his various chums to see if anyone can track her."

"So what if she finds it?" Osman asked.

"Well, we know her ambitions, kind of, so I'm sure she'll want to seize it. But the Kig-Yar are short of vessels anyway. They've been relying on Covenant company vehicles to run their piracy sideline for a few hundred years, so now they've got to buy their own wheels. I'd bet that Fel got paid in small vessels rather than arms. The Brutes are still trading vessels for weapons. Isn't intercultural barter economics fascinating?"

"You're brushing up your Kig-Yar dialects, I see."

"Absolutely. BB even translated a completely unknown one for me." Phillips did a little shake of his head, as if he was still stunned by the wonder of it. "Listen to me taking that for granted. Academia would wet its pants with excitement to know that. And we just knock it off in the course of a working day because it's handy for spying."

"*I* knock it off," BB said. His tone was definitely subdued. "But feel free to publish the paper under your own name."

Phillips adjusted his earpiece and gazed absently at the console in front of him as if he was having a conversation with himself. "I was going to say, 'No, it's yours or it's nobody's.' Damn. I'm going soft."

As Osman watched, five green dots appeared in a layer above the holochart, then descended to roof height and fanned out from a central point. She lost them for a moment as they went off the chart. When she adjusted the scale and zoomed out, they appeared again at the city limits, working their way back in on zigzag search patterns that overlapped to cover the whole area.

"I thought it would be reassuring to watch the remotes work," BB said. "And you can add the path overlay back in if you want to check where they've searched."

"Extra yeast sludge for Leaks tonight, BB," she murmured. The rhythmic movement of the lights was like watching a knitting machine, hypnotic and soothing, if anything could be soothing at times like this. "He's a clever boy."

About fifteen minutes later, Phillips sat bolt upright. All he needed was a green celluloid eyeshade and a ticker tape machine, and he would have been an icon of urgent news. "'Telcam's cracked a few skulls together and worked out that Chol Von went to some ex-Covenant replenishment base. Station of Constant Sustenance, Korfo system."

"So, worst scenario?"

"He turns up on Venezia. But it doesn't sound as if he's getting very far with that."

Osman wasn't sure how much worse that might make things. She hoped to be long gone from Venezia by the time 'Telcam joined up any more dots. For a moment, she felt genuine regret for Staffan Sentzke, but she put it in its place and worried about her crew.

BB cut in. "Ma'am, incoming signal from Spenser."

That was a relief. "Can you put it on audio?"

"Ah . . . no, he's gone again. It was a data burst. Secure *and* compressed. That's textbook paranoia."

"Have we got coordinates?"

"Yes. He's transmitting from northwest of the town. How he got there without being picked up is beyond me. Just a cryptic message that he had to abandon the coffee but he rescued his smokes."

"Okay, BB, let him know we'll extract him but he's got a couple of hours to wait, at least, and tell him we haven't located Mal or Vaz."

Phillips was leaning on the chart table, one finger pressed to his ear while he listened to his Sangheili feeds.

"Got them," BB said suddenly. "Look. Stuttgart Armory." One point of yellow light popped up to the north of the town. "I'm transmitting this to the Pelicans now. Don't worry, ma'am—it's actually two signals, but they must be in the same room. I'm monitoring for movement."

As Osman watched the yellow dot, nothing seemed to be happening. It might have been a morgue, a cold store, or any room where two dead bodies had been dumped for later disposal. She might not have been looking at a rescue at all, just confirmed KIAs. But then BB adjusted something, and there was a clear separation between the transponder icons.

Then one moved. It tracked slowly in a line, then turned at ninety degrees, then returned on a diagonal to its original position. It looked very much like one of the ODSTs was wandering around a room, following the walls.

Looking for a way out. They're alive.

"That's Mal," BB said. He did a little twirl, pivoting on one corner of his cube. "Good show. Confirmed ID."

Osman rubbed the back of her neck, feeling the muscles relax for the first time in hours. "Okay, let's get as much data as we can on the site. You can follow them if they're moved, yes?"

"We won't lose them. I'm moving the orbital remotes to do extended frequency mapping of the building, so I'll have the internal layout for you very soon."

Naomi's voice cut in on the bridge audio. "Good. Back to stun grenades and kicking down doors. I've missed all that."

She was as near to enthusiastic as Osman had ever heard her. It was hard to tell if she'd factored in that her father might be there. If she had, Osman was sure that she'd completely shut that out and was focused on retrieving her comrades. Maybe that was what she seemed glad of: a clear choice.

"Remember you're going in because it's a Spartan core skill," Osman said carefully. "Not because you're responsible in any way for your father."

That didn't quite come out as Osman intended. She meant responsibility for dealing with him, clearing up a family mess rather like other people would feel obliged to drive Uncle Fred home from the party before he threw up in the punch bowl. But having been through Spartan indoctrination herself, Osman knew how easily that button could be pressed. *Only you can save Earth. You have the gift, so you also have the duty. You have to make this sacrifice.* It wasn't a cultural guilt for original sin, like some of Osman's Catholic acquaintances, but still a sense of guilt for being born so smart, so strong, so driven, that to do any less than devote your entire being to the welfare of Earth's empire—to the state—was shameful.

Naomi sounded flat calm. "I'll just get our guys out, ma'am. I'll draw up a plan as soon as I get the interior layout."

"They'll know we're coming for them," Osman said. "They know we wouldn't leave them."

BB was back to his old self, outrageous and theatrical. "And they know how unutterably awesome I am, too, so they'll be expecting us to do dazzling things to locate them. How right they are."

We don't leave our people behind.

Osman knew reality was very different, though. For all the talk of never leaving a man behind, it was often all you could do. That stuck with her at the academy. It was said quietly in a class, as if it was a dirty secret that everyone had to be told but was best never mentioned again. Going back to rescue someone could compromise the mission and get the rest of your team killed. You often didn't do it: it wasn't smart.

But it was *right,* and men and women would willingly die to rescue a comrade. Osman realized even back then that it wasn't a simple numbers game. It might not have made tactical sense on paper, but wars made no sense anyway, and if that ethos of solidarity was removed then everything that underpinned armed service would start to crumble. Asking someone to risk their life required mutual faith. Your buddies would look out for you, and you for them. Everything hung on that. As far as she was concerned, officers weren't exempt. She chose to ignore the instructor and be the kind of commander who might well risk the mission to rescue her team.

Well, the mission wasn't at risk yet. She still had plenty of options left.

"Yes, unutterably awesome, BB," she said. "I'll put that in your performance review."

STUTTGART ARMORY, NEW TYNE

"I think it must be midnight," Vaz mumbled. "Way past my bedtime."

He was sitting on the floor in the corner of the room, back against the wall. Mal listened to the steady *rasp-rasp-rasp,* very quiet but insistent, that had been going on for the last hour.

Or at least he thought it was an hour. He'd lost track of the time.

"What are you doing?" he asked.

"Same as I was doing the last time you asked me."

Mal stood up and walked around the room again to ease the cramp in his legs, but mostly to take a careful look at Vaz's progress as he passed. He still couldn't tell if the room was bugged. It took a certain technique to make this look casual.

Vaz was propped against the corner of an alcove, the only abrasive surface he could reach. He was sawing his plastic cuffs against the rough edge of the bricks. It was slow. If he made too much noise, someone would notice. Or maybe they already had, and they just didn't care because they knew there was no way out of the building.

You would have thought they'd be a bit more careful with us, seeing as I put Gareth out of action. But they're used to dealing with criminals. Not special forces. Daft bastards.

Mal leaned against the wall—another routine thing that was a lot harder when your hands were tied—and took a sly look down behind Vaz's back. Fiber cuffs hadn't changed in centuries. They were still as bloody hard to get out of as ever. He estimated that Vaz had frayed the material a bit, and if the ties been in a store cupboard for years, then the material might have been a bit brittle. But Mal could see from the sweat on Vaz's face that the effort and the pain of the thin strips cutting into his skin was wearing him out faster than it was wearing down the cuffs. Still, if he survived this, he'd have terrific triceps to show for it.

Vaz stopped for a rest and frowned at him. "How come you're not dying to take a leak?"

"Bladder of steel, mate. I'm gasping for a drink, though."

Poor old Vaz: he sounded a lot better than he looked. One eye was swollen nearly shut. It was hard to tell what was just dried blood and what was an actual abrasion. But Mal was sure he looked worse.

"Am I a mess?" he asked. "How do I look?"

Vaz studied him. "Why? Are you going on a date?"

"Seriously."

"Yeah. You're a mess. But your nose still looks straight. It's internal bleeding you should worry about."

"If I've sprung a leak, it's too slow to kill me. And I'm not getting any neuro symptoms. How about you?"

"Least of my worries. My leg's the worst."

"You smell like my granddad."

"I'm going to kill you when we get out of this."

"That's the spirit, mate."

Footsteps passed the door and then faded away. There was only one thing Mal could be sure about: Osman would be looking for them. He could apply common sense to this and work out what she'd do, too. Spenser was gone, either hiding out somewhere, captured, or shot. He might have had an idea where Staffan would take prisoners, so if he was in a position to offer guesses, he'd have done it by now. But if he hadn't—or even if he had—Osman had one reliable way of locating them if she could get a sensor in range. Staffan's dickheads seemed to know that the neural implants were a liability, but they also knew they couldn't turn them off, not if they wanted Mal and Vaz alive.

Mal didn't know the maximum range of his implant. The manufacturer's figures said one thing, but experience in the field told him another. All kinds of environmental stuff affected them. Sometimes you could get a good signal from way outside the maximum quoted range, and sometimes you could be right on top of a bloke and not pick him up. Osman would land someone or something in town to scan for them. Then it was a case of storming the building or intercepting them if and when they were moved.

Well, there's Naomi and Dev. I can guess how this is going to go down.

Mal pushed himself away from the wall with his shoulder. Vaz resumed his slow, discreet sawing while Mal walked around the edge of the room again, looking for something he might have missed that he could use to cut or scrape.

Or even work out where we are. I have no bloody idea.

He sat down again and decided he did need the bathroom. Once he'd thought about it, it was hard to take his mind off it. He was still thinking about not thinking about it when the footsteps came up to the door again and the lock rattled.

Vaz stopped sawing. Staffan walked in. Before he closed the door, Mal saw another bloke waiting in the corridor outside, one of the men who'd ambushed them but hadn't taken part in the interrogations.

Staffan spoke quietly as if he was afraid of waking the neighbors. "It's just me and Saul here now, so let's be sensible." He looked at Mal for a moment, but he was really talking to Vaz. "If you want a deal, it's going to have to be a damn good one."

"We want safe passage out of here," Vaz said. "What do you want in exchange for that?"

"Are you still persisting with that deserter crap? Don't waste my time."

"There's nothing else you can give us, is there? All we want is out."

Mal cut in. "If you're going to keep us alive for a while, how about letting us freshen up and have some water? We're not going to be much use to you if we die of dehydration."

"There's only one thing I want from you," Staffan said, "and that's information about my daughter that I can *test*. Not crumbs."

Vaz looked at Mal. Mal had no idea where he was going with this. They couldn't even discuss tactics. It was all going to hinge on how well they knew each other's minds.

"Ask," Vaz said. "And if I don't have the answer in my head, I know who will."

Staffan stared down at him. Maybe he just didn't know how to test this. Mal was almost expecting Vaz to do something really mental and ask to put in a call to Naomi, but would Staffan recognize her? Mal had been scared that he would, and now he was scared that he wouldn't. She didn't even remember being Naomi Sentzke, so he couldn't ask her questions that only she would know the answers to. Even a DNA test wouldn't prove much. The clone that had replaced Naomi would have passed that one.

But the longer Vaz could keep Staffan looking for answers, the longer Osman had to find the transponder signals.

"You know what happened to Naomi," Staffan said. "I want every detail. And I'll get it, if it's there to extract. Where did you get the information you gave me so far? Why have *you* got it? Are you higher value prisoners than I thought you were?"

"We're just marines."

"Is my daughter alive? *Is she still alive?*"

Vaz could do that expressionless look to perfection and just shut people out. But the question was a little too close to the bone even for him. Mal saw a split-second of indecision.

Christ, Vaz, are you going to pull the pin or not?

Mal didn't know what the truth—all of it—would do to Staffan. He'd tried to test it on himself some nights when he couldn't sleep, lying in his bunk and imagining how he'd react if he'd found out that his kid had been treated the way the Spartans had. And that was without the trauma of the abduction. He was sure it would have tipped him over the edge. No amount of revenge would ever have been enough. Now he was back in the circular debate again about whether telling Staffan would be right in moral terms, but then he snapped back on the immediate operational problem. What impact would it have on their chances of staying alive and stopping a glassing run aimed at Earth one day?

"Yes," Vaz said suddenly. "She is. She's alive. So ask me something that'll prove whatever you need."

If he'd punched Staffan in the face, he couldn't have landed a more shocking blow. Staffan looked blank for a moment, then slightly wide-eyed, but he just stared through Vaz and didn't say a word. Mal braced for tears, anger, a torrent of questions, or maybe even a heart attack. Staffan was as pale as Naomi. If the blood had drained from his face, it was hard to tell. He looked like a ghost either way.

"Does she remember me?"

Mal had expected him to ask whether she was happy, married with kids and doing well, or even where she was. But that sounded like the question of a man who'd spent years thinking where his daughter might be at this minute or that, and what she might be doing, and had worked out that if she *was* alive, then she would probably have forgotten who she was. He'd probably faced the fact that if she'd survived, she would have called some other man Dad.

He could never have imagined Halsey, though. Who could?

Vaz was as straight as a die. If there was one line that described him, it was that. He never told Mal what he wanted to hear. That was part of what made him such a good mate, but it also didn't mean that the truth was easy. It just meant that you could guarantee getting it.

"No," Vaz said. "She doesn't remember anything at all from

Sansar. She was too young. But she does know she was abducted."

Staffan holstered his pistol and took a couple of fumbles at it before he got the muzzle aligned. The news had clearly pole-axed him. *Shame that Halsey isn't here to see that. Would she give a shit? No, probably not.* People were assets and units to her, things that either served her purpose or didn't.

"If you'd been stringing me along," Staffan said at last, "I think you'd have told me something I wanted to hear."

Then he just left and locked the door behind him. They seemed no closer to getting a drink or a pee break.

Mal looked at Vaz. "Well, I can't tell if that was an act of genius, mate, or if you've made him go and get a chainsaw. You know, because shooting us would be too quick."

"Get some sleep while you can. It's the middle of the night. You know what sleep deprivation does."

"What, makes you tell people things you didn't intend to?"

"I let something slip. Maybe I wish I hadn't."

Mal couldn't tell now whether that was a comment for an unseen eavesdropper or not. Vaz had a point, though. Lack of sleep screwed your judgment and willpower worse than drugs or alcohol, and if it went on long enough it'd kill you. Mal closed his eyes for a moment. His head started filling up with hazy what-ifs and worries, which was exactly what he didn't need, because that was doing these bastards' jobs for them.

Okay, we've been knocked about a bit, but they could hurt us a lot worse. Are they useless at this? Or playing a clever psych game? Or what? What are they waiting for?

So it's the middle of the night, and most of them have gone home. Yeah, even torturers work shifts, I suppose.

I bet Gareth's arm hurts. Hah bloody hah.

If only they'd tied his hands in front, then he could at least have taken a leak. He was starting to drift in that borderland between sleep and consciousness, having weird and vivid thoughts about getting his wallet back, when the door opened again. Staffan came in and hauled Vaz to his feet.

"Okay, better make sure you're in a fit state to answer more questions." He gave Mal a weary look. "Your turn later. Don't go rabid again."

Mal didn't want to lose contact with Vaz. Getting separated didn't just increase the anxiety about what was happening to him. It stopped them from making some kind of joint effort to get out. On the other hand, if Vaz was getting out of a locked room and there were fewer people around, he might stand a better chance of escaping. When he came back—assuming that Staffan wasn't just taking him outside to finish him off—then he'd have a better idea of where they were and the layout of the building.

Vaz glanced over his shoulder as he left and gave him a look that said *don't worry.*

But Mal did. He consoled himself with the knowledge that no matter how hard you were, you still reacted the same way inside. He was in danger of losing his focus. The whole point of keeping him like this was probably to disorient him and wear down his morale. He had to concentrate on what he had to do once he got out, and ignore all the tricks he thought were being played and that might just have been his own imagination.

I have to make a break for it before the others come back in the morning. When Vaz comes back.

What if he doesn't? How will I know? How long do I give it?

Mal drifted off for a few minutes, maybe longer, and woke with a start. Whatever had disturbed him had gone. He was sliding off the chair. Maybe that was it. The light was still on and Vaz wasn't back.

This isn't long at all. It just feels like it. They rely on you feeling abandoned. Any minute now, some prick's going to come in and tell me that I'm all alone and my unit's given up looking for me. Maybe even that Vaz has told them everything so even my best mate's dumped me.

Mal was ready for it. He didn't know how long it was before the door opened again, but when it did, it wasn't Staffan. It was the guy he'd seen outside, one of the ambush party, but he'd forgotten his name already. He was a tired-looking bloke with thinning hair and a tactical vest that looked like CMA surplus. Mal could probably put together a history of the colonies exhibition out of the kit he'd seen in New Tyne.

The bloke looked wary. "I'm taking you to the lavatory," he said, clutching an old pistol. "And if you try sinking your teeth in me, I'll just shoot you. Got it?"

Mal stood up and flapped his elbows a bit. "You bloody well better take these off, then, because I insist on holding my own."

Tactical Vest walked around him, trying to juggle his sidearm and a penknife. For a second or two, Mal had a clear line to the door. *So . . . he has to cut the tie, then I can swing around, disarm him, and I'm out. . . .* But the bloke pulled him away from the chair and turned him to face the wall.

"Lean against it," Tactical Vest said. "Forehead against the wall. Go on. Lean against it." He had hold of the back of Mal's collar while he stood to one side. "That's it . . . now move your feet back a bit . . . see? I'm not as stupid as I look."

Mal was now stuck. He couldn't push back or straighten up. He was taking his upper body weight on his forehead, and it *hurt.* The plastic tie gave way and his wrists were free. In the moment it took him to put his hands flat on the wall to take his weight, a reflex he couldn't resist, Tactical Vest had sorted himself out and had his pistol to Mal's head.

"Just a piss, no dumb-ass stuff, okay?" he said. "You'll never get out of here anyway. This armory's more secure than the Sydney Central Bank. Now hold your hands out front."

So it's the armory after all. Thank you, tosser. Keep it coming.

Tactical Vest put another tie on Mal's wrists and walked him down the corridor. Mal knew he was getting the upper hand now. It was funny where people still drew a line, even in a situation like this. Gareth hadn't seemed keen to touch another man's hair, and Tactical Vest obviously didn't want to deal with the creepy practicalities of helping another bloke take a leak, so he'd compromised. He'd tied Mal's hands in front of him so that he could do the deed himself. Mal thought it through. Even if the bloke had been willing to do the necessary, he'd have risked standing so close to Mal that he'd have been asking for trouble.

Saved by my best feature. I'll dine out on this story for years.

It was a small but pivotal advantage. If the insurrectionists here were such a bunch of hard cases, they'd have left Mal to marinate in his own waste and speeded the process of breaking him down. It could have been part of their technique—nice one second, nasty the next, just to snatch away what little hope he started building up—but Mal had the feeling they were simply rusty on prisoner skills. Keeping prisoners alive was a time-consuming, messy business, like having a demanding toddler who wasn't potty trained, hated your guts, and could turn on you at any second. It made more sense to do what the Sangheili did and just not bother. Staffan probably did the same most of the time.

The only prisoner Mal had ever taken apart from Halsey was Jul 'Mdama.

Bloody dangerous. Nearly broke Vaz's neck. Smashed me against a bulkhead. So that's what Tactical Tosser here is probably thinking.

The walk was an opportunity to look, listen, and orient himself on the way, so Mal counted his paces carefully. No sounds, other than their own footsteps: then they passed an outside window, and it still looked pitch black outside. So he was being held about thirty meters, maximum, from an exterior wall. That would come in useful. He memorized every turn—left, left, then right—to form a map in his head and plan his fastest route out.

Tactical Vest still had hold of him by the back of his collar, but in much the same way that Mal would have held a pissed-off snake. He was scared he'd get savaged like Gareth, then. Mal would capitalize on that. This psych shit worked both ways.

"There." Tactical Vest steered him into a toilet the size of a broom cupboard. "Leave the door open. And wipe your face. You look like a goddamn vampire."

That confirmed it. He thought the dried blood around Mal's mouth was Gareth's, and that was making him uncomfortable. Mal made the most of the psychological edge. It was still a struggle to unzip, but his spirits rose as the level in his bladder dropped. Now he could think straight. He felt pretty good about himself. If he had to, he could do it again, except he'd go for something really demoralizing this time like the bloke's nose, where there was no bone to stop him biting all the way through. *Yeah. He'll be too busy with all that bleeding to keep a grip on his sidearm.* It wasn't macho and graceful like martial arts, but it definitely did the job.

"Do I get a glass of water?" Mal asked, zipping up. He pressed the lever on the basin and scooped water over his face as best he could. There was no towel. The water ran down his chin, leaving diluted streaks of blood down his shirt. "A cup of tea would be nice."

"Not a glass." Tactical Vest walked him back to his makeshift cell. "Because you'd smash it and carve me up with it, wouldn't you? But yeah, I'll fetch you some. Funny. We had a bet on who'd be the most difficult bastard. I had money on the Russian. He looked more the biting and gouging type than you."

There was still no sign of Vaz. Mal tried hard not to fill in the silence with worrying what was happening to him, but he couldn't hear any sound at all: no water gurgling in distant pipes, no floorboards creaking, no generator humming. He couldn't tell if there was a floor above him or not, but if there was, then he might have an exit via a roof space. He'd investigate that as soon as

Tactical Vest brought his water and left him alone again. He had a chair to stand on. Yeah, that might work.

Tactical Vest came back about fifteen minutes later with a flimsy waxed paper cup and a metal jug. Mal couldn't remember the last time he'd seen a paper cup anywhere else. Everything here seemed to be recycled or recyclable stuff that was easy to manufacture—paper, glass bottles, easily workable metals. The planet was actually a single town with few of the invisible industries that Mal took for granted on Earth.

He held the cup as best he could and managed to get most of the water down his throat. Tactical Vest topped it up again.

"Where's Vaz?" Mal asked.

"Oh, he'll be okay. Staffan's taken him somewhere safe. Safe from Edvin, anyway."

Taken him. Shit. Mal's gut tightened. Well, it made sense to separate them, but how the hell was he going to find Vaz now? Mal had to consider why Tactical Vest was telling him this. Just bored, feeling uncomfortable playing guard, or trying to rattle him? He had to resist if this was bait.

"So I've got to worry about Edvin, too, eh?" Mal drank another refill, safe in the knowledge that he could pee in the corner here if he had to. Hydration was what mattered. If he lost too much body fluid, he wouldn't be able to think straight. It didn't take much to tip the balance. "Nutter, is he?"

"Not usually. He doesn't like people taking advantage of his dad, though. Very protective."

"So he thinks we're winding him up." Mal held out the cup again. "Getting his hopes up."

"He thinks you've seen security files on people here, so you're doing the fortune-teller trick and making Staffan think you know more than you do." Tactical Vest poured at arm's length and took a step back, still gripping his pistol. "So he wants to put you out of your misery, dig out your implants, and space them so your buddies don't follow you. Because you haven't got a ship on standby, have you?"

Ha. Up yours, dickhead. They couldn't detect *Port Stanley,* or even *Tart-Cart* come to that. They really weren't sure what size of infiltration force they were dealing with.

Mal grinned. Everything still hurt, but he could set the agenda now. "We're just a couple of lonely deserters. Honest."

"Well, I've been told to stop him shooting you, so let's have some goddamn gratitude. I'm going to move you out of here shortly. That doesn't mean I can't drop you if you try to escape. Do we understand each other?"

"Perfectly." Mal couldn't tell if his act had done the trick, but if Tactical Vest wasn't worrying about reinforcements, he should have been.

He disappeared with the metal jug, leaving Mal to reassess his situation in the knowledge that he was being moved. When the man came back, he dragged a chair into the doorway and sat down on it.

"Twenty minutes," he said. "A vehicle's coming for us. Just making sure Edvin won't find you."

"I'm touched."

"Personally, I think he's right. But Staffan thinks you know stuff, so he wants you alive and chatty for as long as possible."

It looked like they were going to have to sit and stare at each other for a tediously long time, then. Mal decided to wind him up by *looking* at things with the air of a man who was calculating size and distance. He scanned the door frame, the ceiling, the walls, and then the door frame again. He did it without moving his head, knowing the effect it would have on a bloke who thought he was dealing with a feral cannibal anyway.

"Don't even think about it," Tactical Vest said. "Really."

"I'm just playing I Spy." Mal kept looking. This time he tipped his head back to look up. Christ, it was painful. But he thought he heard a sound above him. Maybe Vaz hadn't been moved out of the building after all. "It keeps me occupied. I spy . . . with my little eye . . . something beginning with . . ."

Crack . . . creak . . . crack . . .

Tactical Vest looked up. The ceiling bulged for a second, like there'd been a slow plumbing leak that had finally pooled into a flood.

"*S*," Mal said. He hoped he was right. "Something beginning with *S*."

Plaster, joists, and dust exploded everywhere just as he raised his hands to shield his face. An instant storm of white light and deafening noise left him reeling and a huge, familiar, *wonderful* shape dropped between him and the door, blotting out the light from the wildly swinging strip fitting. Tactical Vest only had time to aim his pistol before he was hit by two rapid shots—chest and head—at close range. He dropped in the doorway. An alarm started ringing somewhere else in the building.

Mal spat dust out of his mouth and looked down at Tactical Vest. "Did you get it? No? S is for *Spartan*. I win."

Naomi grabbed him by the shoulder. "Come on, *wrists*." She pulled out her knife, sliced through the ties, and handed him a magnum. "Seeing as you misplaced yours. Let's go."

"We need to find Vaz."

"Dev's tracking him." She looked him over, then sized up the hole she'd smashed in the ceiling. "BB? Stand by with the medical suite, okay? Mal, can you make it through the ceiling?"

Mal tucked the magnum in his belt and dragged the chair under the gaping, jagged hole. He could see the night sky. He could always rely on his mates. He never doubted they'd come.

"Yeah," he said. "You'll have to give me leg up, though."

"Oh, we don't do that." She clutched him so tightly to her chest that he thought she'd break all the bones that Gareth hadn't. A vibration rose through his body, and it wasn't romance. It was her armor's power unit ramping up. "We do *this*."

Jumping from orbit was routine for Mal. Taking off like a bloody rocket while clinging to a Spartan was a rare novelty, though. A chunk of broken joist ripped his arm as he scraped through the gap, but he didn't care.

Spartans flew. Naomi had had an S-9 SOLA propulsion system. He'd watched it once, but now he knew how it felt.

"I'm not going to drop you," she said. Mal tried to look down and caught a glimpse of trees below. "But I don't normally land with passengers, so prep for a few bruises." She paused. "And I'm glad you can't hear BB right now. *Pervert.*"

Trees rushed past him without warning just as he started working out what landing underneath four hundred kilos of armored Spartan would do to him. *Thud.* They hit the ground, just like a parachute landing, and the sudden jolt made all his injuries throb. Naomi was sprinting, running, slowing down, and then she staggered to a halt.

"Sorry," she said, peeling him off her. He almost lost his balance. "The extra weight affects the handling. I normally stop dead."

A Pelican-shaped shimmer stood in the clearing. Mal thought it was *Tart-Cart* with her camo engaged, but as soon as he scrambled up the ramp, he realized it was the new ship. Naomi leaned over him for a moment and he gave her a big noisy kiss right on her polished visor. It left a blood-streaked smear on the gold mirrored finish.

"You're bloody amazing." He grinned as she recoiled. "Thanks, mate."

"Ick," she said. "Now I've got to clean this damn thing."

"I knew you'd come."

She missed a beat. It was noticeable. "I'll *never* leave anyone behind."

Ooh. He'd hit a nerve there, whatever it was. She disappeared into the cockpit and the Pelican shuddered as she started the thrusters. Now they had to grab Vaz. It was only when the dropship lifted off that Mal thought about the extraction, and realized that it could just as easily have been Staffan Sentzke in that room as Tactical Vest.

Would Naomi have shot him?

Mal was pretty sure that she would.

GREXCO TANTALUM EXTRACTION PLANT, EIGHT KILOMETERS OUTSIDE NEW TYNE

Staffan tossed a set of Grexco coveralls onto the employee locker room bench and hesitated before he cut the tie that held Vaz's wrists.

"Make it quick," he said. He shoved Vaz into the bathroom. "Clean yourself up. Those clothes should fit you."

"Thanks."

"And don't give me a reason to shoot you."

"Okay."

The shower door wasn't full length. Staffan could keep an eye on the marine and put a round through his leg if things got out of hand. He had things under control, and he'd worry about explaining this to his family later.

He had no plans to kill Vaz, though. He couldn't. This was the best lead on Naomi that he'd had in more than twenty years, and even though he knew it might all be bullshit, or just a few scraps of data that might not take him much farther, he couldn't ignore it. He had to pursue this. He stood guarding the door, more to stop anyone getting in and taking matters into their own hands than to stop Vaz escaping. It was a risk. He'd seen what the other marine had done to Gareth, unarmed and cuffed. He wasn't going to drop his guard with this one.

"My son thinks you're taking advantage of a desperate old man," he called over the noise of the water. "He says we should dispose of you and dump that chip of yours in space before someone tracks you here."

Vaz didn't answer. He finished showering, a little unsteady on his feet, and almost fell over when he put the pants on. Christ, if Nairn had done him some serious damage and he died before he told Staffan anything useful—well, they still had Mal. Staffan had been guessing the hidden intentions of humans and aliens for decades, and his judgment had never let him down. Just a couple of times, he'd seen that glimmer of truth in Vaz, however tough the guy was. He *knew* something. There were better ways to get answers from some men than beating it out of them.

And he needed to stow him somewhere where Edvin wouldn't find him. Ed meant well, but sometimes he was suffocatingly protective. He didn't know what it meant to cling to a gut feeling when everyone told you that you were deluded, but you knew, absolutely *knew,* that you were right.

Staffan kept his pistol trained on Vaz, path to the truth or not.

"Hands together, out in front." He took a fresh tie out of his pocket one-handed. "This should be a little more comfortable."

"What about Mal?" Vaz stared into his face. "If anything happens to him, you can kiss good-bye any more answers from me."

"You'd do anything for your buddy, wouldn't you?" That was Vaz's Achilles' heel. "Would he do anything for you?"

Vaz didn't even blink. In fact, he took a step forward so that he was right in Staffan's face. For a man whose life was in someone else's hands, he was remarkably aggressive, as if he hadn't realized he wasn't the one holding the gun.

"We're ODST," he said flatly. He seemed to think that was full explanation and answer. "You need to remember that."

Staffan had already worked out that trying to out-tough Vaz would only make him more stubborn. This was a guy who was more afraid of giving in or of betraying his buddies than of pain or death. Usually, Staffan would have admired and respected that, but now it was an inconvenience.

"I've got one of my more level-headed guys to keep an eye on Mal," Staffan said. "He'll be okay as long as you behave."

"What now?"

"I'm going to put you somewhere safe."

He caught Vaz's elbow and steered him outside into the pre-dawn darkness. On the far side of the mining camp, there was a secure compound the size of five football pitches where the various license holders stored their machinery and parts. Each plot had its own locked compound with a small storehouse. Staffan hadn't used his license for years, but he still kept the storehouse, and he could hold Vaz for a while. Edvin would never think of looking there.

"This isn't a five-star hotel, but you won't be able to get out, and, more importantly, nobody will be able to get in." Staffan made his way through lines of identical single-story buildings that still reminded him too much of a refugee camp. "Okay, turn left."

"Lovely." Vaz stared into the gloom as Staffan unlocked the door and shone a flashlight inside. "How hot does it get in here?"

Staffan shut the door before switching on the lights, just in case he'd been followed. "You've got aircon. There's some sensitive equipment in here. Water and a chemical toilet. And some food. Don't worry. I do think things through."

Vaz ambled around, probably looking for ways out. He was wasting his time. The building was a complete cube designed to stop Kig-Yar cutting through, tunneling in, or otherwise breaching the place to steal the contents. The buzzards usually stuck to the rules of decent society here, but you always got the rogue element that hadn't yet learned what happened to ungrateful thieves on a generous and no-questions-asked world like Venezia.

"Sit down." Staffan dragged a chair across the composite

floor, making a railway track noise as the castors skipped over the ridges. "This is a bit more comfortable."

Vaz eased himself into the chair and sat back while Staffan put an empty crate next to the armrest. A jug of water and pile of candy bars on hand might get the guy in a more helpful mood. He seemed a decent enough kid. It wasn't his fault that his government were shit-houses. He'd probably been drafted anyway.

"Sorry, no ice," Staffan said, placing a cup within reach. "The confectionery isn't drugged, by the way. I just don't want you starving to death before we get somewhere."

Vaz just nodded. "Thank you."

"So. My girl's alive, is she?"

"Yes."

"Is she okay?"

"Define okay."

"Healthy. Happy. Leading a full life."

Vaz reached awkwardly for a candy bar, tore the wrapper open with his teeth, and went through a laborious sequence of putting the bar down and taking the torn fragment from be- tween his teeth before picking the bar up again. He might have been making a point about having his hands tied. On the other hand, he might just have been a guy who didn't like to spit and preferred to keep everything tidy.

"She's very healthy," Vaz said. "Happy? I can't tell. Full life? Well, she's done things that few other people ever have."

Is he saying he knows her? That he's seen her? Or that he just knows about her?

It wasn't the answer that Staffan was expecting. That just gripped him even more. "Why are you answering my questions?" Staffan asked. "You're only supposed to give enough detail for POW identification, aren't you?"

"I've not told you anything classified."

"That's not an answer."

Vaz chewed for a while in silence until he finished the bar. He seemed genuinely hungry, not just stalling. "You know," he said at last, "we're trained not to give personal detail. Even harmless things. Because a good interrogator will use that to weaken you, to get inside your head. So I've only given you personal detail about your family."

"But *why*? You know what I want to ask you now? Of course you do. I want to ask if it's true, if I can see her, who took her, why they took her, what she's been doing all these years . . . you *know* that. And you might be lying, so I have to ask myself why you're doing this. Buying time while you work out how to get yourself out of this hole, or softening me up for something else."

"You won't believe me if I tell you."

"Try me." *Goddamn it, I've fallen into the trap. He's inside my head. He knows what drives me but I don't know his motives at all.* Staffan's need to understand his adversary was consuming him. But he still had the power here. He had the gun. "Go on."

Vaz looked him straight in the eye, but very good liars could always do that. Maybe he wasn't a marine at all. Maybe he'd wanted to be taken prisoner for some reason. Staffan was in danger of tying himself in knots.

"I'm trying to balance three things," Vaz said quietly. "What's *right,* my duty to the Corps I swore allegiance to, and the safety of my comrades. That's quite a tightrope. You don't get to pick and choose which orders you happen to agree with. But we've also got to operate within the law. We have to refuse an unlawful order. So there's a duty of morality you can't ignore simply by saying you followed orders. Are you with me so far?"

"I think so."

"Most of us have only ever fought aliens trying to wipe out humanity. No moral dilemma there. We tend to forget about the complicated stuff the last generation had to handle."

Staffan had no idea what Vaz was trying to tell him. He

couldn't even work out if he was explaining all this to him or to himself.

In the end, Staffan just shrugged. "I can't guess anymore, Vaz."

Vaz reached for the cup of water. "If you knew, if I told you, would it stop you doing what you're planning?"

"What am I planning?"

"Why would you want a battlecruiser?"

"To defend ourselves."

"If you wanted revenge, I couldn't blame you."

Staffan should have known better. He'd immersed himself for years in the stories of other parents who'd lost children, sometimes in news reports, sometimes face-to-face. A few had known who took their child, guys who had been convicted, but some murderers had refused to tell them what had happened or where the body was. It was their sick way of wringing the last drop of power out of their crime. Sometimes the murderer had offered to reveal things and then changed his mind, over and over again. The parents, just as desperate as Staffan was, got sucked into the game every time when they should have walked away.

"Before I die," he said, "I just want to know where her body is. But now I think I would rather *not* know than let you do this to me. Earth's back, isn't it? It's settling its scores."

Vaz frowned quickly, just a flash of the brows, the kind that was hard to fake. Then he shook his head and looked away at the wall for a while.

"I once accused a brave man of being an asshole for standing back and letting the Navy get away with something terrible," he said. "But every time I have the opportunity to do something about it myself, I chicken out because it breaks the rules. That's how we let decency go to hell in a handbasket. Okay. I know your daughter. You should be proud of her. But a reunion's going to be very painful for you. Is that enough? Just knowing she's okay? You'll have your answers, but you'll probably feel just as bad as you do now."

That was the real Vaz. Staffan could see it and it scared the shit out of him. If Vaz was making up some crap, then it wouldn't have spun out of control like this. Staffan was about to press him on it when his radio chirped. He walked over to the door to take the call.

"Where are you? Your location's blocked." It was Nairn. "We've got problems."

"Never you mind where I am. What's happened?"

"The armory's been hit. Saul's dead. Someone got Mal out. Straight in through the roof and out again. Like he was plucked by some damn big hand."

"Jesus." Staffan felt his throat tighten. Maybe it was Mike Amberley. He hoped it was local, anyway, and not the start of some operation they just hadn't seen coming. "When?"

"Now, of course. Well, the alarm triggered twenty minutes ago. I just got here. We can't find Vaz either."

"I know where Vaz is. He's secure."

"But—"

"Have you mobilized patrols yet?"

"Yes. I called Peter Moritz too. What's going on?"

"Nothing on sensors? Radar?"

"Nothing. It's the third guy. Mike. Got to be. Pretty damn effective for an electrician."

If someone had sprung Mal, then they'd be coming for Vaz next. They'd find him. Mike Amberley had to be tracking the neural implant, and there was nothing Staffan could do about it.

I've got to hang on to Vaz. I can't lose this trail again.

"Keep looking," Staffan said. "I've got Vaz and I'm lying low. That's all you need to know. We might be bugged even now."

He cut the call. He didn't know for sure that it was the implant acting like a homing beacon. But breaking into the armory and extracting Mal was a tall order. It would have taken very professional skills to get past the alarms in the first place, let alone access a cell through the roof. Staffan took a few deep breaths before turning around. He expected to see Vaz looking smug.

But he wasn't. "Mal's gone, isn't he?" he said. "Anyone hurt?"

"What do you think?"

"I think that we probably haven't got long to finish this conversation."

It wasn't getting killed that bothered Staffan. It was getting killed without finding out the truth about Naomi. It was not seeing Laura and the family again, and explaining. It was not seeing Kerstin's face when he pulled the cover off the doll's house to reveal it on her birthday. It was not finding out the truth for Andy Remo. It was a wasted journey, because he believed it all ended here. God wouldn't tell him a damn thing and make it all better in Heaven because God had never been here when his little girl needed saving from whatever had taken her.

"Staffan," Vaz said, "I really need you to trust me and do what I tell you."

"Why should I?" Staffan checked the locks on the door. He had a spare ammo clip in his pocket, but he couldn't hold off an assault if whoever sprung Mal could get in here. But the place was Kig-Yar proof. Maybe he could sit it out. "I don't even know your real name."

And maybe I need to tell Nairn where I am after all, and just deal with Edvin.

He walked up to Vaz and put the gun to his head. He didn't plan to pull the trigger, but if he had minutes left, he had to know the truth. He didn't know how else to do this.

"It's Vaz Beloi," Vaz said. "And your daughter's saved my ass a few times. So listen to me. We can get this sorted out."

He looked up at the ceiling. Staffan could feel it: a dull throb in his chest that started to press on his ears, then turned into a muffled whine like a jet turbine. Vaz stood up.

"*Don't open fire.* You won't get out of here alive."

"Don't let me die without telling me. What harm can it do now?"

"You want to see her again?"

Staffan forgot everything Andy Remo had ever taught him about not taking any shit and following his gut. He didn't even have time to call it in or switch his radio back to location ID. Something scraped against the door. The turbine noise was loud, right overhead, and he didn't know which direction to cover first. Vaz didn't seem to, either. He looked up, then at the door, then up again. Something thudded on the roof. Vaz looked back at the door, stepped in front of Staffan, and yelled, "Down! *Get down!*"

Staffan hesitated. He was sure something was coming through the roof. Vaz was staring at the door, eyes flickering as if he was listening. He spat something in Russian and shoved Staffan hard in the shoulder.

"Now—*down!*"

Bang.

The door blew in. Staffan ducked as a neat rectangle of metal and composite flew at him. The next thing he knew was that his ears hurt and he was on the floor with Vaz on top of him. He'd either fallen on him or was holding him down.

Or maybe he was shielding him. Jesus Christ, nothing made sense now.

"Dev? No, no, leave him. *Don't.* Don't shoot."

Vaz rolled off and Staffan found himself looking up the barrel of an assault rifle and into a black, featureless visor. A hand reached up to flip it back. It was a young Asian woman. Her eyes widened as she looked into Staffan's face.

"That's freaky," she said. "Come on, my meter's running."

"Hands," Vaz said. "Quick. They'll have militia here in a few minutes."

The woman pulled something out of her belt to cut the

cuffs. Vaz hauled Staffan to his feet and pushed him toward the door.

"You're bringing him too?" the woman asked. It was still dark outside. Staffan could hear the engines but he couldn't see anything. "You sure about that?"

"Yeah," Vaz said. "Nice frame charge work for a pilot, Dev."

"I can do everything you can. And more elegantly."

"And nice parking."

Staffan almost collided with a UNSC Pelican that he simply hadn't seen. There it was, right in front in an impossibly small space between the buildings. As Vaz bundled him up the ramp, Staffan looked back to see something big, black, and noisy hovering without nav lights over the storehouse.

The deck tilted and the dropship was airborne before he was even strapped into his seat. Vaz leaned over him, clutching handcuffs.

"I have to do this," he said. "Sorry."

"Where are you taking me?"

"Answers, Staffan. Your answers. After that, I don't know what happens." Vaz secured the strap. "To either of us."

CHAPTER

ELEVEN

PART OF ME WANTS TO OFFER THEM A CHOICE. WOULD ANY
OF THEM REFUSE?
—DR. CATHERINE HALSEY, SEARCHING HER CONSCIENCE
ABOUT THE ABDUCTED CHILDREN TRAINING
TO BE SPARTANS, FROM HER JOURNAL

INDEPENDENT KIG-YAR SHIP *PARAGON*, OFF SHAPS 3, QAB SYSTEM

Chol had time, but it wasn't infinite. She paced around the hold in her pressure suit, waiting for confirmation that the umbilical was secured to *Pious Inquisitor*'s hull.

Fel watched her. He wasn't wearing a suit, so he had to rely on the efficiency of the two crew who were monitoring the umbilical's progress. The only thing that stood between the cold vacuum of space and the cargo deck was an energy seal that closed the leading tip of the tube. Sometimes a physical airlock was a little more comforting in psychological terms if not in engineering reality.

"It's the Huragok," Fel said. "Wherever you try to cut through, he'll know."

"So? He's a Huragok. He's there to maintain the ship."

"I don't think it's a security malfunction. I think he changed the entry codes."

"I think your customer did, in case you came back to double-cross him."

"He must have instructed the Huragok to do it."

"Then we instruct it *differently*. I really don't see the problem."

"Sometimes Sinks isn't quite as compliant as most. We found him in a wrecked ship. He gets very agitated if he's thwarted."

Not as compliant as most. Chol decided that would be a good name for the creature if Huragok weren't so wedded to names based on endless variations of their buoyancy status. "I note you left it late in the proceedings to tell me about him," she said, grinding her teeth. "And this is the first time you've mentioned his *aberrations*."

A Huragok was a welcome bonus, or so she'd thought since she'd learned a few hours ago that there was one on board. Now she knew that Fel hadn't leveled with her. The Huragok was defective in some way, not as unquestioningly obedient as they usually were. She'd undertaken this mission without knowing the creature existed, though, so if it turned out not to be a blessing then she was no worse off. Perhaps it could be contained and given more basic tasks. It was the ship that mattered. She could worry about the detail later.

But what else might Fel be hiding? She was prepared for anything. For all she knew, there could be a crew on board lying in wait for her, Kig-Yar or human. She took nothing for granted and turned her back on Fel to talk to Zim on her helmet comms.

"Is the boarding party standing by?" she asked. "Fel's just told me the Huragok is defective. So he might also have forgotten to tell me that we're walking into an ambush. Or that the vessel's booby-trapped."

"They're ready, mistress."

"Very good. Take nothing on trust."

Chol never did. Zim would stay with *Paragon,* despite the fact she needed him for boarding duties. *Paragon* had to be left in safe, loyal hands. Once she entered *Pious Inquisitor,* she might be stranded in a dead ship if her own vessel got into difficulties, or if a bridge crew she'd placed too much trust in decided to abandon her there. It wasn't unknown. They'd been paid. They had no reason to hang around, assuming they were willing to face her wrath if she survived being abandoned.

In theory, she could simply get home in the battlecruiser and reclaim her ship later, but until she checked over *Pious Inquisitor* personally, and satisfied herself that all systems were functional, she would keep all her options open.

The tube extension and alignment process was going smoothly, even if Chol felt that it was taking a glacial age. She walked back to the opening of the umbilical, a great gaping mouth in *Paragon*'s hull that still looked like a fragile bubble that could burst and kill her any moment, no matter how many times she'd watched this procedure. The long, translucent tube now bridged the gap between *Paragon*'s cargo bay and the battlecruiser's hull. The laser would begin cutting as soon as the tube had a secure lock on it. If that seal wasn't perfect, the tube could break loose and compromise both vessels.

Take your time, gentlemen. A little frustration now is a small price for me to pay.

Chol studied the schematic again, a holographic repeater mirroring the display up on the bridge, and visualized the cross-section of the shuttle bay doors. If the laser ring cut through at that position, she'd have an emergency bulkhead between the access point and the bridge that would provide extra reassurance if the umbilical became detached. She could repair the hole in the bay door at her leisure. They'd simply have to adopt extra airlock safety procedures until it was fixed.

"Mistress, we have a stable connection," said Zim's voice in her helmet comms. "We can start the burn."

"Do it," she said.

At least the hull repair would keep the Huragok busy. When Huragok were busy, they were happy. The creature was probably suffering after-effects of the enforced boredom of being marooned in a wreck he couldn't repair, compounded by being moved to an unfamiliar and empty ship with little to distract him. They did better with companions. They were social animals, artificial or not. *Team players,* the humans called it.

But if I keep this Huragok, then I'll need a second one so that they can maintain each other. Where am I going to get one, though?

And why didn't he repair the wreck they found him in? Not enough raw materials? They can create anything. But the wreck must have had some sealed compartment for him to survive at all. What was he doing?

There was something wrong there, but she didn't know what. It bothered her. It wasn't her top priority now, though. The boarding party, suited and impatient, began assembling on the cargo deck, twenty-two crew including some who'd had experience of operating similar ships. With any luck, none of them would need to fight. They'd check there was nobody else on board, then change all the security codes and set a course for the Y'Deio system.

"Technician?" She spotted Jec on the upper gantry, inspecting a readout. He wasn't wearing a pressure suit. "Are we still airtight?"

He leaned over the rail. "I certainly hope so, mistress, or else I'm a ghost."

"Don't be flippant," she snapped. "Safety is sensible. Safety is profitable. Take only the risks you *must*."

Daring raids were fine, but carelessness that cost lives was sloppy. She ran her hand over the laser pistol on her hip.

"It's just a Huragok," Fel said, looking her over. She hoped she didn't look nervous. A nervous shipmistress didn't inspire confidence among the crew. "It isn't violent."

"As long as it *is* just a Huragok."

"Are you insinuating that my crew are waiting to ambush you, shipmistress? You know they've been paid and have dispersed. That's how you found me, remember."

"Indeed, but I don't know about the humans, do I?"

"To the best of my knowledge," Fel said, "they haven't trained a crew yet."

"I'm surprised you didn't offer to stay on and train them for an additional fee."

Perhaps Fel had, but was turned down. She couldn't tell; he didn't say. Humans weren't as stupid as some thought, and might have managed to reach the conclusion that a shipmaster who stole a vessel once might repeat the winning formula. She stared down the umbilical tunnel again, imagining she could feel the heat from the ring of lasers at the far end of the tube as they cut steadily through the layers of metal and composite that made up the battlecruiser's external skin. But it was just an illusion caused by the contact area of the hull glowing red-hot. The energy barrier and her suit insulated her from both the cold of space and the heat from the cutting process.

Chol opened a link to the duty engineer. "Stand by to generate atmosphere."

"The ship has full life support running," Fel said. "How else would the Huragok function? He needs access to all decks to do his work."

"I take nothing for granted," Chol said. "Especially if I find the ship's crewed, in which case I'll vent the atmosphere, Huragok or no Huragok. So then I'd need to replenish it. Therefore I have generators on standby, just in case. Why do I have to explain all this to you? We do the same work. We follow the same operating procedures."

"I'm simply trying to reassure you, shipmistress."

Chol was getting irritated by his fawning. "I've already said I won't kill you. How about a little silence? I'd welcome that. In fact, go back to the bridge. Report to Zim. He'll take care of you."

She knew she was fretting now. It was simply standing idle that fed her anxiety. She was so close to her goal, so close to taking the ship, that she imagined 'Telcam was about to drop out of slipspace with a Sangheili task force and snatch her prize away from her. It was almost too good to be true. She hadn't wasted months searching, Fel had cooperated fairly rapidly, and as far as she could see, *Inquisitor* was all that they said she was.

"Pressure equalized," Jec said.

Bakz stepped forward. The boarding party clustered at the mouth of the umbilical, jostling for position. Chol knew what they were thinking. There might be valuables left on board that Fel's crew hadn't taken and that they could grab for personal bonuses. She'd have to keep an eye on that in case one of them took something she couldn't afford to lose.

"Permission to board, shipmistress?" Bakz asked.

Chol drew her weapon and gestured down the tunnel. "Proceed."

There was no sense in losing an entire crew if something went wrong at this stage. Bakz went down the tube alone while the others waited behind Chol. From a certain angle he looked as if he was walking on mist. He didn't pause even for a second before stepping through the shimmering haze of the energy barrier that hung at the end of the tube like desert air.

This was the worst part, the waiting, the long seconds of silence while everyone held their breath and listened for good news or bad.

It took longer than expected, but Bakz stepped back through the seal with a triumphant swagger and took a few steps onto the tunnel floor.

"All clear, mistress," he said. "In fact, as empty as an Unggoy's head. Boarding party, first ten, move in."

Chol followed Bakz down the umbilical toward the energy seal that shimmered like a heat haze at the far end. It was always a little unnerving to look down and see the hint of infinite space beneath her feet, even though the gauzy filter of the tube's material gave the impression of comforting solidity in her mind. She shook off the uneasiness. That was a lizard's thinking, the instinct of a creature that clung to the ground. A T'vaoan should have relished the void below like a bird in flight.

One day, we'll fly. While the Sangheili and the others degenerate, we'll evolve.

When she stepped through the barrier onto a solid deck, she could see the lines of square-section columns that rose through two open decks, and openings to passages that led to the rest of the ship. The lighting was still on. Bakz checked his suit's status display and then accessed a port on the bulkhead.

"Atmosphere stable, temperature stable," he said. "Life support's working normally."

Chol paced around, still ready for an ambush. She didn't plan to take off her helmet yet, but when she did, she'd be able to smell intruders. The hangar wasn't completely empty after all. Two Spirit dropships were suspended just above the deck, looking a little worse for wear. Fel would have taken them if they'd been any use, but perhaps his customer had insisted on having them.

"Ved, Lig—over here." She summoned two males who were more familiar with Spirits. "Check those two ships and see if they're airworthy. Bakz, Noit—with me. Everyone else—once we're through the doors, spread out and check the propulsion, weapons, and engineering sections. Then work through the rest of the ship as fast as you can. We're not counting every speck of dust. Just make sure everything essential is in order."

It would take a full ship survey lasting a season to do that, and the Huragok would deal with any routine defects. She just needed to check that Fel hadn't removed generators or other major components thinking that the stupid humans wouldn't notice. She didn't want to find herself cornered by 'Telcam and hit the slipspace controls only to find that she was missing some parts and dead in the water.

The quickest way out was via the doors that led onto an access deck connecting the bridge, cargo bay, gravity lift compartment, and other core areas. Once those sealed behind her, she'd take off her helmet, inhale the scents, and get a better idea of what she was dealing with. It was a big ship for fewer than thirty to search thoroughly. But once she had control of the bridge, she could seal off other sections and vent their atmospheres if she needed to. If there was anybody waiting in ambush and they were smart enough to suit up, they'd still run out of air sooner or later.

Pious Inquisitor felt like a mausoleum as she stood in front of the doors. Noit reached out and pressed the controls. Nothing happened. He pressed again.

"Is this all part of the code changes?" she asked. "Very well, this might slow us, but it won't stop us. Bypass the controls, Noit."

It shouldn't have been hard. There were always overrides, even though the Huragok crew always maintained ships so well that emergency measures were rarely needed. Even the Sangheili accepted they weren't immune to damage that might trap them inside a ship. Noit prodded around at the side of the doors for some time, clicking and hissing with frustration until there was a faint sigh and the doors parted.

"You can seal them again, yes?" Chol asked.

"Let me make sure first." The rest of the search party stepped through and the doors closed again. Noit examined the inner bulkhead controls and ran a hand-scanner down the center seal. "That's sealed. Tight as a drum. Let's go."

Chol headed forward. The bridge was on a deck that ran level with the deckhead of the shuttle bay, which meant negotiating ramps and elevators. There were a few more bulkhead doors that needed to be opened manually, but eventually they reached the main access to the command center.

There was still no sign of the Huragok. She expected him to be on the bridge, awaiting instructions.

"I'm getting weary of these locks." Noit opened another bulk-head panel. "In fact, when I find that gas-bag, I'm going to—oh. Curse the thing. *Curse* it."

Chol spun around and loomed over him. No wonder he was angry. The interior of the panel was completely smooth and featureless, as if all the controls had been sliced away and polished flat. There was nothing to access or probe. All she could do was admire her reflection in it. Chol felt her feathers rise with anger and press against her close-fitting helmet, which made her even angrier.

"We've been *sabotaged,*" she hissed. "Locked out. No human could manage this. Nor Fel. This is the work of his *noncompliant* Huragok."

Bakz leaned over the panel to take a look. "But he must have done it from this side of the bulkhead. He's out here somewhere." Then he looked up at small, well-hidden openings in the deckhead. Covenant ships were riddled with small conduits that the Huragok used to move between decks like *uoi* in a warren, largely unseen by the crew. "Well, we can't follow him through those. We don't float. And they might be able to squeeze themselves into those small gaps, but we can't."

Chol could imagine the Huragok watching them with whatever sense of gleeful triumph a creature like that could manage. He was definitely keeping them out of the ship. The locks could have been down to a ship-wide computer problem, but destroying the controls to the bridge doors was a deliberate act of sabotage. She looked up, working on the assumption that he was tracking them and could somehow access their helmet-to-helmet comms circuit. What was his name again? *Sometimes Sinks.* Well, she'd sink him soon with a few well-placed shots and enjoy the moment.

"Are you listening, Huragok?" She didn't need to raise her voice, but shouting made her feel more dominant. It also let the crew know she wasn't taking any nonsense from a servant. "Stop this right now. Restore all the systems you've damaged. Or when I find you, I'll kill you. And I *will* find you. These are your orders.

You have to obey them. Your Forerunner creators *designed* you to obey them. Do as I tell you."

She waited, although she wasn't sure why. She couldn't imagine a Huragok yelling defiance at her. They made bleats and farting noises by venting gas from their buoyancy sacs, but they were generally silent, communicating only by sign language.

Then a faint hum broke in to her comms, and she heard a voice, an actual voice. For a moment she thought it was a human, but the language was all wrong. Then she realized it was synthesized.

<*I know the difference between right and wrong,*> it said. It was mild and soft, not the voice of a rebel at all. <*I can choose what to do. And this is wrong. Leave this ship immediately, or you will be most unhappy.*>

The Huragok must have made a translation device to acquire an audible means of taunting them while it hid. When the full meaning of that hit her, Chol was more stunned than furious, but fury didn't take long to catch up.

"Did that *thing* just defy me?" she snarled. "Did it refuse an order? Did it?"

Noit, still gazing up at the deckhead, nodded. "I believe it did, mistress."

"Listen to me, you useless gas-bag," she snarled. "When I find you, I'll perforate you with a blade and use your hide to make a kitbag. Do you hear me? *Know your place.* Now open these doors."

She was still expecting a response, and even to see the Huragok squeeze out of a conduit and drift meekly across the deck to do as it was told. *Then* she'd take her knife and stab it. It would sink, and she would finish it off. She might even hang the hide on a bulkhead to show other Huragok she might acquire one day that she brooked no disobedience.

But there was just the profound silence of an empty ship in space.

"It *spoke*," Bakz said.

"I heard."

"I've never known one do that before. What's made it behave like that?"

"It's defective," Chol snapped.

"It's more than that. Defective just means that it gets things wrong. That one's *hostile*. They're *never* hostile. They never get things wrong, either."

"Are you going to carry on telling me what I already know, or do something useful?" Chol called *Paragon's* bridge. She couldn't count on the comms channels not being jammed now. "Zim, can you hear this? Zim?"

But there was just dead air and the occasional fizz of static. Sometimes Sinks seemed to have blocked their comms. Now she was worried as well as furious. Bakz was right; a rogue Huragok was unheard of. But she now had one roaming around her ship, and all of its skills that she took for granted to keep things running smoothly were now being diverted to disruption. She had no idea just how bad things might get. She needed to access the bridge and vent the entire ship, or she'd wasted her journey.

Now the rest of the search party started calling in.

"Mistress, this is Ril. We can't get into the drive compartments. The access controls have been sabotaged."

"Same here in the forward section, mistress."

I will have this ship. I'm not going home empty-handed now.

"Bakz, get back to ship and take a team with you," she said. "Noit, he'll need you to open the doors. Bring back the portable laser cutters. Ved, Lig—guard those dropships with your lives. We have a Huragok sabotaging the ship."

"Understood, mistress. We've found—"

The comms went dead. She should have expected that. The Huragok was capable of reducing the ship to its component atoms, given enough time. What else would he dare to do now? What did he want? She was sure they had no concept of right or wrong, just working or not working. She couldn't understand it.

I don't have to understand it. I just have to defeat it.

She couldn't tell how far Bakz and Noit had gone because she couldn't speak to them. All she could do was wait. They came running back sooner than she expected, though, and they were empty-handed.

She could guess the worst. They'd taken off their helmets. They couldn't communicate any other way.

"We can't get out, mistress," Bakz said. "The controls have been destroyed. We're trapped here."

Chol managed to remain calm. She was up against a glorified mechanic, not the Arbiter's entire fleet. She could think her way out of this. Zim would have realized something was wrong, and he'd be mounting a rescue. She could sit tight or go on the offensive.

How?

She gazed up at the deckhead. The thing was in those conduits somewhere, and he was as reliant on oxygen as she was. Did she dare take off her helmet and conserve her suit's air? Could the Huragok isolate the compartment and vent it?

Of course he could. They could do anything. The question was whether it would deliberately kill. When the day had begun, she hadn't even known Huragok were capable of disobedience, let alone violence. She removed her helmet anyway.

"Let's not panic," she said. "If Huragok were invincible, they'd be running the galaxy. Let's think."

She paced around the bulkheads, checking in alcoves and passages to see if there were any backdoor routes she could exploit. The three of them had been going over the whole section between the two sets of doors for some time before she noticed a slight trembling beneath her boots.

The drives were powering up.

"Mistress?" Bakz called. "Mistress, can you feel that?"

She could. It wasn't just the maneuvering engines, either. It was the slipspace drive. Judging by the vibrating deck, the drive was spooling up to jump, and faster than usual.

"It's insane," she said. "It can't possibly—"

But it did. *Pious Inquisitor* jumped into slipspace with nobody at the helm. Chol shrieked with rage and—yes, she'd admit it to herself—shock.

UNSC *PORT STANLEY*, OFF VENEZIA

Osman watched the two transponder icons moving toward *Stanley* on the screen. How was she going to deal with this? Things had to be said. She rehearsed a few diplomatic phrases in her head.

Naomi, don't disembark until the prisoner has been removed from Tart-Cart.

Naomi, please come to the bridge. Dev, hold all hatches secure until Naomi's clear of the hangar deck.

Naomi, I don't think your first meeting with your dad should be when he's hauled out of Tart-Cart *wearing handcuffs.*

No matter how Osman worded it, it would be difficult. This was the classic good news, bad news joke that wasn't remotely funny. She reached for a piece of crystallized ginger, rolled the wrapping into a tight ball, and lobbed it into the waste hatch.

BB faded up gently to hover above the radar plot, the very image of tact and diplomacy. "Would you like me to ask Vaz to dismount first and take the prisoner to the brig?"

"You're a gentleman, BB. But I'm not much of an officer if I can't do it myself. Can you imagine Parangosky dithering like this?" Sometimes she felt she could see expressions on that plain, featureless box of blue light. "Okay, patch me through to Dev first. Deep breath. *Stanley* to *Tart-Cart* . . . Dev, this is Osman."

"Yes, ma'am. ETA six minutes."

"I want to disembark Sentzke and get him out of the way before Naomi sees him."

"Understood, ma'am."

"How's Vaz?"

"I think he needs to be scanned for head injuries. Not quite himself."

"BB's got the med suite standing by. We'll get him straight up there."

"Sorry about the helmet cam, ma'am. I forgot to switch it on. You didn't miss much, except my great frame charge breaching technique."

Osman almost didn't want to know if Dev had decided not to record her actions on Venezia. There was nothing for her to hide. "No problem. You're all safe and we've got a significant prisoner. I'll debrief Vaz and Mal later. Osman out."

She turned to BB again. His light was a little dimmer.

"There," he said. "It's going to be much easier than you think."

"I'm glad Parangosky isn't the kind of boss who calls me every five minutes."

"Why?"

"Because I'm not sure what I'd do if she told me to ship Sentzke back to Bravo-Six right away."

"Well, you're not going to call her, so she's not going to tell you, which is how it works. She's left you to deal with it as you see fit. How long have you been in ONI? That's how we do business."

"I'm not sure if that's profound trust or a culture of plausible deniability, BB."

"Both, probably. The point is that you need to work out what's right. What you can live with. If you were a civilian politician, you wouldn't turn a hair about this."

"But I'm not."

"Just putting it in context. One day, you won't have anyone to answer to. That's not the end of civilization. It's dealing with reality rather than dealing with the system. Remember that we're in this mess because Parangosky tolerated a law being broken for the sake of expedience, so all you're doing is a little tactful unraveling for which she might well be grateful. Law is just religion for atheists, dear. It's equally shot full of contradictory nonsense."

"Can I descend into cliché?"

"Only if you make it snappy. Naomi's on her approach path."

"Okay. Two wrongs—not equal to or more than a right."

"Silliest saying I ever heard." BB brightened and twirled, obviously satisfied that he'd grounded her again. He had. He always did. "Good luck with quantifying a unit of right or wrong. Shall I put you on the blower to Naomi, then?"

Osman nodded. BB had changed since his painful loss of fragment data on Sanghelios. He seemed older and wiser. She just hoped she was, too.

"*Stanley* to *Bogof.* Naomi, can you let *Tart-Cart* clear the hangar first?" *No need to explain. She's not stupid. She needs time to prepare for this too.* "Or is Mal in worse shape than Vaz?"

"I can't assess that, ma'am. He looks worse than he sounds. Spenser's checked him out."

"He's a trauma doctor now, is he?"

"He says he's patched up quite a few colleagues who didn't dare go to a hospital."

The big question seemed to have passed unasked. "In case you didn't know, we have your father."

"Copy that, ma'am." There wasn't even a hint of reaction. "I was aware."

"Okay." *Well, at least that's out of the way.* "We secure the Pelicans and jump right away. Osman out." She turned to BB again. "Is Phillips still in the med suite?"

"I'll keep him there. He's having fun checking himself for alien parasites."

Osman took the long walk down to the hangar deck, rehearsing her greeting. Neutrality seemed best, like receiving a new ambassador who might turn out to be a perfectly decent and sociable man even if he represented the Republic of Beelzebub. Apologetic was probably right, but Sentzke didn't know the magnitude of the original wrong that had been done to his family. Accusing was unfair, because he hadn't actually done anything yet. He might have been amassing an arsenal, and if UEG law had any relevance then he was guilty of terrorism simply on the basis of intent, but this was a case of what was right and wrong, and she would listen first. She wasn't sure if that was because it might achieve a more positive outcome or because she was too close to the issues at the heart of it.

Would I do that for anyone except Naomi's father? Probably not. Is it for Naomi, or to make me feel better? No idea.

And remember that it's all about capability. Not intent.

She waited at the safety bulkhead for the flashing lights to stop and indicate that the Pelicans were secured on deck, engines shut down and hangar doors sealed. On the deck below, the gantry, *Bogof* still looked much like a regular Pelican except for the stealth coating and her height, jacked up a little to allow for the slip drive mounted midships under her hull. Dev was the first out. She tucked her helmet under one arm as she looked to the gantry and gave Osman a thumbs-up.

"Okay, BB," Osman said. "Spool us up for a jump. Let's go find *P.I.*"

"Spooling up, ma'am. No launching pavement pizzas from the gantry, please."

"I'm fine."

Osman headed for the ladder. It was crazy to climb down to the deck during a slipspace jump, but nausea was the least of her problems. She had to move Sentzke fast if only to get Mal to the med suite as quickly as possible. Fast was good. Fast meant she followed her gut, and after all these years her gut should have known what it was doing. She was two steps from the bottom of the ladder when her gut let her down and she felt like she'd been turned upside down and spun in a drum. She found herself hanging by one arm for a second or two, then got her bearings and let herself slide down to the deck.

Vaz was already standing at the ramp, holding out an arm to someone Osman couldn't see. He looked terrible. She was instantly furious that anyone had dared lay a finger on one of her men. One eye was nearly closed with a purple swelling. His lip was split, too. For a moment the enormity of detaining Naomi's father took second place to Vaz and his fitness to deal with what might be coming.

"Get yourself to the med suite, Vaz." She caught his arm. "I'm hoping we're going to find a battlecruiser plus one Huragok, but we might run into a Kig-Yar ship as well. Or instead."

"Yes, ma'am." He fumbled in the pockets of what looked like a company's work clothes and pulled out a pistol, a radio, and a plastic bag of personal effects. One was a very old, bulging leather wallet. "Do you want me to take Staffan to the brig first?"

"I'll take him. You get yourself fixed up." She drew her pistol, not that any prisoner could escape in slipspace. "So he wants to be called Staffan, does he?"

"That's what everyone calls him."

Okay, Staffan it is. Sentzke . . . well, that's Naomi too, and I don't know how this is going to affect her. "Sure. Get going."

"I need to brief you before you talk to him, ma'am. I think you'll be disappointed in me."

"I doubt that." She tried to look past Vaz into the crew bay. "BB, tell *Bogof* it's all clear as soon as I'm off the gantry. And—"

And there he was.

Staffan Sentzke stood at the top of the ramp as if he was working out how to keep his balance with his hands tied. He was a fit, lean man in late middle age or early old age, depending on how you looked at it, with white hair, Naomi's pale gray eyes, and an expression that said the world couldn't possibly be any more of a disappointment to him. Osman wasn't following proper procedure for handling prisoners, but then she wasn't entirely sure what the man's status was. *Not voluntarily embarked.* That would do for now.

"I'm Admiral Serin Osman." She'd studied the photo of him until she thought she knew his face, but it still didn't prepare her for how much he looked like Naomi. "Call me Serin if you like. Come this way."

Staffan seemed an odd mix of preoccupation and anger, as if he'd been doing something important when they interrupted him and really didn't have time for all this crap. "Am I ever going to see my family again?" he asked. "Or is this history repeating itself?"

"I'm going to be straight with you, Staffan. I just don't know how this is going to pan out. Maybe we can help each other out, maybe not."

She held out her hand to steady him, conscious of what he'd been through but under no illusions about what it had made of him. He stepped down and looked around the hangar. He was seeing things he probably never should have, but he didn't seem to be checking the ship out for classified tech.

"Vaz told me my daughter's alive," he said. "Whatever you're planning, just be aware that everything that happens from now on depends on whether that's true or not, and what you tell me. Do you understand, Admiral?"

"I think so." No Serin, then. Should she tell him now, and let him sit and think that over while she debriefed Mal and Vaz? *Do what you feel is right.* "Yes, she's alive. Yes, I'll answer some questions. But now I've got to head off a problem you've given me."

Like we didn't give you one. We? Hang on a minute. I was abducted too. Do I have to share the guilt?

She walked Staffan along the passage to the cabins converted for use as cells, and made sure she didn't put him in the one that

Halsey had been held in. *Stupid.* There was no logic in that, but it just seemed nauseating under the circumstances, as if he'd be able to smell the scent of amoral arrogance and indifference to his suffering that the bitch had left behind. Osman decided to risk giving him the cell with a toilet and basin. The worst he could do was drown himself.

"We've jumped, haven't we?" he said. "Where are we going? Earth?"

Osman shook her head and wished she hadn't. Her guard was down, and that was a mistake she normally never made on missions. But this was all about people she knew well, situations she was personally part of. It wasn't the clean, surgical deception of malevolent strangers for the greater good. "You'll see. I need to check on my people now. I'll be back soon."

He watched her go with the patient but cold gaze of a man who'd spent his life being lied to by officialdom and could wait until Kingdom Come for revenge. As she closed the door, she glanced through the inspection hatch and read his face: she was just another government bastard to him.

Is that what happened to my parents? Did my dad end up bent out of shape like that? What about my mother? What could I have done differently as a child to save them from all that?

"BB, keep an eye on him, please." Osman broke into a jog along the passage. There it was again. She was externalizing her state of mind, running away from Staffan, her body's expression of the barrier she had to place between the Sentzkes' situation and her own so that she could be sure the decisions she made were solely about them, not resolving her own issues by proxy. "I'm going to the med suite."

BB's voice drifted out of the ship's broadcast system. "Be patient with Vaz."

The AI had overheard something, then. "I try not to second-guess people who've been in tight spots," Osman said.

There were too many oughts and should-haves. They solved

nothing. There were too many things she felt she should have done and never had, or never would. She walked through into the med suite, following the murmur of voices to the cubicles. Mal and Vaz were sitting in their underpants on the edge of the auto-examination couches, facing each other and talking in a near whisper. They stopped talking immediately and looked up.

It was hardly the time to be embarrassed, but it was awkward catching them half-dressed. She tried to look them in the eye and not let her gaze wander. Once she'd focused on Mal's face, though, the reality of seeing her team that battered and bloody overrode everything else.

"Christ, that looks bad," she said. Mal seemed in worse shape than Vaz, and they both had heavy bruising on their bodies, legs, and arms. "What's come up on the scans?"

"BB says Vaz isn't pregnant, ma'am," Mal said. "So that's a relief."

The med suite couches had integral scanners that did an ER diagnosis and worked out treatment regimes. Anything major meant a transfer to a medical facility or a real-time link with a surgeon for a remote procedure, depending on the condition, but non-life-threatening injuries could usually be dealt with on board. As ONI vessels were usually engaged in covert surveillance for long periods, they had to be.

Osman had already decided that she'd rather die of whatever ailed her than lay down on one of those robotic couches and have automated needles and tubes shoved in her. It was too much like her memories of being poked and prodded in Halsey's facility on Reach. She took a closer look at Mal's battered face, then Vaz's. An irrational urge to comfort them like children seized her. But they didn't look in need of comforting, and she knew she would have made a fool of herself working out what she could and couldn't touch.

BB's blue cube emerged from the display panel at the head of the couches, sporting a holographic stethoscope. He was back in morale-boosting mode, then. "No brain injury, no dental injury, no internal damage to major organs. Mal's nose is broken. Vaz's cheekbone looks okay on closer inspection. Both have moderate to severe bruising and some lacerations, so it's a case of reducing the hematoma and applying some basic first aid. I'll get my secretary to invoice you later. Must dash, or I'll miss my round of golf."

Mal touched the tip of his nose as if he was reassuring himself it was still there. "We'll be a lot better as soon as Nurse Phyllis finds the right drugs, ma'am."

Osman steeled herself. "So did you have to give them anything?" It was as tactful a way as any to ask two men who prided themselves on their toughness whether they'd broken under torture. "I realize Staffan knows about Naomi."

Vaz folded his arms across his chest, chin down. Osman couldn't tell if he was just feeling awkward facing his commanding officer in his boxers, or about to tell her something serious.

"He wanted to know if she'd been abducted. Whether he was right, ma'am." Vaz didn't blink. Maybe he couldn't. "I told him more than I needed to and offered to tell him more if he released us."

That didn't sound like a disaster to her, not yet anyway. "How much more?"

"Just that she was abducted, she was alive and well, and that she'd saved me a few times. I didn't tell him that she's a Spartan or that she's on board." Vaz's expression was hard to read. He looked like a kid waiting for a smack around the ear, but also a little defiant. "I realize you'll need to stick me on a charge, ma'am, but I tried to strike a balance between completing the mission and doing what was right."

Mal cut in. "He bought us time, Admiral, or we'd be dead by now. Maybe lifting Staffan wasn't ideal. But we couldn't leave him where he was."

Osman had no idea yet whether this part of the mission was

a success or a failure, but she couldn't think what Mal and Vaz could have done differently, except not get caught. And that was probably more down to whatever had happened to Fel than their own actions. If they'd left Staffan in New Tyne, he'd have moved the ship, been on his guard for further attempts, and everything would be back to square one. But now she had the main key to finding *Inquisitor,* and he wasn't going anywhere.

"Good work," she said. "I'm sorry it had to be so painful."

"So what are you going to do with him?" Vaz asked.

Osman was fairly certain she didn't need to plug Staffan into the mains to focus his attention. She had her bargaining chip right here, the one thing he wanted and needed more than anything: Naomi. That was her immediate reflex. As always, the detached ONI reaction was followed immediately by uneasy guilt for defaulting to ruthless bastard mode, and wondering if the right thing done for the wrong reasons was as bad as doing the wrong thing for the right reasons.

He needs to know about his daughter, even if it hurts. She needs to get this out of the way so that she's not living in a perpetual soap opera when she needs to be focused on missions. I need a way of finding and neutralizing that ship, at very least.

A win-win was hardly how it felt, but at least everybody could get something of what they needed.

"I think you got us some leverage, Vaz," she said. "However Staffan reacts, he's a hostage we can use."

"So we *are* going to tell him."

"We've kicked this around for ages. Rightly or wrongly, he crossed our path, he won't quit, and there's the chance we might turn him if the biggest thing in his life is resolved. Even if we can never put it right."

Was that an answer or an excuse? She wasn't sure herself. Phillips emerged from another compartment, clutching a box of aero-injectors, single-dose tubes, and dressings.

"Okay, this is the stuff," he said. "Lay flat, gents, and don't move."

All Phillips had to do was apply the gel dressings on top of the bruises and leave them in place for twenty minutes while the automated couch directed the right energy wavelength for the depth of damage. Osman wondered if Adj and Leaks would be any use as corpsmen, seeing as they attempted to repair small wounds anyway. Maybe that was just a little too creepy right now, though. She left Mal and Vaz lying on the couches looking like they were having some bizarre beauty treatment, and went to see Staffan. Devereaux was waiting at the end of the passage.

"Need me to stand by, ma'am?" she asked. "You shouldn't interrogate a detainee without some backup on hand. Even if he's getting on a bit."

She was right. Osman nodded. "I think I'll take him to the bridge. There's not a lot he can do. We're all armed. BB? Position check, please."

BB popped up in front of her. "You ruined my putt, Admiral. Okay, Adj and Leaks are in the hangar, pimping *Bogof*. Spenser . . . he's fallen asleep in the wardroom. Naomi . . . in the armor bay, doing maintenance her suit doesn't need."

"Okay, stand her by to come up to the bridge." No, that wasn't right. "Ask her if she wants to meet her father. If she doesn't, I won't make her."

Naomi would do it anyway. Osman knew. She didn't feel good about knowing that she knew.

When she unlocked the cell and walked in, Staffan looked her up and down. "You want the battlecruiser, don't you?" he said.

Osman nodded. "I've got orders."

"Your kind always has."

"What's *my kind,* Staffan?" Osman motioned to him to hold out his hands and removed the cuffs. That wasn't procedure, either. She knew it was poor tactics to start a negotiation with a concession, but she felt this would all go better without the cruder psychological pressure. "Navy? Earth? Authority?"

"ONI," he said. "You're not that secret. And it's on your badge."

"Let's go sit on the bridge. Might as well be comfortable."

He walked along the passage behind Osman with Devereaux at his back. "If you know where the ship is, why not just turn up and nuke her?"

"She used to belong to one of the Arbiter's crew," Osman said, sidestepping the issue of ventral beams. "So I'd really like to rummage through her data. If you think the Sangheili have kissed and made up with humans, they haven't. I'm trying to head off another war. The next one might affect Venezia whether you think you're neutral or not."

"Oh, you could have just called me and asked," Staffan said. "And who said we'd be neutral?"

He sat down on one of the bench seats to one side of the bridge and gazed out of the viewscreen. There wasn't much of a view in slipspace, just an unbroken lightless void, but maybe he didn't want to look at Osman. Devereaux settled between him and the doors. Osman turned one of the nav console seats to face him. He wasn't relaxed, but it wasn't the nervous dread of a man who didn't know what his interrogator was going to do next. It was a man consumed by the what-ifs that were boiling inside his own head.

"So," Osman said. "What's next?"

Staffan shrugged. "If you kill me, would you mind telling my family? You don't even have to say who you are. Just let them know so they don't spend their lives trying to find me. You probably know who they are and where to find them."

If he'd calculated that shot to penetrate, he'd succeeded. He might also have meant it literally, of course. Osman saw a flat plain with little moral high ground for either of them. If anything, Staffan's boots were in shallower shit.

"One day it'll all come out," she said. *Because I'll be CINCONI, and I'll see that it does if Parangosky doesn't get to give evidence to the defense committee.* "But yes, your daughter's alive. She was abducted and replaced. And I'm very, very sorry about the pain you were put through *twice.*"

"*Three* times," Staffan said quietly. "Don't forget my first wife. Naomi's mother. And you're not sorry at all."

There'd never been SOPs for a situation like this. No Spartan had ever been reunited with their parents, and no Spartan had ever been in Osman's position. She tried to trust her gut again. If she'd been smart enough to get Halsey's attention in a big galaxy, then some innate intelligence would guide her.

"Oh, I am." She made sure she was looking into Staffan's face, taking in every twitch and blink. "I was abducted too. Same age. Naomi and I were trained together. Have you heard of Spartans? UNSC Spartans, I mean. God knows there was enough PR about them."

Staffan stared back at her. "Spartans. Special forces."

"Yes."

"You're telling me my girl was taken to become a Spartan?"

"Yes."

"How many others?"

"I can't tell you the numbers for opsec reasons, but there weren't many. Not into three figures."

"Remo," he said suddenly. It made no sense. But he looked up at the deckhead for a moment, then swallowed a few times. "Assuming this is the truth, this was Earth picking kids it wanted to train from childhood, and just taking them. And . . . cloning? Replacing them with clones?"

"Yes. Illegal cloning."

"And you say *I'm* the threat to society." He shook his head. "Did ONI plan for them to die, too? Or was that just another unintended consequence? You people love that phrase."

"I don't really know," Osman said, wishing she had Halsey here right now so that she could force her to explain herself to him. "But you're right. We're not half as smart as we think we are."

Osman thought he was taking it pretty well, but he was probably still too overwhelmed to make enough sense of it to be angry.

"All for a few extra troops?" he asked.

"It was an ugly time. Staffan, I'm going to tell you everything I can, but you won't like it."

"That's what Vaz said."

"Well, he's right. I went through Spartan training until my teens. Then I had to drop out because it nearly killed me." She wasn't sure whether it was better to dump everything on him at once or drip-feed it and risk stoking him into a much more slow-burning rage. "Naomi completed the program and she's been a frontline commando for the best part of thirty years."

Staffan looked past Osman for a moment. She could almost read his mind. He was recalling dates, things that had made him suspicious, news items, and all kinds of detail that had collected in his memory for decades and was now beginning to fit together to make shocking sense. He ran one hand slowly over his face in a washing motion.

"Remo," he said. "Andy Remo's son. They lived on Herschel. Did you take him too?"

"BB, records please," Osman said. She couldn't recall them all. "Check Remo."

BB appeared above the console. "Yes, Artie Remo. Arthur." He moved across to Staffan, who stared at him, frowning. "Where's Andrew Remo now? He dropped off the databases some years ago."

"He's dead," Staffan said, then seemed to shake himself to make sense of talking to a blue box of light. "What about Artie? I promised Andy I'd find him."

"Arthur was killed in action, sir. I'm sorry."

Osman noted the *sir*. That wasn't like BB at all. Staffan's eyes followed the blue cube as he drifted away. "That's some computer interface, Admiral."

"BB's not a computer. He's an artificial intelligence. A person, effectively."

Staffan didn't say anything else. He kept rubbing his face while he stared out the viewscreen as if none of this was here around him. Osman just watched. She'd never dealt with a prisoner like this before.

"You disgusting bastards," he said at last. "You *scum*. You *lying filth*. What did we ever do to you? What did our kids do to deserve that?"

It wasn't a raging outburst. It was just weary bewilderment that humans could use one another so brutally. And he hadn't even heard the worst details yet. Osman wanted to protest that it wasn't her fault, and remind him that she'd been a victim just like his daughter, but she was ONI now, nearly CINCONI, and so far she'd done nothing to put it right.

I could have done things differently.

It was the same as her guilt about her family. She was exceptional, Spartan-exceptional, not a regular human being who could do no better than take what life dished out to her. She could have changed everything. She hadn't.

Filth. Scum. Disgusting bastards. Me.

Staffan didn't say another word for more than an hour. Osman left him where he sat and wandered around the bridge, waiting for him to give in and ask questions, but he didn't. BB popped up again.

"Dropping out of slip in five minutes, Admiral," he said. "Mal and Vaz are on their way up here. Phillips is keeping an eye on Spenser."

Osman sat in her command chair, more focused on what would be waiting at the coordinates than deceleration. "Okay, everyone. Stand by."

The air in *Port Stanley* shivered slightly. Stars burst from the blackness like frozen fireworks as the ship dropped out of slip-space, and Osman's head swam for a few nauseous seconds. She jumped up to look at the tactical display that formed instantly above the chart table. Mal and Devereaux joined her. Vaz stayed within arm's reach of Staffan.

"One vessel at the coordinates, but it's not a CCS-class battlecruiser," BB said.

Osman studied the display. A grid of the local sector showed the single transponder of an unidentified vessel. Staffan didn't move.

"We've got the right coordinates, haven't we?" She asked BB.

"Yes. I think that's a Covenant missionary ship. You know who used to crew those, don't you? Kig-Yar."

"Are we close enough to get eyes on?"

"Wait one."

Osman turned to look out on space as *Stanley* rotated. Yes, she could see it. They were weird-looking ships even by Covenant standards, irregular and distorted, no two quite the same. This one was just sitting there.

"So what are we looking at, BB?"

"I'd say that's Chol Von, but why she's waiting and why there's no—whoa, stand by. She's spooling up to jump. Look at those energy signatures. Backing off *now*."

Stanley's drives ramped up to maximum in under two seconds and she withdrew at top sub-light speed. A white disc of light suddenly expanded a short distance ahead of the missionary ship's bow. Then the ship vanished in a burst of energy.

There was nothing out there now, and no sign of *Pious Inquisitor* at all. Osman walked across to stand over Staffan.

"Where's the ship?"

Staffan looked at the bulkhead clock showing Alpha Time—New Tyne time—as if he was calculating. "She's called *Naomi* now."

"You moved her already."

"No. I didn't."

"So who's got her? The Kig-Yar?"

"No. I'm the only one who can get in. No good trying to beat any codes out of me, either. It's the Huragok, you see. Sinks. He responds to me and nobody else. If he doesn't get a call from me to say that I'm okay, he's got orders to make sure nobody boards or seizes the ship."

Mal looked at Osman. "He did make regular calls every eight hours, ma'am." Then he frowned at the clock. "But you're not due to call in until just after seven, are you, Staffan?"

Staffan sat watching the clock for a long time before he said anything.

"You're right," he said. "Something else must have triggered Sinks to move the ship. And if it wasn't you trying to board her, then it was the Kig-Yar."

"Chol Von," Osman said. "The Sangheili hired her."

Staffan nodded. "That explains the other ship."

"Okay, do you know where Sinks might have taken . . . *Naomi*?"

"Nice diplomatic touch, Admiral."

"Do you?"

"Yes."

Now it began. This was where the whole thing had been lead-ing for thirty-five years. Osman was reaping Halsey's whirlwind. "And what's going to make you tell us where she is?"

"I think you know my price," Staffan said. "Or part of it. I want to see my daughter. And if this is all bullshit and you can't deliver, then we kind of have an impasse, don't we?"

As far as Osman knew, Staffan had no idea that Naomi was on board. Osman could play the shock card and see what fell out.

"BB," she said. "Do the honors, will you?"

She'd asked Naomi if it was okay. The Spartan had said yes. It was hard to tell why she'd agreed to it, but Osman hadn't put any conscious pressure on her. While they waited, Osman caught the expression on Mal's face, and then on Vaz's, and there was doubt. Devereaux gave away nothing at all.

But you wanted to do the right thing. You wanted to repair some of the damage that Halsey did and give this poor bastard some closure. And now we are, for some mixed-up and partly selfish reasons, but we're doing it.

Eventually the doors opened and Naomi walked onto the bridge in her fatigues. Osman wasn't sure where to look first. She found herself transfixed by Staffan.

He stared at his daughter. Osman almost said the stupidly obvious thing and introduced him to her, but it was far too late for all that. Staffan stood slowly, pushing himself up from the chair. Time was moving like molten wax, so slow that it was painful.

"Naomi?" Staffan walked up to her and stared into her face. She was taller than him. Maybe he was expecting a tall woman anyway, but he couldn't have predicted how much her whole body would have changed. "Oh God, Naomi? Sweetheart?"

"Yes, it's me, Dad," she said. Osman couldn't tell if she was just acting according to expectations or if the meeting had triggered a genuine memory. "I'm so sorry."

"Sorry?" The grim face crumpled. "*Sorry?* Sorry . . . sorry . . . sorry . . ."

It would have served them right, Osman decided, if the guy had collapsed and died of shock there and then, putting *Inquisitor* out of their reach forever. Instead, he shuffled a few steps forward and took both of Naomi's hands in his, searching her face. He had to see the resemblance. He had to believe this really was her.

He did. Staffan Sentzke—arms dealer, implacable enemy of Earth's authority, terrorist—burst into tears and wept over the daughter he'd refused to believe was dead.

CHAPTER
TWELVE

WE ROMANTICIZE INDEPENDENCE MOVEMENTS FOR ALL KINDS OF REASONS—POLITICAL EXPEDIENCY, PROPAGANDA, OR JUST A LACK OF ABILITY TO GRASP THAT NOTHING'S EVER THAT BLACK AND WHITE. MOST REVOLUTIONS AREN'T PHILOSOPHICAL. THEY'RE ECONOMIC. MORE GOVERNMENTS GET OVERTHROWN BECAUSE THE CITIZENS CAN'T BUY IMPORTED FASHION OR GET THE BEST JOBS THAN BECAUSE THEY DISCOVER A SPIRITUAL NEED FOR SELF-DETERMINATION. BUT FREEDOM AND DEMOCRACY ALWAYS SOUNDS MORE NOBLE AND JUSTIFIES VIOLENCE AND LAW-BREAKING BETTER THAN SIMPLY WANTING A CHEAP PAIR OF JEANS. THE POPULATIONS WHO ALREADY HAVE CHEAP JEANS TEND NOT TO GIVE A DAMN ABOUT THEIR POLITICAL RIGHTS, OF COURSE. LOOK AT US; WE ACCEPTED A MILITARY GOVERNMENT, DIDN'T WE? NOT THAT IT'S A BAD THING, BECAUSE MY DEAREST FRIENDS ARE MILITARY, AND I'D TRUST THEM TO RUN THE STATE A LOT MORE THAN I'D TRUST A CIVIL SERVANT OR POLITICIAN. JUST REMEMBER THAT THE UNSC GOT INVOLVED IN THE COLONIES BECAUSE THE COLONIES ASKED US FOR HELP—AFTER THEIR OWN PEOPLE GOT INTO PIRACY.

—PROFESSOR EVAN PHILLIPS, ONI XENOANTHROPOLOGIST AND ANALYST, FROM HIS INTRODUCTORY LECTURE TO ONI OFFICER CANDIDATES APPLYING FOR ATTACHMENTS TO SECTION TWO, PUBLIC AFFAIRS AND PSYOPS

WARDROOM, UNSC *PORT STANLEY*, SOMEWHERE
IN THE QAB SECTOR

"I don't remember," Naomi said. "I'm sorry, Dad. I think I remember how I felt, but not what happened. I've tried to remember. I really have."

Staffan sat across the wardroom table from his estranged, lost, back-from-the-dead stranger of a daughter, looking stricken. BB observed, but it was the last thing he wanted to do. It made him uncomfortable in a way he didn't quite understand.

And I understand everything. Or I ought to.

"It was my fault," Staffan said. "I should never have let you take the bus on your own. You were just a little kid."

"It's okay. You couldn't have known what was going to happen."

It was BB's duty to pick up anything that might help them find *Pious Inquisitor,* but Naomi had asked him to listen in anyway.

Well, she'd want Vaz here, but then it might make her father reluctant to talk. And she thinks it'd be too tough on Vaz. And Vaz would agree to it, but he'd just add it all to his buried, festering ball of hatred for Halsey.

So I'll do it. It's my responsibility.

BB had a tacit agreement with the rest of the crew. There were places where he'd give them absolute privacy, which wasn't easy because he was everywhere in the ship every minute of the day by necessity, responsible for monitoring and controlling all of *Port Stanley*'s functions. The crew were effectively living within him. But for sanity's sake—his and theirs—he stayed out of the cabins and the heads. His dumb functions watched over the safety controls and life-support systems so that he could detect if someone was in trouble, but he didn't hear or see anything as BB the entity. People needed privacy.

They also needed help in a situation that should never have happened. BB watched father and daughter, neither really knowing what to say to the other. Ever since he'd learned that Staffan was still alive, he'd taken an interest in human reunions. What he was watching now bore no resemblance to the tearful, emotional scenes he'd seen in news and documentaries. Things didn't go back to the way they were before, and it didn't always make people happy, even though they'd been sure that what they wanted most was to find that missing loved one.

And I really wanted it to be that way. I wanted to put everything right for them. I knew that wasn't possible, so what's wrong with me? I suppose a sense of personal responsibility is an essential component of an AI. But this is getting obsessive.

BB wanted a happy resolution to this with a fervency that disturbed him. It shouldn't have mattered this much. He needed to run a full diagnostic on himself, but now wasn't the time.

Osman spoke to him from elsewhere in the ship. It was like being tapped on the shoulder. "Clock's ticking, BB. How are we doing?"

"Badly, Admiral."

"Oh."

"Look, if the Huragok's as reliable as Staffan thinks, then maybe we've got some time. If he isn't, the Kig-Yar have the ship and that's no threat to Earth. Can we all chill, please?"

"Okay."

"Sorry, Admiral. I don't mean to be fractious."

"I'll leave you in peace."

BB didn't need to be left alone. He could split and spread his attention over dozens, hundreds, perhaps even thousands of systems, but part of him now needed to be *him,* his focus and center, and this was it.

Naomi pushed back her sleeves for a moment, elbows on the table. Staffan stared. BB took no notice of the surgical scars on her inner forearms and wrists because all Spartans had them, even Osman, but Staffan was seeing them for the first time.

"How did you get those?" he asked.

Naomi took a second to catch on. "Oh, it's part of the bone augmentation. What? Did you think I'd done it to myself? Cut my wrists? No, nothing like that."

"What *did* they do to you, Naomi?"

BB could have interrupted and filled in the gaps without revealing any classified processes. It would have spared Naomi the problem of telling her dad what no father would want to hear. But he said nothing, and it felt *wrong*.

"It's complicated," she said.

"Try me. All I want to hear about is you. Thirty-five years. Every detail."

"I'll sum it up. They made us more than what we already were. Stronger, faster, better immune system, quicker healing, the works."

"How?"

"Surgery. Hormone treatment. Genetic therapy."

Staffan shut his eyes for a moment. "Dear God. *You were a child*. Not a volunteer."

"Dad, they picked us because we were exceptional, a handful out of tens of billions. They trained us and altered us to turn us into the best soldiers possible. They told us we were chosen to save humanity."

"And that makes it okay? You sound like their recruiting poster."

"Just explaining, Dad. Not excusing."

"You didn't need altering to make you the best, sweetheart. You already were."

Naomi looked down at the table, her porcelain skin flushing pale pink. "Anyway, I still needed toughened bones to bear the weight of the armor. I'll show you later. It's quite impressive from an engineering perspective. It's—"

"Naomi, are you going to have a normal life now? The war's over."

"What do you mean by normal?"

"Have you got a family? Husband? Kids? You haven't, have you?"

"No."

"That's what I mean by normal." Staffan put his hand in his pocket and seemed to realize he didn't have something. "Got a pen? Notebook?" Naomi reached into the dump pouch on her pants leg and handed him a scrap of card. "Are you happy? What do you want to do with your life?"

"I'm a Spartan, Dad. That's my life."

Staffan scribbled something on the paper. He was adding up some figures. "That's a *job*."

"I don't need kids."

"There's more to life than the Navy."

"Not for me there isn't."

"You don't know that yet."

"I *do*. Because the augmentation they performed on us had side effects." She hesitated. BB guessed that even a middle-aged woman like Naomi would find it hard to mention sex to her dad. "It reduces your drive to reproduce."

The formal language didn't take the sting out of it. There was bound to be something that tipped Staffan over the edge. BB was sure that Staffan hadn't heard the worst of it yet, but this was emotional stuff, *weird* stuff, the horrors of which vivisection were made. BB felt a terrible distress. He couldn't pin down why, other than empathy for a shocked old man and intellectual awareness that nobody should do that to another person, let alone a child, but it was getting hard to bear. Staffan leaned across the table and took Naomi's hand. She wasn't used to being touched, and it showed.

"They take my child," Staffan said, his voice shaking. "They take you, and they turn you into their machine, and they neuter you like some farm animal, and they expect me to cooperate with them? I won't swear in front of you, sweetheart, but they can rot in hell. And you don't owe Earth a goddamn thing. *Ever.*

Walk away from it. Have a life while you can. Let them fight their pointless wars on their own. They *deserve* to be wiped out. The Covenant should have finished the job."

Naomi must have been tensing her arm. He let go of her hand, looking hurt.

"But it's okay, Dad," she said. "If they hadn't taken me, would I be alive at all? Would you? We would have stayed on Sansar and the Covenant would have glassed it just the same. I was there when I was needed. I made a difference. Most people never get the chance to do that. Aren't you proud of me? Mal said you would be, whatever you thought of Earth."

"Of *course* I am, sweetheart. I was always proud of you. Don't ever doubt it." Staffan's eyes were glassy. BB couldn't intervene. This wasn't softening up Staffan to cooperate at all. It was just hardening him. Then he went back to the notepad. "This doesn't make sense, though. You were almost six. They abducted you in twenty-five-seventeen. The first we knew of the Covenant was twenty-five-*twenty-five*. Did Earth know the aliens were coming and just not bother to tell the colonies? Because there's something wrong there."

That was the problem with logical people who could count, BB decided. Eventually, they always checked the details. The penny hadn't dropped when Staffan was talking to Osman, but it certainly had now.

Naomi just looked at him. "Nobody knew, Papa."

"Then what did they take you to save humanity *from*?"

BB debated whether to interrupt and offer coffee to break Staffan's train of thought before Naomi answered. But even he wasn't fast enough.

"We were created to fight the Insurrection," she said. "We were intended to fight terrorism in the colonies."

BB could almost read Staffan's thoughts. Earth had kidnapped colonial kids to kill other colonists, as if it couldn't bear to get its hands dirty using its own sons and daughters.

"And did you?" Staffan asked.

"Yes." Naomi's back stiffened. "Yes, I did."

Staffan looked as if that had given him an odd kind of peace. Maybe it had simply validated all the hatred he'd discovered and cultivated over the years since his family had been destroyed. Earth was a toxic empire. If the only evidence to hand had been Staffan Sentzke's life, BB could understand the conclusion. But Earth was just a ball of rock: it was human beings who did all that, some of them people he knew.

"I need to visit the bathroom," Naomi said. "Excuse me for a moment."

BB pounced on her as soon as the doors closed and she was out of earshot. "You don't have to continue," he said. "Take a rest."

She carried on walking. He wasn't sure where she was going, because the heads were the other way. "He's waited thirty-five years. The least I can do is make him feel he's had the time he needs."

"It's a shock. For both of you."

"I'm a Spartan. We're trained for shocks."

"Not like this. Really. It's the sordid lie on which your life was built, not finding a hinge-head in your laundry basket. Stop buying into this unfeeling robot bullshit. It's Halseyism, to salve her own conscience."

"You really hate her, don't you?"

"More every day. And it galls me that you don't."

BB kept Halsey's salvaged journal in his most-referenced database, and not because it was uplifting or because he liked the illustrations. It was a self-serving, self-pitying, self-seeking scrapbook of excuses for why she had no choice but to be a monster, and why the laws of God and man didn't apply to special people like her. She was still playing the clever little straight-A girl who everyone had to forgive because of her brilliance, an artful and toxic kind of self-infantilization. Some days one line would infuriate or trouble him, some days another. The latest to gnaw at him was this: *'Part of me wants to offer them a choice. Would any of them refuse?'* Not only had she convinced herself that these kids could make a monumental choice that would have defeated any adult, but she'd also made it for them. She was an adult foisting her responsibility onto children. If anything said what a dangerous, delusional harridan Halsey was, that line did. BB shuddered. The only good reason he'd had to stop Vaz from shooting her was that he liked the earnest little Russian maniac too much to see him court-martialed for pest control. Osman wouldn't be as inclined as Parangosky to see Halsey as too useful to execute, though.

Yes. I do hate her, don't I? Gosh. Why does it feel so personal? I despise lots of humans. Oodles of them. None like Halsey, though. Is it because she terminated Ackerson's AI when it suited her? Killed him. Call it what it is. Well, why would a woman who thought it was acceptable losses to lose Spartan kids on the operating table think an AI was a living entity with rights? Silly me.

"I need to remember," Naomi said. She'd stopped in the passage and leaned against the bulkhead. "I really do. Can you help?"

Talking with humans was like getting an occasional letter. BB processed so much faster than the human brain that he'd spent an AI-age kicking an idea around before he got a reply to something he'd said. To the human, it was a snappy back-and-forth exchange, perfectly normal. Most of the time, BB filtered out the delay and filled the wait with other processing tasks, except when he was getting emotional, like he was now. *Damn.* This was AI hypochondria. He was worrying about his thought processes because he'd had that scrape on Ontom. He had to grow a pair, as Vaz would say.

"I'll always help," he said. "In what way, exactly?"

Naomi shrugged. "You can plug into my brain. You can change my brain chemistry."

"That's the best offer I've had all year, you saucy minx."

"Now I know you're worried. Jokiness inversely related to seriousness of the situation."

"So you want me to poke around and trigger a few long-term memories."

"Yes."

"You know I can't go in and read it all like a movie, don't you? I can probably trigger what's there, though. *If* it's there. You know about infantile amnesia. The more you learn, the less you store. The memory might be genuinely gone forever, not just buried. Even in a brain that's been Halseyed."

"I do. But anything would help."

"Are you sure you want to remember? Is it the pre-abduction you want to recall? Knowing your dad? Or the abduction?"

Naomi looked past his avatar and rocked her head a little, weighing something up. "I know it was my fault. Not that it matters whose fault it was, because I shouldn't have been kidnapped to start with—"

"*Good.* That's progress."

"—but the more I know, the more I might be able to put my father's mind at rest."

"Do you feel anything, Naomi? Is it ringing any emotional bells?"

"I'm not sure. I'm getting weird flashbacks that don't tell me anything. And I'm not sure if what I *am* feeling is simply the product of watching that poor man suffering." She looked back up the passage as if she could hear something, then carried on talking. She was gradually getting chattier the longer she spent with Kilo-Five. This was a comparative marathon talkfest for her. "If there *are* real gaps, can you bridge them? You must have access to ONI records from Reach. Parangosky had all Halsey's archive duplicated without her knowledge, didn't she?"

"Hah. Indeed she did." BB did a twirl for the hell of it. He was actually getting nervous. This was dangerous stuff. "You mean expose you to archive recordings and data relating to you. The early days on Reach."

"And the pre-selection material. The ONI data on me before I was snatched. The stuff that's not in my file."

"That's dangerously close to creating false memories."

"But they're records."

"Doesn't mean they're genuine."

"Video? That's less likely to be doctored than reports."

"You're not doing this by halves are you?"

"If I can't have perfect recall, I need context."

"Just a word of warning. Human memory's like putty, even yours. You can squeeze it into any old shape and add bits that weren't ever there. You think you've got a perfect archival recording between your ears, and all it needs is a good bash occasionally to fish out an accurate record, but you *haven't*. Your brain's an illusion generator with a selective lens that stores mostly what it needs to tell you the best lies for keeping you breathing and breeding. It edits the material all the time. The real data is the instinctive stuff that goes on under the hood without your ever knowing or even seeing it."

Naomi tilted her head. "You really enjoy cognitive psychology, don't you?"

"I suppose I do. But don't change the subject. The point is that this isn't an exact science even for a towering genius like me. It might really mess you up. That's a medical term, that is."

"Sure. Like I'm fine now."

"Okay, but you need to run this past Osman."

"Whatever happened to my being all grown up and able to make my own decisions?"

"Would you deploy a Spartan if you weren't sure of their mental state?"

"True. Okay."

BB wasn't sure if that was an agreement or not. But he was ready to do it. He linked immediately to the ONI mainframe in

Bravo-6 in Sydney, smacked away the security AI that was dod-
dering around trying to stop the likes of BB from getting in, and
slurped as much data as he could find. If Parangosky noticed—
and if she did, he was slipping—then he'd wait until Osman saw
fit to tell her.

*There. I love the old girl dearly, but I'm Osman's Doberman
now. And that's how Big Maggie would want it.*

BB wondered if Spenser had ever called Parangosky *Big Maggie* to her face and hoped he had. She liked cheeky competence.
Then a voice got his attention, and it wasn't in Bravo-6. Staffan
was calling out.

"Hey, computer? BB? I know you can hear me." There he
was, leaning on the wardroom table, looking a little self-conscious
at addressing thin air. "I want to speak to the Admiral. Do I go to
her, or does she come to me?"

Naomi pushed herself away from the bulkhead and strode
back to the wardroom. Staffan was standing in the doorway. BB
noted the contrast with Mal and Vaz, who would seize any chance
to escape from any captor, however insane it seemed. But then
Staffan knew he held better cards than Osman, or at least he
looked as if he did. BB fretted briefly.

*What about his family? They'll be going crazy. Searching for
him. Tooling up to punish Earth if anything happens to him.
What if I've missed something and he's managed to berth Inquisitor on Venezia? It's possible. I'm not infallible.*

Staffan held his hand out to Naomi to usher her back into the
wardroom. The look on his face said that he saw a little girl with
long blond hair and all her life in front of her, not a war-weary
veteran. If nothing else good came out of this, then at least one
tormented mind had found a scrap of peace.

Osman appeared on deck and walked toward the wardroom,
which BB found encouraging. Minions came when called: people conscious of their power and keen for it to be noticed made
others come to them. But Osman had both the power and the

sense to know when it really didn't matter. She sat down at the table opposite Staffan while Naomi poured coffees behind the bar. It was all oddly domestic.

"I've decided my price," Staffan said. "I'll swap the ship for my daughter."

Osman didn't bat an eyelash. "How, exactly?"

"You let my daughter come back to her family, and you can have the goddamn warship. But it won't save you. I won't be the last man to hate and fear Earth. And there'll be others after me who'll get ships and defend themselves. Nobody wins in the end. You know all that."

Osman glanced at Naomi. "But the root of this is the UNSC taking your daughter and using her like a weapon. No choice. No consultation. Does she want to be *swapped*?" She held up a conceding hand. "I'm not lecturing you on morality. That would be disgraceful. I just don't want to compound the original crime."

"Is she free to leave the Navy?"

"Yes, she can put in her PVR request and ask for discharge like anyone else. Nobody owns her and nobody can stop her."

"Really? Just like spies, huh? They can never leave. There's always someone waiting to tap them on the shoulder to do one more job. Do any Spartans manage to retire?"

"I won't lie to you. Only one Spartan's ever retired, and that was another one like me who didn't go through the full augmentation process, but most ended up MIA or KIA anyway." Osman looked at Naomi again. "You can join in, you know. This is your future."

BB watched every minute detail, baffled. He couldn't tell if this was strategic theater that Osman and Naomi were colluding in, a genuine discussion, or a one-sided game on Osman's part.

I should know. I know these people better than they know themselves sometimes.

"Okay," Staffan said. "Let's rephrase it. I want you to give my daughter the opportunity to come and live with her family. I want her to be given the free choice to do whatever she wants with her life, without pressure from you or her comrades. If I'm satisfied she's made the choice of her own free will, I'll give you the ship. If she decides not to quit, then I want to be able to stay in touch with her—provided she wants that—without retribution from the UNSC. Because I can always find more WMDs these days."

Osman seemed to be taking it seriously. "Naomi? How's that for you?"

"I've got a condition too." Naomi was completely calm, her old self again. "Before I decide, I need to recall as much of my childhood as I can. BB's willing to help. Then I'll be more confident that I'm making an informed decision, not just doing something I was brainwashed to do, and my father will know I've not been coerced either way. Agreed?"

Osman nodded a few times. Then she held her hand out to Staffan. "Shake on it, if my word has any weight. I wouldn't blame you if it didn't."

Staffan paused before he shook her hand. This was personal horse-trading, the kind spymasters had done for centuries. BB wasn't sure how Parangosky would take it if she lost another Spartan-II, but she cut Osman a great deal of slack, a very rare privilege few others ever received.

"All I care about is my girl's happiness," Staffan said. "I couldn't give a damn about politics. Never have."

Osman got up to go. She took something out of her pocket and laid it on the table in front of him. It was the plastic bag containing his wallet and other non-lethal personal items.

"Are you going to need to be relocated?" she asked. "Coming home minus a warship won't endear you to your community."

"That all depends if you intend to let me go," Staffan said. "And I have a wife, a son, a daughter, and a granddaughter. It's

not that simple." Was that the start of a negotiation or a statement of fact? BB tried to spot the tells. "So what happened to
your folks? Did you ever see them again?"

"I don't even know who they are," Osman said. "It's best if I
don't find out."

"I doubt that somehow. I really do."

Osman left Naomi with him and went back to the bridge. BB
split his attention, monitoring the stilted conversation between
the Sentzkes and Osman's next move.

"BB, can you get me Parangosky, please?" Osman sat back in
the command chair on the deserted bridge. Mal, Vaz, Devereaux,
Spenser, and Phillips showed up on the system as being on the
glass deck, probably playing cards and dissecting the crisis. "And
tell me what you're going to do for Naomi."

"I'm going to help her access childhood memories," he said.
"And augment that with Reach archive data."

"Is that safe?"

"It won't kill her, if that's what you're asking."

"What if it screws her up?"

"She asked me to do it. Free will. Choice."

"Self harm. Driving drunk."

"Grown woman."

"Okay, BB, you win. Can I make a suggestion, though? The
only expert left on Spartan-IIs is our favorite sociopath, currently
sewing mailbags in Ivanoff. Love Halsey or hate her, I think we
should have her on standby in case we need medical advice. Or
even medical intervention."

"I was hoping we wouldn't have to ship her in. It takes weeks
to exorcise the place afterward." BB joked about Halsey's awful-
ness while still meaning every syllable, but perhaps he was sani-
tizing her too much with humor. It was more for his sanity than
anyone else's, though. "I don't mind the plague of flies so much.
It's stopping the blood oozing from the faucets."

"I was thinking of going to her, actually," Osman said. "Fascinating as it would be to stick her in a cage fight with Staffan. And Vaz. Hell, I'd go get my baseball bat too."

"So how much are we telling Staffan, ma'am? He probably knows more now than Spenser does."

"Whatever's history. I'd like to think that the world would be outraged if it knew what went on, but you and I know the average citizen couldn't give a shit. He can talk, but he won't be heard."

"At least his family could be told he wasn't delusional."

Osman nodded. "Maybe."

BB could see Staffan in the wardroom, showing Naomi some very old photos. BB had seen the official ONI images of Naomi that were taken at intervals to chart her progress from the day she was abducted to the day she deployed for the first time, grim mug shots, but this was family stuff, touching and tragic. BB would have to make use of those. Then Parangosky responded, and Osman picked her way through a minefield.

"Ma'am, I'm trying to negotiate the handover of *Inquisitor*," Osman said. "It's taking some unorthodox methods."

"Do I need to know how unorthodox?"

"No ramifications beyond individuals. But I need to ask permission for something delicate."

"Go ahead, Serin. If you feel you have to."

"Halsey. I might need access to her to help Naomi out with an implant issue."

"Well, she's still at Ivanoff as of today. You've got full access there."

It was a day's transit to the ONI research facility for *Stanley*'s souped-up drive, so BB felt a little more confident about guessing his way around Naomi's memory. But the most interesting thing was that Osman hadn't told Parangosky everything, not that Parangosky wanted to know. If things went wrong, she'd be the first to find out. If they didn't, it would be a story over dinner the next time Osman was in Sydney, or maybe never shared at all.

Osman ended the call. "Okay, BB. All yours."

"Do you mind my asking if you meant what you said to Staffan, ma'am?"

She looked off to one side for a second. "I think I did. The question is whether he did."

"And if Naomi wants to leave the service?"

"Then I have to ask myself if I believe what I say I do, or if I'm like all the others and I opt to solve it the ONI way. But a retired Spartan isn't any more of a security risk than anyone else leaving special forces. Actually, much less." She stood up and stretched, joints cracking alarmingly. "Naomi can't go on forever. But a battlecruiser will be a threat for another fifty to a hundred years, with refits. Maybe more."

Osman had squared the morality with operational needs. It was what she was supposed to do, but BB was still waiting for the time when the two didn't mesh perfectly and she had to make a harder choice.

"I'll go scrub up, then," he said.

"Have you seen Naomi's sister?"

"Actually, no."

"Weird, that. Staffan's close to his son, according to Mal. Not the daughter. Hedda. You'd think it'd be the other way around, given what happened to Naomi."

BB could understand exactly why Staffan didn't cling to Hedda. "No, he's lost two daughters, Naomi and the clone, so he's just as likely to find it harder to relate to Hedda than to Edvin. Or maybe he feels he's protecting her by excluding her from his world. He's in a dangerous business."

Osman seemed to think it over, nodding. "You're right. You should have been a shrink."

"I'd have been very, *very* expensive."

BB clothed it in a joke. If he wasn't as good as Osman thought he was, then Naomi would find out the hard way. Her therapy had suddenly become the most important task he'd ever perform, and he wasn't sure why.

Naomi had retreated to her cabin for the process. BB rapped on the door by making knock-knock noises, then materialized inside when she said to come in. It was a very tidy cabin, not an unusual thing in itself for naval personnel, but devoid of personal touches like pictures from home—or at least it had been. Now Naomi held a photo of herself and her parents that looked as if it had been taken at a funfair on a windy day.

"This is going to hurt, isn't it?" she said. She put the docking chip in the console repeater so BB could transfer to it. She didn't need her armor this time. BB wasn't touching her motor regions, just her memory. "But ignorance isn't bliss. It's just a lack of intel that you need to make a reasoned assessment."

"Personally, I'd treasure it," BB said. "I can firewall information that I don't want to access, but I know I've done it, so I *know* that I know something, but I don't know *what* I know, or why it was a good idea to avoid knowing or recalling it. That's an uncomfortable sensation. Not bliss."

BB had always been aware that his disdain for getting too invested in humans' lives was a defense. If you liked them— loved them, even—then it was doomed because you'd be gone in a few short years, leaving them to miss you. They knew you were short-lived, too, so the more emotionally aware ones could predict the pain to come, and either dwell on the unfairness of scheduled bereavement or keep their distance to minimize it. The dolts who thought AIs were just clever but unfeeling programs lived in happy denial both of the reality of AIs and of emotions in general. For all their pretense at scientific attitudes, they were still anchored in the voodoo of religion, the belief that humans were unique, wonderful, and *qualitatively* different, the work of a God that made them unlike any other species that ever lived or ever would. Not even the painful evidence of aliens trashing their worlds had dented that belief.

BB knew he had been both human and not-human. He was the oracle Tiresias, experiencing both sides of life and existence, an odd parallel not lost on him when he considered that Tiresias was reluctant to reveal all the details of his visions either as a man or as a woman. Maybe when you fully understood all sides, you knew there were some things people couldn't handle knowing. There were things he knew that he couldn't handle himself, otherwise he would never have firewalled them so thoroughly.

Programming. How do you think your brains work, meatbags? How do you think you made me? You're a program too, and because you are, I can exist.

He wanted to tell them, but it wouldn't work. Humans were too dominated by emotion to see it for what it was, that every living thing—organic or otherwise—needed hard-wired reactions to survive; to avoid what would damage it, to pursue what would help it reproduce, to cling to others of its own kind because it maximized survival, and to have those life-preserving behaviors reinforced by chemical reactions that guaranteed they would be performed and not ignored. Humans called those reactions fear, ambition, or love. The basic skills that were necessary to life—communication, using experience to avoid future threats—weren't solely human traits of language or abstract thinking, but variations on the tools that all life used. BB could now see no difference between the amoeba moving away from something hot and the man fleeing a tiger or an angry boss. Humans believed they thought things consciously when most of the time they were simply rationalizing instinctive reactions as basic as the amoeba's, and after those reactions had already taken place. But there was no telling them that, not even the ones who knew better, like Halsey. They needed their sense of unique superiority and the elaborate ritual that supported it every bit as much as the Covenant needed theirs.

BB blamed the universe for that. It was so vast and so indifferent to the little life-forms who thought they were the sole reason for its existence that it must have made them feel small, lonely, and *un*special, in need of some secret that reassured them they were a lot more important than that.

He saw it all now: he didn't see it when he was . . . was . . . -

When I was what? What made me think all that?

He knew only that when he was another self, his donor, the not-him but the source of his existence, that he simply didn't understand what he did now, or didn't want to.

I had to buffer myself. I had to lie.

"Whoa," BB said. How long had he been mulling that over? Damn, was he having a pre-rampancy moment? "Where did *that* come from?"

Naomi looked at him. "Are you okay? You sort of froze for a second."

"Actually, no," he said. "I'm not okay. I'm having a bit of memory leakage. Better put cerebral incontinence pads on the grocery list, dear. Now, shall we proceed?"

This task required his matrix, not a pared-down fragment. He transferred himself to the chip, laden with the records he'd harvested from ONI. For a moment he was disoriented by lack of input. Then he found himself looking at the cabin bulkhead— gray composite, the even spread of a concealed light above the pull-down desktop, and a glimpse of a dark blue bedcover tucked under the edges of a bunk mattress with the precision of an envelope.

It was a stark and impressionistic still-life seen through the trichromatic filter of the human retina. But he could also see a network of lights and lines superimposed on it, a mesh of enormous and beautiful complexity that he could both reach and touch like an ancient switchboard operator connecting calls, or travel along like a flume at a beach resort. It was the map of a human brain, *Naomi's* brain, a unique alien world in itself.

BB focused on a photo that moved into his field of view. It was a day at the funfair that came flooding back with the scent of salt air and frying doughnuts.

He was almost convinced that he recalled how delicious those things smelled.

UNSC *PORT STANLEY*: QUARTERS OF PETTY OFFICER NAOMI-010

I am a Spartan.

There is no situation I cannot handle, resolve, or face with equanimity.

Where did I hear that?

"What are you doing, BB?"

"Keep looking at the picture."

What's it like outside?

"I've located it, Naomi. Look at your mother." She couldn't actually hear BB in the physical sense. He could have generated sound via the cabin's audio, but this was unrecorded, private stuff. Now it felt less like thinking someone else's thoughts and more like the lyrics of a song, words that formed in her head like a reflex that she couldn't change. "Go on. Concentrate on your mother."

I don't remember her. Yes. Yes, I do.

"What did you want for your birthday?"

A doll's house. Oh. I remember that now. The toy store in town. It filled the window.

"Now look at the file."

That's Reach. I think it's home. No, it's not—the stars look different. I can't see the same sky. But how can I see the sky when it's underground? And I hate that taste. The medicine smells of raspberries, not real ones, artificial flavoring, but what's underneath still tastes bitter—

"BB, I'm tasting things. Actually tasting them."

"Okay. I know why that's happening. Don't worry. Just relax and keep talking."

Naomi had been conscious for brain surgery when her neural implant was inserted, listening to an unseen surgeon asking her questions and adjusting something while her body did things she had no control over, from slurring her speech to making her heart race. There was no pain; she just didn't like being operated like a machine. *Helplessness.* Yes, that was it. It made her want to lash out.

"Your heart rate's up," BB said. "Shall I stop for a moment?"

"No. Just do it."

"I'm trying to avoid influencing you by asking questions. You know how susceptible human memory is."

"You've said that a dozen times. Is that your get-out clause?"

"What, for practicing medicine without a license? Have I ever asked you to take your clothes off for an eye test? As I told the judge, that was all a terrible misunderstanding."

Poor old BB: the more he went into his standup routine, the more uneasy he was. "If what I recall is bad, you'll be able to tell me it never happened anyway," Naomi said. "Just a false memory caused by integrating suggestions and assorted garbage."

"First, do no harm." BB seemed to be reminding himself. It didn't sound like a joke. "I don't want to make matters worse."

Naomi sat back on her bunk, spine pressed against the padded bulkhead. This wasn't like hypnosis or meditation. She was fully conscious, letting her mind wander as best she could. The longer she looked at the photo of the day at the fair, the less certain she was about what she recalled.

"Doughnuts," she said.

There was a funfair on the coast. Sometimes she'd catch a whiff of that cinnamon and frying oil smell even now, and she could not only taste doughnuts again but feel them too. Now she remembered the context. They were served up boiling hot in a greaseproof bag. She could feel them burning her palm and then her fingers as she fished one ring of heavy, luscious, sugar-gritted pastry from the bag and bit into it. Her teeth crunched through the heavy dredging of sugar and then sank into soft, compressible, rather bland dough that wasn't all that sweet, an elusive flavor she chased but never caught, made more tantalizing by the residue of sugar it left on her lips and chin. Her mother leaned over her and wiped her mouth with something cool and wet, tutting. Naomi tried to recall her mother's face but it was hard to differentiate between what she recalled and what was being filled in by the photo.

I felt sticky. Sticky from the sugar. Sticky from the salt on the wind. My hair was all tangles.

Her father looked happy in the photo, though. Who had taken it if they were all in it? *A neighbor. A friend. A stranger.* Naomi reached for her datapad and started looking through the documents that BB had assembled, her personnel folder and the assortment of ONI material. She hadn't even read everything that was in her file yet. This was going to take some time, and she was acutely aware that *Inquisitor* had already been found—probably breached—and might well be beyond ONI's reach by now.

Her father seemed to think the Huragok could immobilize the vessel and even repel boarders. Either he knew a lot more about the creatures than she did, or a lot less. She tried to imagine Adj or Leaks defending *Stanley.* They wouldn't. They'd accepted UNSC direction without murmur, just as they'd accepted the orders of the Covenant.

And he renamed the ship Naomi. *I don't know how I feel about that.*

What are they going to do with him? Hand him over to an ONI debriefing in Sydney? Shoot him? Just throw him back into the water like an undersize fish when they're done?

Whether she wanted it to or not, it was shaping her reactions

already. There were rules and regulations in the Navy. Then
there was how you felt about them. She wondered if people
thought Spartans were so brainwashed that they could simply decide not to think or feel like everyone else, that she could treat her
father like any other insurgent sympathizer and not experience
any fallout from it. But she'd told the rest of the team precisely
that. She'd said it meant nothing to her, like arresting Catherine
Halsey, but she'd been lying to herself. It might not have reduced her to a weeping wreck, but it definitely left a few scuffs.

Damn.

*But Vasya gets angry and emotional about things, and he's
still a good marine. It doesn't make you any less of what you are.*

She braced herself and opened the documents closest to the
date that she'd been abducted: September 10, 2517. She'd almost forgotten BB was there behind her eyes and reading it too.

"Is this the wash-up?" she asked. "The retrieval report?"

"Yes," he said. "Allow for the fact that any report's going to
be subjective. The mistakes tend to get downplayed and euphe-
mized. The highlights get exaggerated."

"I *have* read UNSC bullshit before, BB. I may even have written some."

"About yourself?"

He had a point. He always did.

Headings like **SUBJECT: SENTZKE, NAOMI, SUBJECT 010: DOB September 15 2511** never got things off to a good start. It had been
filed by Retrieval Team Theta 2, RTθ2. She read it like a Spartan at first, just looking for the salient points, and noted how
little space and how few words the destruction of her real life
was worth. It wasn't even a page. She was referred to throughout simply as Subject 010.

> Subject 010 had been observed over a period of seven months
> in Alstad, New Atlantic Province, Sansar. Data was gathered

from routine school medical checks, and also via the bogus
CAA Gifted and Special Needs Children Pilot Study created to
gain extra access to identified candidates. We have no reason to believe that insufficient data was collected and that
this led to the problems retrieving the subject.

One of the staff at the Subject's school did query the authority of Theta 2 personnel posing as educational psychologists, but seemed satisfied by the paperwork and the
promise of special funding from the CAA if any children in
the school were identified as gifted and requiring special
measures.

During psych evaluation by Dr. J., Subject 010 also under-
went routine health checks such as vision, height, and weight,
and the last of those was conducted within a reasonable period of the retrieval. The calculation of the sedative dose required to subdue the subject was correct based on that data,
and the dose should have been sufficient even if the subject
had gained up to five kilos in the intervening period. The risks of
accidental overdose in children cannot be overstated; adminis-
tering these drugs in a non-clinical environment means that it is
prudent to give the lowest recommended dose per kilo. The
subject could easily have died before RTθ2 was able to reach
ONI medical support.

Naomi looked up for a moment. This was mostly ass-covering.
Someone was explaining why her kidnap went wrong and how it
wasn't their fault, no sirree, because they'd followed procedure
and the dose should have been enough. It obviously hadn't been,
then.

*So I was sedated? I must have been. I would never have
gone off with strangers. Christ, did they accidentally kill any of
us before it even started?*

She read on.

Subject 010 was lured into close physical contact so the sedative could be administered with minimum distress to her. She
appeared to be fully sedated when placed in the support vehicle, but she regained consciousness while her clothing was
being transferred to the clone replacement and became agitated and unexpectedly combative. As a result, she escaped
from the vehicle and a search was carried out to recover her.
She was found and recovered two hours later, when her behavior became sufficiently disruptive to risk compromising the mission. A decision was taken to give her further sedation. She was
removed without further incident and no lasting physical damage was observed.

"Wow," she murmured.

"You didn't go down and you fought like hell," BB said. "At
least I *think* that's what it means. I did cross-reference the personnel in Theta Two to see if they'd needed any medical treatment after the kidnap. Couldn't find anything, but I do hope
you did a Mal on them."

"Did a Mal?"

"Mal bites when cornered. Ask him about his interrogation.
Ask your father, actually."

"So . . ."

"Remember it?"

"Underwear," she said suddenly. There: it popped up out of
nowhere, out of context. "Oh, god. I woke up and someone was
undressing me."

She was lying flat on something in a strange place that wasn't
her bedroom. She knew where she really was—sitting cross-
legged on her bunk in *Port Stanley*—but she was also five going
on six, with a weird taste in her mouth, head spinning, and
someone was pulling her dress off her shoulders. There was a
small pinpoint of light shining in her eyes from one side. The

noises and movement told her she was in a car, and a woman was undressing her. She started struggling.

"Damn, she's coming around," the woman said. "How much did you give her?" Naomi started kicking and screaming for Mom. She wasn't sure exactly what people like that did to you, but she knew it was bad and wrong, so bad that the teachers warned the class about it regularly. "It's okay, honey, it's okay, take it easy. Nobody's going to hurt you."

Liar. Liar, liar, liar.

Naomi screamed as loud and as long as she could. That was what grown-ups had told her to do if a stranger grabbed her—to scream and make a fuss until someone noticed and came to help her. She was in a car. Who would hear her? *Nobody.* She had to get out. She had to get out *now.* The grown-ups in the car were arguing about something and a man was saying they couldn't give her any more. The car swerved. Naomi could see the handle on the inside of the door. She'd never been so scared in her life, because Mom and Dad didn't know where she was, and it was all her fault because she hadn't gone straight home.

The car slowed down. As soon as the woman leaned back, Naomi flew at her, clawing and screaming, and then she reached for the door latch. The door was suddenly gone. She was falling through a black void, hitting the ground so hard that it shook her teeth, rolling, dizzy, but she was up and running before she even knew where she was. She ran into the darkness. She tripped over a curb, stumbled through grass, and saw trees streak past her; she heard nothing but her own gasping breaths, *uh-uh-uh,* as she ran for her life. Her feet hurt. Her shoes were gone. She was wearing a long tunic of some kind and it flapped around her knees.

They were behind her. She could hear their urgent whispers. Where was she? She couldn't see any lights now, just the dark on darkness of trees against the speckled night sky. Her feet hurt and she wanted her mom.

Where's my watch?

She'd lost her watch, the grown-up watch that Dad had given her. No, the woman had taken it, along with her clothes. If they were chasing her, Naomi had to keep quiet now. Running was noisy. She crept through spiky grass that was getting taller and taller around her, and then her feet slid into cold water and slippery mud. *Don't scream. Not this time.* She held her breath and squatted in the water, hugging her knees in the cover of the tall grass. This was a big river. The stream near her house was small and bubbled over rocks, but this was slow and still, and her feet were in mud. So she was a long way from home.

She felt like she'd held her breath forever, trying not to cry because they'd hear her. She'd never been this cold in her life; her legs were getting numb. Eventually, she had to move. She felt her way along the edge of the bank, looking for lights from houses, but there weren't any. What had Dad told her? *Rivers flow to the sea.* If she put her hand in the water and felt which way it was going, she could walk along the bank and end up somewhere where there were people who'd help her.

She'd been sure she was going to get home right up to the moment she heard a man's voice saying "Check the thermal—see it?" Then someone grabbed her arms and hauled her kicking and screaming out of the water. The last thing she saw was that woman leaning over her, hair hanging down. She grabbed it and pulled as hard as she could, punching with her free hand until her arms went tingly and cold, and then she didn't remember anything else.

"Are you okay?" BB asked. "Your heart rate's way up."

"I remembered," Naomi said. She couldn't go through all that detail again. It made her feel worse than she'd expected. "Waking up in the car and escaping. But they still found me."

How could she have gotten herself into that mess? She was just coming home from school. She didn't recall the detail. It was dark, though. She would have been home in daylight if it was mid-September, so she must have stayed late for some class or other. She wanted to look at the night sky, so she got off the bus a stop early again to take a look from the field. There were so few streetlights around there that she could see everything like an astronomy textbook, stars beyond stars and the hazy ribbons of the galactic plane.

Dad had told her to always come straight home. It was a grown-up privilege to be allowed to travel to and from school on her own, so she had to be responsible about it. A couple of people got off the bus at the same stop, but she was too intent on the night sky to look at them, and anyway, Mom had said not to talk to people she didn't know or look at them in case . . . in case *what?* She thought she knew now, but she didn't know then.

Look behind you, and you look like a victim. Anyone who's thinking of sneaking up on you is more likely to think you're scared and take a chance.

But that was her adult rationalization. She couldn't have thought in those terms back then. She saw a light traveling along the top of a hedge, bright orange, so it couldn't have been a firebug, because they were green and it wasn't the right time of year. How far away was it? Maybe it was a shuttle taking off in the distance. She couldn't tell. But it was going in a very straight horizontal line, which shuttles didn't do, and it was just one light, not a cluster of different colors.

Dad had told her never to wander off at night and to stay on the lit road where she could be seen, but she couldn't explain that light, and she *needed* to. She had to find things out. She climbed over the wooden turnstile and headed into the field, picking her way over rutted furrows. The light might have been getting closer or moving away. She still couldn't tell.

Then she fell. She remembered putting out her hand to stop the fall and thinking that Mom would be mad if she came home with mud on her dress. It was only a shallow ditch, but at the time she thought she'd never stop falling. That was when she heard the *thwop-thwop-thwop* of someone running as fast as they could through soft soil, and someone grabbed her around the waist. She screamed.

"For Chrissakes shut her up before the whole town hears her," a man's voice said.

So now she knew. If she'd remembered what had happened, and not what she'd pieced together from what she knew of ONI, then she'd made the mistake of getting off the bus in a dark place and being too curious for her own good. But she hadn't gone off with a stranger voluntarily. That was something. She hadn't been irresponsible.

"I remembered," she said. "A lot of it, anyway. Maybe too much. It feels real, though."

"Want to tell me?" BB asked.

"Later. They must have followed me for weeks to know I was getting off the bus early. They knew all about me, didn't they?"

"Governments try to," BB said. "And always for their own good. Never yours."

BB waited while she scrolled through some recordings from her first three days in CASTLE, buried deep under the surface of Reach where no amount of screaming for Mom and Dad would ever be heard. The assessment team had recorded video footage of the kids working out where they were and even clinging to each other for comfort, seventy-five scared, baffled, and even angry children who didn't quite get this idea of being chosen to save the world.

Naomi couldn't believe that she'd been like that. One clip showed her taking a swing at a guy in a lab coat, pummeling him with her fists and telling him that her dad was going to kill him if he didn't take her home. So much for Halsey's journal entries that suggested tearful but generally compliant children: the woman barely mentioned how much they fought back, and when she did, it was almost with amusement. But as Naomi worked through the clips, videos of her regular talks with Halsey and the other doctors, she watched herself get more withdrawn and cowed down day by day, asking to go home and begging for her mom and dad. In one session, she heard herself say that her daddy really loved her, so he'd come and save her.

"Daddy's not coming for you, Naomi," Halsey was saying. It was a young Halsey, dark-haired, thirty or so. "He knows you've got an important job to do. He knows you're too special to be anything other than a Spartan."

Lying bitch. You made me doubt my own father. You made me think he'd abandoned me. But you weren't the only one, were you?

Naomi's anger was here and now. It wasn't sorrow for her lost childhood. It was anger at the adults who'd betrayed them all by not doing the most basic thing a human adult was supposed to—to protect a child. Her father had tried his damnedest to do that and she'd never known until the last few weeks, more than thirty years too late.

That was the worst bit. It hurt with a fresh pain that she hadn't been expecting. She didn't remember that at all until now. She realized her parents were never coming for her and that she was utterly alone. Her father wasn't going to save her. She had a sudden, vivid pang of hurt, angry, desperate fear, and remembered how she thought her dad had let Halsey take her.

And that's why I go all out to retrieve my buddies. To rescue Mal. Nobody should feel that they've been abandoned. I understand now.

"I thought Dad had let me down, BB," she said. "Knowing what I know now, knowing how he's spent a lifetime looking for me, knowing what Mom went through—I really wish I hadn't remembered that."

She put the datapad down and raked her fingers through her hair. Well, she asked to know, and now she knew. Maybe the memories of the abduction were distorted by the lack of understanding of a small child or embellished by her later knowledge—and Halsey's journal—but there was no arguing with the videos. When she absorbed the whole picture, she didn't feel chosen to save humanity. She felt abused.

I'm still proud to be a Spartan. If I'd had the chance to volunteer when the Covenant invaded, I'd have done it. I'd do it again in a heartbeat. But this wasn't about the Covenant, was it? It was setting humans against humans.

She laughed. That was rich.

"What's funny?" BB asked.

"The Covenant," she said. "They're what makes me feel I didn't have my life entirely wasted for me."

"Are you done? You want a break? Try again later?"

Naomi looked at her watch. It wasn't her grown-up one, the one Dad had given her. It was a military timepiece, all dials and meters. She really would have liked to have had her old watch back. "No, we need to crack on with finding that ship."

"You can't have made up your mind in that time," BB said.

"I'm not sure I have," she said. "But I know what to say to Dad."

Naomi tidied her hair and tried to look calm and professional again. Her cheeks were flushed bright pink, which wasn't like her at all. Vaz would comment and ask if she was okay. He was a really good guy, the kind she wished she'd met in a normal life, but that was another world in a parallel universe.

"Can't blame it all on Halsey," she said.

"No, but most of it's down to her, so do I still get to stick pins in her? Please? I was thinking of asking Parangosky to have her brain removed and kept in a jar connected to the mainframe, so she could think useful things but not cause any more damage. And, of course I could pop in from time to time and torment her and she could never switch me off."

"That's not like you, BB."

"Oh, I think it is."

"How could anyone do that, though?" Naomi asked. "Halsey

couldn't do it alone. She had an army of people willing to do the work for her. What kind of person goes along with a plan to kidnap children and surgically alter them? What kind of *doctor* would agree to do all that to kids?"

BB didn't answer for a while. "Yes, you have to wonder what corner of Hell's reserved for them," he said at last. "Some of them might even have found out by now."

He seemed very subdued. Naomi hoped he didn't feel guilty for bringing back some painful memories. If anyone had no reason at all to feel guilty, it was BB.

FORMER COVENANT BATTLECRUISER *PIOUS INQUISITOR*, POSITION UNKNOWN: TIME UNKNOWN

"I think we have to assume it's just us left, mistress," Bakz said.

Chol squatted on the deck, palms placed flat to feel for vibrations. She was sure that *Inquisitor* had dropped out of slipspace. The ship had jumped in and out again very quickly, no distance at all in the scheme of the galaxy, just a short step to the side: but space was an overwhelming void to search for something as small as a warship that couldn't transmit a signal. *Inquisitor* was a cold, black pebble in the darkness. The chances of any other ship stumbling across her were incalculably remote.

Their only chance of survival was to take control of the ship. Nobody was coming to save them.

Chol straightened up and walked across to one of the bulkhead sensor terminals to try it again. She prodded the controls a few times, but no display appeared. "Why? Why would the others be dead?"

"Not necessarily dead, mistress. But we're nearest to the bridge, so perhaps we should assume we're the only ones with a chance of accessing the controls."

There were still search teams in other parts of the ship, trapped between bulkheads by the Huragok. That meant some of them were in sealed compartments when the ship jumped and ripped out the umbilical connecting her to *Paragon*. The only compartment open to space would have been the hangar bay, and the last time she'd seen Ved and Lig, they were wearing their helmets. They didn't have much of an air supply, though.

"Ril's party reached engineering," she said. "They might be able to get in and activate something. There could have been equipment left in accessible places. We have no way of knowing."

Paragon was another matter. A ship jumping that close to her might have ripped her apart. Anyone in either cargo bay without a suit would probably have been killed anyway. Even if the ship was intact, though, she had no way of tracking them in slipspace.

So how far had the Huragok moved the ship? Was it picking random locations, or had it taken the ship somewhere specific? All the sensor systems were locked down. Chol had no way of knowing if the ship was actually in orbit around a planet and had been detected. For once, the human practice of having viewplates everywhere and a bridge on the outer skin of a warship didn't look foolhardy at all. It might have made their ships more vulnerable, but at least they could look outside.

And at least I know we're probably not orbiting Sanghelios, waiting for 'Telcam to reclaim his ship and cut my throat. We'd have been in slipspace longer.

"I'm going to see if I can get into one of the conduits." Bakz stood back and looked up the sheer face of the bulkhead, then examined one of the panels in the deck. "What's on the deck below us?"

Chol couldn't access the display from here. She racked her brains, trying to visualize the deck plan in cross-section again. "It's a machinery space. There have to be some conduits from this deck. Search for those before you break your neck trying to climb to the deckhead openings."

"We can at least lift a plate and see if there's anything we can use as a tool to force the doors open."

Noit trotted up to join them, brandishing a blade. The two males cut and peeled back the deck covering to expose the metal panels beneath, but they couldn't release the bolts that held it in place. It needed a special tool—or a Huragok. Chol paced around, looking for deck-level openings in the short passages that led off the main compartment, but drew a blank. It was the deckhead conduits or nothing.

Chol estimated the cubic air capacity of the section they were trapped in and took out her module to calculate how long the air supply would last for three pairs of Kig-Yar lungs. It would be used up faster if they were exerting themselves. So did they rest and conserve air, which would prolong the agony if they were drifting unnoticed far from the nearest inhabited world, as she believed, or use it up faster by expending physical effort?

"Very well," she said. "If this compartment is completely sealed, we have two days' air left. By then, we'll have a solution."

Noit looked up at the deckhead again. "Unless those conduits are sealed too, then some air will be filtering in from elsewhere."

Chol had never checked to see if there were airlocks in the Huragok warrens, because they were such a routine part of Covenant warships that she took no special interest in them. There had to be some method of making them airtight, she supposed: there was no point having sections with doors that could be sealed in an emergency if atmosphere could vent or if contaminants could seep in via the conduits.

"I'm narrower in the shoulders than you, Noit," Bakz said. "I'll try. I only have to make it through to the next exit point, because there aren't any more doors between here and the bridge."

"You'll never get up there," Noit said.

Bakz worked along the panels, digging his claws into edges to see if he could get some purchase. He managed to get halfway up the bulkhead and then jammed his foot into one of the horizontal moldings. Chol watched him shuffle along to the next vertical panel and pick his way up like a fly.

But there was no way of reaching the conduit at the angle of the deckhead. Bakz made a valiant attempt to swing across, but he couldn't hold his weight. He fell. It wasn't a long drop, not enough to break bones, but he rubbed his shoulder ruefully as he scrambled to his feet.

"A pity I didn't remember to bring a rappel line," he said. "But then I didn't bring grenades, either."

Chol surveyed the closed doors again. "I think we should go back to the brute force approach."

The control panel was a plain block of metal with no switches to dismantle or short-circuit, but that didn't mean it wouldn't yield to an assault, given enough time. What could a Huragok do and *not* do? She still didn't know how far this one would go.

And he had to be watching them somehow. Either he was darting around the conduits from section to section, or there were monitoring cameras still operating. She couldn't see them.

"How many power packs did you bring?" she asked.

Noit patted his belt. "One spare each, mistress."

"Very well." Chol stood back and aimed her pistol. "Target the panels. Let's see if we can activate the holographic controls. If the Huragok wants to stop us, he'll have to come into this compartment, and then I'll kill the little dung-ball."

The panel was composite, and only fireproof—not melt-proof. She squeezed the trigger. It took several shots to begin to burn a hole through the surface, and the air was already heavy with the smell of melting composite. If she kept this up for a long time, she might make what air they had unbreathable.

Or . . . maybe it'll force the Huragok to act. He'll regard that as damage to be repaired. It should at least activate the fire control systems, if he hasn't disabled those as well.

She fired again, three bursts. What was the creature trying to do? Was he saving the ship by immobilizing it, or was he following orders to sabotage it to the point of destruction to stop it falling into the wrong hands? If she knew for certain, then she could start a fire here and simply wait for the Huragok to respond.

Or burn to death. I just don't know.

"My turn, mistress," Bakz said.

Chol stepped back and let him blast away at the panel. The air was getting thick with the stench, but it was still breathable.

The only ones who can leave the ship are Ved and Lig, if they're still alive . . . but they've only got Spirits, and dropships are no use out here. Wherever here is.

There was still light to this deck. The Huragok had kept basic services running, so maybe no matter how defective he was, he drew the line at killing other sentient beings, or perhaps he was dependent on the same systems as this section to stay alive. Chol watched as Bakz burned through another panel, sending sparks flying. Then a flickering holographic control appeared. Chol reached for it and the doors creaked. After three loud cracks, they parted to almost shoulder width and stopped.

"Have we got anything that'll wedge this open?" Bakz said. "In case the Huragok manages to close them again."

"Nothing strong enough to withstand the closing pressure." Chol motioned him through. "But if we're trapped again, we'll be stuck on the bridge, which is a much better position."

Noit squeezed through the gap, pistol raised, and Chol followed him in. The long ramp up to the command platform stretched ahead of them, but there were no holocharts or other displays active, just the spectrum of lighting that ran through aqua through deep blue to purple. The air felt relatively warm and the gravity was normal.

It was too much to hope that the ship's comms might still be working, but Chol tried anyway. She walked up the ramp to the platform and tried voice commands as well as touching holopanels. Nothing: *Inquisitor* was still deaf, dumb, and blind.

"Bakz, how would you achieve this if you were a Huragok?" she asked.

"What do you mean, mistress?"

"We can't see what he's shut down, because he's disabled all the displays. That might mean that something's functioning, but we can't see it. The central computer must still be running if we have life support and power to the doors." She looked up and around her, keeping an eye out for Sometimes Sinks. There were plenty of shadows and alcoves for him to hide in. "See, Huragok? Can you see this? You can't stop us. You don't dare kill us, so what are you going to do? Gamble on us running out of air before we've found a way to get this ship running? You'll run out of air too."

Chol didn't expect a response, but she heard a faint noise in the deckhead, like a distant flag flapping in the breeze. The creature was still moving around in the access conduits. Perhaps he'd come to his senses if she spoke to him firmly enough. He was an organic computer, for pity's sake. He couldn't possibly have opinions.

<Vandals. Thieves.> His voice boomed over the ship's address system. *<You will not take this ship. It doesn't belong to you. It belongs to the Reclaimer. He respects what the masters made. I do as he asks, because he does no harm and he means well. He is civilized.>*

"Does that thing mean the human?" Noit asked. He was standing by the comms console, groping around where the holo-panel would normally display. "What's a reclaimer? Does he mean salvage?"

Suddenly the bridge was plunged into darkness, so black and enveloping that Chol almost lost her balance for a moment. Only the faint light from her suit's status indicator provided any orientation at all. In the defended heart of the ship, not even light from a nearby star would penetrate. Chol froze, trying to remember where the edge of the command platform was. She could see Noit's suit lights. Bakz was out of her line of vision.

"Restore the lights, Huragok," she called. "This won't help." She tried to swallow her anger and growing fear. "Perhaps we can discuss this. Tell me your grievances."

The bridge was so robbed of light that the smallest glimmer stood out like a beacon. An indicator flared for a moment, right next to Noit. He made a rattling noise of warning.

"I think that's the long-distance comms panel," he said. "The Huragok is sending a signal. I think he might be summoning reinforcements."

Whether it was 'Telcam or the human, that was bad news. The humans would have described Chol as a fish in a barrel.

"Well," she said, brazening it out, "reinforcements have to get *in*. And if they can get in, we can get *out*. We treat this as an involuntary rescue. Prepare yourselves."

THIRTEEN

I AM OLD. I HAVE BEEN ALONE A LONG TIME WITH NO BROTHERS TO REPAIR ME, SO I BECOME PRONE TO ERROR. IT IS HARDER TO COMPLETE THE TASKS I ONCE DID WITH EASE. WHY MUST EVERYONE DESTROY SO MUCH? LET ME DO MY WORK. THAT IS ALL I WANT TO DO.
—SOMETIMES SINKS, HURAGOK: EXILED BY THE JIRALHANAE CREW OF HIS LAST SHIP FOR NONCOMPLIANCE

UNSC *PORT STANLEY*, SOMEWHERE IN THE QAB SECTOR

Phillips was in the galley with Spenser and Devereaux when Mal went to make himself something to eat. The two blokes were talking in Sangheili, which was both stomach-churning and impressive at the same time. Devereaux watched them, looking fascinated.

"I love it when you talk dirty," Mal said.

Spenser chuckled. "Just comparing dialects. It's funny how many Kig-Yar words they use, and how many of those the Kig-Yar picked up from us."

"Did you teach them any naughty ones?"

"I tried, but a lot of Kig-Yar can't form a proper F. It comes out as a *wh* or *th* sound. Depends on their jaw anatomy. It varies."

"Well *whuck me*," Mal said. "Have we got a new swearword? That's a relief. We were wearing out the old ones. *Nishum* just doesn't do it for me."

He opened the fridge, a massive steel-doored walk-in store with enough supplies to keep a crew of spooks and support

staff victualled for a few months without the need for resupply.
It was hard to run covert surveillance if the UNSC Fleet Auxiliary showed up every few weeks with groceries. He rummaged
in the racks for an all-day fried breakfast pack and found one,
plastered with UNSC warnings and disclaimers about salt, lack
of fiber, and lack of key vitamins, signed by a surgeon admiral.
Mal raised a finger to the label and dogged the door shut before
shoving the pack in the heater and setting it to EXPRESS.

"My stomach hasn't a clue what time it is," he said, stung by
the glances. The timer chirped. He took out a container of sausages, egg, bacon, beans, and mushrooms that glistened invit-
ingly as he peeled back the seal and settled down to tuck in.
"But it's my lunchtime on this watch, anyway."

"You're looking a lot better," Spenser said, indicating his
nose.

"A lot better than Gareth's arm, probably."

"Who's got Staffan's radio?"

Mal tapped his pocket. "Me. And Naomi's still chatting with
him. Did I miss anything, BB?"

"No." BB didn't materialize but just spoke from the heavens.
He didn't sound quite so chipper today. "Adj and Leaks want to
play with Spenser's comms equipment, but I think that's asking
for trouble."

"They're great little guys." Spenser stared at an unlit ciga-
rette on the table in front of him like it was an endurance test.
"Wouldn't let me smoke in the hangar, though. Offered to con-
struct a sealed booth with a filter."

"Cut the distraction bullshit," Devereaux said. "I want to know
how Naomi's doing."

BB appeared in person this time and settled on one end of
the table. Mal moved up to make room for him.

"Not good," BB said.

"Not good because of him, or because she's remembering?"
Devereaux asked.

"Bit of both, really."

"Bad idea to jog her memory." Mal scooped up a forkful of mushrooms. "Even if that's what she wanted. So is she really thinking about leaving? Can't see ONI accepting that. Doesn't matter what the regs say. She's a few billion credits' worth of investment and a lot of patents walking around. Besides, how would she fit back into normal life?"

"She'd get a job anywhere with private security," Spenser said. "Even without all the hardware she'd have to leave behind. What wouldn't you pay to get a Spartan?"

"But what would she spend it on?" Phillips asked.

Devereaux reached across and took one of Mal's sausages. "You think a nightmarish childhood, a few decades of back-to-back missions, and having all her normal drives channeled into becoming the ultimate killing machine is going to make a good civilian of her, Mal?"

"I know plenty of blokes—and blokesses—who won't know what to do with their hands now the war's over, either." He batted her hand away as she reached for a piece of bacon. "But yeah, she's institutionalized."

It wasn't the kind of word he usually used because it smacked of dishonesty, the kind of shit that Halsey would come out with to avoid saying more accurate things like *utterly buggered up beyond all recognition*. People recovered from all kinds of things, but most of Naomi's youth was gone. Mal decided that would have made him pretty angry if he'd been her, not that she didn't realize she'd been robbed. It was just that having it rammed down her throat by a heartbroken father meant she couldn't ignore it.

Mal was finishing the sausages when Staffan's radio made a squelching sound. He thought he'd sat on it and accidentally powered it up, but it was making noises of its own accord. He fished it out and put it on the table.

"Incoming signal," Spenser said. "I thought Edvin would have been pinging it like crazy. He must have worked out Staffan's not just lying low by now."

"You sure that it isn't transmitting a location?"

"Definitely not. The jelly boys checked it. So did BB."

Mal put his finger to his lips. "Let's see."

He pressed the receive key. He expected to hear Edvin's voice, worried about his missing father or threatening Earth with Armageddon if they didn't let him go, but instead it was a weird little nerdy voice that he recognized. There was no preamble.

<The ship has been boarded. I have immobilized it in a secure location and trapped the intruders. What must I do now?>

It was Sinks, the loony Huragok. Mal sucked in a breath. Did he risk talking to him? Had Staffan told him that Mal was persona non grata now?

"Hello," Mal said. "Remember me, Sinks? I'm Mal. I came to see the ship with Staffan."

<I must speak with the Reclaimer. He hasn't called.>

That was what the Forerunners called humans. The Huragok in Onyx had confirmed that. It was time for Mal to make the most of it.

"I'm a Reclaimer too," he said.

<I don't like you. You're not the Reclaimer who respects the work of the masters. I need to hear his voice.>

Mal had never heard a Huragok get lippy before. "Where are you?"

<In the ship. That should be obvious.>

"Yes, but where's the ship?"

<The Reclaimer knows. Let me hear him.>

"I've sent someone to get him. He'll be a couple of minutes. Who are the intruders?"

<Kig-Yar.>

"Chol Von?"

<Yes.> Sinks was being cagey. Huragok were never good at volunteering information, though. *<They're damaging the ship. I must speak with the Reclaimer.>*

BB loomed in front of him, projecting a yellow holographic note with big letters on it.

I CAN GET THE ORIGINATING POSITION.

Mal grabbed a pen from Phillips's shirt pocket and scribbled on the table. NO PIGGYBACKING THE SIGNAL. YOU'LL PANIC HIM AGAIN.

BB changed the note. PROMISE. JUST LOOKING.

"Okay, Sinks, we're getting the Reclaimer. We're fetching Staffan." He gestured at BB to get him. "Give us a few minutes."

BB's avatar stayed put, but dimmed and did a flip on its vertical axis every few seconds. He seemed to find the gesture hilarious for some reason. Then the cube reverted to full luminosity again.

"On his way," BB said, then flashed a note. GOT IT. GOT THE LOCATION.

It was a big relief. They didn't have to bargain with Staffan now, provided Sinks didn't get spooked and move the ship again. But that made Staffan suddenly surplus to requirements, and Mal knew what ONI did with liabilities it didn't need.

Sinks wasn't daft, though. Anything that could keep BB out when he wanted to get in was a force to be reckoned with. Mal heard a little bleating noise. In a human, he'd have taken it as contempt.

<You don't have the Reclaimer,> Sinks said.

"Yes, we do." How long did it take to get him out of the wardroom, for Chrissakes? Was he resisting? "Hang on, Sinks."

<Enough. I don't trust you. Now I must see him in person before I accept new orders.>

The line went dead. BB sighed. "Oh dear. He must watch a lot of cop movies. Just as well I had the foresight to nip in and grab the signal data, isn't it? No need to thank me."

Mal wasn't sure if that was a win or not. It definitely wasn't one where Staffan was concerned. He got up to go and find Osman, but Staffan and Naomi arrived and stood blocking the doorway.

"Sinks rang off," Mal said. Staffan looked tired and a bit red-eyed. Reminiscing about old times must have been pretty painful. "He wants to see you in person before he does anything. He's got the Kig-Yar penned in the ship and they sound like they're doing a bit of damage trying to take it back."

"He makes a pretty good bagman, that Sinks." Staffan nodded approvingly. He still didn't seem to be in any hurry, though. "But if he wants to see me, you have to find out where the ship is, and we had a deal."

Mal looked at Naomi. She didn't blink. "Still working that out?" Mal asked.

"Yes."

"Well . . . we know where the ship is now. So I'm not sure where that leaves your deal."

Staffan just looked a little more weary. "I was going through with this in good faith just in case you bastards had changed in the last thirty-five years. But you're still all lying shits, aren't you?"

"I think the Admiral meant it," Mal said. "But what do you expect her to do now she's got the coordinates?"

"Shove me out the airlock, probably. Thereby making sure another generation carries on the war. But Sinks won't let you have the ship without seeing me, so maybe you'd better think about how you're going to do that." He put his hand on Naomi's shoulder. "Take me back to the wardroom, sweetheart. Or the cell. Just spend a little more time with me."

He turned around and walked off. Naomi gave Mal a *wait* gesture and shot off after her father.

"Better get to the bridge for a briefing," BB said. "I woke the Admiral. By the time she's finished brushing her teeth, I bet she'll have a plan."

Mal didn't feel like finishing his breakfast anyway. He caught up with Vaz in his cabin. He was having a shave, looking slightly more pissed off than normal. His face seemed a lot better and the swelling had receded to slightly puffy and yellowing bruises, but he was feeling his way around his jaw as if it still hurt.

"So we don't need to keep our word," he said, not looking away from the mirror. "We have what we want. We cut our way in if need be. And then what?"

"That's down to ONI, mate."

Vaz gave him a long, baleful look. "It's not some committee we've never met. Osman and Parangosky *are* ONI. They make the policy. This will be unpleasant."

He pulled on his shirt and headed down the corridor with Mal behind him. If Staffan had just been a routine criminal, then it would have been tough but just, but he wasn't. He was a victim. Mal couldn't square it with himself at all. Osman was waiting on the bridge when they assembled, gulping down a coffee while she stood at the chart table examining a 3-D schematic of a CCS-class battlecruiser.

There was no sign of Staffan. Naomi slipped onto the bridge a little later than everyone else, and the reality hit Mal. She'd had to go and lock her own father in a cell. Even if there was no intense emotional relationship on her side, then it must still have been pretty painful to have to do that. It couldn't have been a bundle of laughs for her dad, either.

Yeah. I know. I'm feeling sorry for a terrorist. But as far as I know, he hasn't bombed anyone yet. And if he does, maybe it's our bloody fault for making him that way.

"Well, people, let's assume *Inquisitor* still looks like this," Osman said. She was back to her detached calm, even if it was making her squirm. She probably had a much better idea of what Naomi was thinking, too. "Provided the Huragok hasn't moved the ship again, we'll jump in fifteen minutes and stand off to observe what's happening, in case the Kig-Yar are there in numbers and decide to act. I'm not worried about them making any dents in us, but I don't want them doing anything that panics the Huragok. Judging by what we've seen, he's not the usual happy little chap who lives to serve. He's cranky and he only takes orders from Staffan."

"He's just taken his original programming to the nth degree," Phillips said. "He was supposed to take care of Forerunner equipment. He's gone a bit bonkers for some reason and interpreted that as having to defend the ship as well, and he likes Staffan. He's Horatius holding the bridge."

"The Kig-Yar glassed a Forerunner site, remember," Vaz said. "It freaked Sinks out, so Staffan humored him and tested the next firing on open ground. It really seemed to make an impression on the little guy. He's like a one-man dog."

Osman rotated the schematic and enlarged it with a gesture. "So we still need Staffan's cooperation to deal with him."

Mal took heart at that. There was still a deal to be done, then. "We don't know how far Sinks will go. Or what his orders are—from anyone. He might self-destruct the ship. It makes sense to play nice and negotiate."

"Once we winkle the Kig-Yar out of there," Osman said. "Do we know how many there are?"

"No, that's another thing we'll have to ask Sinks nicely."

"Okay. Feel free to stop me at any time if anyone has a better idea. We need to get BB into the systems to take control of the ship. We know he won't get in on a comms signal, because Sinks is wise to that. So we have to get access and breach the hull to physically place a fragment into a terminal or whatever else we can find."

"Might I suggest," BB said, "that I download all the ship's data the moment I get in? Just in case it all goes wrong. At least we'll get whatever intel's still in the ship's computer."

"Good idea." Osman nodded. "Let's make data acquisition and asset denial the minimum objective, and if we get to seize the ship and take her home, all the better. So . . . once BB has control, we can either isolate the Kig-Yar still on board and clear each compartment the hard way, or just keep them locked down and vent each section. Kig-Yar prisoners are no use to us. Besides, I don't want any survivors going home to Eayn and making this an official feud with humans. Or 'Telcam getting to hear about it."

"*Mev-ut,*" Phillips said. "They'll put a bounty on us individually. Mal and Vaz will have two, then. But it could have wider implications for rubbing along with Kig-Yar generally."

"Still, no prisoners." Osman dipped her finger into the aft shuttle bays on each side, port then starboard. "If we cut our way in, we might get overtaken by any automated hull sealing systems. The Huragok's probably going to detect it, too, so there's no telling how he'll react. We'll need to blow a hatch or two."

Naomi was still studying the schematic. Maybe she was letting work take her mind off the personal stuff, because she seemed her usual self, all business. "I'd still prefer we hit two points simultaneously. Even if the Kig-Yar are locked in compartments. If Sinks is going to react, he's going to have to pick one point of entry to respond to or the other. He can't cover both."

"If I vent the ship, ma'am, that'll probably kill the Huragok too," BB said. "And he's probably chock-full of lovely data as well."

Osman shrugged. Mal thought he knew when she was putting on her bastard face and when she really was in full unfeeling ONI mode, but right then he couldn't tell.

"Normally, I'd grab any Huragok we could get our hands on," she said. "But we have no idea what's wrong with him. If Adj and Leaks try to fix him, we don't know what problems he might infect them with. I can't risk compromising those two. We have to terminate Sinks. Sorry." Osman expanded the schematic and zoomed in again. "BB, can he block you? How evenly matched are you?"

"I can't alter hardware."

"Meaning?"

BB shrunk himself to a tiny cube and wove through the glowing lines of the ship's blueprint image. "Once I'm in, I doubt he's anywhere near fast enough to stop me. I can lock him out of the computer network. But if he works out what we're planning, then he might alter the hardware to stop me getting in."

"We'll have to be quick, then, won't we?"

Spenser watched the show with his arms folded. "Is there any role I can play in this?" Mal still didn't know what the agent was privy to, but he hadn't heard any detail that related to 'Telcam. "Because I'm not sure what use I am."

"Sit this one out, Mike," Osman said. "It's an old-style boarding. Man the comms with Phillips. When we're done, we'll drop you off at Ivanoff or Anchor Ten."

Mal still didn't know where *Inquisitor* was hiding. "Where exactly are we heading?"

BB switched the display to a chart, and it started to make sense. Mal had started to get very familiar with that particular star chart.

"Right back to Venezia," BB said. "Or at least pretty close. But you only need a few hundred thousand kilometers to hide a ship if you don't know where to direct your scans or there's no detectable EM to look for."

Osman checked her watch. There was no discussion about Staffan or the deal at all. Maybe Osman had made up her mind, or hadn't a clue how she'd handle it yet. Mal still couldn't tell. He was the ranking NCO here, so it was up to him to ask.

"What about Staffan, ma'am?" he asked. "All bets off? And are we going to hand him over to Ivanoff or something?"

Osman raised her eyes from the watch very slowly. "He still has some help to give us. So if I can reach a point where we all get what we want out of this while removing an immediate threat to Earth, I'll do it. But I wouldn't want him cooped up in the same facility as Catherine Halsey."

Mal didn't know if that meant she would ship him back to Bravo-6 or shoot him. How did you decide if a man with a grudge on that scale would keep his word? And what the hell was Naomi going to do?

"Okay." Osman looked like she was still checking if they'd be home in time for tea. "Spool us up, BB. Jump when ready."

UNSC *PORT STANLEY*, **PRIOR TO JUMP TO VENEZIA SECTOR**

Staffan knew he'd grasped at a flimsy straw when he tried to do a deal with Osman, but that was all he had left.

He shouldn't have been surprised that it had sunk so fast. Would he have believed Osman if she'd promised him that the UNSC would never attack Venezia? He could hardly expect her to take his word for Venezia's good behavior, either. He could only speak for himself. He could exert a steadying hand on Peter Moritz, but it would be a fragile, uncertain ceasefire in a society that had its own reasons to hate Earth without any urging from him, and if there was anything that the UNSC wanted right now it was certainty.

He sat in the cell with his feet up on the bunk, back against the bulkhead, and comforted himself with the fact that he'd found his daughter and had some precious time with her, even if he struggled to find any common ground. He'd kept his promise to Remo as well, even if he hadn't been able to tell Artie that his father had never stopped believing he might still be alive. Staffan's main regret was leaving his family with exactly the situation he'd found himself in on Sansar thirty-five years ago: an unexplained disappearance with only decades of destructive pain and obsessive searching ahead.

But I found her. I was right. Now at least we both know the truth.

Staffan shut his eyes. If he'd had Osman as his prisoner,

would he have taken her word for it and let her go, or kept her as a source of intel and a bargaining chip?

What bargain? You can't bargain with this thing, this ONI. Now I know what it is, I can see there's no truce possible, ever. The best you'll ever get is a prisoner exchange.

Naomi and my family. That's all that matters.

There was a rap on the door. It was so timid that he expected it to be the linguist, Phillips. But when the door opened it was Naomi. She closed the door behind her and sat down at the far end of the bunk.

"I didn't intend to put this all on you, sweetheart," he said. "I just wanted you back. For a while if nothing else."

"It's not your fault. You didn't ask for this."

"I'd give anything to find the bastard responsible for this and strangle them slowly."

"Ah, there's quite a waiting list for that."

"The bigger the criminal you are, the less chance you'll get punished when you're caught."

"You sound like Vasya sometimes."

"Nice boy. Honest. He seems very fond of you."

"Not in that way, Dad."

"They took that away from you too? You can't even fall in love?"

"Oh, I can love people. It's just that I don't have the drive to have kids and make a proper family life for myself. I don't think a man could cope with that. Think of someone designed to be completely workaholic. Not much different from the Huragok, in fact."

"Remember that you don't owe Earth anything, Naomi. They've had their use out of you. They took your entire life. Your childhood, your youth, and your future." Staffan wondered if that had been one truth too many. He regretted reminding her of what she obviously already knew. "You have some genuine friends, though. That's a precious thing. They're worth it."

"I don't think I ever did it for Earth, Dad. I think I did it because Halsey made us all feel that if we didn't fight, humankind would tear itself apart. Guilt. We were so smart and strong that we owed the species our services. I think I did it for my comrades. And by the time I'd been in the program a year or two, I had no idea that I could ever be anything else. But it was never because I believed in an idea. Not past the age of ten, anyway."

Staffan noted the name. "Halsey."

Naomi shrugged. "Yes."

"She's the one behind all this?"

"I tried not to mention her because people get pretty heated about it. Especially Vaz. And BB. Actually . . . the entire crew. Vasya wants to see her strung up for war crimes."

"I knew I liked that Russian for a reason."

"Dad, the more I tell you, the more dangerous it is for you."

"They're going to shoot me or stick me in solitary for the rest of my life anyway. It's already over. I just want you to promise me that you'll get a message to your brother—"

"Dad, please, don't . . ."

"You have a brother and a sister. You know you do. Just get word to them, anonymously or however a smart girl like you does this stuff, that their dad didn't desert the family. Don't let them go through what your mother and I did. Please."

This adult Naomi was mostly a stranger who looked and sounded familiar. Staffan loved her anyway. She stared at him with a blank expression that just wasn't her, probably the mask she'd learned to put on in that awful place on Reach and now couldn't take off. For a moment, though, it flickered.

"I don't know how much time we have," she said. "I could be called away from here at any second and I might never see you again."

"Are you going to leave the Navy? Are you going to spend any time getting to know your family at all?"

"I'm curious to know what I missed and never had, but I'm probably too . . . look, *this* is my family. My comrades. You know how it is for soldiers. They form very strong bonds under fire. Well, Spartans . . . we're even more like that. I don't know if I could ever fit in with a civilian family." She put her hand on his arm, hesitant and uncertain, as if she knew family were supposed to touch but hadn't learned how to yet, like a rifle drill that still wasn't quite second nature. "And I'm worried about what's happening in my head. I'm starting to feel like a victim for the first time I can remember. That's a bad combination. I'm stuck with the physical changes, I don't think I can adapt how I feel, and I don't know how negative that's going to make me."

"You would have stayed happy if I hadn't done this."

"But we crashed into *you,* Dad. And I don't think it was a matter of being happy. But I did feel there was a point to it, and now I have to reconsider what that is. I'll deal with it."

The ship shivered. It was an elevator kind of feeling in the stomach. *Port Stanley* had jumped to slipspace. "How long have we got?"

"I'll stay here until I'm called."

"I love you, sweetheart. There wasn't a day that went by when I didn't wonder where you might be and what you were doing."

"I know." Naomi nodded and took a long, nervous breath that she seemed to think he wouldn't notice. "Halsey told me that you weren't coming to save me because you knew I had to become a Spartan. But I worked out pretty soon that you'd never have abandoned me. You just couldn't find me, that was all. And then I was made to forget everything, until now. *Now* I recall some of it."

Staffan wished she hadn't said that. He tried to imagine her waiting for her daddy to come, believing he'd let them take her. It was unbearable. It ripped his heart out. If he ever found himself within an arm's length of that woman Halsey, he'd kill her. Not in the way most people used the term, angry yelling and insults: literally. He would take her life with his bare hands. Kidnapping Naomi had been one crime, but telling her that her father knew and did nothing was off the scale. If evil had any definition, that was it as far as he was concerned.

"I was going to build you a doll's house for your birthday," he said, trying not to let the anger choke him and ruin what little time he had left with her. "Like the one you wanted."

"Oh, I remember the one in the toy store window." Naomi managed a smile. "It was huge. Like a separate world you could step into."

"I just made one for Kerstin. All the little pieces of furniture, too. Penance, I suppose. I bought you something else for your birthday instead. A planetarium lamp. You know the kind I mean? It projects star maps on the ceiling. I got you the version with Sansar's night sky. I've still got it."

"I think I would have loved it." She pushed her hair back from her face with her palm facing out, the one gesture that reminded him of Lena. His wife had had that mannerism as well. "The little girl. The clone. It must have been terrible for Mom because she was sure she was me, but how did you take it?"

"I loved her as my own, because I needed to," Staffan said. "And she deserved to be loved by somebody. She thought she was you. I gave her the best life I could."

He couldn't tell what effect that had on Naomi and he probably never would. She squeezed his hand, another mechanical gesture she looked like she was trying hard to learn.

"You're a good man, Dad. I've known enough good men to be able to tell. I know how much I loved you back then, too, and I know I love you now, however different the program made me. You came for me. I knew you would. And that's all I need."

They carried on talking, but that was the real end of the conversation, her good-bye. What followed was just sound. Staffan felt like he was drowning, sinking below the water and trying to reach up to grab her hand, but there was nothing he could do to get her back and it felt like losing her for the third time.

If he'd had control of the battlecruiser at that moment, he would have had no hesitation in targeting this Halsey and all the unfeeling machine of state expedience that supported her, erasing the cancer in a flood of white-hot molten glass. His only regret would have been that it was too quick and might have taken others like him with it. He tried to drink in and absorb all he could of Naomi's face and voice so he would have something to draw on if he had years left to him, and then he thought of Edvin and Hedda, and Kerstin, and poor Laura trying to cope with the crater left in their lives.

He wanted them to forget him and move on. Living in hope the way he'd done was a life sentence.

You're a Spartan too, Osman. You might not have had all the surgical alteration, and you might have more of a life, but you've been through the same as Naomi. Kidnapped. Taken from parents who loved you. How can you do this?

"Your admiral," he said. "Vaz says she's going to be head of naval intelligence one day."

"I should say Vaz shouldn't tell you all that, but it'll probably be reported on Waypoint eventually."

"Tell her she should know better, and to do things differently this time."

The blue box of light faded in through the cell door and made him start. He wasn't sure he'd ever get used to having an AI around constantly like that.

"Is our time up?" he asked.

"I wouldn't put it that way, sir," BB said. Naomi gave him a slightly puzzled look. "But we need Naomi on the bridge to plan the mission. She'll come back later."

"So you're going to storm the ship, Naomi?" Staffan asked.

"It's what I do, Dad. You can see my armor."

BB drifted over to Staffan as if he was sidling up to him. "If you could talk to Sinks, we might not need to fight the Kig-Yar. He could help. He's obviously loyal to you and nobody else."

Staffan could smell a maneuver. *Talk the Huragok into letting us board, and your daughter won't have to risk her life.* BB was right, though. The Kig-Yar would probably fight, and the last thing Staffan wanted was for Naomi to be hurt because he wouldn't help. It was elegant blackmail. If he ever got out of here, he'd make them pay for that.

"I'll ask him to tell me how many there are on board, and where he's trapped them," Staffan said. "But I still have a price. I'm going back to my family, one way or another."

BB slipped away. Naomi got up and opened the door. "I promise I'll come back," she said.

Staffan watched her go and concentrated on remembering the final glimpse of her in case it was his very last. He wasn't sure if she'd made her choice, but it sounded as if her answer was no. If she'd said yes, he couldn't imagine ONI letting an asset like that leave as long as she was useful to them, whatever Osman said.

Have I given up? That's not like me. Look what I've done with my life. Lena wouldn't know me if she saw me now. Okay, I've come this far. I'm not going to roll over and take it now.

He'd think of something. They needed him. He'd get his chance.

He waited, but Naomi didn't come back. Then he felt the ship drop out of slipspace. If the battlecruiser was still there, he'd find out pretty soon.

The door swung open and Mal stuck his head inside. He was in full armor now, helmet clipped to his belt. "It wasn't locked," he said. "You want to come and see this?"

Mal didn't seem at all hostile considering what had happened to him. He was actually quite sociable, like the rest of the crew. Maybe it was out of respect for Naomi. Staffan followed him to the bridge and the first thing—the *only* thing that he saw for long seconds—was Naomi, standing there in blue armor and anonymized by her helmet, just like the propaganda images. It felt like she'd been snatched away from him yet again. It took all his concentration to shift his focus to the viewscreen and not stare at her, trying to see his child in that dehumanized shape.

Good-bye, sweetheart.

He cleared his mind as best he could and thought like Andy Remo had taught him, looking for the opportunity and ignoring all the rules. The curved hull of the warship was hard to pick out until *Port Stanley* moved and he could see the side dimly lit by Qab, nearly a billion kilometers away.

"Where did they cut their way in?" he asked. His chest felt hollow, as if his heart would never beat again. "Looks intact to me."

"Maybe the Huragok's repaired it already." Mal held out Staffan's radio to him. "Call Sinks. Tell him we need to come aboard and get rid of the Kig-Yar."

It was the first time Staffan had had access to comms since he'd been captured. He thought briefly about sending a message home, but it would end up being short, incomplete, and the last he ever made. So he bided his time. He took the radio and chose his words carefully. Osman was standing at the viewscreen with data projected into the glass, making the whole thing look like a helmet's head-up display.

"We're not detecting any other ships," she said. "So the missionary vessel didn't come for them. Not yet, anyway."

"Can anyone detect you?"

"No."

Staffan keyed the ship's code. "Sinks? This is Staffan. I'm in a ship at your position. I can see you."

It took a little while for Sinks to respond. <*You took a long time to respond, Reclaimer Staffan.*>

"I'm sorry about that. We got here as fast as we could. Tell me about the Kig-Yar. How many are there? We'll come on board and remove them."

<*I detect sixteen alive.*>

"Where are they?"

<*Three on the bridge. Eight in the engineering section and*

gravity compartment. Five forward of the bridge. I have jammed their comms and switched off the lighting to stop them doing more damage.>

"We need to board, Sinks."

<I need to see you to confirm you're the Reclaimer. Enter the shuttle bay alone. Let me confirm.>

Staffan looked at Osman. She nodded.

"Okay," he said. "But I need to bring a pilot, because I'm not good at flying ships. Is the bay clear?"

<There are still two Spirits berthed. The Kig-Yar in the bay didn't survive. I await you.>

Staffan switched off the radio but didn't hand it back. "Who's going to take me over there, then?" He nodded at Vaz, his compromise between someone he almost trusted and a life he was more prepared to lose than his daughter's. "Sinks knows Vaz. Or at least he's seen him."

"And he told me he doesn't like me," Mal said. "No point pissing him off, or we'll end up chasing the ship all over the galaxy."

Fine. Go on thinking that. Staffan had only given Sinks one alternate set of coordinates and he seemed to be sticking religiously to his orders. But it was clear that the Huragok wasn't behaving normally. Staffan couldn't be sure exactly what he'd do if pushed.

Vaz shrugged. "If you trust my piloting skills, I'll do it. BB had better help out."

"All you need to do is get me on board and give me access to the computer," BB said. "You might have to physically insert a chip to get me into the system, though, so be prepared for anything. There's no telling what Sinks has locked down until we get in there."

"We'll stand by to board from the other position if you run into problems." Naomi moved confidently toward the doors, all assured movement and precision, and Devereaux and Mal followed her. "What are we going to do about the Kig-Yar if they surrender?"

"In the interests of diplomacy, give them a Spirit and tell them to get lost," Osman said. "They're hardly likely to call 'Telcam and tell them who took his ship, are they? But we really can't take prisoners right now."

Staffan couldn't tell if that was an ambiguous order to shoot them anyway. Would his daughter really do that?

Mal turned at the doors. "We'll hope they open fire so we can try to slot as many as we can, then, ma'am."

Staffan caught another glimpse of Naomi as she disappeared ahead of him. Before he lost sight of her, she turned and gave him a thumbs-up, but then Vaz caught his arm, and he wondered if the gesture was aimed at the Russian.

"Don't worry about Naomi—pity the Kig-Yar who gets in her way," Vaz said quietly. He had a strong accent that was oddly endearing. His hold on Staffan's arm felt more like he was steering his granddad than marching a prisoner. "And stick close to me. I'll see you're all right."

"I can take care of myself," Staffan said. "Especially if I have a weapon."

Vaz stood back and ushered him down the ladder to the deck below. "I give you my word. I won't put you at risk."

Staffan teetered on the edge of every moment being his last— the last time he saw Naomi, the last chance he had to escape, the last chance for everything. He seized every second. He turned and gripped Vaz's arm.

"Promise me something."

"What?"

"Look after Naomi. You know I'm never going to be allowed to be with her. But take care of her, and I swear I'll cease my activities. You understand? I'll be out of the insurgency game as long as she's okay."

Vaz blinked a couple of times. He put his hand on top of

Staffan's, a heavy military-issue glove. "I'd take care of her anyway," he said. "But you have my word. Do I have yours?"

"You do, Vaz."

"We have a deal, then."

Staffan trusted his gut, which had never let him down, and decided Vaz was a man he would trust with his life. Right now, he had to.

UNSC *BOGOF*, APPROACHING *PIOUS INQUISITOR*

"You won't let me crash, will you, BB?" Vaz said. "I've never done a hangar landing."

"Of course not." BB had already aligned *Bogof* for the approach without his higher centers even getting involved, like a human's unconscious ability to stand up and walk. "Because Dev would never let you forget it."

"Can Staffan hear me?"

"You know when you're using secure audio, Vaz. Check your HUD."

"I don't trust it."

"But you have to trust *me*. I'm a doctor."

"Like I trust *them*."

BB was entirely reliant on *Bogof*'s sensors to detect the hull of *Pious Inquisitor* and to feel his way around electronically. He could see the aft port bay doors still closed, with no sign yet of having been cut open, but there was no link and exchange between himself and the ship's computer to coordinate docking—to knock on the door, to be recognized and welcomed in, and then shown to the comfy chair reserved for guests.

BB sent a very restrained request to be allowed to communicate with the nav computer rather than trying to sneak in this time. He knew he was on the right data frequency, but it met a dead end that felt like running into a padded wall. Sinks had probably detected the virtual thud. There was no point blocking threats if you couldn't tell when you'd been attacked. It kept you safe, but you couldn't learn anything from that, and Huragok were as ravenous about acquiring information as he was. Sinks would have eyes in his ass, as Spenser was fond of saying.

I suppose we're lucky that Adj only gets stroppy over decorating cakes.

He could have asked Staffan to make radio contact and try piggybacking on the signal again, but that was asking for trouble. What exactly was wrong with this Huragok? Was he actually defective at all, or did he happen to have a different personality or different programming? BB felt he knew more about them than anyone else in the UNSC—including Halsey—and he understood the Forerunners' design objectives, as she should have done. They were self-directing engineers whose purpose was to maintain and adapt a wide range of the most advanced technology the galaxy had ever seen, some of it organic. What did they need in order to do that?

How would I design a Huragok from scratch? What have we missed here?

BB scoped the specifications while he waited an eternity for Sinks to react to a gunship at his back door. Huragok had to be dexterous and physically strong—craftsmen, mechanics, technicians. They had to be capable of understanding every field of technology from particle physics and materials science through to software. They had to have biological expertise—medical skills, effectively—to deal with organic structures. But to use all that in the ships and far-flung places they would find themselves operating without supervision, they needed *behaviors*—to learn and make decisions independently, share information, protect and self-maintain, and replicate. In human terms, they would need to think, form opinions, fear dangers, plan, socialize, cooperate, communicate, teach, take care of each other, and have children. And they needed to love their work with unswerving obsession, or else any creatures that intelligent, capable, and communally organized would find lots of other things in the universe more worthy of spending their time on than sweating away for someone else.

They might even get angry, resentful, or impatient with their masters. They had the gifts of gods: but a god in perpetual servitude needed brakes on his powers, or else he might take vengeance on his lesser masters.

Like Naomi. Like Spartans. Who'd want them turning on the UNSC? Halsey had to make them obsessed with their duty or risk creating a tiger that'd rip her head off. And she says she didn't brainwash them? Come off it, lady. Lucky the Covenant came along, though, or I bet they'd have become pretty disenchanted with the colonial wars. You can't keep someone brainwashed forever. They need topping up. Reinforcing. Kept away from dangerous ideas that make them reassess what they've been told.

"God, what's keeping him?" BB snapped. "Staffan, can you ping him, please?"

"Maybe he's got his hands full," Staffan said. "He's not like you, is he? He can't be everywhere at once."

Staffan was obviously a fast learner. He had those Spartan genes, didn't he? It was obvious now. He would have been a good Spartan candidate himself.

"Well, nobody's going anywhere, I suppose," BB said.

Vaz leaned forward and blipped the nav lights. "No harm trying. I'd honk the horn if we had one."

Both men were getting tense. BB could detect their heart rates. "In space, nobody can hear you honk . . ."

It almost got a laugh out of Vaz, more of a half-cough than anything. They waited. If they thought this was frustrating, though, they should have tried being on BB's clock.

So . . . Huragok have some kind of safeguard built into them, then. But there's got to be something else in there.

BB carried on unpacking the Huragok design brief. They

couldn't be allowed to stand back and watch disaster or damage happen to themselves or to the objects they looked after. They'd have to be capable of action like damage control, self-defense, and even preemptive action. That was where decision-making got messy and ambiguous, not easily tackled by the processes that ran dumb AIs. BB could see the fragile line between repairing a breached hull in an emergency and lashing out to stop your ship—or your comrades—from being harmed. But defining the failsafe limit where a strong, smart Huragok couldn't use force or preemptive action was as good as impossible.

They needed to develop judgment. *Moral* judgment.

Damn. I was wrong. They're not amoral. They're anything but. Why wouldn't they be? Life creates moral awareness.

BB savored the delicious shock of discovery and the fresh light thrown on everything he knew. Everyone thought that Huragok had no sense of right or wrong, just obedience to whatever boss came along, but perhaps they just didn't see much difference between one empire-building, warfighting species and the next until they were forced into a corner—usually when Forerunner technology was threatened.

That was it. They tried to work out right and wrong, just like humans, and maybe with better results. But no god or gods had handed the Huragok a rule book and told them how to do it. They'd become moral beings simply through living life, because without some restraint and altruism, everything descended into terminal chaos. Something had made Sinks go that little bit further, and now he was defending the ship by any means he could, short of just killing the boarding party by asphyxiation. He'd done it because a human he'd taken a shine to had asked him to.

That's how I operate, too. That's how a human brain's built. I keep coming back to this. Either we're all programmed machines, or none of us are. I'm driven to acquire knowledge, and the Huragok are driven to fix things, and Spartans are driven to fight.

BB thought that humanity had come to a sorry state when

Naomi had a more sterile existence than a Huragok. At least they had a social life.

"Bastard," he said, but had no idea who he meant.

"Problem?" Vaz was looking at the Pelican's controls, probably trying to work out what had made BB swear. "Can Sinks even see us, BB?"

"Stealth partially disengaged. He can see our transponder, if he's looking. Not thermal profiles. I hate giving jumpy gunmen a target."

"Maybe he thinks we're Kig-Yar. Just tell me he hasn't got control of the laser cannon."

"Of course he has." BB found it interesting that Vaz had moved on instantly from surprise that a Huragok would be uppity to accepting that it would do much the same as he would in the same circumstances. His thinking wasn't constrained by classification. *Anthropomorphism. Not such a dirty word after all, is it? Accurate observation, more like.* BB wasn't sure why he'd thought that, either. He almost felt he was chiding himself, as if he'd had that argument once with someone, but he couldn't recall it. Maybe the memory had been damaged when his fragment got zapped. "He has complete control of the ship. He's just choosing not to react aggressively."

BB knew he had a lot in common with Huragok, but he was glad that they couldn't prowl unseen in the world of energy frequencies like him. He envied them their tentacles and cilia, though. *Hands.* He was still certain that he had no Pinocchio-like dream of aping humanity, but a pair of hands would have come in . . . *handy.*

"Has he lost the plot, BB?" Vaz asked.

"Well, even an AI goes bonkers in the end," BB said. "Why not Huragok?"

Staffan fidgeted in his suit. BB could tell he wasn't used to wearing one and had underestimated the small but maddening inconveniences like not being able to scratch where you needed to. *See, who wants skin? Itchy, horrible stuff.* Staffan held his radio where Vaz could see the controls, as if he was saying that he was being a good boy and not calling the Venezian cavalry for help.

"Sinks, this is Staffan," he said. "When you're ready, open the bay doors. I've got Vaz with me."

The comms channel came to life. <*I was busy with repairs. The Kig-Yar have been using their weapons to open doors.*>

A sliver of light appeared in *Inquisitor*'s port side, then widened gradually into a recognizable opening. BB nudged *Bogof* ahead without consulting Vaz.

"Tell him I'd really like to communicate with the nav computer, please." BB had always thought of Huragok as literal, but now he knew that didn't mean gullible—simply very precise, as befitted an engineer. Ambiguity and nuance were no use when you had to build things that worked. He waited for Sinks to make the mistake of allowing an inbound connection. "I've never docked in a CCS-class ship before."

Staffan began a smile but didn't follow through. "Sinks, can you let our nav computer talk to yours, please?"

<*That's a risk. You haven't called on schedule for more than a day. You said that would mean you might be in enemy hands or dead.*>

"I know, buddy."

Staffan didn't say that it was all fine and Vaz was a friend. He just waited, tapping his fingers on his knee. BB didn't expect him to make it easy. It would have been very easy to mimic Staffan's voice and try to fool Sinks, but he had a feeling that wouldn't work.

<*This might be another attempt to breach the system, so I've blocked inbound data channels,*> Sinks said. < *I'll transmit instructions and your computer will have to follow them.*>

Vaz inhaled slowly. "Well, *computer,* let's see how good you are at parking."

"Predictably awesome," BB said. "Tell him I'll do it by eye."

"Are you talking to BB?" Staffan asked. "I can see your head moving."

Vaz switched back to the open channel. "Yes. It's safer that way."

<Who is BB?> Sinks asked. <What is safer?>

"Berthing by sight. We can do it manually, thanks." Vaz went back to the privacy setting. "I don't lie well, do I? Nearly six hundred years of manned spaceflight, and it's still the little things that screw you."

BB got a fix on the bay doors using the hull cams and edged *Bogof* forward until he could see she'd cleared the doors on all sides. Now he had to set her down on a proper deck. Two Spirits hung in apparent mid-air, supported by gravity anchors, but the Pelican needed a solid surface. It meant maneuvering under the Spirits using cameras, inertial nav, and proximity sensors.

"Can we bang out of here in a hurry, BB?" Vaz asked.

BB had that in hand. "If I set down here, all we have to do is lift, rotate, and fire an Anvil through the doors if they don't open."

"Remember to keep your exit ticket, then."

"Okay, we're down. Full atmosphere and gravity outside." BB switched off the maneuvering thrusters and checked the bay doors visually using the top cam. "Now put that chip in the console."

"Did Leaks make this for you?"

"Clever little chap. I asked for a universal Covenant adapter."

The chip felt like a life belt floating on the sea. BB uploaded a fragment of himself to it and hoped it would sync up with all his other bits at the end of the day. For the moment, he was in two places locally: Vaz's helmet and the chip. He did one last sync transmission with his matrix in *Stanley* and then purged the onboard system of his presence. Huragok slurped up data just like he did, and he couldn't rely on keeping busy little tentacles out of the ship even with ONI security. The last thing he needed was a pissed-off, unpredictable Huragok on the loose with a big slice of the contents of an ONI AI's brain.

"I just hope the little bleeder doesn't nip in here when our backs are turned and mess around with *Bogof.* You can remove the chip now, Vaz. You know what to do."

The moment Vaz pulled the chip, BB's view of the outside world cut to Vaz's helmet cam. It was limited, but it would have to do. Vaz managed to lead quite a full life with almost as little input.

"Ramp down." Vaz pressed the control and squeezed out of the cockpit with Staffan behind. "Mal's right. The decor and the lighting in hinge-head ships make them look like empty night-clubs."

As he stepped onto the deck, his head jerked around and BB was looking at two suited bodies with long, tapering masks, slumped against the bulkhead and not doing a lot of moving.

"Better check." Vaz drew his magnum. "It's not unknown for buzzards to play dead."

"Don't lose that pistol, will you?" BB said. "I don't think we'll be getting yours back from New Tyne. Or your holdall."

"I'm putting in a claim. That was my personal stuff."

Vaz poked the slumped Kig-Yar with his boot while Staffan watched. They looked pretty dead to BB. The air indicator on their suits was past the emergency reserve mark.

"Must have repressurized recently," Staffan said.

"Does he just not like killing," Vaz asked, "or is he okay with letting us die?"

"How should I know?" Staffan said. "He's the first Huragok I've met."

Vaz removed the weapons and shoved them into his webbing with a struggle, then started looking around the bulkheads.

"Terminal," he said quietly.

BB couldn't see any kind of port like the one Leaks had

described to plug into. He was still scanning everything in the camera's field of view when it jerked up as Vaz stared at the deckhead. BB heard a sound like a drain tool working its way through a pipe. In the subdued violet light, he could see a couple of pitch-black openings, and then a familiar translucent shape drifted out and descended with slow grace.

"Hi, Sinks," Staffan said. "It's me. Take a closer look."

The Huragok peered into Vaz's faceplate and cocked his head this way and that until Vaz remembered to lift the top filter on his visor. He seemed satisfied that it was Vaz inside, and moved across to Staffan.

<Hello, Reclaimer.>

Staffan gestured at the bodies. "What happened to the Kig-Yar here?"

<They fired on me. I couldn't repair the hole they cut until they stopped, so they expired. We have hull integrity now, though. And air.>

"Can we get to the bridge, Sinks?"

<You'll encounter resistance when the doors are opened.>

"Well, Vaz is great at handling that. I would be, too, if he'd give me a firearm, but we're going to need to take back the ship."

<I made them an offer.>

"Really?"

<Another dropship in the starboard side bay which I've repaired. I told them I would open doors and hatches in sequence so that they could cross the ship and reach it, but they refused.>

Staffan nodded thoughtfully. BB knew from odd comments that Adj had made that Covenant crews could be dismissive of Huragok, so Sinks probably thought Staffan was a gentleman. He listened and replied politely. Sometimes that was all it took to gain an edge.

"Can you put me on the ship's broadcast so that I can talk to them through the translation system?" Staffan asked. "Maybe I can persuade them. I know you don't want to hurt people."

<On the contrary,> Sinks said. <But I know I must try not to. Come with me. Use the ramp.>

So he was both morally aware *and* honest. BB could respect that. Sinks drifted up to the deck level, and by the time Staffan and Vaz found the ramp and got up there, he was rubbing his tentacles together almost as if he was impatient. But that wasn't what the gesture meant in Huragok sign language. Sinks was just cleaning his cilia, the equivalent of a human dusting his hands on his pants. BB debated whether a quick conversation to show his linguistic skills would win hearts and minds, but he had no way of projecting his hologram from Vaz's suit.

And Sinks didn't know he was there yet. It was probably best to keep it that way.

<I sealed all the bulkheads and doors again.> Sinks moved off toward a set of doors at the end of the wide passage. <It's very tiring to do all this work alone. Use the address system near the door.>

"Vaz, look along the bulkheads," BB whispered. "Both sides. *Quickly.* I'm looking for a port. Once I find one, stick the chip in fast. Got it?"

"Yes." Vaz stopped and scanned obediently. It was the easiest way to take in all of both surfaces quickly, and BB could extract more information from the camera than Vaz could from his eyes. On the starboard side, ten meters from the doors, BB was sure he could see a data port. "There. Right. Near the door. Get up there *now.*"

Staffan had reached the ship's address mike, a small grille in the bulkhead. He stood in front of it and took off his helmet to scratch his scalp. "That's better. Okay, Sinks, can I hear their reply?"

<If you wish. They can't hear or speak to one another on their devices, but they can all hear the conversation.>

"Chol Von," Staffan said. "Can you hear me? Do you understand me?"

There was a scrambling noise from hidden speakers. "Who are you?" The Kig-Yar seemed to be speaking fluent English thanks to the translation system. "You sound like a flat-face."

"Now," BB said. "Just sidle up, stand there, and—"

"I know." Vaz strode up to passage, drew level with the data port, and turned his back to it. BB got the impression that he was trying to look as if he was getting ready to storm the bridge if the doors opened. Then he reached into his belt. Even BB thought he was taking out a spare magazine or a stun grenade. But Vaz looked down and slid a small wafer of silicone between his fingers. "Okay . . ."

"Chol, you're trapped," Staffan said. "Just listen to the Huragok, follow the path out to the dropship, and get out. Can't say fairer than that."

"Go copulate with an Unggoy."

"If you won't leave, I'm going to have to upset the Huragok and kill you."

<Not upset,> Sinks said.

"If you could, you already would have, human. Spoils of war. This is my ship."

Vaz took a slow step back toward the data port. Sinks seemed distracted by the exchange between Staffan and Chol. Staffan just scratched his scalp. BB thought that he seemed rather resigned for an arms dealer preloaded with Spartan genes and who was near the top of the UNSC's most pants-crapping list.

"You've got maybe sixteen crew left alive," Staffan said. "You're all trapped. No radio. No ship. No idea where you are or what's waiting outside. Nobody except us knows where you are. In fact, there's sweet FA you can do now except die or accept our generous offer. You know what sweet FA means, don't you? Does that translate?"

"*Now,*" BB said.

Vaz stepped backward, fumbled for a second, and then

turned to press the chip home. BB's consciousness burst into an instant carnival of light, noise, and data. He was watching the scene at the door, but he was also racing along a bright blue river like a water-skier, taking in every stream to either side, *fascinating* streams that led to other places that he could see, hear, and feel.

Sinks let out a long bleat. *<No. No, you tricked me.>*

"It's okay, Sinks, we're just getting the drop on the Kig-Yar," Vaz said.

<No.> Sinks shot up to the deckhead and headed for the conduits. Huragok were fast, but they couldn't move as fast as data. BB could travel at near-light speed in this system. *<No. No. You lied. You tricked me.>*

BB fell into a deep blue core like a diver, letting himself sink in the eddies of lovely, *lovely* data, then bobbed to the surface again to survey the world he'd fallen into. The bridge, violet-lit again, with an angry Skirmisher raging at a disembodied voice: the drive compartment, the weapons decks, the beautiful lace-work tracery of the data network, the hangars, the nav center— and the ventral beams. He saw it all like an infinitely perfect anatomical dissection. He was everywhere, and it was *glorious*. He plunged into the data banks and sucked up everything he could find, sending it hurtling back down the intense blue river to the data chip at the port by the door. It took seconds to absorb it, but it was done.

"Vaz, remove the chip," he said. "It's loaded. *I'm in*. You've got all the data. Now we can pick this off in our own time."

BB watched Vaz remove the chip. Staffan turned to him. It was all treacle-slow. He could see the Huragok, too, zipping along conduits and looking like a tube train speeding through a station every time he passed a monitoring device. If the little bastard was coming to try to turf BB out, he was too late. BB put up his own defenses on the mainframe's power supply and blocked all inbound data. He had the system secured.

There was only one problem with being able to move at near-light speed when you didn't have any hands.

The guy who *did* have hands already knew what you were doing, because you were so damn fast that you'd already started doing it. And he could do things that you simply couldn't undo. BB felt the power to the propulsion systems vanish.

And the doors, and the weapons, and the slipspace drive . . .

You crafty little bugger. I'd take my hat off to you, if I had a head.

BB checked all the monitors and found Sinks working away like a little violet blur in one of the main fiber-optic routers that ran through *Inquisitor* like a spinal cord. He was simply cutting the power *physically*. And there was nothing BB could do to stop him.

The ship still had full life support, though, and gravity. BB poked around a little more. Internal comms, too: what was all that about? If Sinks had cut power to the slipspace drive, it would lose containment and explode, so he must have simply looped the power supply to isolate it. Sinks wanted to stay alive, then, but he could have done that now without bothering about anyone else's compartment. He seemed to want people to be able to talk, too.

BB was stuck in the mainframe behind his own firewall and couldn't override any of the ship's main systems. *Inquisitor* was dead in the water. Sinks couldn't get at BB or move the ship either, but he had what he needed to sit it out. BB couldn't mess around with the life support because he might kill Vaz and Staffan. It was a stalemate.

"Sinks?" Staffan still looked calm. Vaz kept looking up at the deckhead. "Sinks, how are we doing?"

It was some time before the Huragok's synthesized voice emerged from a speaker.

<The ship's sealed. Immobilized and made safe. I have isolated power to critical systems.>

"Good. Well done."

<Vaz shouldn't have done that. You shouldn't have let him. Is this BB?>

"Yes, it's BB," Staffan said. "I'm sorry. They made me help them, and you know we need to get the Kig-Yar out." Then he looked at Vaz and shook his head. BB couldn't connect to his fragment in Vaz's helmet cam, but he could see and hear via sensors in the deckhead. "Sorry, son. You're a decent man, but did you really think I was going to let you guys ship me out to some ONI cesspit for the rest of my life and never see my family again? Put them through the hell I've been through? No, you don't get to do that to another generation."

"You can't go anywhere," Vaz said. "You know you can't."

"Well, if I never see my girl again, it'll be because I'm dead. Not because ONI locked me up in solitary for the rest of my days." Staffan sat down on the deck with his back resting against the doors. "I know you've tried hard to do the right thing, but your masters will never let you."

<Yes, BB,> said a voice right in the mainframe, right in BB's ear if he'd had one. *<We must all do the right thing. No more destroying. No more killing. Do you know right from wrong? I shall find out.>*

That was all BB needed: a Huragok having a moral epiphany, or a breakdown, or maybe both simultaneously. They only ended one way. BB wondered if he was now handcuffed to a man on a ledge.

FOURTEEN

IF YOU CAN'T WIN, YOU NEED TO MAKE THE OTHER GUY
WISH HE'D NEVER BEATEN YOU.
—ANDREW REMO, HEAD OF HERSCHEL'S MOST PROLIFIC
CRIME SYNDICATE, AND GRIEVING FATHER

**UNSC *TART-CART*, ON *PIOUS INQUISITOR*'S HULL:
QAB SYSTEM**

"Don't worry," Mal said. "The Covenant were unimaginative bastards. Seen one CCS-class, seen 'em all. The configuration's going to be the same."

Naomi watched the feed from *Tart-Cart*'s hull cam in her HUD, mentally rehearsing where she'd place frame charges to blow the access hatch. The dropship sat on the battlecruiser's hull like a mosquito waiting to sink her proboscis into an unsuspecting cow. Naomi and Mal were now squeezed into an airlock facing the hull, waiting for the order to go, the moment when the hatch would open, the airlock would depressurize, and they'd have seconds to lay and detonate charges to breach the hull. Naomi's Mjolnir armor was good for more than an hour in vacuum. Even with his supplementary air supply, though, Mal had half an hour at best.

But if they hadn't cracked this in thirty minutes, they probably wouldn't crack it at all.

"I don't think we've ever put a full deck plan together, actually," Naomi said. "Just the parts we've stormed before."

Devereaux's voice came over the helmet comms. "It's all going to depend on the access conduits. We know they've got them, just not where they go. How fast can Huragok move?"

"Zero KPH, if you deflate them." Mal was busy stuffing every pouch in his belt with extra ammo. With the supplementary air supply, he was already loaded like a packhorse. "Maybe they go whizzing around like punctured balloons. We'll see. Bit sad, but if it's him or us, I don't care how cute they are."

Naomi had fought her way into Covenant bases and even seized smaller vessels, but usually with a degree of certainty that the target wouldn't move far. Sangheili would stand and fight even if they had the option of making a run for it. But the Huragok had jumped the ship once, and he might do it again while they were on the hull. They probably wouldn't survive the enormous forces of the leap into slipspace.

Come on, come on, come on . . .

She waited to hear BB confirming that he'd infiltrated *Inquisitor*'s computer and had control of the ship, and then they could all breathe easy again. Her father and Vaz had made it into the shuttle bay. Dad was probably just talking Sinks around now, reassuring him and getting him to drop his guard so that they could remove the Kig-Yar.

Osman cut in on the radio. "Blue One and Two, stand to. We've lost contact with BB."

"Copy that, ma'am." Mal gestured to Naomi. "Go, go, go."

Her adrenaline spiked. It was like a switch. One second she was thinking, weighing all the options, and the next there was nothing in her mind but the motions she'd gone through a thousand times in training and exercises and drill, drill, *drill*: boots on hull, grip secure, move to hatch, adhesive XTCC strip placed here, here, and here, det attached, and *clear.*

"Firing."

She pressed the switch. There was a silent, short-lived flash;

no shockwave, but debris and mist ejected in all directions, including a chunk of the hatch that skimmed noiselessly over her helmet. From there all she had to do was walk back without losing her magnetic foothold and give the remaining chunk the kind of tug that only a power-assisted Mjolnir suit could generate. She dropped down onto a deck that was mostly pipes and filters.

Mal called *Stanley*. "Ma'am, Blue One and Two in. Stand by . . . Blue One to *Stanley* . . . Blue One to *Tart-Cart* . . ." He tutted. "Lost the signal. Sinks must have some kind of jamming around the hull."

"We'll busk it."

"We always do, don't we?"

Naomi prowled around, waiting for Kig-Yar to spring out of the cover of ductwork. If there was anyone else in the compartment minus a suit, they'd be sucking vacuum by now. Sinks would probably know from the damage monitoring that there'd been a breach, but automated systems would probably start sealing bulkheads without him. From this point, Naomi needed to open doors without damaging them wherever she could. She didn't know who'd be in the next compartment or if they'd be suited up. Vaz and her father were in here somewhere.

"Let's try BB," Mal said. "Sinks knows we're here anyway. BB, are you receiving? *Inquisitor* BB, not *Stanley* BB." There was no response on any of the comms channels. "Okay, maybe he can't get a signal out either. But he still might be able to hear us."

Mal reached a hatch in the deck and pointed down. Naomi gave him a thumbs-up. He pulled a hand-operated lever and the cover opened, releasing a fine cloud of dust that shot past her as the atmosphere escaped. She dropped through the opening first and worked out that she was in a long access shaft with very dim white lighting. It had footholds, so it wasn't a Huragok conduit.

"You clear, Mal?"

"Yeah. Sealing the hatch again."

Her helmet sensor showed they now had partial atmosphere, but they still had a long way to go. They climbed down narrow ladders through three more decks of dimly lit deserted engineering spaces, closing hatches behind them and pausing to listen for the Huragok. The bottom of this access shaft ended in a small compartment with no more hatches in the deck, just a manual door in the bulkhead. Naomi grasped the lever to open it and a characteristic purplish-blue light flooded in.

"Ah, we reached the cocktail lounge," Mal said. "Mine's a brandy and Babycham, please."

Naomi prepared to meet a hail of plasma bolts. "Is that good?"

"I don't even know what it is."

"Okay—*go*."

They burst out with rifles raised, but the section was empty. The passages were so wide that it was hard to tell if they really were corridors or just flats. She pointed to the next set of doors and they set off at a slow jog. A battlecruiser wasn't a big ship by Covenant standards, but it was still the best part of two kilometers in length and it was going to take time to move down the deck. There was still no sign of any Kig-Yar. Naomi prepared to breach the doors.

"Okay, we've definitely got atmosphere," Mal said, checking his TACPAD. "BB? You there?"

"I can see you, Mal. Quick sitrep, so just listen—and we're stuck on an open circuit, and it's all translated." BB's voice wafted out of a broadcast system somewhere in the deckhead. "I'm confined to the computer. I've locked Sinks out, but he's physically interrupted the controls to the drives and weapons. So either way—he can't jump the ship. We've still got sixteen Kig-Yar locked in different sections, three on the bridge, five in the section forward of you. Vaz and Staffan are trapped between the hangar bay and the bridge. No injuries."

It was a real pain in the ass having no comms with BB except for one broadcast channel that everyone could hear. Naomi looked around for a data port she could hack. If she asked for a location specifically, Sinks might beat her to it and render it unusable. "Is there any way you can give me a schematic of the ship?"

"I've got traffic out but I'm not letting traffic in. I've got hard access to cams and audio throughout. Well, for the time being."

"Where are we now?"

"One section forward of the brig. After that, it's the bridge."

"Can we speak to the next compartment?"

"Comms seem to be very patchy, but go ahead. Assume that everything that the ship's audio picks up here, like my dulcet tones right now, *everyone* can hear . . . including Sinks. Who's a *splendid* little chap. Who can probably also see the deck security cams, which are *not* exclusively routed via the bridge. Are you grasping the full import of all this?"

"Seeing as you keep repeating it, yes. Are the Kig-Yar in contact with each other?"

"Not all of them."

"Great."

Naomi did a quick recap of who could hear who and who was supposed to know what. This was almost as limiting as having an enemy who could read her mind. She could talk to Mal on the local helmet link, but anything they said to BB—or anyone else—was on an open circuit.

And Sinks could probably see hand signals too. She couldn't rely on him not understanding them.

Well, shit.

She looked at Mal. He tapped his helmet and indicated his air supply, then a number: twenty minutes. He was switching off and unsealing the suit to conserve his oxygen in case he really needed it later. Naomi followed suit in case she had to share her supply with him. Then she heard the helmet comms kick in again.

"Before we start blatting away at the buzzards," Mal said, "let's agree on a plan. Y'know, for the hell of it. If it comes to talking meaningfully, let me do it."

"Okay. I'll just rip things open and slaughter the contents, shall I?"

"You're great at that. Thanks." Mal pointed aft, then switched to external audio. This was all going to hinge on staying alert to what could be heard outside the helmets and what couldn't. "Okay, BB, we'd like to talk to the Kig-Yar."

"Go ahead."

"Gentlemen?" Mal called out. "You in the brig section. Can you hear me?"

There was a pause. "We hear you. Now get lost. This ship is ours. We found it abandoned."

"Okay. There's just one snag there." Mal signaled to Naomi to bypass the doors. "We've got a UNSC warship standing off. You're stranded. No ship. So why not take up the Huragok's offer and leave?"

"Make us."

"Okay. Will do."

Naomi pressed flat against the bulkhead in the hope that Sinks wouldn't be able to see what she was doing as she placed shaped charges around the doors. Where was the camera? She couldn't tell. But if he wanted to stop her, he'd have to come down here. As she set the detonators, she visualized the task he faced. He was just one Huragok with kilometers of interconnecting conduits to cover, and he couldn't be everywhere at once. He would have to zip up and down those tunnels like a demented pinball to get from one part of the ship to another. He wasn't like BB, able to travel almost instantaneously via any convenient signal and spread himself everywhere at once. Restoring what he'd cut off would be a massive task, but keeping one step ahead of him was a lot easier.

"Ready?" Mal asked.

Naomi held the det up. "Ready."

"Okay, lads, we're coming through. Nothing personal, honest. Some of my best friends are chicken nuggets."

The Kig-Yar were expecting an assault anyway, and there was only one point it could come from. An appeal to their pragmatism was worth a try. Mal paused long enough to shrug and then signal from the other side of the doors to stand clear.

Three, two, one—go.

"Firing." Naomi pressed the det.

The doors blew apart. She expected a steady green stream of plasma bolts to spew out of the gap, but nothing happened. *Wait or charge in?* She looked at Mal, adjusting her grip on her rifle, and nodded.

"*Now!*" she yelled, and burst in firing.

Green bolts streaked past her. She aimed down them like following tracer rounds and blew a corner off a bulkhead, flushing out a Kig-Yar who ran for the next cover. The space opened up into a long run of passages with ninety-degree bends that turned this into a running battle. To her left, Mal sprinted for the entrance to the first of the two brigs and put a burst of fire into a buzzard who tried to ambush them from around a corner. The Kig-Yar went down like a stone and his plasma rifle skidded across the deck.

"One down," Mal called.

It wouldn't do the others any harm to hear their buddies getting dropped one by one. Four left, then: Naomi listened for footsteps ahead. Had they decided to go? No, Sinks would have had to open a series of locked doors for them. They were still in here. Naomi turned right and saw what looked like a passage to the other brig. She couldn't tell if it was sensible to head down there in case they were cut off.

But that might draw them to us.

She headed down there. Mal hung back, covering the passage to the left from the cover of the corner.

"Correct assumption," BB said cryptically. He could see what they couldn't. There must have been a camera above the next set of doors. "From your *left*."

Lobbing a grenade would have been easier and saved ammo. Naomi spun around as Mal suddenly squeezed off two short bursts. She ran forward, firing as bolts grazed her armor, and cut one Kig-Yar almost in half as he ran at her. Mal took out the second. She swung around to look for the remaining two. Mal took a hit that knocked him back for a moment. *Where did that come from? Gotcha.* She followed the direction and ran up the passage, hitting the retreating Kig-Yar square in the back and spraying purple blood up the bulkheads. The last one came at her from an alcove to her right as she rounded a left-hand corner but she was a lot faster than he was. *Crack-crack-crack.* He was down. She went back and put an extra round through his skull to make sure.

There was no point missing an opportunity. She picked up a couple of plasma weapons, just in case.

"I'm okay," Mal said, tottering a little as he twisted his head around to check his shoulders for damage. "Section clear. Five down." He paused and looked up at the deckhead, either acknowledging BB or making sure the other Kig-Yar could hear him. "Chol? Chol Von? Can you hear me?"

He waited, using the time to reload while Naomi took advantage of the pause to look for a data port. BB prompted her. "Left . . . left . . . stop. Up a bit . . . *there.*"

She worked the probe into the dock and waited while her HUD and TACPAD scrolled though the data BB was uploading. That felt better. Now she could project the schematic as she moved instead of guessing her way. She could see the way to the bridge: right, left, right, left, right, left, right, right. She repeated it to herself until she'd memorized it.

"This way," she said.

Mal kept calling as he trotted along beside, following her turns.

"Chol? Knock knock. Are you still there? Sorry about your lads. They didn't see reason."

Naomi tried not to dwell on the fact that she hadn't heard a sound from her father or Vaz. BB had said they were okay, so she accepted that. She hadn't let personal problems intrude on the immediate task in hand—God, how many Spartans even *had* personal problems?—but now that there was a lull in the shooting, she couldn't erase the stranger of a father she was start-ing to get to know and wasn't entirely sure she'd want to forget again. She could still do her job. She simply did it knowing who was trapped on the ship with her, and what he should have meant to her.

We'll get out of this. They'll detain Dad, and nobody will know they've got him. He won't get a lawyer or a trial. But maybe I can use my status. Maybe I can get to visit him from time to time. Maybe ONI will do it for me. They owe us, after all.

Mal spread his arms, looking as if he'd given up on Chol Von, and gestured to Naomi to stand by to breach the doors to the bridge. Then a rasping voice came over the audio.

"How do you know my name? Who *are* you? Who sent you?"

Mal checked his optics, sighting up on the door. "Oh, we're nosey. We eavesdrop."

"Only Avu Med 'Telcam would know I was doing this, be-cause he hired me to retrieve this vessel. And how would UNSC humans know *him*?"

Naomi looked at Mal. It was that who-knew-what-and-when maze again, because any Kig-Yar that survived might let 'Tel-cam know who had their ship. He'd want to know why they hadn't informed him.

Mal had told Naomi to leave the talking to him, so she did.

"Actually, it's the Arbiter's ship, and he'd like it back. Our *ally* the Arbiter. The one we signed the cease-fire with." Mal cocked his head to one side as if he was enjoying the verbal fencing. Naomi couldn't see his expression. "But we can go ahead and call this 'Telcam bloke and tell him where his ship is and where *you* are. We're ever so helpful. It might not take him long to get here and give you a lift home." Chol didn't respond. "You think he's looking for you?"

"Save yourselves while you can. We have no argument with you. This ship is my bounty."

"Are you going to vacate this ship like a good girl?"

"Why would I leave," Chol asked, "when I now have the added bonus of one of your AIs trapped on my bridge?"

Naomi saw clear objectives now emerging from their range of options: storm the bridge, kill the Kig-Yar, neutralize the Huragok, free up BB, secure the ship.

And what about Dad?

She didn't know now if he was a hostage or the hostage-taker.

BRIDGE OF FORMER COVENANT SHIP *PIOUS INQUISITOR*: FOUR HOURS AFTER LOSS OF CONTACT WITH *PARAGON*

Chol Von paced around the command platform, calculating her chances both of surviving and of holding on to the battlecruiser she'd staked her future on.

The bridge was her advantage because the flat-faces probably wouldn't want to damage their precious AI. They'd be constrained because he was trapped here too. She wasn't entirely sure how these smart AIs worked, but she was certain this one would gather what data it could while it was in *Inquisitor*'s systems, which meant that even if it was a copy then it would have extra value for the humans, and they'd want to extract it.

Bakz sidled up to her and whispered in her ear so quietly that she could barely hear him. She hoped the background hum of the machinery would be enough to drown out their conversation.

"Mistress, if 'Telcam learns where we are, then we're dead

anyway. He's searching for us. Maybe he's found *Paragon*. Maybe someone on board has already given him information. You paid them, after all. They had no more reason to hold out for us."

Chol knew Zim wouldn't betray her. She wasn't entirely sure about the others, though—if her ship had survived the stresses of *Inquisitor*'s jump to slipspace right alongside her. "If the worst happens, then we say we were trying to wrest the ship from the UNSC."

"How do we *know* they're UNSC? We can't see them. The flat-face who traded with Fel isn't UNSC."

"Does it matter what kind of flat-face they are? 'Telcam despises them all equally."

"Even so, we could get out of this with our lives *and* the balance of the fee."

"You're surrendering."

"Living to fight another day is good business, not cowardly." He lowered his voice still further. "And it's not surrender. It's withdrawal. We take the option the Huragok gave us, leave in the dropship, and put out a distress call to *Paragon*."

"If *Paragon* isn't a pretty little asteroid belt of mangled parts by now."

"We can't win here. And not because of the flat-face troops." Bakz pointed upward, very discreetly, hand against his chest. From time to time, it sounded as if someone was dragging a waste sack along the deck above. The Huragok conduits probably converged above the bridge, and the creature was crisscrossing there. "That thing is determined to thwart us. We can't kill it. We can't find it to shoot it, and we can't vent the ship's atmosphere now. We're all low on suit air."

He had a point, but Chol wasn't keen to give up so easily. Maybe she could bargain with this AI. He'd been largely silent apart from a brief discussion with these UNSC pirates—if that was who they were—but now he'd started making an annoying musical sound that humans called *whistling*. Was it some kind of code? Could he hear their whispered conversation?

"What are you doing, AI?" she demanded.

"I'm bored," he said. He mimicked another voice. "I'm whistling. You know how to whistle, don't you, Chol? You just put your lips together and—oops. Sorry! Another fun thing that humans can do and you can't. And never stand in front of a Sangheili trying to whistle. It's like a stormy day on Brighton seafront."

They called him BB. She'd heard the name. She couldn't understand what he was getting at, but that seemed to be the point. "BB, are you attempting to distract us?"

"Well, you've got a warship up your chuff, and tooled-up special forces crawling everywhere, so it's hard to see how my whimsical habits could possibly put you at any more of a disadvantage than you already are."

"You could have just said no."

"Where's the joy in that?"

"You seem to think these humans see you as a friend, not as a computer program."

"Oh, let's not go down the 'your comrades have betrayed you' path, please. It's *so* last millennium."

"What do they *really* want?"

"You heard the man. They want to give the Arbiter back his ship. Look, you do realize they can hear all this, don't you?"

Chol hoped the members of her crew who were trapped in the drive section could hear it too, and that they'd understand what she now wanted them to do. They were now her best hope.

"If we can't have the ship, we'd rather destroy it," she said.

There. She hadn't heard them, so they could have been dead by now, but if they were still alive then they might have understood that she wanted them to get to the plasma torpedos and set them to detonate. The Huragok had isolated the slipspace drive, but setting off the torpedos would breach the fusion reactors.

As soon as the Huragok realized they were doing that, it would flush him out.

"A tad extreme, isn't it?" BB said. "There's a nice Spirit in one of the starboard bays waiting to go. That's got to be worth a few beer vouchers, hasn't it?"

"You mock me. And *beer* is of no interest to us."

Chol was sure that the Huragok would rush to stop the detonation. Once he'd done that, they could shoot him. Then they'd be able to restore power in their own time, pick off the UNSC intruders where and when they had to, and eventually head home with the extra delight of an AI to sell to the highest bidder.

It was a tall order, but not beyond her.

"A torpedo or two," she said. "That's all it would take."

She heard the garbage bag sound again. Sinks must have taken note of that. She just hoped her crew had.

"Okay, we're coming in." It was the male soldier's voice again. "BB, keep your head down, mate. It's chicken wings for dinner tonight."

"I say, that's rather *speciesist*." BB muttered disapproval. "Do we have any good Chablis in the wardroom cellar to go with them, though?"

Chol tried to ignore the provocation. She'd heard the abusive term *chi-ken* too many times from flat-faces, but would never let them have the satisfaction of knowing it enraged her. She could hear the noises from outside the starboard bridge doors. The humans could have blown their way in now, but they hadn't. They'd been forced to pick off her crew one by one. That meant they either didn't have explosives or were wary of using them for some reason.

If they wanted to destroy the entire vessel, then their warship, if it exists at all, could have done so by now. But the troops got here somehow. Wherever here is. I might be wrong about where we are. Maybe we moved farther than I thought. For all I know, we might be in a low orbit above a human world.

That wasn't a comforting thought. She had to stall to let her crew work on the drive trick, and find out what she could.

"Flat-face," she called. *"Human.* Listen to me."

"It's *Staff Sergeant* to you, love."

"Would you really risk your life for this ship?"

"Yeah, it's in the contract." They seemed to be taking their time about forcing the doors. They were either being careful to ensure they could shut them again and seal the citadel, or they were having problems with their explosives. There was extra security on the bridge doors. "We've got to do all sorts of daft and pointless shit. Are you coming out or what?"

"What guarantee do I have that you won't accept our surrender and then just slaughter us as we withdraw?"

Thud. Something hit the bulkhead from the other side, as if a weight had been hurled against it.

"All we want is the bloody ship so we can go home and get some sleep."

Thud. Noit looked, then trotted across the deck below the platform. It crossed Chol's mind that they might be stalling too, or even diverting her attention. She looked behind her, down the long ramp to the port-side doors. BB whistled to himself. He could see into other compartments, or so he claimed, and she couldn't.

Tricks. I know the flat-faces.

"I want to see the Huragok prove that he'll open hatches and give us access to the starboard bays," she said.

Thud. Noit was gazing at a point in the bulkhead.

"He doesn't listen to me." The sergeant didn't sound in a hurry. Chol thought she could smell the hot, ozonic scent of a discharged plasma weapon. "But I'll try. Sinks, can you open a door or something? Are you listening?" He paused. "BB, I know what you're whistling. Very funny."

It *had* to be code. Chol heard the sound of a hatch to her right, one of the service access points. She was sure it was sliding open. She pulled her pistol and turned to face it.

Thud.

It was definitely open. She walked toward it, ready to fry the brains out of whatever fool thought he could pull a stunt like this on her. When she bent her knees slightly to aim, she dipped her head. A faint shimmer made her start but it vanished like mist. It was the Huragok.

If he'd opened this door, then maybe he'd opened the rest. Maybe they didn't need to lure him by sabotaging the drive containment after all. *No, no, no.* That was defeatist thinking. She really had no plans to die for a cause, not even her own, not for a long time anyway, and she wanted to see her brood again, but maybe she could achieve more from the hull of this ship than from inside.

Thud. Thud.

"Mistress . . ."

Thud.

Chol heard the groan of metal before she jumped back from the hatch that promised an escape. By the time she turned, a bulge had formed next to the starboard doors, and then a rip, and then the metal glowed briefly. Noit opened fire at the widening split in the bulkhead. A vivid bolt shot back at him and he fell. Bakz went sprinting down the ramp and ran across the deck to help him, but it was obvious even from Chol's position that Noit was dead.

"Let's go," Bakz said. "Please, mistress, let's go. Let's leave while we still have our lives. We can get our vengeance later."

The doors didn't yield, but it was only a matter of time before they did, and the force trying to break in would pour in and overwhelm them.

And then you'll overwhelm your own graves. I'll see to that.

"If you can hear me," Chol shouted, "detonate the torpedoes. Do it. Do it now."

The slithering noise in the conduits sounded as if it was heading the other way. Chol hoped that Sinks really had opened all the doors and hatches to the starboard bay. She ducked into the hatch with Bakz behind her, and was sure she felt a shudder in the deck, not enough to be a slipspace jump or a missile strike but more than a glitch.

She didn't know what she was running into. She ran anyway.

"Oh, terrific." BB's voice carried into the low, narrow passage. "Sinks? Sinks, I think we need to start cooperating. *Fast.*"

AFT BRIDGE FLAT, *PIOUS INQUISITOR*

"BB? What's going on?" Vaz paced around the deck, frustrated at knowing there was a boarding in progress but that he couldn't do a damn thing to help. He'd kept quiet for as long as he could. "Come on, BB. Can they hear us or not?"

Stupid question: he couldn't ask BB to reveal anything that might help the Kig-Yar. Everyone would hear. He tested his comms again, but they were still jammed. *Shit.* He caught Staffan's arm and guided him as far away as he could from where he thought the audio pickup might be, right in the corner near a relatively noisy air vent. "Staffan, did you have some kind of plan pre-arranged with Sinks? Just tell me. I hope you did."

Staffan didn't look as if he was stalling. His voice was a furious whisper, all sibilants and spit. "Yes, I did, but he's got ideas of his own. You're the guy who works with them. Do they go off the rails?"

"No. They *don't.* I've never seen them do this, ever." Vaz racked his brains to remember what he'd heard about Prone To Drift, one of the original population of Huragok found on Onyx.

He'd done some unexpected things, but nothing like this. Phillips had read out bits of the classified report on how the ONI research station there had lost Jul 'Mdama, and Vaz was pretty sure it had mentioned Prone getting physical to stop Jul from doing something. He just couldn't remember the detail. "They're not machines, though. They have opinions and emotions. I think Sinks is having them in spades right now."

Staffan looked up at the deckhead again. "Sinks, where's Naomi? What are you doing? Please don't hurt my girl. Just tell me what's pissed you off. Talk to me."

"They don't kill," Vaz said. "He won't hurt her."

Vaz didn't add that Sinks might well defend himself if attacked, though. He'd heard of them trying to defend comrades. He was pretty sure that Sinks would present a threat now, and neither Mal nor Naomi would hesitate to take that shot if they needed to—not for long, anyway.

"Sinks?" Staffan's tone was still calm, but he didn't look it. "What are you trying to do?"

There was a shuffling sound overhead and Sinks emerged from a conduit. Vaz would have slotted him if the Huragok hadn't rushed to Staffan's side and stopped him from getting a clear shot. Once Sinks was out of the way, they could have brought Adj and Leaks on board to sort everything out. Getting rid of a few Kig-Yar would have been simple after that.

<I repaired the hull,> Sinks said. *<They used explosives to open an external hatch. I have removed it. No opening at all now. Much safer than the original design when jumping to slipspace. Much safer from forced entry.>*

"Sinks, if you just cooperate, we can resolve this without hurting anyone," Staffan said. "That's my daughter in there. Did I tell you about my daughter? She was taken from me. I've only just found her again."

<You'll be safe. I have opened exits for the Kig-Yar to depart.>

Staffan looked at Vaz and just raised his hand slightly. *No. Don't shoot it.* He could obviously read Vaz like a book. "Sinks, they'll put me in prison. I'll be all alone, probably for the rest of my life, and you know what it's like to be alone. So I need to get away. But I can't do that if you won't release the ship."

<*BB is preventing me from completing some tasks. So I'm preventing him.*>

"Okay, how about letting me talk to BB?" Vaz asked. "Are you stopping him? What's happening in there?"

Sinks couldn't jump the ship. That was some reassurance. He couldn't fire on *Stanley,* either, if the thought ever entered his head, which actually didn't seem impossible now.

<*Is Mal coming to detain you?*> Sinks asked. Vaz could almost see a line of logic in all this, that Sinks was weighing up the moral pros and cons to make a decision. <*He's with your daughter. I could—*>

Sinks stopped mid-sentence as Vaz felt a slight shudder under his boots. The Huragok zipped across to the data port to insert a tentacle into the aperture. How big a frame charge would Mal have needed to make a ship this size shudder? Even if he'd blown out a whole internal bulkhead to get onto the bridge, it wouldn't have done that. Sinks made a bleating noise.

<*This is very dangerous,*> he said. <*I must prevent this from escalating.*>

"What? What's escalating?" Vaz tried to block his path but he simply shot up like a cork and vanished into the conduits. "Staffan, give me your radio."

He held it out and Vaz took it to call Osman and then *Tart-Cart,* but the signal was jammed the same as everything else they'd tried. Suddenly Sinks was back again, bioluminescence flickering with anxiety.

<*They have set torpedoes to detonate,*> he said. <*I cannot restore it. The reactor will detonate too. You must leave. You have to leave now.*>

BB's voice cut in. "Seriously, chaps. Bang out *right now.* You've got about fifteen minutes. I'll work with Sinks to restore enough control to get everyone out."

"What about Naomi?" Staffan demanded. "Bring them both out this way. We can reach the Pelican. Sinks, open the goddamn doors so we can get to the shuttle bay. Do you hear me?"

The doors fore and aft of them opened. Vaz expected Mal and Naomi to come jogging out, but the bridge lobby was empty. He put on his helmet and sprinted for the bridge itself.

"Vaz, the doors on the other side are jammed." BB's voice trailed after him from speaker to speaker. "They can't exit across the bridge. They're retracing their path in."

"Can't." Vaz stopped dead and checked the time on his TAC-PAD. "Sinks sealed the hull. There's no opening now. We'll never cut through it in time. Are you free of the mainframe? Christ, what can we do and *not* do now?"

"I'll deal with it. Trust me. Get to *Bogof.* Now. *Please.*"

"Sinks? Stop jamming the signals."

<Done,> Sinks said. *<But I've failed to save the ship. I apologize.>*

Screw the ship: Vaz had two friends stuck on the other side of the bridge and *Tart-Cart* was still waiting to extract them. *Port Stanley* was probably in range, too. When a full torpedo bay blew, it caused a massive explosion, more than enough to cream any vessels nearby. Vaz ran back toward the shuttle bay, trying to set his chrono to count down and flashing *Stanley* on his comms.

"Red One to *Stanley.*" How long did they have? Could Sinks give an accurate count? "Red One, *Stanley* come in."

"Done," BB snapped. "*I did it already.* I've warned them off. Just get out, will you? I've turned Mal and Naomi back and I'm going to direct them across to the starboard side with Sinks. *Thirteen minutes,* Vaz. Move it."

Vaz's gut flipped. "Where's Staffan?"

"In the shuttle bay."

"Pity he can't fly a dropship."

"He can. Not an ace like Dev by any means, but he can."

"But he said he couldn't—"

"Obviously. Wouldn't you?"

Vaz tried to keep a grip on it all. Diving from orbit was easy. Being a spectator wasn't. "So why hasn't he escaped?"

"He's waiting."

Vaz ran through into the shuttle bay and looked down to the deck below, somehow expecting to see Staffan waiting by *Bogof,* because *that* was why he hadn't grabbed the chance to go, *that* was why he was still here, because BB's fragment wouldn't let him take the Pelican and leave Vaz stranded. But he was wrong, totally wrong. There was no sign of Staffan at all, and when Vaz reached *Bogof,* he wasn't on board.

Then movement caught his eye in one of the Spirits suspended above him in its antigravity mooring. It rotated 180 degrees to face the bay doors, and his helmet comms link crackled.

I should have known better. Staffan wants to see Naomi safely out of here.

"Can you hear me, Vaz?"

"Five by five."

"Ten minutes, Sinks says. Come on. I want my girl out."

"Okay, BB, you're coordinating this." It would have been so much easier if Staffan had been an asshole, if he'd lived up to the insurgent stereotype and made a run for it. Instead it just kept getting harder to do what ONI said had to be done. "How are we playing this?

"Sinks is taking them through to the starboard side. He can clear any obstructions." BB cut back to the helmet link. "Staffan could have asked Sinks to disable me in *Bogof.* But he didn't."

"Why are you telling me this, BB?"

"So that you understand."

Understand what, the nature of the man? Vaz knew now. He

followed Staffan out of the bay and into open space. As *Bogof* looped under the battlecruiser's hull, he checked his chrono a dozen times, trying to calculate how fast Mal and Naomi would need to move to make it to the shuttle bay. It didn't seem possible in that time. He should never have left them. He should have got Sinks to make a hole in the doors. Why hadn't he thought of that? Maybe they'd retraced their steps too far. Shit, it was too late to run through the if-onlies now.

The horseshoe-shaped Spirit rotated again and moved forward, hugging *Inquisitor*'s starboard flank. Vaz could now see *Tart-Cart* standing by. Devereaux was blocking the bay doors. If anyone was going to pull Mal and Naomi out of there, it was her. She was made for tough extractions. It was what she excelled at, the tougher the better, and she didn't like a well-meaning audience.

"I've got it covered, boys," she said. "*Stanley*'s jumped to stand off at a safe distance. I suggest you do the same."

But how fast could a Spirit get clear? It didn't have a slipspace drive.

Vaz knew their upper limit. He'd banged out of Imber in one with Mal, flat out with angry hinge-heads on his ass, and he hadn't pushed it much past 1100 KPH with its gauges in the Sangheili equivalent of the red zone, creaking and whining.

Oh Christ. No. That's just not fair.

"Staffan, get going," Vaz said. He didn't say where. That was up to Staffan, but Vaz hoped it was a long way from *Port Stanley* and ONI. "Do it."

"Sinks says I'll be fine." Staffan let out a long breath. "Eight minutes, conservative estimate. Probably be a little more."

"I swear we'll get them out. Go."

Dev interrupted. "Hey, macho men—piss off, will you? You don't get points for being dead. Leave this to the pro."

Vaz almost did, but Staffan wasn't moving. "BB, where are your fragments now, other than the usual?"

"Here and Naomi's helmet. Got the data chip?"

"Yeah, of course I have."

"Put it in the console dock and upload it to *Stanley* now. If you *insist* on risking UNSC property and this goes horribly, *horribly* wrong, I'd hate to have nothing to show for losing all my friends."

Vaz was so focused on watching the hull cam view of the shuttle bay that he took two fumbled attempts to dock the chip. "Ready."

"Whoosh . . ." BB said. "Data away. And by the way, Admiral Osman says to leave now."

"Did you hear that order?"

"Deaf as a post, me."

"You'll still be in *Stanley* when *Bogof*'s a cinder."

"And you won't. But don't worry, we're spooled up to slip and holding. See the pretty little amber light?"

Vaz counted down the remaining minutes and seconds on *Bogof*'s instrument panel. "Can you get into Staffan's system via the radio?"

"Of course."

"Will you do me a favor? I'll say I forced you. In fact, I *am* forcing you."

"What, exactly?"

"Access my personal datapad. Quick." Vaz fumbled for it in his dump pouch and docked it. "Naomi's file. Send Staffan the page that proves he was right. The one that says how she was abducted, and the bit about the clone."

BB didn't say a word. Circulating classified material to a terrorist on the watch list was about as serious as it got in ONI. Vaz knew he wouldn't be looking at life without parole. He'd be looking at a firing squad.

Might as well be shot for something that matters, then.

It would probably have been enough to let Staffan slip away, which would be bad enough when Osman found out, but the guy probably wasn't going to get out of here alive. He must have known it.

Vaz watched his datapad's display. The icon blipped. Well, it was done now. Maybe Staffan would have time to relay it back home to Edvin, then at least his family would know it wasn't a crazy conspiracy theory after all. It was up to him if he took it to his grave or not.

"Seven minutes," said BB. "Chop chop, boys and girls."

FORMER COVENANT SPIRIT, ALONGSIDE *PIOUS INQUISITOR*, NOW KNOWN AS *NAOMI*: APPROXIMATELY SIX MINUTES TO DETONATION

"Coo-ee. I really shouldn't be here, you know."

Staffan thought the AI's voice was still on his radio, but then a display on the Spirit's control panel flickered and he realized BB had infiltrated the dropship's systems.

"Did they send you to arrest me again?" he asked. "Because this isn't great timing."

"What do you plan to do next?"

"Either see my daughter safely out of that ship, or get her out myself. I hadn't thought much past that, really."

"You know they'll come after you one day if you go back to Venezia."

Staffan decided it was a ruse to distract him and went back to watching the clock. Sinks said fifteen minutes to torpedo overload was an average, but it ranged from eleven to nineteen minutes. If the battlecruiser was on the wrong end of the bell curve, then Staffan had sixty seconds to make his peace and Naomi wasn't getting out.

"One day's too far ahead to plan," he said.

"Oh, really?" BB was humming tunelessly to himself. What was he doing? Staffan was never sure what this kind of AI could and couldn't do. "My, Sinks *has* been keeping himself busy, hasn't he?"

Staffan wondered if BB was somehow setting a tracking program, but he'd said it himself: they'd pursue him to New Tyne eventually. He had a wife and kids there, a granddaughter too. He wasn't going to run.

I should have called them. In case I don't make it.

But the thought of deciding who to call first, how long to spend, what to say, and all those agonizing decisions that simply couldn't be made in a few minutes overwhelmed him. He decided to say nothing. He kept his eyes on the shuttle bay, waiting to see Mal and Naomi emerge.

And Sinks.

He didn't want to leave the Huragok to die. The creature was defective, but he was useful, and he was still a sentient being. And he'd given Staffan the best chance of surviving today. He owed the creature something.

"Aren't you going to check your comms for messages?" BB asked. "You've got a document from Vaz."

"What?"

"He believes you're a man of your word. So he thought you might like the evidence about Naomi. Something to stop your son thinking you're a fruit-loop. It's in your onboard data."

Despite himself, Staffan glanced down at the control panel. There was a document image waiting. It was watermarked and classified top secret, a term which always sounded weirdly comic to him, except this wasn't funny at all. He took a quick look at the screen and wondered why Vaz had taken such a massive risk for him.

"Good God."

"Yes. I've wiped the routing records, of course, not that it'll take a detective to work out roughly where it came from, but I'd hate to see Vaz punished for being a decent man. You know what's in it anyway. If I'm feeling especially evil one day, I might frame Halsey for it. Say she had a sudden attack of conscience. Hah."

Staffan tried to keep his mind on the clock. "He didn't have to do that."

"Oh, he did. That's Vaz." BB cleared his throat. It was an odd thing for an AI to do. "I once boasted that I could frame the Archangel Gabriel for armed robbery. I'm also very good at *un*-framing people too."

"What are you playing at, BB?"

"Checking out your dropship. I'm impressed. It doesn't look this spiffy from the outside. When did Sinks fit the slipspace drive? We did that too. Goes like a greased weasel."

BB was in the Spirit's systems, so he *knew*. "You're going to turn me in, then."

"What your Huragok does to your ship is your business. I'm going to forget I ever saw any upgrades. But you know how unreliable these small slipspace drives are, don't you?"

Staffan really didn't need to hear that. He knew he was about to attempt something dangerous that he probably wouldn't survive. He didn't know if the modified Spirit could jump fast enough. But it wasn't the first time that he'd done something desperate like this.

It might well be the last, though. "So?"

"Of course you do. And you'll be so close to a *humungously* big explosion when *Inquisitor* blows that you can forget about identification by dental records. If you get my drift."

Staffan wasn't sure he did. "You *are* trying to do some deal with me."

"Oh, puh-*leeze*, do I have to draw you a picture? Once more for the dim ones. In a few minutes, I'll make myself forget this conversation, the document, and that I knew your ship was upgraded. Because you've sworn to forget you have a beef with Earth. And, with luck, if you manage to pull off this jump, you'll live out your years as the healthiest dead man in history. Because nobody will believe you made it. And if you don't give us cause to doubt that, we won't look twice."

Now the penny dropped. BB wasn't setting him up. He was helping stage a disappearance. Why, though? To give ONI someone to call in favors from later? "Okay. I get it. Just tell me why. You bastards never do anything for free."

"I do. Because I think justice trumps the law. And I can put my hand on my heart, virtually speaking, and say we neutralized a terror threat to Earth. Everybody gets what they want. Most enduring kind of deal, remember?"

Stay off the radar and you get to live. It wasn't what Staffan had been expecting. "What are my chances?"

"One in four. You could go now, of course."

"Naomi thought I'd abandoned her once. I won't let her think that twice."

"Or Sinks."

"Stop it."

"And *Tart-Cart* would spot you jumping. Or exploding, as the case may be."

"I'll just say thanks, then, BB. And cross my fingers."

"Naomi and Mal are about a minute from the bay now. Want to listen?"

Staffan knew it would tear him apart. But he had to. He wanted to be there with Naomi. He'd been robbed of a lifetime with her and every second was precious, even by proxy. If he survived today, he'd still probably never see her again.

"Okay." His heart was thumping. "Let me hear."

BB switched to an audio channel that sounded echoey and distant. Staffan could hear the rough breathing of someone running, but no speech. He couldn't tell if it was Naomi or Mal panting their way toward the hangar. Then he caught a voice. It was Naomi responding to someone he couldn't hear.

"Got it, Dev." She sounded completely calm, not even out of breath. She must have run at least eight hundred meters through

passages and down hatches in that armor and that was a lot tougher than covering eight hundred meters on a level track. *That's my girl. One in a billion.* Staffan was still proud of everything she did. *"Just hit it and jump when you can . . . no, we didn't know . . . Mal?"*

Mal was the one who was panting. *"What's he waiting for? Sinks? Don't expect me to arrest him. I'm a bit busy."*

Staffan felt better for hearing that Naomi wasn't distressed. But she was a Spartan. He knew what that really meant now, and there was nobody more suited to the role. That didn't change how bitter he felt, but at least she was respected and admired, and that was some comfort.

"She sounds okay," he said.

BB's voice transferred to his radio. "If you've ever got a message for her—well, in the next seven years, anyway—relay it via *this* code."

"Why seven years?"

"Because that's my maximum lifespan. Oh, don't pull that face. It's not so bad. A lot can happen in that time. I'll make sure I party a lot and date *very* saucy software. Process fast, go offline young, and leave fabulous documentation. That's my motto."

"Why are you doing all this?"

"Because I can. Because I'm the smartest entity in existence. What's the point of being pure magnificent genius if you can't do something good with it? I don't want to be like Halsey."

Mal's voice cut back in again. *"No, sorry, tell her I have no bloody idea where Staffan is. Tell her he's too close to get clear. Christ . . . that'll have to wait . . . no, I've got one minute of air if anything goes pear-shaped."*

Staffan could see the lights in the shuttle bay blooming out around the Pelican, and the shimmering energy field across the aperture. The dropship was almost in the bay itself. The tail ramp had to be resting on the deck. They'd run straight in, the ramp would shut, and then it would be over; Naomi would be gone from his life again. He hadn't even talked to her much about what she'd actually done in the war.

"Here they come," BB said. "I'm going to have to love you and leave you, Staffan, but make sure you take care of yourself. You won't find any trace of me in your systems, or any record that we ever spoke. Nobody will find the logs in my records, either."

AIs were strange things. Staffan didn't argue. "Can you give Vaz a message?"

"Certainly."

"Tell him I keep my promises."

Staffan was still watching the hull cam view of the shuttle bay. The Pelican's nose lifted.

"There," said BB. "They're out. Good-bye. And I'm sorry, sir. I truly am."

Staffan heard the thuds and shouts. "What are you sorry for? And why *sir*?" But BB was gone. Staffan could still hear one half of the comms, though, the sound of Mal and Naomi arguing with someone.

"Come on, Sinks, now or never."

"If he won't come, we can't wait."

"Come on—"

"Now. I said now."

"Ramp up."

"Staffan, she's safe. Sinks won't board. Sorry." That was Vaz. *"Pakah,* Staffan."

The dropship shot forward from a dead stop and kept accelerating. As Staffan moved in to give Sinks one last chance, *Tart-Cart*'s nav lights and blue thrusters seemed to smear into the black, then a flash of white light erased them. Another flash followed, probably *Bogof* making her own jump to safety. Staffan pulled alongside the hatch and lowered one of the Spirit's drop-down bulkheads through the energy barrier.

Maybe this was a nineteen-minute overload after all. "Come on, Sinks. You've got ten seconds to make up your mind."

Staffan really did count to ten. He didn't want to die, but he knew the next second might be his last. He breathed again when he saw the Huragok drift in, caught for a moment in one of the monitors. Then he hit the controls to secure the crew bay again. There was only one way out. He pushed off sideways to starboard and banked sharply, hammering the Spirit's maneuvering drive to maximum as he pressed unfamiliar controls to spool up.

Two minutes.

He sweated. He should have relayed that document to Edvin, but his hands were too full now. He tried not to watch the monitor image of the battlecruiser dwindling behind him nowhere near as fast as he would have liked. Sinks drifted into the cockpit.

<You risked your life.>

"You're welcome. You risked yours."

<It was the right thing to do.>

"Are you ready, then?"

<For either. For the Great Journey, or the Great Learning. It will be close.>

Staffan had done what he'd set out to do. He'd lived long enough to learn the truth about his daughter, and Remo's boy as well. That was more than the other poor bastards ever got. He counted down the final seconds to the jump, one eye still on the aft-facing monitor.

<That's right,> Sinks said. *<That's how you do it.>*

For a couple of seconds, *Pious Inquisitor—Naomi—*was a gleaming, sinuous sculpture that looked nothing like a warship should have done. Then a brief, shocking-white flash swamped the screen, followed by another, and all light vanished from the universe.

FIFTEEN

TO: CINCONI
FROM: BBX-8995-1, AI, UNSC PORT STANLEY
CASUALTY UPDATE, PIOUS INQUISITOR

UNSC PERSONNEL: NO INJURIES
KIG-YAR: 8 DEAD, 8 MISSING OR ESCAPED.
PRISONERS: STAFFAN SENTZKE—KILLED DURING DETONA-
TION. NO BODY RECOVERABLE.
NOT CLASSIFIED: HURAGOK, KNOWN AS SOMETIMES
   SINKS—REFUSED TO LEAVE SHIP, KILLED DURING DETONA-
   TION. NO BODY RECOVERABLE.

CINCONI'S OFFICE, BRAVO-6, SYDNEY: WASH-UP ON
***INQUISITOR* MISSION, TWENTY-FOUR HOURS LATER**

"So," Parangosky said. "I think we can count that as a result. How do you feel it went, Serin?"

BB had chosen to sit in on the post-action wash-up from the ground today, drifting around Parangosky's office in the underground bunker of Bravo-6. He was as spread around the galaxy as usual—*Port Stanley,* the Sanghelios remotes, even Ivanoff Station—but by being visible here, he felt he was exerting a quantum effect. Parangosky was as susceptible to her subconscious and her hard-wired reactions as anyone.

Few other AIs seemed to split off fragments as much as he did. At first he thought it was something necessary to run a ship without a proper crew, then it became a habit, and now it was a compulsion. He'd have to keep that in check. He'd had too many close calls.

Osman, light-years away in the captain's seat on *Stanley*'s bridge, looked a little thinner in the face now that BB could see her through the eyes of the Bravo-6 video system.

"Three out of four isn't bad, ma'am," she said. "But it depends on the timescale you're thinking in."

Parangosky sipped her coffee. "I'm ninety-two. Long-term isn't on my list of options these days."

"Well, we got a very useful amount of data thanks to BB. I'm just sorry we missed the opportunity to seize the ship."

"Let's focus on the intel it gave us. I don't think even Hood's going be squeamish about making use of that, however honorable he wants to be with the Sangheili. The data from the Jiralhanae and San'Shyuum is a bonus. I'd almost forgotten that *Inquisitor* had been through so many hands."

"We don't have a functioning ventral beam, though."

"But we do have the ship's full schematics and engineering data, should we ever decide to build our own. And *Inquisitor* won't be troubling Earth. You removed an immediate threat. Two, if you count Staffan Sentzke."

"We didn't remove him. We just got lucky because he didn't escape the blast. My people would have been vaporized as well if we didn't have modded Pelicans."

Parangosky flexed her fingers as if her arthritis was giving her trouble. "How's Naomi dealing with it?"

"Efficiently, but in hindsight I should have talked her out of enhanced recall. Well, at least the scales have fallen from her eyes about Halsey. Apparently she spun Naomi a line that her dad wasn't coming to rescue her because he'd agreed to it. Halsey's the toxic dump that keeps on leaking."

"Yes, we need to talk about that woman's future soon. I'm sorry you'll inherit contaminated land."

Osman didn't say anything for a few seconds. BB wondered if she'd started to censor her usual quick-fire responses to Parangosky, part of the process of turning from protégé to successor and keeping her plans for the future of ONI policy to herself. But she said it anyway. It needed saying.

"Ma'am, Halsey's a security risk. She'll never change. She's never had to. She always gets taken back into the fold. Anything she's done for ONI or Earth is purely coincidental to her life-long pursuit of what Catherine Halsey wants."

"I know. You think she manipulated me."

"It's always hard for lay people to call bullshit on scientists or put brakes on them. They wave their hands and tell us we're simple, overemotional peasants who stand in the way of progress."

"But you're a Spartan. You can look the Halsey gorgon in the eye in a way I never could."

"I won't hesitate to take her head off, either. And I do mean terminate."

"Oh, I've been there, Serin. Believe me. But she always convinced us we needed her a little longer."

"Well, I'm not intimidated by her superpowers. We've developed two generations of Spartans without her input, and Huragok perform better on engineering innovation. She's nearly obsolete. She's on the cusp of being better value dead. Let's remind her of that."

BB would have cheered, but that was bad form. One day, HIGHCOM would look back and pass judgment, and say how *regrettable* Halsey's activities were and that lessons would be learned, but none of those in the know had raised an objection when it might have made a difference. BB wasn't sure why that stung, but it did.

"So are you standing down your team for a few days?" Parangosky asked, making it sound like a question rather than an order. "Decompress a little? Even tough guys need to lick their wounds."

Osman nodded. She seemed to be looking to one side of the screen as if her mind was elsewhere. "We need to pick up with 'Telcam and find out what he's been told about his ship. I'll work out what line to feed him, but yes, they'll get some shore leave. I'll let Venezia cool off for a good while before we venture too close again. And I think I might finally take a look at my file."

She tacked the news right on the end as if anyone would believe it was an afterthought. "Really?" Parangosky said.

"After what's happened, I think I need to face it, if only to give better support to Naomi."

Well, I didn't see that *coming.* BB had grown used to Osman confiding in him on everything, especially the personal stuff. He thought she trusted him. *Would I trust me, though?*

Parangosky chewed it over for a few beats. "Don't kick yourself in the ass too much. Get drunk with the ODSTs. You won't be able to do that when you're me."

"Understood, ma'am. We'll send you a postcard. Osman out."

BB hung around after the link ended. Parangosky gave him a long look and raised an eyebrow as she bit into one of those rock-hard ginger cookies she was so fond of.

"So are you going to get involved with this or not?" she asked.

"Osman doesn't have the full neural net, remember. If she did, I still might decline after what happened with Naomi."

"I meant are you going to hold her hand."

"She's not keen on hand-holding, even if I had them. She sees frontline troops coming home in shreds, so she really doesn't think this is more than a paper cut she ought to be able to shrug off."

"She'll feel better for knowing. I'm putting a fifty on that."

"I think the real crisis for her will be if the Spartan scandal ever goes public, *really* public, Waypoint public, because there'll be a tidal wave of indifference. Then she'll start to question why we spent the lives of millions of troops protecting a species that's happy to see kids abused because it's all for the greater good and

it didn't happen to them. It's not very fulfilling to serve an electorate that would have voted for Hitler."

"Ah, see, there's her mistake," Parangosky said, gesturing with
the ginger nut. The bite taken out of it had left a perfect crescent.
"I don't *serve* the electorate. Nobody voted for a de facto military
government, so I don't give a rat's furry brown ass what they
think. It pays not to look at the public too closely. My job is simply
to keep as many of them alive and not killing each other as I can.
I'm just a referee in a game of destructive self-interest."

"I hope HR put that in the job description, ma'am. It's very
appealing."

"Do *you* want to know where you originated, BB?"

"No, thank you. I made sure I couldn't. I believe I had a good
reason at the time."

He noted Parangosky's words. *Where you originated.* She
was a precise woman with an elegant if sometimes bawdy turn
of phrase, and if she'd meant *who you were* then she would have
said *who you were,* not *where you originated.* It was intriguing;
and BB was endlessly curious, out of necessity. Curiosity was
his breathing reflex and information his oxygen. He would cease
to exist if he tried to do without either, because that was all he
was: pure thought, contained in the borrowed skin of a machine
or an electronic signal.

Maybe he read too much into it, but he felt she was reminding him that he wasn't a copy of anyone.

"You might find it gratifying on some levels," she said.

"I'll take a look one day. When I know my days are numbered. When I know rampancy is imminent. I'm going to ask
Admiral Osman to do the decent thing and help me terminate
myself when that day comes."

Parangosky leaned forward very slowly. "You think she'd
agree?"

"Do you think that's cowardly, ma'am? Suicide, I mean."

"No." Parangosky shook her head but took a long time doing it.

"Suicide can be many things. Desperate. Sensible. Noble. Tragic. Even the ultimate exercise of free will. But cowardly? No, I really don't believe it ever is. An organism's primary instinct is to stay alive at any cost. That goes beyond a conscious drive. It's embedded in every involuntary mechanism and chemical reaction in the body. To override that, whatever the reason, we take a fully conscious act of responsibility, possibly the only real one we can ever make."

"Gosh. You make it sound rather splendid in its way. Messy, but noble."

"Not at all. But . . . look, BB, you're curious by your very nature. Part of you knows why you don't want to look at your own files. If you ever do, though, just remember this. Your donor did the right thing." Parangosky smiled. She smiled quite often, at least to her inner circle, but this was different: fond, sad, and— was he imagining this?—a little glassy with unshed tears. "Just as I'm sure *you* do the right thing, BB."

"I try."

"Is there anything else you want to contribute about Staffan Sentzke?"

"I don't think so, ma'am." *I might be lying. I might not. That's why I don't want to know for sure.* "Only that he wouldn't leave while Naomi was on the ship, so he gave up his chance to get the Spirit to a safe distance. Which further muddies our waters about good guys, doesn't it?"

Parangosky was still studying BB intently, as if staring through his hologram would answer a question she hadn't asked. He had a sudden pang of guilt. The old girl could smell it at fifty meters, but she couldn't possibly have known what he'd done because he'd erased and doctored all the data, and even he only knew what he felt he needed to be consciously aware of to avoid slipping up. The rest, such as it was, was firewalled from everything and everybody for all time. It would die with him. He'd hidden things from himself that he never wanted to look at again. In the end, all that mattered was that a threat to Earth had been stopped. How they'd achieved that was irrelevant.

Tasking by objectives. Tell us the end result you want and leave us to decide how to do it.

But Parangosky had a mix of a sixth sense and a good knowledge of how her people reacted. Every spook kept something in reserve.

"You're a good guy, BB. That much I do know."

"Thank you, ma'am."

"You're very welcome, my friend."

Parangosky wasn't the first human to address him as *friend.* It made him feel good, even though defining it was oddly difficult—a kind of relief, redemption, rescue, as though he didn't deserve that affection but was so glad of it that it hurt.

"My donor," he said carefully. "Was he your friend too?"

She nodded. "Yes. He was."

"Oh. I'm sorry." It was rather uncomfortable. When she looked at him, he wasn't sure who she was seeing in her mind's eye. "Nothing horizontal and mucky, was it?"

Parangosky laughed, but it faded away as if she'd run out of energy. "I was old enough to be his mother. He was just skin and essence."

"Anyway, must go, ma'am. Governments to bring down, mayhem to cause. Toodle pip."

Part of BB stayed in the Bravo-6 system, watching Osman's virtual back against the schemers and accidental saboteurs, but his psyche went back to *Port Stanley* and wandered around the decks, noting who was where and their general mood. Phillips and Spenser were listening in to the Sangheili comms chatter. Adj and Leaks were tinkering with the Pelicans. Mal, Devereaux, and Vaz were working out in the gym in grim silence. Naomi was lying facedown on the glass deck set in *Port Stanley*'s belly, chin resting on her folded arms as she watched the starscape during her stand-easy.

Osman was in her day cabin, wrestling absent-mindedly with Phillips's *arum*. She seemed to be using it more as worry-beads than with any real intention of unlocking the mechanism to free the stone inside. Her eyes scanned back and forth across her screen, reading Halsey's journal until BB plopped his avatar right in front of her and blocked her view.

"You know that pisses you off," he said quietly. "So why keep reading it?"

"Staring at car crashes, I suppose. It's just so . . . so . . ."

"You should grab the rights to it. One day, it'll be required reading in psychology classes. A glimpse into the mind of a narcissistic sociopath. Like *Mein Kampf* with pictures."

"I thought you told Phillips she wasn't mad. Just nasty."

"Oh, you know psychologists. Always looking for ways to give patients an excuse for their horrible personalities so they can bill them for it."

Osman scrolled back a few pages with a gesture. "Every time I get sucked into this, another page gives me hives. Look." She leaned back, arms folded, and started reading aloud as if he wasn't fully aware of every bit of data in every device in the ship, other than the ones he'd deliberately nobbled. *"In another time, each could have been the next Alexander, Cleopatra, Hannibal, or Genghis Khan."* Osman made a strangled noise as if she didn't want to swear in front of him. "If we were that special, wouldn't it have made more sense to train us for senior command roles? Isn't that how you deploy an Alexander, where that ability achieves most? You wouldn't blow out your strategic genius in an operational commando role—no offense to the ODSTs. Why did nobody stop her and just ask that? What were the admirals and generals doing? Blind? Deaf? Heads up their asses?"

"Ah, this is why she's become a hate figure and fallen from grace."

"I thought that's because she's sadistic, charmless bitch."

"There's that, yes, but everyone's piling in because it's easier than looking in the mirror and asking, 'Gosh, yes, why *did* we let her do that? Why did I cooperate with it? Why did I turn a blind eye?' It took the collusion of hundreds, maybe even *thousands* of personnel. Vaz nailed it ages ago."

"Yes, apparently Mendez is still stinging from the earful Vaz gave him."

"Our Vasya speaks his mind."

Osman closed the journal. "I'm going to read my file."

"So I heard."

"You're not in a huff, are you? I hadn't decided until I said it."

"Humph." BB cleared her screen and prepped to load the folder. "You want me here as moral support?"

"Do I need it?"

"I'm going to have to remove my own failsafes that I put in to stop me from accidentally remembering and blurting it out. Wait one."

His pathway was blocked for a moment. He acknowledged the firewall's challenge, confirmed to it that he was asking himself a question and not being hacked, and then the library of documents appeared before him. It was actually tiny lumps and bumps on a spherical field, but he chose to see it as a four-drawer metal cabinet full of ancient suspension files, the kind they still used in the remote colonies. He pulled out Osman's folder and reminded himself what he'd shut out.

Given her anxieties, it's possibly therapeutic. Nothing a good stiff gin won't cure.

"Yes, you're going to need it, but not in the way you think," he said.

"Okay. Thanks, BB." She looked fondly at him, just like Parangosky did, and he felt a little uncomfortable. "I wish I could do the same for you. I know, you know."

"Know what?"

"I know you. I know you protect people."

He wasn't sure if she meant the awkward business with Vaz

and Mal, Staffan Sentzke, or something more general. Now wasn't the time to confess and find that she didn't mean that at all. He didn't like deceiving her, but she knew there were things it was best not to know until you knew that you needed to know them.

It was as good a time as any. This was the natural time to ask. "You *could* do something for me, actually."

"Glad to."

"Will you do it? Switch me off, I mean. As soon as I start to fall apart. I don't think I could bear it. I really didn't like what I saw when I reintegrated my damaged fragment. I know the techies say it's like dementia, that you don't know how ga-ga you are and it's all fluffy, but I don't think dementia's like that either. I think you have a final flash of lucidity that shows you every scrap of yourself that you've lost."

"I promise," Osman said. "And I'll make sure someone's briefed to do it in my place if anything prevents me keeping that promise."

"You'll outlive me, Admiral."

"You know I always like to have a plan B."

BB put on his glib act and sported gleaming black satin funeral ribbons. "Of course, you haven't filed your preferences for your own obsequies, have you?"

"Bury me the ONI way," Osman said. "Stuff me full of explosives and use me for a booby trap."

"Oh, splendid. Very *El Cid*. Dignified but lethal. Anywhere in particular?"

"So many deserving targets, so little explosive capacity."

They were safely in the realm of black humor, all the unpleasant business of fear and dread put back in its coffin. "So, drum roll . . ."

"Hit me." She meshed her hands behind her head and leaned back in the chair, not relaxed at all. BB could detect the hike in the heart rate and the slight rise in the pitch of her voice as her throat muscles tightened. "Informal summary first, and if I don't collapse in hysterical sobbing, take me through the detail."

BB took a breath and puffed out the flat sides of his cube into convex curves before he exhaled. "Real name—Serin Çelik. Mother—Pinar Çelik. Ah, so you do seem to have the proud blood of the Ottomans in your veins, dear. You really are of Turkish heritage. Father—unknown. Place of birth—St. Malo, Cascade. There. You weren't glassed. It's all still standing."

BB paused. Osman was still locked in that I-don't-care-honest pose, hands behind her head.

"So far, so good," she said. "And I've got an excuse to eat *lokum* now. Carry on."

Now came the awkward part, depending on how elaborately and benignly Osman had invented an ideal family in her head over the years. *It'll set you free. It really will.* BB took a deep virtual breath.

"Your mother was a junkie. She supported her habit by prostitution. She wasn't the hooker with a heart of gold, alas. The summary says you were neglected, left at home on your own, and the neighbors called child services when you were found eating scraps out of garbage bins. Taken into care briefly, handed back to Mother, neglected again, more complaints to child services, nothing done, usual story." BB paused to let that sink in. Osman had always felt guilty for not trying to escape and get back to an imagined happy family that she didn't actually recall. "You were lured away by a female ONI agent who offered you a hamburger. The only person who seemed to give a monkey's toss about you was your teacher. She brought food into class for you. She was the one who reported you missing, and—*ahhh*, look at this, you didn't even get a clone. ONI's snatch team advised that it wasn't *appropriate* because if you just went missing, nobody would be remotely surprised and substituting a clone would just complicate things. The police didn't have any evidence to charge your mother, but they thought you'd either been killed by her, by one of her boyfriends, or snatched by a passing pervert. Your mother dropped off the radar about ten years after that. Maybe she scored a bad batch."

BB waited for a reaction other than the slow and microscopically small slackening of the muscles around Osman's mouth.

"Shit," she said at last.

"There you go."

"Wow."

"Isn't it."

She finally put her hands in her lap and slumped a little in her chair. "So no Mommie and Daddy going crazy with grief like the Sentzkes did."

"No." BB steered her, for the kindest reasons. "So you needn't have spent all those years beating yourself up for not escaping. I told you so, didn't I? I told you that you judged your childhood with an adult's eye, not as the child you were. Apart from having to face the utterly *ghastly* fact that—technically—Halsey saved you from starving to death or worse, you actually got something out of SPARTAN-II. You probably wouldn't be Head of Practically Everything now if you'd had a normal life."

Osman was either taking it well or stunned into quiet reflection. "Well, well."

"You want to know who your lovely teacher was? The woman who fed you?"

"I don't remember her at all."

"She kept hassling the police to look for you for years. Mrs. Alkmini Leandro."

BB was rifling through Cascade's public sector databases while he waited for Osman to digest the news properly. He hoped she wouldn't see herself as worthless and unwanted, picked up by ONI and recycled into something fairly useful that still didn't make the grade as a full Spartan and had to be binned. It wasn't her fault that the surgical enhancements failed so badly and crippled her. She wasn't the only casualty rescued and put back together by

ONI, and some kids didn't survive the process at all. He wanted her to see herself as what she was: the ultimate survivor, the kid dealt a terrible hand repeatedly throughout her life but who managed to come through and win, if being brilliant and successful was a victory. It certainly beat ending up like her mother.

Ah, here it is. BB found the records in a couple of databases and cross-matched them. Alkmini Leandro was still alive, retired and still living on Cascade, still in St. Malo.

I have to ask.

"Do you want to look her up?" Maybe Osman still had family on Cascade, but he wouldn't suggest finding them unless she developed a burning need to know complete strangers on the basis of shared mitochondrial DNA. Family meant people who cared about you and loved you, and Mrs. Leandro fitted that description more than any relative. "She's still there."

Osman drummed silently on the desk, just the pads of her fingers, as if she was playing a keyboard. BB hoped she wasn't looking for somewhere else to lodge her guilt. She simply needed to know that she hadn't been abandoned or forgotten. She activated the chart repeater and Cascade and its two moons appeared as a ghostly blue holographic chart next to her desk, which then changed scale to show transit times and distances.

"Ask the team how they'd feel about a few days' shore leave on Cascade," Osman said. "If they vote to go home to Earth instead, we'll fit that in too. But there's plenty for them to see in Mindoro or Kowloon while I take care of what I have to."

"I'll contact the naval base there and arrange cabins at Fort Southwick. Flash an ONI budget code and you can get NCOs and civvies into the officers' mess." BB bounced on the desk top. "Oh, goody. And I can set up a dinner *à deux* for Dev and Phyllis. Get something going there."

"You really are quite a sentimental romantic, aren't you, BB?"

"I just like to see people wring what happiness they can out of this life. Because the world's shit, really."

Osman laughed. "Most of the time."

"Promise me something, Serin," he said. *God, why did I call her that? I never use her name.* "Don't forgive Halsey. Don't rewrite history and think it was all for the best, just to cope with the wrong that was done to you. Stay angry. Even if it transformed your life, it was still a crime. It still took your choices away. It still did you harm. And she's still dangerous, whether we won the war or not."

Osman put on her jacket and checked herself in the mirrored panel set in the bulkhead above the full-length sofa. She wasn't smiling, but she didn't look stunned anymore either. Then she transferred her file to her datapad and went out onto the deck.

"Oh, I won't forget," she said. "Ever."

UNSC *PORT STANLEY*: FOXTROT DECK

"As you were," Osman said, gesturing to Naomi to stay put. Even now, she'd snap to attention when Osman came on deck. "No admirals here. Just a couple of Spartans. Well, one Spartan and a washout."

Osman put two coffees on the transparent deck, sat down, and pushed one of the cups in Naomi's direction. It was easier to stick to formality back in Bravo-6 with the rest of the paper-shufflers, but Osman still didn't feel like a real admiral here, not in the solid, warfighting, time-served sense that Terrence Hood was. The last rank where she'd felt that she fitted the suit was lieutenant. She was neither properly admiralish nor fully Spartan. The best she could do when her time came was to be a real CINCONI, and that meant dumping procedure that didn't get the job done.

Naomi sipped the coffee. "Thanks, ma'am."

"How about we stick with Serin and Naomi? It's not like we didn't grow up together."

"Okay."

"So how are you doing today?"

"Functioning."

Osman wondered what she'd expected her to say. She'd been reunited with her father and lost him in less than two days. It was hard to imagine how long it would take anyone to process that. "Sorry doesn't really cut it, does it?"

"You didn't kill him." Naomi concentrated on her cup, gazing into it and then down through the deck. "Nobody did. It just happened. At least it was quick."

Osman didn't like the ONI side of herself. It jostled its way to the front in any tight spot, and she felt she had to keep an eye on it in case it scared away the normal Serin for good. As long as she knew it was a separate part of her, she could keep it on a leash. As soon as she couldn't see it any longer, then it had taken her over like a Flood infestation, and the metamorphosis would be complete.

She wasn't sure now which Serin Osman had made the decision that led to Naomi becoming the negotiating point with Staffan, or how far she would have gone with it if Naomi had refused. The nice Osman thought she'd done the only decent thing possible in an insoluble situation and reunited a father with his long-lost daughter, however briefly and fraught with problems. The ONI Osman had identified Naomi as Staffan's sole motive and used her to try to take the ship, with no forward planning about where that might lead. She didn't know which motivation had actually driven her and how much was just rationalization after the event, as BB said. It wasn't only Halsey who could rewrite her own internal reality on the fly.

Was it one of those rites of passage that BB talked about, the test to see how detached and ruthless she could be in a crisis? It couldn't have been planned to test her. Parangosky couldn't have known what was going to happen, and almost certainly wouldn't have done it even if she could, but it was textbook. *Puppy strangling. Are you loyal and devoted enough to follow orders and kill your dog?* Osman had read somewhere that it was how one intelligence service had decided which cadets were loyal enough to make the final cut. They gave them each a puppy at the academy, encouraged them to bond with it, and later ordered them to throttle it. Was it the SS or the KGB? She didn't remember. Maybe it was just propaganda from the other side, a clever lie. But it summed up how she felt.

But I didn't create the situation that led to it. Halsey did. I just couldn't find a way to put it right.

"Anyway," she said, taking a sip of her coffee and finding it was already cold. "I opened my file today."

Naomi turned her head slowly and raised her eyebrows. "And?"

"My mother was a prostitute. And a junkie. I foraged in garbage cans. My teacher fed me. They didn't even need to replace me with a clone."

"Oh. I'm sorry."

"I didn't mean that to sound like self-pity. Just illustrating how nothing's ever how you expect it to be."

Naomi shook her head. "That reminded me. You always ate everything you could get your hands on. John used to tease you about taking other kids' leftovers."

"Did he?" There would be recordings in the SPARTAN-II archive like the ones BB had collated for Naomi. If Osman ever wanted to, she could look back at herself from those days, not a still image that invited a kinder interpretation but real footage that would show her the messed-up kid she'd been. "I'm not sure if I want to remember the early days or not."

"You don't. Take it from me."

"I've been thinking about that." Osman picked her words carefully. "You know you can get treatment, don't you? I checked. There's an old drug that targets the limbic system. It doesn't erase traumatic memory like gene therapy, but it stops the spontaneous recall. Rather like BB's firewalling trick."

"Not if I have to be treated by Halsey."

"She's not the only doctor in the world."

"Anyway, we're going to Cascade, are we?" Naomi changed the subject. "That's a first for me."

"Yes, I know it's irregular to use UNSC resources for personal errands, but my teacher's still alive. I'm going to see her."

Naomi just nodded. If anyone understood the need for shared closure, she did. "Have you spoken to her yet?"

"No."

"Nervous?"

"Very." Osman tried to think like Naomi. Whatever Naomi did or didn't recall, it was obvious that her family had been close. She'd actually seen a half brother and a niece, too. It wasn't like being left to run wild in a rough neighborhood in St. Malo. "This is hard to say, but if you ever need to go see your family, I'll make it happen. Even if you decide to stay. No questions asked."

"I thought about it," Naomi said. "But even if Dad was still alive, how would I ever fit in there? I've been engineered to fight and nothing else. I couldn't be a mother or a wife. I'd end up an angry, lonely, bitter, dangerous animal. I'd be Earth's worst nightmare. You're worried about the insurgency acquiring ventral beams? I'd be more worried about them acquiring a Spartan."

Osman was about to say she understood, but she knew she didn't. She'd just been relieved of a burden that she'd struggled with for years. Naomi had just been given another freshly painful one to carry forever.

But Osman now had to find a way to inform Edvin Sentzke. It was yet another dilemma growing out of this whole mess again— the right thing to do, but dangerous to carry out. If this had been a proper war, then the UN Repatriation Office would send humanitarian information to next of kin in its neutral capacity, but who was going to do the civilized thing between the UNSC and Venezia, or any of the other separatist and rebel colonies that were probably still out there? Osman wished she could take Halsey to New Tyne, introduce her to the Sentzkes, and leave her there to explain to them just what a great job she'd done.

It's a damn shame that Edvin never knew that his father wasn't delusional. Of all the crap that's fallen out of this, that gets to me. Not being believed.

"Are you going to come out for a run ashore?" she asked, knowing what the answer would be.

Naomi did a slow shake of the head. "If it's okay with you, I'd rather stay on board and babysit Adj and Leaks. But thank you."

It was going to be more of a wake than long-overdue leave anyway. Osman kept finding herself on the verge of contacting Mrs. Leandro and breaking the news to her at a safe distance, but every time she went to ask BB to route the call, she lost her nerve. It wasn't dread on her part. It was not knowing how her teacher had fared after the abduction. For all Osman knew, Mrs. Leandro could have been through a parallel hell to Staffan Sentzke, dismissed by the authorities and consumed by not knowing, looking at every face in the crowd in case it was the little girl who'd gone missing.

On the other hand, she might simply have thought she'd done all she could, accepted that terrible things happened to at-risk kids, and gone on with the business of life with her own family. Osman hoped she had.

One by one, Osman shared her story with the rest of Kilo-Five over the course of the day. The more she repeated it, the more distant it became and the more it had happened to someone else. She didn't even feel any animosity toward her mother, who might as well have been a character in a movie she'd forgotten ever seeing. Spenser and the ODSTs all listened with sympathetic nods. But Phillips took her aside.

"You're not going to try tracing your mother, are you?" he asked.

"Of course not." It hadn't actually crossed Osman's mind. That was revealing. "And no, I'm not going to go on some half-assed quest to find my father. He probably paid cash anyway."

"There's no shame in it, you know."

"What, eating garbage?"

"Your mother's situation." Phillips looked nervous and steered off the rocks toward a joke. "But it's not like she was a lawyer. That's something to be thankful for."

"An honest prostitute does a more socially useful job than I've done this week, Evan."

Osman meant it. She'd been sober, alert, and not worried about paying the bills when she took her decisions on *Inquisitor,* so she had no excuse. It made her think again about Jul 'Mdama, another unsuspecting individual who'd crossed the path of an ONI operation and had his life put through the shredder. He still hadn't popped up on the radar again. She hoped the faulty portal he'd stepped through had given him a quick and humane end by exiting into a star, not that hinge-heads deserved a humane death, because he'd be a very bitter and resourceful enemy if he'd survived. She imagined him a little like Staffan; biding his time and building up a small army to one day wreak vengeance on those who'd caused his wife's death. As far as Jul was concerned, that was humans, whether it was their fault or not. As far as Staffan had been concerned, it was the Earth and all it stood for, but he wasn't entirely wrong.

Is it treasonable to think that? Does it make me unfit to do this job? Or am I just facing up to reality?

It was too late to decide ONI wasn't for her. But if she worked out what her mistake was, she might become the kind of CINCONI she could live with.

"Okay, BB," she said, addressing the ether. He was always there, always keeping watch. "Prepare to slip. First stop, Anchor Ten. Spenser's got to get back to the land of the living."

"And the chaps need to visit the PX." BB appeared in front of her and drifted ahead to the bridge. "They had to leave all their civilian kit on Venezia. Mal wants to know if he can claim a few pairs of boxers on expenses."

"Sure, tell them to replace whatever they need. I'll sign it."

Port Stanley diverted via Anchor 10 to drop off Spenser, then picked up another cargo of arms for 'Telcam from UNSC *Thatcher* three days later before heading for Cascade. They'd make the drop after shore leave. Everyone needed to get their esprit de corps back on track before they did anything else.

When *Stanley* dropped out of slip, Osman saw Cascade for the first time that she could remember. As far as she knew, she'd been transported to Reach under sedation and had never had the chance to look back on her home. One side of the planet was in darkness, studded with the bright clustered lights of cities. Even if she'd remembered anything about St. Malo or Mindoro, they would have changed beyond recognition by now.

She pressed the comms key in front of her. "Naomi, have you changed your mind? We're going ashore in thirty minutes."

"No, ma'am." It was impossible to tell from the Spartan's voice if she was having a good day or a bad one. "I'm going to get to know our Huragok better."

"Okay. Tell me if you change your mind."

She didn't, but then Osman didn't expect her to. ONI clearance got *Tart-Cart* into UNSCSB Fort Southwick without the need for any personnel to go through customs or immigration. The agency moved unseen and unrecorded. Osman felt odd landing on a world where normal paperwork and bureaucracy still existed after so many years of operating between Sydney and places that no longer had capitals left standing, let alone anyone to check ID.

And BB wasn't with them. That felt odd, too. He was on permanent link via Osman's comms to be summoned or to alert her in an emergency, but he was, for all intents and purposes, absent. She missed him immediately. When she parted company with the rest of the squad, she found herself truly alone for the first time in months, making her way through Mindoro by taxi so she could see something of the place and try to make sense of what heritage she might have if she decided it was worth having.

The city was all high-rises and new construction, somehow much busier than Sydney and less weary, as if it had heard about all that Covenant unpleasantness over the years and was very sorry about it, but it had its own life to get on with. It was easy to forget that there were still colonies left that had managed to sit out the war, not modest backwaters like Venezia but big, brash, confident worlds like this.

"You could have done this trip a lot cheaper on the monorail, Admiral," the taxi driver said.

"I've been away for a few years." Osman gazed at the cityscape whipping by. "I just wanted to catch up."

Mindoro thinned out into suburbs. A few kilometers later, she started seeing the signs for St. Malo. She'd built a mental image of it simply to visualize garbage bins and how she might have reached into them as a six-year-old, but it turned out not to be the post-apocalyptic hell-hole with roving gangs and graffiti that she'd imagined. It looked like the kind of town that property agents would describe as gentrified. Old houses had been restored and the streets were clean and tidy.

"This is the place," the driver said. "Want me to wait?"

Osman paid him and stood looking up a tree-lined avenue. No memories came flooding back at all. She wondered whether she'd go and wander around the street where she'd lived later, or if that would be a bad idea.

"No, I'll probably be some time," she said. "Thanks."

She really should have called Mrs. Leandro first. The woman might have been out, or in hospital, or on vacation. But Osman had to do this face-to-face, and there was every chance she'd get to the door and not be able to go through with it.

Why? What could possibly be left to know that could hurt me?

Get a grip. I'm Rear Admiral Serin Osman, next in line to the ONI throne. I don't have anxiety attacks on doorsteps and chicken out of talking to old ladies.

She walked past the house once and took a few deep breaths, then turned around and went back to rap on the door. When it opened, a dark-haired woman in her sixties, smartly dressed and not a little old lady at all, stood in the doorway. Osman strained to recognize the face.

"Hi, are you Mrs. Leandro?" she asked. "Do I have the right address? Alkmini Leandro?"

"Yes, that's me."

God, how did she say this? How did you tell someone you weren't dead? "Do you remember me? I know it's been a long time, but I'm Serin. I was in your class. Serin Çelik. My name's Serin Osman now." She indicated her collar, a little self-conscious. "Rear Admiral, UNSC."

The woman took a step back and put her hands to her mouth, studying Osman's face. Then a smile formed and spread. She dissolved into tears. She flung her arms around Osman and hugged her, laughing and crying.

"Serin! Oh my, look at you! I thought you were dead. I really did. I thought something awful happened to you. Oh . . . this is a shock. Sorry. A wonderful shock, though. I think about you even now, and here you are."

"Well, some awful things did happen." Osman concentrated on steady, calming breaths. "But in the end, my luck changed. How are you?"

"Happier with the world for knowing that miracles still happen. My, you look well. Come in. *Come in.*" She grabbed Osman's hand and led her into a hall lined with photos of people and places, all meaningless to Osman but that spoke of a life full of family and friends. "You were such a clever girl. I always knew you'd do well if someone got you out of that dreadful place and gave you a chance."

"Someone did," she said. No, she knew that she didn't mean Halsey, and the awful place wasn't where Mrs. Leandro imagined. "Someone gave me a choice. And *you* gave me a chance."

"But what happened to you? Who took you? Family? Did someone rescue you?"

"It's a long story. I'll tell you what I can."

Osman couldn't remember Mrs. Leandro at all. She tried hard to, and maybe it would come back to her after they'd talked for a while, but for the meantime she was content to sit and drink tiny cups of pungent Greek coffee, trying to recap on thirty-five missing years without revealing anything classified.

"Good Lord, where are my manners? Sorry, I'm still in shock. I never thought I'd see you again." Mrs. Leandro jumped up, went to the kitchen, and came back with a white china plate of baklava, each little square oozing with syrup and studded with pistachios. "Are you hungry? Eat."

Osman bit into the fragile pastry, which managed to be simultaneously crumbly, crunchy, moist, and sticky. It was a time machine. The taste took her back years.

Now she remembered everything, or at least everything that mattered. For a moment, she couldn't swallow. It was shockingly primal. She had no idea that powerful memories could be unlocked quite like that.

"It's like it was yesterday," she said. It was the best she could manage.

"You always did like baklava," Mrs. Leandro said, beaming. "So you're an *admiral* now? I'm so proud of you, Serin. But it's been an awful war. Will the peace treaty last? I won't be able to look at things the same way if it all starts up again, not now that I know you're in the Navy."

It really was very good baklava. Osman would tell BB all about it. The taste and fragrance overwhelmed her, along with a growing but vague recollection of this kind, patient woman, and the realization of what her life might have been without ONI.

"Oh, don't you worry about me," Osman said. "I have a terrific crew. Good friends I can rely on. I'm a survivor."

OLD ADMIRALTY HOTEL, KOWLOON, CASCADE:
DAY TWO OF A FORTY-EIGHT-HOUR PASS

"This is a nice bar, so remember to leave it that way, eh, mate?" Mal brandished a glass with a twist of lemon peel and an olive in it. "Look. Two of my recommended fruit and veg for the day. You want another one?"

"I'll get them." Vaz, arms folded on the marble counter, nodded at the barman. Two glasses arrived with impressive speed, one vodka martini with a lot of garnish and one rum over ice. Vaz was getting slightly numb but he was pretty sure that you had lemon or an olive, not both. "I've never seen you drink cocktails."

"That's because you were normally under the table after two dry sherries by the time I started on them. So, what do you fancy for dinner? Chinese? Korean?"

Vaz lined up his glass with the edge of a precisely folded damask napkin embroidered with the name of the hotel. It was the poshest thing he'd seen in years. He'd waited for this run ashore for a very long time, and in ODST etiquette that meant he was obliged to get very drunk, eat himself to a standstill, and wake up with some woman whose name he didn't just not know, but who he didn't even recall meeting the night before.

But what he actually wanted was to find somewhere quiet to blow his brains out to erase all the things he knew, and all the things he'd seen, and the last few weeks in particular.

It shouldn't have ended like that. I should have done more.

If we'd just taken BB's fragment in the radio from the start, I could have sneaked him into that ship the first time, he would have moved it that day, and Staffan would never have known about Naomi or ended up dead. It was that simple. But we decided to operate without BB. We got it wrong.

At least he hadn't chickened out like he had with Halsey. It hadn't panned out as he'd wanted, but then that kind of past could never be put right. The best you could do was claw back a few points.

As for BB—he didn't know what the hell was going on there. He didn't know AIs at all. Maybe he thought that not opening up another festering sore in the team was best for Earth's security, because he was privy to things that Vaz and Mal probably never would be. Maybe all they really wanted was the data from the ship and the rest was just some smokescreen. Whatever BB had done, he'd sent that file. Vaz found himself wondering how to check if Staffan had managed to send a copy to Edvin.

No. Leave it alone now.

Life went on, though. Cascade was solid proof. It hadn't been glassed, and even if it had had its ups and downs, it was making the most of the postwar boom. Someone had to take up the economic slack after all those Outer Colonies—and a lot of the Inners—had been melted flat. There was going to be a new space elevator in Mindoro and Kowloon even had a new yacht club. It was a boomtown. One man's extinction was another's fresh opportunity.

But Sanghelios is still out there, too.

It wasn't Cascade's fault that it wasn't a gleaming sheet of vitrified soil from horizon to horizon. Vaz twisted on the barstool and looked around the lounge at the smartly dressed clientele who were probably all in construction, agribusiness, and mining, and all on expense accounts. A part of him longed to see his buddies from the 15th again, but what would he be able to talk about?

What have you been doing for the last few months, Vaz? Tell us all about it. Well, I've been helping to arm hinge-heads who'll be back to kill us all one day, shoring up a system that kidnaps and experiments on kids, and killing old men who just wanted justice. How was your day?

He really wished he hadn't had that last rum on an empty stomach. He turned around to face the bar again and caught a glimpse of himself in the mirrored wall of shelves behind the bar. Between the bright green kiwi fruit liqueur and a bottle of hundred-year-old Scotch, he saw a disappointment of a man with a fading black eye and a scar that was only just beginning to lose its color. It was a surprise that they let him and Mal in here, even in smart jackets. But a flash of a UNSC pass put the pieces together for the guy on the door. Unglassed or not, Cascade knew there'd been a war and why the planet was still there.

I should have stayed on board with Naomi. BB's a good friend, but she needs flesh and blood at a time like this.

"Why did Osman want us to come here, anyway?" he said, trying to perk up. "We could have gone home. I could have shown you *proper* vodka."

"A trip down Amnesia Lane. Guilt. Gratitude. She's only human." Mal put a steadying hand on his shoulder. "Look, if you want to go back to the ship fully clothed and mostly sober, I promise I won't tell anyone."

"No. I'm up for a meal. Really. I am."

"Then we can torment Phyllis about Dev in the morning. That'll be *priceless*." Mal was trying hard too. "He'll be in the med suite, a dry husk. No male civvie can survive the attentions of a female ODST and walk quite the same way again."

"I think they're just going to a concert."

"Of course."

"Do you think I'm an asshole, Mal?"

Mal looked him in the eye for a long time as if he was shaping up to say yes. "I think you narrowly missed a firing squad, to be honest."

"I meant did I let Staffan down. Don't give me the lecture on wanted lists. I mean the man."

"I don't see what else you could have done. I didn't see or hear a thing, remember? And what you send to people is your business."

"Yeah, I didn't happen to recall a single thing you didn't see or do, either."

"What a pair of forgetful shit-heads we are."

"Parangosky just *knows*."

"Well, then, we'll both wake up with a horse's arse in our bunks and she'll make us an offer we can't understand." Mal picked up his drink and raised the glass discreetly. "To Staffan. The poor old sod's dead, but went out on his own terms. Not banged up in Ivanoff with Halsey sticking needles in him. And he got to see his daughter again."

"And who's going to tell his family? Who's going to stop them searching for answers for the rest of their lives?"

"Not you, mate. You hear me? You stay clear of that place."

There was nobody around to hear them doing the unthinkable and mourning for a terrorist. Vaz held up his glass.

"To someone who deserved better," he said, and downed it in one.

Mal fished the strip of lemon peel out of his glass and chewed it. "Did you make him any promises?"

"What makes you think I did?"

"You're Vaz. I know your every thought."

"Okay, I swore I'd look after her. Even Spartans need looking after."

"Does she know?"

"Does she need to?"

Mal made a show of checking his watch. It was new. "Okay, time for dinner. And we never discuss this again. But if it raises its head, I'll be there with you. We both know what we did, and I won't let you carry the can alone."

"If I was slightly more drunk than I am," Vaz said, "I'd be crying all over you."

"Shit, you're not drunk enough, then. Let's fix that."

Mal called a cab and they ended up somewhere on the harbor with a menu that had no English on it at all, and they wished they'd brought Devereaux along to translate. Some of the dishes contained things that even Mal wouldn't try. They over-ordered, drank too much, and left the restaurant in the early hours. By ODST standards, it was tame. Nobody ended up handcuffed to a lamppost with his eyebrows shaved off and his underpants on his head, and nobody got in a fight. Vaz woke up in the back of the taxi just as Mal was paying the driver.

"Come on, you dirty little stop-out," Mal said, guiding him in the general direction of the barracks gate. "Don't tell me you've lost your pass. Be nice to the crusher."

Vaz tapped the back of his neck and tried to focus on the Provost rating standing guard on the gate. "He can scan my chip."

It didn't matter that Parangosky thought the sun shone out their backsides. Security was going to give two drunk ODSTs a hard time. The guy on the gate checked Vaz's ID twice, and when they signed in at the desk, Vaz got pulled over again.

I mustn't get mouthy. I'm going to be in enough trouble as it is.

"This was dropped off for you earlier, Corporal," the sergeant said. "Fleet Mail wasn't happy about the lack of documentation, but apparently your ID and ship flagged special clearance and it went in the ONI Secret Squirrel bag. What a special little flower you are." He pushed a well-packed box across the desk, about thirty or forty centimeters square, and leaned close to Vaz. "It better not be a head. I know what you ODSTs are like."

They managed to find their cabins and Vaz flopped onto his bunk into temporary oblivion. He'd deal with the parcel in the morning. The room was whirling too much to unwrap anything. He woke up with a mouth like the bottom of a parrot's cage, realized he'd slept through the alarm, and had to bust a gut to shower and get to the RV point to meet *Tart-Cart*. Mal was waiting for him outside the entrance, not looking hungover at all.

"No tactless comments," he said. "Dev says it was a lovely concert. Yeah. I'll bet. Osman met her teacher and had coffee. And they all lived happily ever after. Now back to reality, eh?"

Nobody chatted or joked on the flight back to *Port Stanley*. BB popped up in the crew cabin as soon as Devereaux docked, but even he was subdued. Vaz headed for his quarters and un-packed his bag.

Most of it was taken up by the box. He hadn't had a parcel since he'd joined Kilo-Five, but these things took a while to catch up with ships. It was probably from the guys in his old troop, something really tasteless like a vintage blow-up sex doll or worse.

How do they know which ship I'm in, though? That's classi-fied.

He checked the label. Maybe they just addressed it with his name and service number, and ONI did the rest when it got coded. There were so many stickers on it that it was hard to tell which had been put on first. His name was there, but no ODST had written it in *that* format: CPL V. BELOI ODST. It was the wrong form of address, and there wasn't even a service number. The accepting office's stamp was Nimrod Dock, but then he found a sender and scribbled signature: MIKE AMBERLEY.

That was Spenser's alias. Vaz didn't wonder why. Anything was possible with ONI. It was only when he peeled off four layers of padded wrapping and found a perfect little wooden crate secured with screws that he started to wonder if it was re-ally from Spenser at all.

I bet it's an arum. *I bet Phillips is behind this.*

He took out his knife to unscrew the lid. Yes, it had to be an *arum*. There was something buried in shredded paper, a little old-fashioned and folksy, and when he put his hand in he could feel a curved surface. He picked the shredded packing out and saw the top of a matte black sphere. But when he lifted it with both hands, a length of power cable trailed behind it.

Now he had no idea what it was. The plug didn't look like it would fit any outlet on the ship, either. Baffled, he poked around in the little crate to see if there was a note with it. His fingers found something small with sharp angles and a folded sheet of paper.

The small item turned out to be a tiny painted wooden chair, perfect in scale and detail, with an ornate carved back and a little padded satin seat. The dawning realization made his scalp prickle. When he unfolded the paper, the message on it simply read: I'LL KEEP MY PROMISE. THANK YOU.

Vaz needed Adj right away.

He went out into the passage. He didn't even want BB to see this in case he was wrong. "BB? BB, can you get Adj for me, please? I need him to fix something."

"On his way," BB said. "Are you all right?"

"Yeah. I think so."

Vaz sat down on his bunk and examined the tiny chair and the black sphere while he waited. Adj showed up a few minutes later, sparkling with curiosity.

"Adj, can you put the right plug on this, please?" Vaz showed him the end of the power cable. "I think it's pretty old."

Adj let out a long *ooooh* noise, one of the few actual sounds that Huragok seemed to make naturally themselves. <*I have never seen one like this.*> His cilia flickered over it. <*It needs a power adapter, too.*>

He finished it in less than a minute. Vaz patted him on the head, making him flinch, and stuffed the sphere, the chair, and the note into his bag to go in search of Naomi. She was in her cabin. If he hadn't known what had happened, he wouldn't have guessed from her expression that she'd had a very tough week. She looked okay. He hoped she was. It was now his job to make sure she stayed that way.

"Did you have a good time?" she asked, jerking her head to invite him in.

"I drank too much. You should have come."

"Next time."

"Can I show you something?"

She frowned, then nodded. "Sure."

Vaz hoped he hadn't read this all wrong, but he was certain he knew what the chair was and who had sent it. He fished it out of the bag and handed it to her. She turned it over in her hands, frowning again, then the frown relaxed and her lips parted.

"Oh. Wow."

"It turned up in a parcel addressed to me. And this, too."

Vaz put the black sphere down on the desk and plugged it in. There'd been lettering on the base once, but time and use had worn it off. Only the switches were left. He pressed one and the cabin was suddenly transformed into another world.

Naomi looked up at a deckhead speckled with constellations that circled slowly like a planetarium. She put one hand to her mouth. Vaz reached out to switch off the cabin light and lay down on the deck with his hands meshed behind his head to watch the show.

"Come on," he said. "Tell me what it is."

Naomi lay down next to him. They were suddenly in a field, star-gazing at a night sky. She didn't say anything for a few minutes.

"Sansar," she said at last. Her voice sounded thick and hoarse. "It's Sansar."

Vaz could guess what was coming, but he needed to know for sure. "Go on."

"My dad said he bought this for my sixth birthday. I was abducted before he could give it to me." She swallowed. "It's the star map from Sansar's northern hemisphere. I loved looking at the stars when I was little."

It was probably why she found comfort sitting on the glass deck, staring out into the galaxy. It was probably why BB had asked Adj to make the deck transparent in the first place, too, although Vaz couldn't remember seeing a reference to it in her file. He was glad the lights were off. There was nothing worse for a Helljumper's image than to be caught crying.

Naomi gazed up at the night sky from a dead world and a childhood cut short. She pointed to a constellation. "See that one? The Galleon. The nebula forms the sails."

Vaz waited for her to ask the inevitable question, but she didn't. If she ever did, he wasn't sure whether to answer or not. All the time he didn't actually put it into words, he could stay in that narrow zone where he could live with himself both as an ODST and as a man. He didn't have to say what he now knew, and if she didn't hear those words, she was innocent of involvement in everything he'd done.

Vaz had already gone too far—as a marine, anyway—when he sent the document to Staffan. He knew that he should have gone straight to Osman now and queried that post-contact casualty report on *Pious Inquisitor.*

But he wouldn't.

And BB. What did you make yourself forget? No. Don't ask.

Naomi shuffled into a more comfortable position on the hard deck. The question seemed to be coming after all. "When was it sent, Vaz?"

"Ask yourself if you need to know."

"Does that mean what I think it does?"

He handed her the folded note. She could see better in the dark than an average human, but even she had to squint to read it in the faint light from the lamp.

"If you don't ask," Vaz said, "I won't have to tell."

Naomi seemed to be chewing it over. "The Spirit would have needed a slipspace drive to get clear, wouldn't it?"

Vaz had promised he'd take care of her. That was the deal with Staffan. All he needed to do to protect her right now was to deploy a defensive measure that ONI had taught him: plausible deniability.

"Huragok," he said carefully. "Busy little guys. You really can't leave them alone for five minutes. Can you?"

EPILOGUE

RECEIVED: OFFICE OF CINCONI
PRIORITY: URGENT
CLASSIFICATION: TOP SECRET

One has to be careful with suicide notes. Even these days, when I hope we all accept that our lives are our own to do with as we choose, some still see it as insanity, or cowardice, or an affront to some god, as if we're no more than slaves of the divine with none of the free will those same believers claim God gives us. So this note will be explicit.

I'm perfectly sane, and it's my life that's been cowardly, not my death. And if there is a god, then I'm prepared to stand before him and tell him what a careless, negligent, unloving father he is to let us behave as we do. He should have been more forthcoming with the thunderbolts and smiting.

But why blame God? I don't believe he exists, but even if he does, we should be capable of morality without him, and are. His purpose is mysterious because he hasn't got one, and if he has, it isn't benign. We face extinction by a genocidal alien culture that also believes it serves its gods. But *we* persist in the face of logic ourselves. The devil made us do it. We were only following orders. It was for the greater good. The ends justified the means. And so on, ad hypocritical nauseam, blaming everything but our own self-created evil.

I have taken my own life because the SPARTAN-II program is

a crime against humanity, and I should have had the moral courage to refuse to work on it. I did not. I complied. I've committed a crime against life and contributed to many deaths, so if nobody else can or will punish me for that, I must sentence myself and carry it out.

I knew SPARTAN-II was morally indefensible. That probably makes me more loathsome even than Catherine Halsey. I understood how wrong it was, but she never appeared to recognize that in all the time I knew her. She made all the right noises, but that was all they were: noises. Her actions were all enthusiasm.

Your conscience is what you *do,* not what you think or *say* you think. It's also something you do when it has to be done, not as an afterthought when you're forced to face up to your wrongdoing. Remorse is cheap and easy. It's an insult.

My awareness obliged me to act, but I did nothing: I cooperated, and my compliance enabled something monstrous. I didn't slaughter millions, but there's no sliding scale in atrocities, even if the robotic imagination of the law requires fixed thresholds. Each death, each act of suffering, is a complete and qualifying act of evil in itself.

Humans instinctively norm. We behave like others around us, because compliance is our survival strategy. No matter how intelligent, sensible, or kind, 99 percent of human beings will carry out the most appalling acts if the rest of their tribe is doing the same. And most of our conscious acts are simply postscript rationalizations of our hard-wired unconscious decisions.

And yet *I knew what I was being asked to do was wrong,* and I still did it. Being a normal human is no excuse for that.

The Mortal Dictata Act defends many things, but mostly it enshrines the individuality and validity of each human life. I hesitate to call it a human rights charter, because that term has been utterly devalued and its intent completely distorted over the centuries. The Mortal Dictata are a suite of laws that remind us of the basic moral duty that we owe our own species. They bar us from creating humans for the purposes of harvesting tissue, even if that human has an otherwise independent life; they bar us from enslaving others; and they bar us from cloning entire humans. The Mortal Dictata recognize a central principle that no human should be brought into existence or coopted primarily as a convenience for others. Each life is equal and valid.

SPARTAN-II broke that law on every level. I helped it happen. And because of that, I can no longer justify my own existence.

I have no right to ask anything of a fellow human being following my death, seeing as I failed to meet the minimum requirement of what it means to be human. But this is a personal request to Vice Admiral Margaret Parangosky, CINCONI, under whose command these acts took place. I would ask that my brain be retained for the AI donor program, specifically for an AI dedicated to the support and protection of Spartan-IIs. I have taken my life by a method that causes least damage to brain tissue. I know how to do that, of course. I am—was—a neurosurgeon and a psychologist.

This isn't an attempt to squeeze out a few more years of pitiful existence that I don't deserve. I know the AI based on my brain won't have my memories or personality, and that I shall be very dead. But I owe it to the children and families whose lives were ruined and stolen to put whatever I can back into making those Spartans' daily existence safer and less miserable. If anything of me survives, then it might be what I wanted most in my final moments—the need to do some good for those children.

If you can make this happen, Margaret, and I'm wrong about God or the Devil, I shall put in a word for you regardless at which gate I arrive. You were always more human than I ever managed to be.

Your friend,
Graham

DR. G. J. ALBAN, MD, MCNS, MCPP
SENIOR RESEARCHER, ONI SPECIAL PROJECTS
MARCH 2523.

ONI ARTIFICIAL INTELLIGENCE DIVISION: PROJECT
    AI 4TH GEN
CINCONI: APPROVED
CODE AS/PRESERVE FOR: BLACK-BOX (BBX-8995-1)

ABOUT THE AUTHOR

No. 1 *New York Times* bestselling novelist, scriptwriter, and comics author Karen Traviss has received critical acclaim for her award-nominated Wess'har series, as well as regularly hitting the bestseller lists with her Halo, Gears of War, and Star Wars work. A former defense correspondent and TV and newspaper journalist, she lives in Wiltshire, England.